Capital Crimes

Capital Crimes

London Mysteries

Edited and Introduced
by Martin Edwards

Poisoned Pen Press

Introduction and notes copyright © 2015 Martin Edwards

Published by Poisoned Pen Press in association with the British Library

First Edition 2015 First US Trade Paperback Edition

10 9 8 7 6 5 4 3 2 1

Library of Congress Catalog Card Number: 2014958043

ISBN: 9781464203770   Trade Paperback

Poisoned Pen Press
6962 E. First Ave., Ste. 103
Scottsdale, AZ 85251
www.poisonedpenpress.com
info@poisonedpenpress.com

Printed in the United States of America

Contents

Introduction

London has been the home to many of fiction's finest detectives, and the setting for mystery novels and short stories of the highest quality, throughout the genre's history. The very first detective fiction, written by Edgar Allan Poe, may have been set in Paris, but the book usually described as the first detective *novel* was Charles Warren Adams's *The Notting Hill Mystery*, republished recently by the British Library. As this collection of vintage London crime stories demonstrates, the city has inspired many of the genre's stellar names.

In the first chapter of Arthur Conan Doyle's *A Study in Scarlet* in 1887, Dr Watson conveyed the allure of the capital in vivid if unflattering fashion:

> I had neither kith nor kin in England, and was therefore as free as air—or as free as an income of eleven shillings and sixpence a day will permit a man to be. Under such circumstances I naturally gravitated to London, that great cesspool into which all the loungers and idlers of the Empire are irresistibly drained.

While in search of suitable lodgings, Watson meets his old friend Stamford at the Criterion Bar, and is duly introduced to Sherlock Holmes, who has his eye 'on a suite in Baker Street'. Before long, 221B Baker Street would become as famous an address as Scotland Yard. The way in which Conan

Doyle conjures up the foggy and often menacing atmosphere of the gas-lit London streets contributes to the power of the Holmes stories, and set the bar for his successors.

The city soon became home to several of Sherlock's rivals, including Martin Hewitt, a private detective created by Arthur Morrison, an East Ender from Poplar, whose evocative *Tales of the Mean Streets* and *The Hole in the Wall* drew on his inside knowledge of the capital's darker places. Baroness Orczy's 'armchair detective' the Old Man in the Corner took up residence in an ABC teashop, and his early cases included 'The Fenchurch Street Mystery' and a murder on the London Underground, which has been a popular haunt for fictional crime for many years—think of the James Bond film *Skyfall*. This anthology contains a marvellously sensational Victorian serial-killer thriller set on the Underground, while a Tube station murder is at the centre of *Murder Underground* by Mavis Doriel Hay, whose three whodunits from the 1930s have been republished as British Library Crime Classics.

Hay was at work during the 'Golden Age of Murder', which introduced readers to a new generation of detectives, many with homes or offices in London. It helped to be handy for Scotland Yard, whose hapless senior officers regularly needed to pick the brains of gifted outsiders to solve the knottiest murder mysteries. Lord Peter Wimsey, whose brother-in-law was a chief inspector, lived in luxurious surroundings at 110A Piccadilly. In *Murder Must Advertise* he takes a job under an assumed name at Pym's Publicity, the scene of a recent unexplained death. Pym's was modelled on Benson's, an advertising agency in Kingsway where Wimsey's creator Dorothy L. Sayers worked during the 1920s. Albert Campion, Margery Allingham's enigmatic sleuth, lived not far from Wimsey, in Bottle Street. Several of Campion's cases, most notably the post-war classic *The Tiger in the Smoke*, make fine use of a sinister metropolitan background. 'The Smoke', of course, is London.

Agatha Christie's Hercule Poirot shared rooms with Captain Hastings at 14 Farraway Street before moving to Whitehaven Mansions, 'one of the newest type of service flats in London.... [He admitted] having chosen this building entirely on account of its strictly geometrical appearance and proportions'. This sounds rather like the Isokon Building in Hampstead, also known as the Lawn Road Flats, where Christie herself lived during the Second World War. Among Poirot's most notable investigations in the capital is *Lord Edgware Dies*, which opens at a West End theatre.

Sayers, Christie, and Allingham were among the members of the world's first social network of crime writers, founded by Anthony Berkeley. The Detection Club had a meeting room in Gerrard Street, Soho, and it says something for the bias of detective fiction in the first half of the twentieth century that the club was frequently called the *London* Detection Club. In 1939, its membership consisted, with very few exceptions, of men and women who had a home either in London or within easy reach of it. Nine of them are represented in this collection.

With its fascinating mix of people, rich and poor, British and foreign, worthy and suspicious, London is a city where anything can happen. The possibilities for criminals and for the crime writer are endless. In real life, Whitechapel witnessed the Ripper killings in the late nineteenth century, and the unsolved crimes inspired Marie Belloc Lowndes' *The Lodger*, which became an early film directed by Leytonstone-born Alfred Hitchcock. The first two British serial killer whodunits of any significance, Anthony Berkeley's *The Silk Stockings Murder* and John Rhode's *The Murders in Praed Street*, were set in the capital. In terms of short stories, Thomas Burke's contribution to this anthology is the outstanding work of short fiction inspired by the Ripper killings.

Increasingly, the fictional exploits of gifted amateur sleuths were superseded by more realistic accounts of detective work, and senior figures from Scotland Yard did their bit to help the process. Sir Basil Thomson, who wrote novels in the 1930s recounting the rise through the ranks of a police officer named Richardson, was a former head of the CID. Sir Norman Kendal, an Assistant Commissioner of the Metropolitan Police, became an honorary member of the Detection Club in 1935, and a year later, ex-Superintendent G. W. Cornish collaborated with Detection Club members including Sayers and Allingham to produce *Six against the Yard*.

Henry Wade, another Detection Club member, was responsible for a ground-breaking novel of police procedure, *Lonely Magdalen*, which is set mainly in London, and opens with the discovery of a prostitute's body on Hampstead Heath. This remarkable book, which did not flinch from the reality of brutal police interrogation techniques, featured Inspector John Poole, a forerunner of the more credible crime solvers found in modern detective fiction.

Capital Crimes is an eclectic collection of London-based crime stories, blending the familiar with the unexpected in a way that I hope reflects the personality of the city. We have classics by Berkeley and Burke as well as almost unknown, and excellent, stories by three fine women writers, E. M. Delafield, Ethel Lina White and Anthony Gilbert (yes, Gilbert's real name was Lucy Malleson). The stories appear roughly, although not precisely, in chronological order, to give a flavour of how writers have tackled crime in London over the span of more than half a century. Their contributions range from thrillers and horrific vignettes to cerebral whodunits. What they have in common is a nonpareil setting for crime fiction, and enduring value as entertainment.

Martin Edwards
www.martinedwardsbooks.com

The Case of Lady Sannox

Arthur Conan Doyle

Arthur Conan Doyle (1859–1930) created, in Sherlock Holmes, the most famous of all fictional detectives, but the colossal success of the Holmes and Watson stories frustrated him, because he took more pride in some of his other work, especially his historical fiction. Authors may not be the best judges of their own achievements, but it is certainly true that some of Conan Doyle's tales of terror, such as 'Lot No. 249' and 'The Leather Funnel' are masterly.

This short, snappy story of a horrifying crime is another example of the power and economy of his best writing. Note how skilfully the key revelation is clued. The eponymous Lady Sannox is the loveliest woman in the capital, and the city's cosmopolitan nature, even at the time of publication in 1893, was such that it is entirely credible that Douglas Stone should receive an urgent summons from Hamil Ali from Smyrna. What happens next is unforgettable.

The relations between Douglas Stone and the notorious Lady Sannox were very well known both among the fashionable circles of which she was a brilliant member, and the scientific bodies which numbered him among their most illustrious *confrères*. There was naturally, therefore, a very widespread interest when it was announced one morning that the lady had absolutely and for ever taken the veil, and that the world would see her no more. When, at the very tail of this rumour, there came the assurance that the celebrated operating surgeon, the man of steel nerves, had been found in the morning by his valet, seated on one side of his bed, smiling pleasantly upon the universe, with both legs jammed into one side of his breeches, and his great brain about as valuable as a cup full of porridge, the matter was strong enough to give quite a little thrill of interest to folk who had never hoped that their jaded nerves were capable of such a sensation.

Douglas Stone in his prime was one of the most remarkable men in England. Indeed, he could hardly be said to have ever reached his prime, for he was but nine-and-thirty at the time of this little incident. Those who knew him best were aware that, famous as he was as a surgeon, he might have succeeded with even greater rapidity in any of a dozen lines of life. He could have cut his way to fame as a soldier, struggled to it as an explorer, bullied for it in the courts, or built it out of stone and iron as an engineer. He was born to be great, for he could plan what another man dare not do, and he could do what another man dare not plan. In surgery none could follow him. His nerve, his judgment, his intuition, were things apart. Again and again his knife cut away death, but grazed the very springs of life in doing it, until his assistants were as white as the patient. His energy, his audacity, his full-blooded self-confidence—does not the memory of them still linger to the south of Marylebone Road and the north of Oxford Street?

And his vices were as magnificent as his virtues, and infinitely more picturesque. Large as was his income, and it was the third largest of all professional men in London, it was far beneath the luxury of his living. Deep in his complex nature lay a rich vein of sensualism, at the sport of which he placed all the prizes of his life. The eye, the ear, the touch, the palate, all were his masters. The bouquet of old vintages, the scent of rare exotics, the curves and tints of the daintiest potteries of Europe, it was to these that the quick-running stream of gold was transformed. And then there came his sudden mad passion for Lady Sannox, when a single interview with two challenging glances and a whispered word set him ablaze. She was the loveliest woman in London, and the only one to him. He was one of the handsomest men in London, but not the only one to her. She had a liking for new experiences, and was gracious to most men who wooed her. It may have been cause or it may have been effect that Lord Sannox looked fifty, though he was but six-and-thirty.

He was a quiet, silent, neutral-tinted man, with thin lips and heavy eyelids, much given to gardening, and full of quiet, home-like habits. He had at one time been fond of acting, had even rented a theatre in London, and on its boards had first seen Miss Marion Dawson, to whom he had offered his hand, his title, and the third of a county. Since his marriage this early hobby had become distasteful to him. Even in private theatricals it was no longer possible to persuade him to exercise the talent which he had often shown that he possessed. He was happier with a spud and a watering-can among his orchids and chrysanthemums.

It was quite an interesting problem whether he was absolutely devoid of sense, or miserably wanting in spirit. Did he know his lady's ways and condone them, or was he a mere blind, doting fool? It was a point to be discussed over the teacups in snug little drawing-rooms, or with the aid of a cigar in the bow windows of clubs. Bitter and plain were the comments among the men upon his conduct. There was but one who had a good word to say for him, and he was the most silent member in the smoking-room. He had seen him break in a horse at the University, and it seemed to have left an impression upon his mind.

But when Douglas Stone became the favourite, all doubts as to Lord Sannox's knowledge or ignorance were set for ever at rest. There was no subterfuge about Stone. In his high-handed, impetuous fashion, he set all caution and discretion at defiance. The scandal became notorious. A learned body intimated that his name had been struck from the list of its vice-presidents. Two friends implored him to consider his professional credit. He cursed them all three, and spent forty guineas on a bangle to take with him to the lady. He was at her house every evening, and she drove in his carriage in the afternoons. There was not an attempt on either side to conceal their relations; but there came at last a little incident to interrupt them.

It was a dismal winter's night, very cold and gusty, with the wind whooping in the chimneys, and blustering against the window-panes. A thin spatter of rain tinkled on the glass with each fresh sough of the gale, drowning for the instant the dull gurgle and drip from the eaves. Douglas Stone had finished his dinner, and sat by his fire in the study, a glass of rich port upon the malachite table at his elbow. As he raised it to his lips, he held it up against the lamplight, and watched with the eye of a connoisseur the tiny scales of beeswing which floated in its rich ruby depths. The fire, as it spurted up, threw fitful lights upon his bold, clear-cut face, with its widely-opened grey eyes, its thick and yet firm lips, and the deep square jaw, which had something Roman in its strength and its animalism. He smiled from time to time as he nestled back in his luxurious chair. Indeed, he had a right to feel well pleased, for against the advice of six colleagues, he had performed an operation that day of which only two cases were on record, and the result had been brilliant beyond all expectation. No other man in London would have had the daring to plan, or the skill to execute, such a heroic measure.

But he had promised Lady Sannox to see her that evening, and it was already half-past eight. His hand was outstretched to the bell to order the carriage when he heard the dull thud of the knocker. An instant later there was the shuffling of feet in the hall, and the sharp closing of a door.

'A patient to see you, sir, in the consulting room,' said the butler.

'About himself?'

'No, sir, I think he wants you to go out.'

'It is too late,' cried Douglas Stone peevishly, 'I won't go.'

'This is his card, sir.' The butler presented it upon the gold salver which had been given to his master by the wife of a Prime Minister.

'"Hamil Ali, Smyrna." Hum! The fellow is a Turk, I suppose.'

'Yes, sir. He seems as if he came from abroad, sir. And he's in a terrible way.'

'Tut, tut! I have an engagement. I must go somewhere else. But I'll see him. Show him in here, Pim.'

A few moments later the butler swung open the door and ushered in a small and decrepid man, who walked with a bent back and with the forward push of the face and blink of the eyes which goes with extreme short sight. His face was swarthy, and his hair and beard of the deepest black. In one hand he held a turban of white muslin striped with red, in the other a small chamois leather bag.

'Good evening,' said Douglas Stone, when the butler had closed the door. 'You speak English, I presume?'

'Yes, sir. I am from Asia Minor, but I speak English when I speak slow.'

'You wanted me to go out, I understand?'

'Yes, sir. I wanted very much that you should see my wife.'

'I could come in the morning, but I have an engagement which prevents me from seeing your wife to-night.'

The Turk's answer was a singular one. He pulled the string which closed the mouth of the chamois leather bag, and poured a flood of gold on to the table.

'There are one hundred pounds there,' said he, 'and I promise you that it will not take you an hour. I have a cab ready at the door.'

Douglas Stone glanced at his watch. An hour would not make it too late to visit Lady Sannox. He had been there later. And the fee was an extraordinarily high one. He had been pressed by his creditors lately, and he could not afford to let such a chance pass. He would go.

'What is the case?' he asked.

'Oh, it is so sad a one! So sad a one! You have not, perhaps, heard of the daggers of the Almohades?'

'Never.'

'Ah, they are Eastern daggers of a great age, and of a singular shape, with the hilt like what you call a stirrup. I am a curiosity dealer, you understand, and that is why I have come to England from Smyrna, but next week I go back once more. Many things I brought with me, and I have few things left, but among them, to my sorrow, is one of these daggers.'

'You will remember that I have an appointment, sir,' said the surgeon, with some irritation. 'Pray confine yourself to the necessary details.'

'You will see that it is necessary. To-day my wife fell down in a faint in the room in which I keep my wares, and she cut her lower lip upon this cursed dagger of Almohades.'

'I see,' said Douglas Stone, rising. 'And you wish me to dress the wound?'

'No, no, it is worse than that.'

'What then?'

'These daggers are poisoned.'

'Poisoned!'

'Yes, and there is no man, East or West, who can tell now what is the poison or what the cure. But all that is known I know, for my father was in this trade before me, and we have had much to do with these poisoned weapons.'

'What are the symptoms?'

'Deep sleep, and death in thirty hours.'

'And you say there is no cure. Why then should you pay me this considerable fee?'

'No drug can cure, but the knife may.'

'And how?'

'The poison is slow of absorption. It remains for hours in the wound.'

'Washing, then, might cleanse it?'

'No more than in a snake bite. It is too subtle and too deadly.'

'Excision of the wound, then?'

'That is it. If it be on the finger, take the finger off. So said my father always. But think of where this wound is, and that it is my wife. It is dreadful!'

But familiarity with such grim matters may take the finer edge from a man's sympathy. To Douglas Stone this was already an interesting case, and he brushed aside as irrelevant the feeble objections of the husband.

'It appears to be that or nothing,' said he, brusquely. 'It is better to lose a lip than a life.'

'Ah, yes, I know that you are right. Well, well, it is kismet, and it must be faced. I have the cab, and you will come with me and do this thing.'

Douglas Stone took his case of bistourie from a drawer, and placed it with a roll of bandage and a compress of lint in his pocket. He must waste no more time if he were to see Lady Sannox.

'I am ready,' said he, pulling on his overcoat. 'Will you take a glass of wine before you go out into this cold air?'

His visitor shrunk away, with a protesting hand upraised.

'You forget that I am a Mussulman, and a true follower of the Prophet,' said he. 'But tell me what is the bottle of green glass which you have placed in your pocket?'

'It is chloroform.'

'Ah, that also is forbidden to us. It is a spirit, and we make no use of such things.'

'What! You would allow your wife to go through an operation without an anæsthetic?'

'Ah! she will feel nothing, poor soul. The deep sleep has already come on, which is the first working of the poison. And then I have given her of our Smyrna opium. Come, sir, for already an hour has passed.'

As they stepped out into the darkness, a sheet of rain was driven in upon their faces, and the hall lamp, which dangled from the arm of a marble Caryatid, went out with a fluff. Pim, the butler, pushed the heavy door to, straining hard with his shoulder against the wind, while the two men groped their way towards the yellow glare which showed where the cab was waiting. An instant later they were rattling upon their journey.

'Is it far?' asked Douglas Stone.

'Oh, no. We have a very little quiet place off the Euston Road.'

The surgeon pressed the spring of his repeater and listened to the little tings which told him the hour. It was a quarter past nine. He calculated the distances, and the short time which it would take him to perform so trivial an operation. He ought to reach Lady Sannox by ten o'clock. Through the fogged windows he saw the blurred gas lamps dancing past, with occasionally the broader glare of a shop front. The rain was pelting and rattling upon the leathern top of the carriage, and the wheels swashed as they rolled through puddle and mud. Opposite to him the white headgear of his companion gleamed faintly through the obscurity. The surgeon felt in his pockets and arranged his needles, his ligatures, and his safety-pins that no time might be wasted when they arrived. He chafed with impatience and drummed his foot upon the floor.

But the cab slowed down at last and pulled up. In an instant Douglas Stone was out, and the Smyrna merchant's toe was at his very heel. 'You can wait,' said he to the driver.

It was a mean-looking house in a narrow and sordid street. The surgeon, who knew his London well, cast a swift glance into the shadows, but there was nothing distinctive, no shop, no movement, nothing but a double line of dull flat-faced houses, a double stretch of wet flagstones which gleamed in the lamplight, and a double rush of water in the gutters which swirled and gurgled towards the sewer gratings. The door which faced them was blotched and discoloured, and a faint light in the fan pane above it served to show the dust and the grime which covered it. Above, in one of the bedroom windows, there was a dull yellow glimmer. The merchant knocked loudly, and, as he turned his dark face towards the light, Douglas Stone could see that it was contracted with anxiety. A bolt was drawn, and an elderly woman with a taper stood in the doorway, shielding the thin flame with her gnarled hand.

'Is all well?' gasped the merchant.

'She is as you left her, sir.'

'She has not spoken?'

'No, she is in a deep sleep.'

The merchant closed the door, and Douglas Stone walked down the narrow passage, glancing about him in some surprise as he did so. There was no oilcloth, no mat, no hat-rack. Deep gray dust and heavy festoons of cobwebs met his eyes everywhere. Following the old woman up the winding stair, his firm footfall echoed harshly through the silent house. There was no carpet.

The bedroom was on the second landing. Douglas Stone followed the old nurse into it, with the merchant at his heels. Here, at least, there was furniture and to spare. The floor was littered and the corners piled with Turkish cabinets, inlaid tables, coats of chain mail, strange pipes, and grotesque weapons. A single small lamp stood upon a bracket on the wall. Douglas Stone took it down, and, picking his way among the lumber, walked over to a couch in the corner, on which lay a woman dressed in the Turkish fashion with yashmak and veil. The lower part of the face was exposed, and the surgeon saw a jagged cut which zigzagged along the border of the under lip.

'You will forgive the yashmak,' said the Turk. 'You know our views about woman in the East.'

But the surgeon was not thinking about the yashmak. This was no longer a woman to him. It was a case. He stooped and examined the wound carefully.

'There are no signs of irritation,' said he. 'We might delay the operation until local symptoms develop.'

The husband wrung his hands in incontrollable agitation.

'Oh! sir, sir,' he cried. 'Do not trifle. You do not know. It is deadly. I know, and I give you my assurance that an operation is absolutely necessary. Only the knife can save her.'

'And yet I am inclined to wait,' said Douglas Stone.

'That is enough,' the Turk cried, angrily. 'Every minute is of importance, and I cannot stand here and see my wife allowed to sink. It only remains for me to give you my thanks for having come, and to call in some other surgeon before it is too late.'

Douglas Stone hesitated. To refund that hundred pounds was no pleasant matter. But of course if he left the case he must return the money. And if the Turk were right and the woman died his position before a coroner might be an embarrassing one.

'You have had personal experience of this poison?' he asked.

'I have.'

'And you assure me that an operation is needful.'

'I swear it by all that I hold sacred.'

'The disfigurement will be frightful.'

'I can understand that the mouth will not be a pretty one to kiss.'

Douglas Stone turned fiercely upon the man. The speech was a brutal one. But the Turk has his own fashion of talk and of thought, and there was no time for wrangling. Douglas Stone drew a bistoury from his case, opened it, and felt the keen straight edge with his forefinger. Then he held the lamp closer to the bed. Two dark eyes were gazing up at him through the slit in the yashmak. They were all iris, and the pupil was hardly to be seen.

'You have given her a very heavy dose of opium.'

'Yes, she has had a good dose.'

He glanced again at the dark eyes which looked straight at his own. They were dull and lustreless, but, even as he gazed, a little shifting sparkle came into them, and the lips quivered.

'She is not absolutely unconscious,' said he.

'Would it not be well to use the knife while it will be painless?'

The same thought had crossed the surgeon's mind. He grasped the wounded lip with his forceps, and with two swift cuts he took out a broad V shaped piece. The woman sprang up on the couch with a dreadful gurgling scream. Her covering was torn from her face. It was a face that he knew. In spite of that protruding upper lip and that slobber of blood, it was a face that he knew. She kept on putting her hand up to the gap and screaming. Douglas Stone sat down at the foot of the couch with his knife and his forceps. The room was whirling round, and he had felt something go like a ripping seam behind his ear. A bystander would have said that his face was the more ghastly of the two. As in a dream, or as if he had been looking at something at the play, he was conscious that the Turk's hair and beard lay upon the table, and that Lord Sannox was leaning against the wall with his hand to his side, laughing silently. The screams had died away now, and the dreadful head had dropped back again upon the pillow, but Douglas Stone still sat motionless, and Lord Sannox still chuckled quietly to himself.

'It was really very necessary for Marion, this operation,' said he, 'not physically, but morally, you know, morally.'

Douglas Stone stooped forwards and began to play with the fringe of the coverlet. His knife tinkled down upon the ground, but he still held the forceps and something more.

'I had long intended to make a little example,' said Lord Sannox, suavely. 'Your note of Wednesday miscarried, and I have it here in my pocket-book. I took some pains in carrying out my idea. The wound, by the way, was from nothing more dangerous than my signet ring.'

He glanced keenly at his silent companion, and cocked the small revolver which he held in his coat pocket. But Douglas Stone was still picking at the coverlet.

'You see you have kept your appointment after all,' said Lord Sannox.

And at that Douglas Stone began to laugh. He laughed long and loudly. But Lord Sannox did not laugh now. Something like fear sharpened and hardened his features. He walked from the room, and he walked on tiptoe. The old woman was waiting outside.

'Attend to your mistress when she awakes,' said Lord Sannox. Then he went down to the street. The cab was at the door, and the driver raised his hand to his hat.

'John,' said Lord Sannox, 'you will take the doctor home first. He will want leading downstairs, I think. Tell his butler that he has been taken ill at a case.'

'Very good, sir.'

'Then you can take Lady Sannox home.'

'And how about yourself, sir?'

'Oh, my address for the next few months will be Hotel di Roma, Venice. Just see that the letters are sent on. And tell Stevens to exhibit all the purple chrysanthemums next Monday, and to wire me the result.'

A Mystery
of the Underground

John Oxenham

John Oxenham was a pen name often used by William Arthur Dunkerley (1852–1941), a journalist, poet and prolific writer of fiction. Like Conan Doyle, he was not a native Londoner; born in Manchester, he moved to Ealing in 1882, and lived there for the next forty years. His six children included the well-known writer of stories aimed mainly at girls, Elsie J. Oxenham.

This is an abridged version of a story originally serialised in To-Day, *a weekly magazine edited by Jerome K. Jerome. The idea of a Tube-travelling serial killer caused such a sensation that passenger numbers slumped, and the Underground authorities wrote a letter of protest to Jerome. Dunkerley worked for the magazine, but had not revealed his authorship—the episodes of the story purported to come from an author in Scotland who insisted on anonymity. Dunkerley persuaded Jerome to continue to publish the serial, but did not come out as Oxenham until a couple of years later.*

>>>

The underground station at Charing Cross was the scene of considerable excitement on the night of Tuesday, the fourth of November. As the 9.17 London and North-Western train rumbled up the platform, a lady was seen standing at the door of one of the first-class carriages, frantically endeavouring to get out, and screaming wildly.

The station inspector ran up to the carriage, and pulled open the door, when the lady literally sprang into his arms. She was in a state of violent hysterics, and it was with difficulty that he assisted her across the platform to a seat.

Meanwhile, a small crowd gathered round the open carriage door. The guard of the train had come up, elbowed his way through, and entered the carriage. The spectators could see a man sitting in the further corner, apparently asleep, his hat over his eyes, his head sunk forward.

'Drunken brute! he's frightened the lydy!'

'Pitch him out, guard, and we'll jump on 'im!'

The guard shook the man roughly, his hat rolled off, and the crowd jeered.

Then, suddenly, the guard came back to the door, waved his flag to a porter, and said hurriedly:

'Block the line behind—quick—and send the inspector.'

The porter hurried off, shouted to the inspector, and ran down the train to the signal-box.

The inspector left his charge in care of some ladies, and pushed his way into the carriage. The guard said a word to him, and they bent over the man in the corner. Then, with startled faces and compressed lips, after a momentary hesitation, they stopped and lifted him out of the carriage. The head fell back as they carried him awkwardly across the platform, and the crowd shrank away, silent and scared, at sight of the ghastly limpness and the stains of blood.

'Where to?' said the guard.

'Upstairs, I suppose,' said the inspector; and then added: 'Best thing would be to take him right on to Westminster. It's a Scotland Yard job, is this!'

'That's so!' said the guard. 'And her, too?' nodding towards the hysterical lady on the seat.

'Yes. Put him in again, and lock the door. I'll see to her. Tell Bob to keep the line blocked till they get the word from Westminster.'

They put the body back into the carriage, locked the door, and the guard went off to the signal-box, while the inspector took in hand the more difficult task of getting the lady, still in a state of hysterics, back into a carriage.

Finally, he had to have her carried in; he stepped in himself, and the train rolled off through the fog, past the line of scared faces on the platform, into the darkness which led towards Westminster; and the red stern light blinked ghoulishly back at the crowd, and tremulously disappeared up the tunnel like a great clot of blood.

Within seven minutes of the arrival of the train at Westminster, Scotland Yard was in possession of the facts, and of the chief factors in the case—the body—and the lady—by this time in a state of extreme nervous prostration. A couple of detectives were minutely examining the carriage as it sped on its journey, and the traffic on the Underground resumed its normal course.

The morning papers contained a brief announcement of the discovery. The evening papers imaginatively worked up all the details they had been able to obtain, and promoted the item to a prominent position among the day's news, in large type, well spaced out. But with the inquest, held next day, the excitement increased. Briefly, all that was learned was this:

From letters and papers found upon the deceased, the body was identified as that of Conrad Grosheim, a financier and speculator in the City. The identification was confirmed by Grosheim's clerk, and by the landlady of the room he occupied in King's Road, Chelsea.

The station inspector at Charing Cross and the guard of the train spoke to the finding of the body.

Maud Jones stated that she had a race to catch the train at Temple station. She was running up towards the second-class carriages when the train started and the inspector flung open the door of a first-class and assisted her in, telling her to change at the next station. She had not noticed anything wrong with the gentleman in the corner—thought he was asleep—remembered his cigarette had slipped from his fingers, and was still smoking on the floor, when suddenly her eyes caught sight of blood dripping from his coat, and it flashed upon her that he was dead. She was so horrified that she nearly lost her senses. Was positive the cigarette on the floor was smoking when she got in. No, she did not smell anything like powder—nothing but the cigarette. The window next to the dead man was up. She touched nothing in the carriage, and got out of it as soon as she could. She was a waitress at Belloni's Restaurant, in the Strand. She had never seen the gentleman before, and was only sorry she had ever set eyes on him at all.

The inspector at Temple station confirmed Miss Jones's story as to her being put into the carriage.

The ticket porter at Temple station swore positively that no one whatever got out of the train. He had watched the young lady helped into the first-class carriage by the inspector, and there was not a single person on the platform when the train went out, except the inspector. Nobody could possibly have got up the stairs while he was watching. He had snapped the ingress gate as the lady passed through, and had not opened the egress one.

Dr Mortimer stated that he had examined the body, and was of the opinion that death had taken place not more than fifteen minutes, certainly not more than half an hour, before his examination. Cause of death was a bullet through the heart. It had entered the body level and straight, passed through the heart, causing instant death, and was found inside the ribs on the right side of the body. Bullet produced. It was of an unusually conical shape, and by impact with the ribs had been slightly flattened. In its natural shape it would be sharper, almost pointed. There were no signs of singeing or burning on deceased's clothing. The bullet made a clean cut through coat and vest, and did its work. If, as he understood, deceased was sitting in the corner of the carriage facing slightly towards the corner which Miss Jones occupied, the shot must have been fired from the seat exactly opposite where deceased sat.

'Or through the window?' queried the coroner.

'Or through the window,' granted the doctor. 'The exact spot from which the shot was fired would depend upon the angle at which deceased was sitting, but I understood the window was found closed.'

'Could the wound have been self-inflicted?'

'It could, of course, but not without singeing the clothing.'

'Could deceased have shot himself, thrown the revolver out of the window, and raised the window?'

'Absolutely impossible; death was instantaneous.'

Miss Jones, recalled, stated that the window was up when she entered the carriage. She was quite certain of that. It was a close, muggy night, and she felt half-suffocated. The window nearest her was jammed, and she could not let it down. She had looked across at the other, and thought of trying to open it. Then she saw the cigarette smoking on the floor, and then she saw the blood, and then she remembered screaming.

Detective-Sergeant Doane, of Scotland Yard, stated that the case had been placed in his hands; that he had taken possession of the carriage within a few minutes of the discovery of the body. It had been examined most minutely by himself and a colleague, both inside and out. Beyond the cigarette, trampled flat, probably in the removal of the body, and a few drops of blood on the floor, nothing whatever had been found. There was no weapon, no sign of a struggle. The contents of deceased's pockets, including a valuable watch and chain, had not been touched. He had questioned the passengers in the next compartments, but no one had heard a shot, or any sound whatever, except the screams of Miss Jones. Further stated that if Miss Jones was correct in stating that the cigarette was still burning on the floor when she entered, and he had no reason to doubt it, he judged that the deed was committed in the tunnel between Mansion House and Blackfriars, and he arrived at it thus. A cigarette of that brand would burn on the floor for five minutes; the train took one and a half minutes to travel from Temple to Charing Cross, half a minute's stoppage at Temple; two minutes from Blackfriars to Temple, half a minute's stoppage at Blackfriars took them into the tunnel between Mansion House and Blackfriars, and there the shot must have been fired. That tunnel had been searched inch by inch, so had the others, but nothing whatever had been found. He had his own ideas on the subject, but declined at present to make them public. Deceased's ticket was from Mansion House to Sloane Square.

The jury returned a verdict of wilful murder against some person or persons unknown; and so one more was added to the long list of undiscovered crimes of the Metropolis.

(From the *Link*, 12 November 1894)
ANOTHER MURDER ON THE UNDERGROUND
THE *LINK* MAN ON THE SPOT, AS USUAL

At 9.21 exactly, last night, as the weary *Link* man, having finished his appointed tasks, was patiently travelling in an

Underground train to his humble abode at Chelsea, a piece of great good fortune befell him. Great good fortune to one man generally means corresponding bad fortune to some other man, and so it was in this case. Without desiring to appear over-presumptuous, it does seem providential, that is, to the readers of the *Link*, that the *Link* man was right on the spot, and is therefore able to give an eye-witness's account of the very strange occurrence which took place at St James's Park station on the Underground railway last night.

Our contemporaries have published more or less garbled versions of the matter. They have done their best. The *Link*, however, was the only paper actually represented, and able, therefore, to give an absolutely exact account of what happened.

The *Link* man entered the train at Blackfriars, travelling third-class, as usual. He always travels third—not, as you might imagine, from necessity, but from choice. He thereby sees and feels, and, in every sense of the word, comes so much more in contact with his fellows, than is possible in the cold, refined, varnish-and-saddlebag atmosphere of the first-class. After standing patiently past three stations, the *Link* man had just managed to gently insinuate his person into the sixth place on a seat intended for five, and was jocularly remarking to his scowling neighbours, upon portions of whom he was sitting, that the tighter you sat the less you joggled, when a series of piercing screams from the next carriage forward rent the darkness of the tunnel, and heated all the *Link* man's professional instincts to boiling point. He sprang to the door. Something was happening—something untoward and out of the common. Such screams—off the stage—were an outrage, or implied one.

His first intention was to climb along the footboard till he arrived at the screams. But thoughts of Mrs *Link*-man and all the little *Link* men and women deterred him, and he decided not to risk his precious life, but to be first on the scene, all the same.

The screams had ceased. The silence seemed even more pregnant. While the screams continued something was happening. With their cessation, it—whatever it was—had happened. As the train slowed up at St James's Park, the *Link* man dashed forward to the next carriage—the rearmost first-class—and this is what he saw on opening the door—a lady lying apparently lifeless in the corner seat nearest the platform, and on the floor face downwards, the body of a man.

A crowd rushed to the door almost as soon as the *Link* man, but his were the first eyes that witnessed the scene. The station inspector came up, and was for ordering the *Link* man away, but, upon the latter disclosing his identity, became the courteous official the *Link* man has always found him, except upon that one unfortunate occasion when he (the inspector) found him (the *Link* man) riding first with a third-class ticket, and only let him off imprisonment for life with a reprimand, which still tingles in the *Link* man's ears, on the *Link* man's proving to him by ocular demonstration that every third-class carriage was carrying thirty per cent more humanity than it had any right to do.

The guard came up, too, and *ex officio*, the *Link* man was privileged to share the labours and cogitations of these officials.

By virtue of her sex, the lady claimed their first attention. She was in a dead faint, and was carefully carried through a double line of curious faces by the *Link* man and the guard to one of the station seats.

The *Link* man left the guard in charge, and hurried back to the carriage.

The inspector was stooping over the prostrate man, and as the *Link* man stepped in, he looked up with scared face, and said, 'It's another murder!'

'Good God!' said the *Link* man, involuntarily, for this was getting exciting. Then he saw blood on the inspector's hands.

'Better block the line behind, and wire to Scotland Yard, hadn't you?' he suggested.

'It blocks itself,' said the inspector; 'but we'll make doubly sure. Stop here in charge, will you, and I'll wire Scotland Yard at same time.' And he went off at a run, leaving the *Link* man in full charge.

Notebook and pencil came out of their own accord, with the following results: 'First-class carriage No. 32. London and North-Western train, St James's Park; time 9.25 p.m. Body dressed in dark grey overcoat with velvet collar—dark trousers—black diagonal coat and vest—patent leather shoes—Lincoln and Bennet hat, bruised from a fall. Face, so far as visible, dark and pale—age about forty-five—four-coil snake ring, with ruby and diamond in head, on third finger of left hand. In vest, exactly over heart, small, clean-cut hole, no singeing or burning, no smell of powder—no signs of struggle—window furthest from platform closed. Note—Exactly a week, to the minute almost, since discovery of the murder at Charing Cross last week. Is this accident or horrible intention?'

Link man acknowledges to creepy feeling. Door opens. Inspector returns, and a few minutes later, Scotland Yard, in the person of quiet, stern-faced Detective-Sergeant Doane, who has the previous case in hand, arrives with a colleague. They examine carriage minutely, inside and out, rear-side and off-side, under and over. They say little, but make many notes.

Carriage is locked up, and train sent on. *Link* man notices that most carriages are about half as full as when train came in, as though many had conceived sudden distaste for underground travel—that no single travellers are to be seen—general mistrustful gregariousness observable. *Link* man feels himself that sooner than travel in a carriage alone, or with only one other person, he would stop on the platform all night, and sleep on Smith's bookstall.

Body is carried to ambulance. Lady, now reviving, is placed in cab, and all drive off to Scotland Yard.

The unfortunate victim of this second outrage has since been identified as George Villars, commercial traveller, residing at West Kensington. The lady is Mrs Corbett, manageress of the ABC shop in Albert Street, Westminster.

Her account is simply that she entered the train at Westminster, and had barely got seated when the gentleman opposite lurched forward in his seat, presumably with the shaking of the carriage, and then fell prone on the floor. She saw blood on the floor, and screamed, and then fainted.

What may be the meaning of this exact repetition of the murder at Charing Cross exactly a week ago it is impossible to say. The time, the manner, the general conditions, are as nearly as possible identical.

Are both murders the act of the same hand; or is Number Two but one more proof of the epidemic nature of abnormal crimes—the result, in fact, of the action of Crime Number One on some weak intellect, with a morbid craving for notoriety?

One thing is certain: travel on the Underground is less attractive than of yore, and the homely 'bus is rising in public estimation.

(From the *Daily Telephone*, 19 November 1894)
A THIRD MURDER ON THE UNDERGROUND

The appalling discovery last night at Ealing Broadway station, on the District Railway, places beyond possibility of doubt the fact that a cold-blooded murderer is at large in our midst, and that travellers on that at all times depressing line are completely at his mercy. The police, we are willing to believe, are doing their best in the matter, but so far their efforts have apparently been fruitless. Every Tuesday night for the last three weeks, at, as near as can be told, exactly the same time to the minute, the mysterious death-dealer has chosen his victim, fired his fatal shot, and vanished. Whatever his motive and whatever his method, he has succeeded in instilling such a sense of dread into the public mind that the District Railway is beginning to be shunned by all persons of nervous temperament.

This curious state of things recalls to mind a similar series of crimes perpetrated on the Ceinture Railway, in Paris, about seven years ago. There, too, the victims were smitten down by an undiscoverable hand, and it was only when the seventh had fallen that the slaughter stopped. If it had not, the traffic on that line would have ceased, for the excitement was indescribable, and travellers shunned the Ceinture Railway as they would a pesthouse.

Much the same feeling is growing in the minds of travellers by the District Railway, and especially so on Tuesday nights, which is the time fixed by the mysterious one for his horrible work. Last Tuesday night the trains ran nearly empty. Numbers of people, so curious is the hankering of the morbid mind after sensation, gathered in the stations most likely to afford the chance of a thrill. The platforms at Charing Cross, Westminster, St James's Park and Victoria were crowded with sensation-seekers, who had taken tickets which they had no intentions of using, but simply with the idea of being on the spot in case anything happened. And a very curious study those platforms were.

Throngs of people, waiting silently, in a damp fog, peering into carriage after carriage as the almost empty trains rolled slowly, like processions of funeral cars, in and out of the stations. In one carriage a party of young roughs had ensconced themselves, and endeavoured to make things lively by chaffing and jeering the silent crowds on the platforms as they passed through. They met with no encouragement, however, and had things all their own way. We wonder how those lively youths feel now when they know that, beyond a doubt, the mysterious murderer looked in on them, and could, had he so chosen, have launched his deadly bullet into their midst. But, as usual, his fatal choice fell upon a solitary wayfarer occupying a corner seat in a carriage by himself, and within three compartments of one occupied by the rowdy gang referred to.

Many of the crowd on the stations remarked on the temerity of the occupant of that corner seat. He might well sit so quiet. The fatal bullet was in his heart before he reached Victoria, at all events. But he journeyed peacefully on until he reached Ealing Broadway station, the terminus of the line. There, one of the principal duties of the porters is to arouse all the passengers who have succumbed to the monotony of the journey from the City and there John Small, the Ealing porter, tried in vain to arouse Carl Groeb, the occupant of the corner seat in the rear compartment of one of the first-class carriages, and found him dead—murdered, in the same way, and, beyond all doubt, by the same hand which struck down Conrad Grosheim, at, or about, 9.15 on the evening of Tuesday, the fourth inst., at Charing Cross, and which struck down George Villars, at 9.15 on the evening of Tuesday, the eleventh inst., at St James's Park.

The crowds at the stations up the line had dispersed with a sigh of disappointment, or let us take a charitable view, and say of relief. But the tragedy was there all the same, and the victim had passed beneath their eyes, though the public had to wait till Wednesday morning to get its thrill.

It is a terrible fact, but one that has to be faced that, in the greatest city in the world, in this year of grace 1894, such an appalling series of crimes can be perpetrated with impunity.

The police seem powerless. We give them credit for doing their utmost, but, up to now, nothing, so far as they let it be known, has resulted from their efforts.

One thing is certain, if the criminal cannot be brought to justice the directors of the District Railway can close up their line. It would pay them to run the electric light through every tunnel, and to line the route and sprinkle the carriages with detectives, in the style of an Imperial progress in Russia. The matter is really too gruesome for a jest, but *Punch* certainly hit the case off admirably in Bernard Partidge's clever sketch of the young City man attracting all the attentions of all the beauties in the drawing-room by the simple assertion that he had travelled from town by the District Railway, in a first-class carriage, *all by himself*, while the season's lions scowl at him from a distance, and twirl their moustaches, and growl in their neglected corners.

While, in another portion of the same journal, Mr Anstey's 'Voces Populi', describing the scene at Victoria station on Tuesday night, while the crowds waited for what they feared, and made simple bets on the basis of murder or no murder, and more complicated ones as to the age and nationality of the expected victim, the station where the discovery would be made, and so on, is immensely clever, but grim in the extreme. It proves the identity of one of the crowd at all events, and it will afford matter for much wondering comment on the part of readers of this year's *Punch* twenty years hence.

To return to the facts which confront us, however. Murder, grim, cold, calculating, glides unchecked in our midst. No man's life is safe. You yourself, reading this, may be the next victim—that is, if you are so unwise as to trust yourself alone in a carriage on the District Railway. And this in London, AD 1894! What a satire on our boasted civilisation!

The official report of this latest crime is, with the necessary alterations of names, places, and dates, a mere duplication of the previous ones.

Carl Groeb took ticket at Mansion House for Victoria on the evening of Tuesday, the twenty-fifth inst., at 9.20. Before he reached Victoria he was dead—shot through the heart, in identically the same manner as the previous victims, and not a trace of the murderer is discoverable.

It is beyond belief, and yet it is horrible fact.

(From the *Daily Telephone*, 23 November 1894)

More light has been thrown on the dark corners of the Underground railway during the last few days than at any period of its existence, and yet the mystery remains unsolved. Travellers between 9 and 10.30 p.m. have been few and far between. Indeed, between those hours the service has been almost suspended, not more than one train in ten being run, and that running practically empty. But such hardy voyagers as have ventured, at risk of their lives, to run the passage from the City to Earl's Court, have travelled through a torchlight procession. Every tunnel has been filled with men with flare-lights, and the grotesque effects of the continuous blaze and the weird gigantic shadows are things to be remembered for a lifetime.

Not only is traffic on the Underground disorganised—business and pleasure alike are interrupted in their regular courses. Never, during the last twenty years, has London worked itself up into such a state of excitement as it has done over these mysterious crimes on the Underground. Suburban residents find words even of the most cerulean hue quite inadequate to express the annoyance and inconvenience they are being put to.

Scotland Yard has had a detective patrolling the foot-board of every train. This, however, is to be stopped. The sensation of suddenly finding a strange face peering in at your ear as you sit harmlessly reading your evening paper in your favourite corner seat, is enough to startle any man. It has given rise to some most ludicrous scenes. Going home in a Richmond train last night, the writer sat opposite to a quiet, nervous-looking old gentleman. He happened to raise his eyes from his paper just as the patrol on the footboard passed the window. The old gentleman made up his mind at once that he had been selected as the murderer's next victim, and that the deadly bullet was just about to be launched. He instinctively sheltered his head behind his newspaper, and sank suddenly off his seat, and remained flat on the floor, nor could he be induced to rise till the next station was reached. Many ladies have been driven into hysterics in the same way, and the patrols are to be abolished.

In connection with the murder of Carl Groeb, it is now proved beyond doubt that the murderer has added to his other crime the meaner one of robbery. Groeb's pockets were empty when he was discovered—money, watch, chain, all were gone, though the evidence is conclusive that, when he left his office in Houndsditch, he carried a good round sum, and wore a good gold watch and chain. There is more hope of catching the murderer if he is driven by the exigencies of want, or the desire for gain, to unite the functions of footpad with those of self-constituted executioner. At all events, he descends from the sphere of the supernatural, into which popular credulity has been inclined to elevate him, and becomes a mere murderous thief.

(From the *Daily Telephone*, 25 November 1894)

We have received the following letter:

To the Editor of the *Daily Telephone*.
    Sir,—You are wrong. I never touched the money or effects of Carl Groeb, or any other of my victims. I kill; I do not rob.—Yours truly,
    The Underground Murderer.

The letter is post-marked 'London, SE, 24 November,

1894'. Is it a grim jest, or is it a genuine document? We give it for what it is worth.

(From the *Daily Telephone*, 26 November, 1894)

To the Editor of the *Daily Telephone*.

Sir,—The Underground Murderer has enough on his conscience. He did *not* rob Carl Groeb of his watch, chain and money. I did. I entered the carriage at Sloane Square. The attitude of the figure in the corner startled me. When we had passed South Kensington I spoke to him. He did not answer. I touched him. He did not move. I saw he was dead. I was stone-broke myself. I had bilked the ticket-man at Sloane Square, and intended doing the same at Earl's Court. The opportunity was too good to be missed. The man in the corner had no further use for his money. I had. I relieved him of it, and also of his watch and chain. The latter I pawned in Liverpool, and I enclose you the ticket. I am a bad lot, but, thank Heaven, I am

(Signed) Not the Underground Murderer.

The above letter was received by us two days ago, post-marked 'Liverpool'. We sent the pawn-ticket on to Liverpool. The watch and chain, recovered from the pawnbroker, have been sent to London, and have been identified beyond all doubt as Carl Groeb's!

Both letters are in possession of the police.

(From the *Daily Telephone*, 27 November 1894)

What, in Heaven's name, is this monstrous thing that is waging cruel, remorseless and indiscriminate warfare with that section of London that travels by the Underground? Is it against the Underground railway itself, as a system or as a corporation, that this foul fiend is fighting? Or is it some lunatic registering in this gruesome fashion his protest against the influx of foreigners into English business life?—for it is a noticeable fact that three out of the four victims have been foreigners.

Last night was 'Murder Night', as Tuesday night has come to be grimly dubbed on the Underground, and two more victims fell to the assassin's bullet—one in the usual neat and finished style to which we are becoming accustomed, but with a change of locality, necessitated, no doubt, by the close and incessant watch kept on every corner of the murderer's old haunts; the other was a gratuitous slap in the face—or, to be precise, bullet in the leg—of one of the guardians of the public safety in charge of the tunnel between Victoria and Sloane Square.

As the train which left Mansion House at 9.16, and left Victoria at 9.31, was running through the tunnel between Victoria and Sloane Square, it passed an up-line train proceeding to Mansion House.

The flare-light men are mostly concentrated between Victoria and Mansion House, in the tunnels of which section all the murders have hitherto been committed. As a precautionary measure, however, half a dozen men have been told off for duty each night in the tunnel between Victoria and Sloane Square. As the two trains passed, one of the flare-men standing in the six-foot fell to the ground, shot through the leg. No report was heard. Nothing but the rattle of the passing trains, which drowned the man's groans as he sank to the ground. His mate down the line saw a blaze of light as his flare fell over, and the oil caught fire and spread along the ground. Running up, he dragged the wounded man away from the flames, and yelled to the other men further down the tunnel.

Among them they carried this latest victim up to Victoria

station, where their arrival caused a stampede of all except the officials.

The men's accounts of the matter are confused.

The bullet, of course, came from one of the passing trains, but which they cannot say. Even the wounded man is not certain how he was standing when the bullet struck him, but in any case only the very promptest action could have thrown any light on the matter. Had the men promptly wired to the next stations, both up and down the line, at which both trains would stop, strict search might have led to some discovery. But their wounded mate absorbed all their attention, and the chance, such as it was, was lost. We may, however, conclude, without doubt, that the shot came from the down train. That train reached Baker Street at 9.58, and four minutes later the murderer's fifth victim was discovered in a first-class carriage at Gower Street, in the person of John Stern, merchant, of Jewin Street, who was discovered shot through the heart, in exactly the same way as all the previous victims of the Underground fiend.

How much longer this state of matters is to continue depends, apparently, entirely on the will of the mysterious and bloodthirsty perpetrator of these atrocious crimes. The arm of the law seems powerless. It only remains now for the Underground fiend to shoot down an engine driver and his mate to bring about a catastrophe too horrible to contemplate. The bare possibility of an Underground train deprived of its natural controllers, and crashing madly along at its own sweet will, is enough to make one forswear for ever the delights of travel on that much-maligned line.

(From the *Link*, 4 December 1894)
another outrage on the underground
the *LINK* man the sixth victim

To all intents and purposes, I am a dead man.

To all intents and purposes, I am victim No. Six of the Underground Demon.

That I am here alive to tell the tale is no fault of his, but is due to a little precautionary measure of my own.

I have passed through a very strange experience.

I have done what no other man has done. I have looked Death in the face—the Death of the Underground. I have looked down the barrel of the weapon with which the Underground Death-dealer slaughters his victims.

I myself was the victim.

I am free to confess that I am shaken in nerves and sorely bruised in body.

After the detailed account given below of my experiences last 'Murder Night' I have done with the matter. I have had enough of it. My constitution cannot stand the exigencies of up-to-date travel on the Underground. The facts I am about to relate are so passing strange, that I may state at once that they are vouched for by the one man who has had more to do with the Underground Murders (except, of course, the chief actor of all) than anyone else—Detective-Sergeant Doane, of Scotland Yard. Sergeant Doane, into whose hands, from the first, has been entrusted the discovery of the mysterious murderer, has been greatly exercised by the failure of all the ingenious plans laid for his capture, and the apparent impossibility of coming to grips with the invisible one.

It is obviously impossible to have a detective on the step of every carriage of every train on the Underground railway. It is impossible to line the whole length of the system with flare-light men, even on 'Murder Night.' As a matter of fact, since the shooting of John Cran, the flare-man, in Sloane Square tunnel, it is not easy to induce the men to undertake the duty at all, for every one of them feels that he takes his life in his hand when he picks up his lamp. Every man of them knows that, as like as not, he may be the next victim.

I came into contact with Sergeant Doane over the second murder, the one at St James's Park, as readers of the *Link* will remember. I have met him many times since, and we have discussed the matter from many points of view.

On Saturday last I laid before him a scheme which seemed to me to offer at least the chance of a solution of the mystery.

My proposition was this: I offered to take my place, alone, in a first-class compartment in the train leaving Mansion House at 9.12 on 'Murder Night,' and to afford the Underground Fiend every facility for selecting me as his next victim. As a precaution, I was to wear inside my waistcoat a breastplate of solid steel; I was to have the company of an armed detective beneath the opposite seat within reach of a kick, and on top of the carriage, lying flat on the roof, directly over each window of my compartment, were to be two other detectives.

Sergeant Doane turned this idea over in his mind before cautiously venturing the remark that it might do—might do for me, in any case, he grimly added.

The idea was carried out precisely as given above, and 9.13 last Tuesday night found me comfortably ensconced, steel breastplate and all, in the rear first-class compartment of the London and North-Western train from Mansion House to Willesden, gliding through brilliant tunnel after tunnel into the comparative obscurity of the stations, and patiently waiting to be shot at. Beneath the opposite seat, within easy reach of my toe, was one of Doane's trusty followers, armed with a revolver. Flat on the roof, feet to engine, and head over my window, with the cold night wind ploughing up his back hair, was Sergeant Doane himself and over the opposite window another of his men, both armed with revolvers. A slight iron framework had been fixed to the top of the carriage to prevent their rolling off.

Now, a scheme of this kind—I speak from experience—is all very well in the heat of inception and preliminary discussion, but, in the carrying out of it, one's temperature is apt to fall.

I must confess to feeling distinctly nervous as I took my seat in the carriage, and, as the train rumbled along through the weird, irregular illumination of the flare-light men, an odd idea grew upon me that the compartment I was sitting in was somehow unpleasantly familiar to me.

The sensation grew, and the feelings of discomfort increased in proportion. It was likely enough I had ridden in that same carriage dozens of times, for I use the Underground freely, and occasionally go 'first' when, in my opinion, the 'thirds' are full. I was arguing myself into the idea that it was just the natural nervousness incidental to the job I had in hand, when my eye, roving around, caught the number of the carriage—No. 32—on the small enamelled plate above the door, and I experienced all the sensation of a cold douche down the spine.

'Nonsense!' said I to myself. 'Don't be an idiot!'

But I sat and stared at that small enamelled plate till it began to hypnotise me.

To prove myself a fool, and disperse the blue devils, I hauled out my notebook, and turned over the pages till I came to what was in my mind. And then—I had a strong inclination to get out of the carriage, and have done with the business.

I was sitting in the exact spot of the very compartment of the very carriage in which George Villars was shot exactly five weeks ago to the day, and almost to the minute. As readers of the *Link* will remember, I was the first to discover his body at St James's Park station. It was distinctly unpleasant, but it could not be helped.

For companionship's sake, I landed a kick on a tender portion of the recumbent detective under the seat opposite, and he grunted wakefully. Then, feeling deucedly uncomfortable, I sank my head down into the pose of a tired man, drew my hat down over my brow, and turned my eyes almost upside down in the endeavour to keep a bright look-out from under the brim of it.

Blackfriars, Temple, Charing Cross, Westminster, St James's, Victoria, Sloane Square: I heaved a sigh of relief. We were through the original murder zone, and looked like drawing blank this time. Still, as the murderer had broken fresh ground at Baker Street last week, there was no knowing where he might strike this time. And so the train rumbled on.

Earl's Court, and tickets; Addison Road, Uxbridge Road, Shepherd's Bush, and we were rushing across the wilds of Wormwood Scrubs, when my eyes, wearied almost to blindness with the unnatural strain, closed for a moment's rest.

When I opened them, to my amazement, the window on my left, which I had carefully closed, was down, and wind and rain were pouring in. It sank to the bottom. Every drop of blood in me was tingling with excitement. My heart was going like a sledge-hammer. I wanted to kick the man under the seat, but could not move a toe.

As I glanced at the window, along the polished framework of the part that slides down, there came gently and silently into view a shining steel barrel, pointing straight for my heart. I caught just one vague glimpse of a face beyond it, then—without any report, or any warning, an awful shock—and—blank.

They tell me that I was lifted out at Willesden, and that I was unconscious for upwards of four hours.

I take their word for it; at present I will take anybody's word for anything. As far as I am personally concerned, I have done with the Underground Murders. I hold a season ticket on that abnormal line from Blackfriars to Sloane Square. Anyone who wants it, and will take it with all risks, including its non-transferability, is welcome to it. I would suggest that whoever takes it, should also take out a £10,000 Life Policy for the benefit of his widow and children.

For myself, as I said at the beginning. Underground travel is not adapted to my peculiar constitution. I now go home by 'bus.

As this story is passing strange, and may, in some quarters, be received with incredulity, Sergeant Doane has very kindly offered to add a few words concerning his experiences on Tuesday night.

If any of my fellow-journalists desire ocular demonstration of the truth of my story, and will call at St Bartholomew's Hospital, they can see for themselves the documents in the case, viz.: one steel shield, and one journalist, with a bruise, of the dimensions of a soup-plate, round about the spot where his heart is supposed to be.

Sergeant Doane's account is as follows:—

'I have read the foregoing statement, and endorse it in every particular which came under my own knowledge. Journeying on one's stomach, stern foremost, on top of the Underground train, is not a mode of locomotion that I can recommend. The motion of the train, much more violent up there than in the body of the carriage, the peculiar position, and the horrible atmosphere, produced a feeling of nausea to such an extent that my colleague, on the other side of the roof, when he descended at Willesden, was white as a sheet, and was practically in the throes of sea-sickness.

'Nothing happened on our journey till we reached Wormwood Scrubs. It was blowing half a gale. The heavy rain stung like pellets, and, combined with the rattle of the train, drowned every other sound.

'Half-way between Wormwood Scrubs station and Willesden Junction, the gale seemed to seize the train and shake it, and it was all we could do to hang on by main force. It was at that moment that I heard a shout in the carriage below; then my colleague, Detective Trevor, who had been hidden under the seat, put his head through the window, shouting, 'Doane, Doane, he is shot.' Half a minute more, and we ran into Willesden station. Mr Lester was insensible from the impact of the bullet, which was flattened on the shield like a shilling. I heard no report, and feel sure there was none. Trevor confirms this fact. Beyond the 'ping' of the bullet on the shield, he heard nothing. On hearing that, however, he crawled out, found Mr Lester with all the breath knocked out of him, and yelled for me.'

(From the *Daily Telephone*, 10 December 1894)

We feel like accessories before the fact—like partners in the horrible work of the Underground Murderer.

Ten days ago we hinted in these columns at the appalling catastrophe which might result from the massacre of an Underground engine driver and his mate by the Underground Murderer.

Last night, William Johnson, driver of the 9.1 Outer Circle train, was shot at and wounded, fortunately not fatally, as the train ran through the tunnel beyond South Kensington station.

When the train steamed into Gloucester Road station, it was seen at once that something was wrong. Charles Jones, the fireman, was hanging on to the brake lever, white as a sheet, shouting for help. As the train came to a stand, and the inspectors and guard ran up, Driver Johnson was found lying in a heap on the floor of the cab.

Jones explained hurriedly that, as they ran through the tunnel Johnson suddenly clapped his hand to his side, and cried, 'My God! I'm shot!' and fell all of a heap.

'I'm off,' said Jones, when he had finished his story. 'I'll have no more o' this—a man's life isn't safe.' Neither threats nor persuasion availed to induce him to resume his place on the engine. Another driver and fireman were eventually procured from Mansion House, and traffic was resumed.

Matters, however, have come to a pretty pass when such an occurrence is possible, and something has got to be done, and at once, to put an end to this unheard-of state of affairs.

The authorities offer a reward of £1,000 for information leading to the arrest of the killer, and no further murders are committed on the Underground. However, the Link *reporter, Charles Lester, discovers that the culprit is about to flee for Australia on a ship called the* Bendigo. *Lester joins the other passengers on board, but two more murders occur at sea before Lester deduces that the unlikely culprit is an elderly man called Hood, who is accompanied by his pretty grand-daughter. Hood arouses the suspicion of Shannon, the ship's doctor, whom he tries to kill. But Shannon fights back, and Hood falls to his death. His grand-daughter, an unwitting accomplice to the old man's crimes, invites Lester to Hood's cabin.*

The girl was kneeling on the floor, amid piles of books, papers, clothing, etc., which she had taken from his boxes.

She beckoned me inside, and bade me close the door.

'You have a right to see some of these things, Mr Lester,' she said. 'When you have seen all you care to, will you help me to get rid of them? I only learned this morning from Captain Joram that you were the Mr Lester who—' She faltered, and the large eyes, turned pathetically up to mine, were swimming with tears.

'Try and forget all about it,' I said, 'and let me help you.'

She stooped hurriedly, and picked up a bundle of papers.

'Read those—and those—and look at these,' putting into my hand some strange steel instruments, quite unlike anything I had ever seen before. One had a horse-shoe clutch at the end, and, at the other extremity, it was pinned on to another long, thin steel rod, one end of which terminated in four fine sharp teeth, like the prongs of a fork.

I turned it over in my hand, but could make nothing of it, so proceeded to look over the papers. And, reading them, I arrived at old Hood's story.

A mechanical engineer, of quite unique powers, he had patented a number of inventions, and offered them to the District Railway Company, in whose employment he had spent the best part of his life. Nothing had come of them, however, and I gathered from some of the company's letters in reply that the old man had accused them of using his ideas, but giving him no benefit of them. Then he left the company's service, with his brain bursting with grievances, and it was easy to conceive that he determined to strike at them in a way that was as horribly effective as it was, for him, easy of accomplishment.

I was puzzling over the strange implements, and trying to get at their use. In thought, I went back to one of the murderer's journeys along the swinging footboards, and suddenly it all flashed upon me. A long steel rod, with curved top—that hitched on to the edge of the carriage roof, and had enabled him to pass rapidly along, without troubling to grasp each handle. That spidery implement, with the curved horse-shoe clutch and the pronged lever—I could see the sharp teeth inserted quietly into the window sash, the clutch fitted to the bottom outside frame, the pressing of the lever—and my closed window was sliding quietly down, the wind and rain of Wormwood Scrubs were beating in on me again, and my paralysed eyes were looking once more down the deadly death-tube. I could see myself lying bruised and stunned in the corner, and, in imagination, could follow the murderer as he rapidly made his way back to the carriage he had issued from, and, perhaps, concealed himself under the seat, or, riding between two carriages, dropped quietly off as the train began to slow up to the station.

There were other curious contrivances, whose meaning I could not fathom, but had no doubt they all tended to the same end—the boarding of, or hanging on to, trains in motion.

I looked up at the girl.

'What do you want me to do with all these things?'

'Throw them all overboard—clothes—books—papers—everything. I have kept the only papers I need. Please get rid of them all for me.'

I did. Shannon, however, claimed the air-gun, and certainly no one who wanted it had a better right to it.

It was a wonderful weapon, the only remaining monument to the old engineer's skill. With two twists it came into three pieces, and was easily stowed in one's ordinary pockets. The first day Shannon appeared on deck, Miss Hood being below, he tried that demon air-gun on the main-mast with a bullet of his own making. It buried itself out of sight, and a three-inch probe failed to reach it.

'No wonder it knocked the wind out of you, old man,' he said; 'if you hadn't had that breastplate on, you wouldn't be here now.'

We cleaned our memories of Old Man Hood as far as we could, as we had cleaned the ship of himself and his belongings, and Mary Hood grew brighter every day. Her burden lay behind her at the bottom of the Indian Ocean, and her sweet face was set bravely and hopefully towards the new life that awaited her in the unknown land that lay beneath the rising sun.

The Finchley Puzzle

Richard Marsh

Richard Marsh was a pseudonym for London-born Richard Bernard Heldmann (1857–1915), whose most famous creepy thriller, The Beetle, *was published in the same year as Bram Stoker's* Dracula, *and was at first more successful. His grandson, Robert Aickman, was also a talented author of 'strange stories'.*

Marsh ventured into the detective genre from time to time, and he created Judith Lee, an interesting and early example of the female sleuth. She is a teacher of the deaf whose ability to lip-read makes her an unexpectedly formidable adversary. Although Marsh's fiction requires a certain amount of suspension of disbelief, his ability to tell a good tale compensates for an occasional lack of credibility.

As I cut the string, and, unfolding the brown paper, saw what the little package contained, some trick of memory bore me back to an incident which had happened nearly two years before. I had been with a girl friend to the theatre, and had come back alone in an omnibus which put me down at the corner of the road in which I then had rooms. There had been a promise of rain all day, and just as I descended from the vehicle, something seemed to happen to the clouded heavens which caused water to descend in pailfuls. I was lightly attired; owing to some stupidity I had omitted to take an umbrella. I had to take refuge somewhere; I found it in the entry to a mews which was at the beginning of the street.

It did rain! I wondered what would happen if it kept on. I was only a couple of hundred yards from my dwelling-place, but if I had to approach it in that downpour I should be drenched before I got there. All at once I heard footsteps coming along the pavement from the direction in which my rooms were. Presently a man came quickly past. He had no umbrella; his billycock hat was pressed close down on his head; his coat collar was turned up to his ears—he must have been soaked. Just as he passed the entry in which I stood a man came rapidly across the road, who wore a waterproof and carried an umbrella. At sight of him the other paused. There was a lamp-post on one side of the mews; in spite of the deluge they paused under its glow to exchange a few sentences, standing in such a position that both their faces were visible to me. I heard nothing, but I saw quite plainly what the new-comer said.

'Did you give it her?'

The other shook his head. 'She wasn't in. I said to the girl who opened the door, 'Give this to Miss Lee directly she comes in.''

'If the girl does and we have any luck, Miss Lee will be where there are no deaf and dumb in the morning.'

The man with the umbrella held a part of it over the other, and the two went striding off as if they were walking for a wager, leaving me to wonder. I was quite certain that they had mentioned my name, and, though I had heard nothing, something in the expression of their faces convinced me that it had been in no friendly fashion. I was sure that they were strangers to me. The wet man was an undersized, pale-faced, mean-looking youth, whose appearance did not appeal to me at all; the other was a scarlet-visaged, bloated individual, who looked as if he might have been a publican. What had he meant by saying that if they had luck I should be where there were no deaf and dumb in the morning? I was quite sure that those were the precise words which he had used. I am not a supersensitive person, but—something made me shiver.

When at last I did get in—I could not wait for the rain to cease entirely, but so soon as it showed signs of slightly slackening, I made a dash for it—among other matter lying on the table in my sitting-room was a small, oblong-shaped package, addressed in a bold hand, 'Miss Judith Lee.' In those rooms a maid always sat up to let in late-comers; she had admitted me. As she commiserated with me on the state I was in—I was rather damp— I asked her, since it had clearly not come by post, how that packet had got there. She said that a young man had brought it who said it was most particular that she should give it to me directly I came in.

When the maid had gone I looked at that parcel for some moments before I even touched it. Although to the superficial glance it was the most commonplace-looking little parcel, there was something sinister about it to me. Had its contents anything to do with that red-faced man's observation about my being where there were no deaf and dumb in the morning? I opened my other letters first, and left that parcel to the last. Then, telling myself that my hesitation was absurd, I took a pair of scissors, clipped the string, removed the wrapping, and there was an ordinary, white cardboard box within, bearing the imprint of a well-known manufacturer of sweet things. I opened it. It was filled with chocolates; on the top was a scrap of paper on which was written, in the same bold handwriting: 'To Miss Judith Lee, from an Humble Donor. This Little Present Long Overdue.'

Nothing could seem more innocent. I did receive presents at times from anonymous givers, to whom, I presume, I had been so fortunate as to render services for which they felt they would like to make some sign of recognition. Had I not seen those two men under the lamp-post I should probably have put one of those chocolates into my mouth at once and scrunched it thankfully; but I had seen them, and I did not wish to be where there were no deaf and dumb in the morning.

I took one of the chocolates out of the box. I could hardly receive any hurt from the mere touch. It was a good-sized chocolate, looking as if it might contain a walnut. I was really curious as to what it did contain, and was regarding it attentively when some slight noise behind caused me to look round. I suppose I started; the sweetmeat fell from my fingers, and as it reached the floor there was a blinding flash, a sudden, extraordinary noise, a most unpleasant smell. I was left in a state of doubt as to whether I was alive or dead.

The advent of the maid made it clear that I was still alive. In a few seconds the whole household was there to learn what was the matter. I could not explain; I was myself without information, and actual, tangible information I have remained without until this day. Who sent that box I have never learned; what was the secret of the construction of that toothsome delicacy I do not know. I sought light from a friend who was a famous chemist; he declared that that seeming candy was a bomb in miniature, and that if I had put my teeth into it it would have blown my head off; so it was lucky I had refrained. It was the only candy in the box about whose construction there was anything peculiar; it had been so placed that it was nearly certain that it would be the first I should take. Analysis showed that all the other contents of the box were simple, albeit excellent chocolates, manufactured by a well-known maker, and were in the exact state in which they had left his hands.

Some one had tried to murder me. I caused inquiries to be made on lines of my own, but since nothing came of them, and for reasons of my own I was unwilling to place the matter in the hands of the police, the affair remained 'wrapped in mystery"; and now, nearly two years afterwards, under altogether changed conditions, there had come addressed to me another seemingly innocent package—whose innocence I gravely doubted.

Two or three evenings before I had been with some friends in a box at a popular variety theatre. Glancing round the crowded house through an opera-glass, the lenses had rested for a moment on two men who were leaning over the partition in the promenade, and in that brief instant I distinctly saw one of them shape my name upon his lips, 'Judith Lee": just those two words. The lenses passed on before he had a chance of saying more. It was a curious sensation—to see my name being uttered all that distance off. I brought the lenses back again, just in time to see the second man asking a question, rather a full-flavoured one.

'Who the blazes is Judith Lee?'

I had been right; no doubt the first man had pronounced my name, because here was his companion doing it also. I allowed the glass to rest upon his companion's face. He was in evening dress, a crush hat was a little at the back of his head; he had a cigar between his lips, which he took out to answer the other's inquiry. I saw as clearly what he said as if he had been in the next box.

'Judith Lee is a young woman who calls herself a teacher of the deaf and dumb; in reality she is the most dangerous thing in England. The police aren't in it compared with her: they make blunders, thank God; she doesn't. If she catches sight of your face at a distance of I don't know how many miles, and you happen to open your lips, you are done. The other day she saw—I won't mention his name; he was talking business to a friend; before he knew that she was there he said something—only in a whisper, to his friend, you understand—which, when dealing with a sharp young devil such as she is, was enough to give himself clean away. He's had the fidgets ever since, and I'm bound to say that I think he's right. I shouldn't like her to have half that hold on me.'

'What's he afraid of? Is she connected with the police?'

'Not ostensibly; one would know where one was if she were. She has spoilt more good men and more good things by not being connected with the police than I should care to talk about. There has been more than one try to get her out of the way; now there's to be another. It's her or—him; and it's going to be her. She's going, and she'll never know what struck her.' The other man looked round. 'Take care, there's a chap behind who seems to be all ears. Let's stroll.'

They strolled, or, at least, they moved away from the partition and passed from my sight leaving me not at all in a suitable frame of mind to enjoy that variety show. That I should have lighted on such a conversation in such a place and in so odd a fashion was amazing. By what fortuitous accident had my opera-glass rested on that spot at just that moment? What would that speaker's feelings have been had he known that quite unintentionally I was watching him from below, and that he was furnishing an illustration of his own words, that I had only to catch a glimpse of a man's face, though only from afar, and if he opened his lips he would give himself away.

Whom the speaker had in his mind when he spoke of the man whose name he would rather not mention, and to whom I was supposed to have given the fidgets, I had not the vaguest notion. I have an idea that since more people know Tom Fool than Tom Fool knows, I might often give the 'fidgets' to persons who might suppose that I had obtruded myself upon their confidence without my having, actually, done anything of the kind. Possibly the speaker, being himself a person of doubtful character, had acquaintances like himself; if I had given one of them a scare it served him right; only—I did not relish that reference to getting me out of the way. As he said, there had been 'more than one try,' though I did not know how he knew it, and I did not desire that there should be another—just yet awhile.

Nearly two years before some one had tried to 'get me out of the way' by means of a bomb in the shape of a chocolate bonbon; a shiver would go all over me when sometimes I thought of how narrow my escape had been. It was not the sort of thing one is likely to forget, so when I received that little package, of which I have already spoken twice, I hesitated before I inquired into what it contained.

It had come by post, the address was typed, the post-mark Fleet Street, the wrapping coarse brown paper, within was a box of stiff brown cardboard. In the box there were four roses, arranged so as to form a small bouquet. Whether they were real I was not sure, imitations are, nowadays, so exquisitely done. They looked like four lovely Maréchal Niel blooms which had just been taken from the bush, deep golden yellow. It might seem very silly, but I was reluctant to take them out of the box. I raised it to enable me to eye them more closely. They must be real, imitations could not be so perfect. I had a strong impulse, as any woman would have had, to take them out and smell them; it was absurd to be afraid of roses.

I took them out and was advancing them towards my nose, when I saw something gleaming in the very heart of them, something which sprang out towards me. I gave the roses a swift twirl, and something went whirling out of them to the floor, a curiously coloured something which lay for a moment as if stunned, and then began to move across the carpet. About a week before some one had given me a Pomeranian puppy, the queerest, daintiest morsel of living jet. It had been asleep on a cushion. The noise of that thing being thrown to the ground disturbed him. He jumped up. Seeing the thing wriggling across the floor, imagining, I take it, that it was some new plaything, with its funny little bark the puppy dashed towards it. The thing on the floor reared itself, leaped at the puppy, not once or twice, but again and again.

It all happened so quickly that I hardly grasped what was taking place. Then all at once I realized that that simple-minded puppy was being attacked by that hideous little snake which had been contained in my bouquet of roses. When I rushed to its assistance it was already too late. I struck the creature with a poker I had snatched up, and with that one blow killed it; but the puppy was dead.

That was one of the most dreadful moments I have ever known when it was borne in on me that the puppy was actually dead, and how easily its fate might have been mine. I am not fond of snakes; to die from the bite of one—that is not the sort of death I would choose at all. If I had advanced those roses only a few inches nearer that creature would have struck me in the face—the puppy's fate might have been mine. This was the second time I had been saved from attempted murder by what seemed very like a miracle. If I had not seen through the opera-glass those two men talking in the promenade I should have known no hesitation, I should have at once advanced those roses to my face, as most women would, and I should have been dead.

The whole episode, as may be imagined, set me furiously thinking. When something of the same sort had happened before I had not taken any special pains to discover the guilty party. But this time I had a feeling that it was a sort of challenge, that I was on my mettle; I had got off scot free, but my puppy had been slain, and for that some one should pay dearly. The question I had to put to myself was—who?

As I was casting about in my mind to find an answer, I had what seemed to me at the time to be almost an inspiration, though, as I realized afterwards, it was open to the most commonplace interpretation. I recalled a fragment of a conversation I had seen when crossing on the boat from the Isle of Wight. Two men had been walking up and down, talking together, apparently in undertones and very earnestly. I had been seated. I glanced in their direction while they were still at some distance, but were coming towards me along the deck. One was a shortish man with very fair hair and pink-and-white complexion. It was he who was speaking. He had a slight moustache, which was so fair as to be almost white, and which did not prevent my seeing his lips distinctly; his words came back to me from some forgotten cell in my memory with a vividness which—as I surveyed that dead puppy—almost frightened me. I had paid scarcely any attention to them at the moment; how they had got themselves stored in my brain I had no notion. Now they seemed so apposite.

'Get a man asleep, or unconscious, introduce the proper kind of snake to the proper part of his body, and that man will be dead inside sixty seconds, and I doubt if half a dozen doctors in the world would be able to tell you what had happened. Look at Finchley—'

I remembered that at that point he looked towards me, and, seemingly for the first time, saw that I was there. As he did so he brought himself up with a sudden jerk, put his hand in his companion's arm, turned him right round, and led him off the upper deck somewhere down below. At the time I was idly amused. The man was a stranger to me; I had no reason to suppose that I was not a stranger to him. Perhaps, conscious that he was talking in rather a curious strain, unwilling to be the object of a stranger's observation, he had taken himself and his friend away. If I thought about it at all, that was the hazy conclusion I arrived at. But such episodes are so common. I endeavour not to look at people's faces, since I suffer from a sort of obsession which suggests that, becoming conscious of my glance and the revelation of self which it portends, they remove themselves to where I cannot see them. I more or less vaguely took it for granted that this fair-haired man might be a case in point. I do not remember seeing him again on the boat, or when we landed. I never thought of him again until, all at once, he and his words came back with such terrific suddenness as I was looking at my dead puppy.

He had been speaking of how very easy it was to kill with the proper kind of snake. I had seen that fact illustrated. I wished he had not seen me; I might have heard more. Could the man in the promenade at the music-hall by any chance have been alluding to him? Could he have been the man to whom I had given the fidgets? Experience had taught me that coincidences are the rule rather than the exception, but what an astounding one that would be! And, in any case, why should he have been fidgety because of me?

Then, with the same odd suddenness, something else occurred to me. What was the word he had pronounced when, at sight of me, he stopped short? Was it not Finchley? I was sure that it was Finchley. But if that were so—again, how odd! Were not the newspapers still referring to what they had christened 'The Finchley Puzzle'?

A Mr and Mrs Le Blanc had lived in a house called The Elms, in Hill Avenue, Finchley. They were elderly folk, of rather eccentric habits—he was a naturalized Frenchman, and she was a Frenchwoman who had not been naturalized.

One morning both of them were found dead in bed, each in a separate bedroom. They were alone in the house. They generally kept a French maid, but were for the moment without one. The question was how they died; it came out at the inquest that nobody was able to give a clear explanation. They had died, said the doctors, of shock, but of what sort of shock, and how it chanced to visit them simultaneously, there was the puzzle. The vital organs were fairly healthy, they had no congenital disease, they had been seen together the night before, they were supposed to have retired to bed about ten o'clock; according to the medical evidence about two hours afterwards they were dead. The medical theory was that while they lay asleep in bed something had happened to them of so astounding a nature that both of them were smitten with death. Eminent authorities were called, not one of whom was willing to bind himself to an exact definition. The inquest had dragged on, and finally the jury, acting under the coroner's direction, had returned what he called an open verdict.

I regretted that that fair-haired man's discovery of my presence on the boat had caused him to cut his observations short; he might have added something about Finchley which would have shown that the Le Blanc tragedy was not in his mind. I did not say, even to myself, that it was. I picked up that snake, put it back in the box in which it came, concealed in those Maréchal Niel roses, and paid a visit to the Zoological Gardens. I went straight to the snake house, and made inquiry of an attendant if there were any one about who might be regarded as an authority on its occupants. The chief authority, it seemed, was not there, but I was introduced to an elderly gentleman who, I was told, knew probably as much about snakes as I wanted to know. Opening my box I showed him what was in it. He regarded it with considerable interest, took it out, turned it over and over, examining it closely from tip to tip.

'Where did you get this from?' he asked.

I told him it had come to me that morning through the post.

'Alive?'

'Very much alive,' I said. 'I killed it after it had killed my puppy.'

'Your puppy? It might have killed you. I can't tell you exactly what it is, because I have never seen one quite like it before. There are probably a large number of snakes of which we have no record; I fancy this is one of them. But I can tell you it is one of the *Viperidæ*, and possibly West African. I have never seen one anything like so small before, but I have no doubt that it's one of that family, and I should say all the more dangerous because it is so small. But I can tell you who might be able to give you information, that's Dr George Evans. He is not only an authority on snakes in general, he has made the *Viperidæ* his special study. He doesn't live very far from here; he is always in and out. Here is his address.' He wrote something on a card. 'Although it may seem odd to you, snakes are the things he chiefly lives for, and he's always glad to see any one who wants to know something about them.'

I called on Dr George Evans then and there, with the snake in the box. His house was within a quarter of a mile of the Zoological Gardens. He was at home, and came to see me at once: a big, burly man, with a quantity of grey hair which hung over one side of his forehead like a sort of mane. I told him what I had come about, showing him the snake, and asking what it was. The sight of it affected him in a manner which, by me, was unexpected. His naturally sanguine countenance turned purple.

'Good God!' he exclaimed. 'Where did you get that from?' I told him. His surprise seemed to grow. 'That thing came to you by post ? But, my dear young lady, how came it to do that?' I told him that I hoped shortly to find out. 'You don't know? What object could an anonymous person have had in sending it to you? I don't know your name, but, my dear young lady, are you aware that if that dreadful creature had bitten you it would certainly have killed you on the spot?'

I told him how I had escaped being bitten, and how it had killed the puppy. He dropped on to a chair and seemed positively gasping for breath.

'It's one of the most terrible things of which I ever heard. It almost looks as if some one had designed to do you mischief; but what a terrible means to have chosen!'

I had already felt that myself; as I listened to him I felt it more strongly every moment.

'This is a hitherto quite unknown member of the *Viperidæ* family. It is the smallest I ever met, and what is worse, I believe one of the most deadly. Until a little time back I was the owner of what I supposed to be a unique specimen. It was brought to me from the West Coast of Africa. It killed a native, and then, while trying to escape, got entangled in a quantity of calico which lay upon the ground, in which it was made a prisoner. The man who captured it was a friend of mine, who, knowing my tastes, and being aware that it was something unusual in snakes—although he knew the district well, he himself had never seen one like it before— refused to have it killed. At considerable risk to himself he transferred it to a metal case, in which he brought it home, and in due course presented it to me, and in my keeping it has been until a month ago last Sunday. I had it on the Sunday evening, but on the Monday morning it was gone; and do you know I am half inclined to suspect that the one you have here in this box is the one I had. I cannot see any other solution, since I am convinced that mine was the only specimen of the kind which has been seen in England.'

'How do you account for its getting out of your possession, since it was clearly a very dangerous thing to handle? Do you think that it escaped?'

It struck me that Dr Evans seemed to be very curiously distressed.

'My dear young lady, that's—that's the trouble. I—I'm afraid that it was stolen.'

'Stolen? A thing like that? For what purpose—by whom? I should have thought that an attempt to steal it must have meant death to the thief.'

The doctor got up from his chair, he brushed the mane of hair off his forehead; his manner became what I should have judged to be more normal.

'Exactly; you put the case correctly. Under ordinary circumstances it would have meant sudden death to the thief. Have you no idea who can have sent it to you, not even a remote suspicion? I have not your name. May I ask who you are?'

'I am Judith Lee.' He stared at me hard.

'Not the—the young lady of whose lip-reading capacity I have heard so many tales which seem to me to border on the miraculous?'

'The same. I don't know what tales you may have heard, but I assure you that there is nothing about me which is in the least miraculous.'

Then I told him all about it—about two men whom I had seen talking in the promenade. He stopped me at once.

'My dear Miss Lee, you say there's nothing about you that's the least miraculous, and then you tell me that you followed a conversation between two men who were removed from you by the whole auditorium of a great theatre, and that without hearing a word they said. That seems to me to be a miracle to start with.'

I laughed. 'I assure you it is nothing of the kind. I assure you it is simply a question of constant practice. Given ordinary perception, and as much practice as I have had, with the greatest ease you would be able to do just the same.'

'I doubt it. I very gravely doubt it. However, that is by the way; that is a matter about which I should like to have a long talk with you presently. In the meantime, do I understand you to suggest that from what you saw those two men saying you draw the deduction that they may have had something to do with this?' He touched the box in which the snake was.

'Dr Evans, I am making inquiries. I do not like to draw deductions, I prefer to deal with facts. Will you please to tell me, so far as you can, just how that snake came to pass from your possession? You see what importance anything you may say may have for me, and under the very peculiar circumstances of the case you must have your suspicions.'

'I don't like suspicions any more than you like deductions, Miss Lee.' He turned quickly towards me. 'Do you know anything about snakes?'

'No more than the average person, and you know that that is practically nothing. A little while ago I saw—not heard—a man say something on a boat about a snake, which was news to me. He seemed to hint that an artist in murder might find one rather useful.'

I told him precisely what I had seen. It seemed to me that the doctor's eyes opened wider as he listened.

'What sort of man was this you saw—not heard?' I described him as well as I could. The doctor's eyes grew more expansive. He plumped down on his chair again. 'And yet you say, Miss Lee, that you are no dealer in the miraculous. What you saw I have heard him say. Because of him I have been suffering what I really believe to be much more than I deserve.'

The doctor looked furtively about the room as if in search of an unseen listener. He went to the door and looked outside; closing it carefully he came towards me with what was very like an air of mystery. He even lowered his voice as if he feared that the very walls had ears.

'Miss Lee, what I am about to say to you I perhaps ought not to say, and in any case I must beg you to let it go no farther. Have I your assurance?' He looked at me with an odd sort of disquietude.

'I tell you quite frankly that I would rather give you no assurance till I know what you are going to say to me.' Perceiving that he was about to speak, I stopped him. 'Permit me to explain. You say you know this man who was on the boat; you are probably thinking of telling me something about him. Is it not possible that it may have something to do with this?'

I placed the tip of my finger on the box which contained the snake.

'Well, that was not at the moment in my mind; at least, not quite in that form.'

I had one of those inspirations which do come to me every now and then.

'Has it anything to do with Finchley?'

The bow had been drawn at a venture, but the arrow hit the target; he obviously started. He positively glared at me.

'With Finchley? What—what do you mean by 'Has it anything to do with Finchley'?'

'I mean what you mean, Dr Evans. Is it not odd that the same embryonic thought should have taken root in both our minds? That snake was meant to kill me; is it not possible that it killed some one else before it was sent to my address, two persons, say, at Finchley?'

'Miss Lee, what a horrible thought; how you jump at conclusions! I thought you liked to deal with facts?'

'So I do. I am about to deal with them. With your permission, Dr Evans, we will deal with them together. The same thought in embryo is in both our minds; let's leave it there. Now, tell me, please, all you know about the man I saw on the boat. I have only to go to the police—I have had a good deal to do with them in my short life—and tell them my suspicions. You will find it more agreeable to answer my questions than theirs. You must see for yourself that I have been in danger of my life, probably from your snake; I think I am entitled to ask you to help me from running a similar risk again.'

When Dr Evans and I had said all we had to say to each other—and it took us an unconscionably long time—I paid a visit to The Elms, Hill Avenue, Finchley, the residence of the late Mr and Mrs Le Blanc. There were certain theories which I wished to test by an actual inspection of the premises. Hill Avenue proved to be a broad, old-fashioned road, in which private houses were interspersed with shops. I walked straight past The Elms—I saw the name on the gate-post as I went—because, just as I reached it, a young lady alighted from a taxi-cab which had stopped at the gate. There were four more houses, and then a stationer's shop. As I stopped to look at the window I kept one eye on the young lady who had descended from the taxi-cab. She was a distinctly pretty young person, about eighteen or nineteen years old, with something about her which told me that she was probably French. She appeared to be in a state of much agitation. From my post of vantage I saw her say to herself, in French—

'Why is the gate locked?' She had tried the handle and found that it refused to yield. 'I have never known it locked before. And all the blinds are down. What does it mean?'

An elderly woman came out of the adjoining house.

'Why, Miss Le Blanc,' she exclaimed, 'so you have appeared at last? I have been wondering what had become of you.' She stood on the pavement in front of the house with her mouth sufficiently visible to enable me to see what she said. The girl turned towards her; I could see her plainly.

'Oh, Mrs Green, what is the matter?'

The woman turned more towards her so that her lips were hidden. I had to guess at her words from the other's reply.

'Dead!' said the girl. 'My parents dead!' She seemed to reel. 'Since—since when are they dead?'

Again I had to guess at Mrs Green's words from her answer.

'How could I know? I have been staying with my friends in different parts of France. My parents do not often write, they are not fond of writing, but when I had no letters from them at all I supposed they had gone astray because of my so often moving about. But when I could get no answers, not even to my telegrams, I began to wonder if anything were wrong. I hurried back to see. I have been staying in a little village where there come no news at all. It is now more than a month since I heard from them, and when I did last hear they were both well. I could not guess that they were dead, I only imagined it was too much trouble to write. I knew they did not like writing, especially when they had nothing to say.'

The girl's distress was evident; she seemed bewildered by the sudden shock of the news which she had learnt from Mrs Green, too bewildered to know what to say, think, or do. Mrs Green said something. I fancy she was urging the girl to come into her house, but before the girl could reply another taxi-cab drew up in front of the house, from which still another woman alighted. This was a very gorgeous person indeed, very tall and big, dressed in the very latest fashion. The fact that she wore a veil rather obscured her mouth, but I saw enough of it for my purpose. She was all warmth and enthusiasm.

'My dear Freda,' she began. I could fancy the affectionate emotion which was in her voice. 'Of all the lucky things, to have come on you like this. You poor, dear darling, to think that you have only just come home—to this!—without the slightest warning of what you were coming to.'

It was, perhaps, small wonder that the girl burst into tears. There was quite a little scene on the pavement. Mrs Green was apparently urging her to go into her house, a suggestion which the new-comer did not endorse.

'My dear Freda,' she said—if here and there I missed a word because of that veil of hers, I did my best to fill in the hiatuses—'you must come home at once with me. A little bird whispered that you would be here to-day, so I simply had to come in the hope of catching you. And now that Providence has brought me here in the very nick of time, I am not going to lose sight of you for a single instant. I will tell you everything there is to tell when we get home. If you only knew how anxious Harold has been. Have your luggage put on my cab and we'll start at once.'

'But can't I get into my own home?'

'My dear, I believe the police have the keys and they've locked the whole place up. When you've heard what I have to tell you, you'll know what it will be best for you to do. Come, let's lose no more time. Driver, put the young lady's luggage upon my cab.'

The driver did. The cab, with the gorgeous lady and the girl in it, departed. The other was about to start when I hailed it. The position was developing along unexpected lines. So far as I could recollect there had been no mention at the inquest of a daughter. It seemed terrible that she should come back in this haphazard way from a pleasure jaunt to find both her parents dead, and her own home shut by the police against her. I could quite understand how news from London might never reach a remote French village. I wondered who the lady might be who had turned up at such a very opportune moment. I thought, as I was making investigations of my own, that it might be worth my while to see where that fine lady was taking her. I asked the driver of my cab to keep the other in sight. He did. The vehicle in front took us right across London, but we never lost sight of it; my driver did it very well.

The cab ahead led us to Warwick Gardens, Kensington, stopping before an old-fashioned, detached house, guarded in front, as it were, by lofty iron railings. My cab drove on; the occupants of the other cab got out. My driver took me home. I, at that time, had a flat in Sloane Gardens. I had made a note of the address of the house at which that other cab had stopped. I looked it up in the directory. According to that encyclopædia of knowledge the tenant's name was Harold Cleaver. I found the news a little startling. According to Dr George Evans that was the name of the fair-haired man whom I had seen saying how easy it was to use a snake as an instrument of murder while crossing on the boat from Ryde to Portsmouth. Matters were beginning to take rather a peculiar shape. My search for the person who had sent me that specimen of the *Viperidæ* was taking me where I had never expected to go. I had to collect my thoughts, to put two and two together, from such facts as I had collected to draw—in spite of what I had said to Dr Evans—my own deductions.

On a certain day Dr George Evans missed a snake which, the night before, had been in his possession—a very deadly snake. Only a few persons knew that he had it; they knew what a very dangerous thing it was to handle. A few days before, Mr Harold Cleaver, a well-known taxidermist, had brought back a case of stuffed snakes which he had been preparing under the doctor's direction for exhibition in a museum of natural history. The doctor had shown him the West African snake. Mr Cleaver had regarded it with singular interest. It appeared that he knew more about it than the doctor himself. He spoke of some of its peculiarities, pointing out that though it was a very deadly creature, whose bite was instantly fatal, yet it scarcely left any mark, and the poison it had injected into its victim's body vanished almost directly it had done its work, leaving practically no traces behind.

How the snake was taken the doctor was unable to determine. He kept it in a glass case; the case was left, the snake was gone. He thought at first that in some inexplicable way the creature had escaped, and had some very anxious minutes while searching for its whereabouts. After a while he came to the conclusion that its escape, unassisted, was impossible. It is true that the case was found open, but the creature was so small—less than ten inches long—and so slender that it could be concealed in a bouquet consisting of four roses, that the idea that, unaided, it would force the case open was absurd.

The doctor's ophidians were housed in a sort of conservatory, which was heated by hot air. Close observation led him to suspect that the door which opened into the garden had been tampered with. Since it was extremely unlikely that a thief would care to enter a building which contained such singular inmates, he was content, at night, simply to turn the key in the lock of the outer door. When he looked into the matter he found that the key was missing. He could not remember if he had locked it the previous night, which was Sunday. What had become of the key he could not learn—he never learned. The door was locked; he had to summon a locksmith to open it. It was an ordinary lock, the workman had no trouble in finding another key to fit it. The door was open.

Dr Evans said nothing about his loss. The members of his household were already sufficiently nervous on the subject of his pets; he had difficulty in getting servants to stay. If he had mentioned that a dangerous snake was missing, quite possibly his staff would have left him on the spot. Snakes are not popular; no maid would like to run the remote risk of finding a particularly deadly specimen between her sheets at night. A few days afterwards Mr and Mrs Le Blanc were found dead in their beds. The more Dr Evans read about the Finchley puzzle, the more uncomfortable he grew. At one time he nearly applied for leave to view the bodies. He had received from his friend a very vivid account of how the negro had looked whom that little snake had slain. He was haunted by a gruesome notion that Mr and Mrs Le Blanc would be found to look very much as that black man had done. He remembered what Mr Cleaver had said about the snake leaving no marks, and the vanishing of all traces of poison from its victim's body.

Then he told himself it was absurd; the whole notion was too far-fetched. He did not know what had become of his snake; strange things had happened to his specimens before, which he had not plumbed to their deepest depths. How could that missing reptile have played such a prominent part in that Finchley puzzle? So, in spite of his first impulses, he said nothing, and he did nothing, until I appeared upon the scene.

Now I was confronted with the new fact that when they died the Le Blancs were alone in the house, not only because they were without a servant, but also because their daughter was visiting friends in some remote part of France. Somebody must have known of this; quite possibly some one knew her address, yet no communication was made to her until she stumbled on the truth on her return. It also looked as if some one knew that she was coming back. That gorgeous lady had talked about the whisper of a little bird, but little birds do not impart information which enables people to appear on the scene quite so pat as she had done.

There was one new fact, or series of facts; but there was still another, and that was the most curious of all. The gorgeous lady was presumably a relative of Mr Harold Cleaver; she had actually taken Miss Le Blanc to a house of which he was the tenant.

So, to string facts together, the case stood thus: Mr Cleaver shows interest in a snake with whose deadly properties he is better acquainted than its owner; that snake vanishes; shortly afterwards two people die in a lonely house without any doctor being able to give an adequate explanation of the cause of death; Dr George Evans almost applies for permission to view their bodies, but is restrained because there is nothing to show what has become of his snake, because he has no reason to associate his interference with any act of Mr Cleaver's, because he has no notion that Mr Cleaver has any acquaintance with the Le Blancs. Then, all at once, I discovered that he must have some acquaintance with the dead husband and wife, because their only daughter is taken to his house.

There was the man on the boat. He was Mr Harold Cleaver. Was it not possible that he was the unnamed person whom the man in the promenade had said had the fidgets because he had given himself away to me? Quite possibly he knew very much more about me than I did about him. If, having something on his mind, having said what he did say to his companion on the boat, seeing me, all at once, sitting there and watching him, might he not jump to the conclusion that I was there for a purpose, and that, inadvertently, he had supplied me with the missing clue? He had certainly vanished with remarkable rapidity. Dr Evans thought he recognized the snake. If it had been used in Hill Avenue, and the man who had used it had afterwards had reason to suspect that I was aware of the fact, might he not, in desperation, have sent it on to me, to do again what it had done at The Elms?

At this point I drew a long breath. Once more events seemed to be shaping themselves after a fashion of which I had never dreamt, as I had learned they had a trick of doing. I might, and probably should, never have concerned myself with the Finchley puzzle had it not been that the criminal's conscience caused him to make a horrible attempt to destroy a peril which only existed in his own guilty imagination. I should never have touched the business had my hand not been forced in such a fashion. Now that I had been compelled to move I would not stop until I had seen the matter through.

As the day went on I paid another visit to the neighbourhood of Warwick Gardens, certain vague ideas floating through my head which I had a notion to develop. But when I got in sight of the house at which Miss Le Blanc had taken refuge, they went by the board. I had gone by rail to Earl's Court Station, and from thence had proceeded on foot. As I entered Warwick Gardens I saw an old-fashioned four-wheeler cab approaching, on the top of which was piled a quantity of luggage. A feminine head protruded from the window, giving directions to the driver. It was when I saw that head and that luggage that, all in an instant, an idea came to me. I hastened forward; I stopped the cab; I addressed the feminine head.

'Pardon me, but are you the new maid who is expected at Mr Cleaver's?'

'I am,' she said. 'I am Eliza Saunders, the new house-parlourmaid. Are you from Mr Cleaver's?'

'Will you allow me to get in the cab with you for one moment? I have something to say to you which is of very great importance.'

She allowed me, not too willingly, but she at least offered no active resistance. About an hour afterwards a second four-wheeled cab drew up at the servants' entrance of Mr Cleaver's house, from which I descended. I flatter myself I was a good deal altered. I rang the servants' bell and announced myself as Eliza Saunders.

'That's all right,' the maid said. 'Come in; we expected you before this.' So I went in.

Presently I was taken to a room upstairs—in the roof—a minute, scantily furnished apartment, in which, if there was only a tiny window, there were two beds.

'That's for you and me,' said the maid who had answered my ring. 'It isn't a large room, but we at least do have a bed each, and that's something. You'd better be as quick as you can and come downstairs. Miss Cleaver is sure to want to see you when she comes in.'

I was not afraid of Miss Cleaver. I had learned that she was Mr Harold's sister, and that the brother and sister formed the household, together with a Miss Le Blanc, who had arrived earlier in the day as a guest. I had made myself up to resemble the real Eliza Saunders as nearly as I could. I had little doubt that so far as appearance went I should be able to pass muster with the lady; it was from her brother's keen eyes that I feared detection. I was put to the test almost directly. As I went downstairs there was a knock and ring at the front door, and the maid who was to be my room mate informed me that I should have to answer the door. I answered it, to find on the doorstep the fair-haired man whom I had seen talking on the boat, and, of all persons in the world, the man whom I had seen leaning over the partition in the promenade.

To find myself so suddenly confronting such a pair was rather nerve-shaking. I had not the slightest doubt that together they had planned the attack upon my life, and deemed it extremely probable that if they penetrated my identity I should find myself in a very parlous position. Luckily, neither of them so much as glanced at me. They came into the hall; and both marched off and disappeared through a door which was at the other end of the hall.

'What an escape!' I told myself. I found that I was positively trembling. 'Don't be an idiot,' I added. 'How are you going to get even with that pretty pair if you shake at the mere sight of them?'

A few minutes afterwards Miss Cleaver entered by the same door, which I opened to admit her. With her was Miss Le Blanc; apparently they had been out to buy mourning, for the girl was attired from head to foot in black. Miss Cleaver looked me up and down, as I never had been looked at before.

'So you've come.' Her manner was distinctly curt. 'I thought you were taller and not so thin. I hope you are strong. I will talk to you in the morning; in the meanwhile the housemaid will give you an idea of what your duties are.'

I said nothing; plainly I was not expected to. The two ladies passed up the stairs, and I was left with a feeling that I did not like being talked to in quite that tone. I wondered what the room was into which Mr Cleaver had vanished with his companion. It might have been by accident that, instead of returning to the kitchen I found myself in what I took to be the drawing-room. It opened into a conservatory, which I entered for purposes of exploration. It was rather spacious; in the centre was a bed which was full of magnificent Maréchal Niel roses. The sight of them gave me quite a shock. Had four of them been sent to me that morning? Proceeding a little farther I came upon a window which looked into a room in which were Mr Cleaver and the man of the promenade. Had I taken another step they must have seen me. As it was I drew up just in time, where I could see them without their having the faintest notion that they were observed. The man of the promenade was drinking something out of a tumbler. As he removed it from his lips I saw him say—

'Any news of the fair Judith?'

Mr Cleaver was less courteous.

'Darn her, none; at least, as far as I know.'

'The roses reached her?' The speaker grinned.

'So far as I know, unless something happened to them on the way. In which case, something probably happened to a Post Office official. It would be quite in the order of things if something did. Luck is on her side.'

'I shall believe it if she gets off this time; she certainly can have had no warning, and she couldn't possibly guess what was in that box, and you say that what was in it was quick enough.'

'No mistake about that; it would probably be at her as soon as she had the lid off; one touch on the hand, wrist, anywhere, would be enough.'

'That young woman has got on your nerves.'

'She has, and she'll keep there till I've got on hers, once and for ever. I doubt if there's anything I wouldn't do which would result in wiping her off the face of the earth.'

'I believe you,' said the man of the promenade.

And I believed him also. As I drew away from the window—for the two men had moved, and I had certainly no wish to be discovered at that particular moment—I told myself, not for the first time, that I would not stick at a trifle to dispose of him; my presence there proved it. Shortly afterwards, as I was on the landing of the floor above, the door of that room opened, and the two men came out. Mr

Cleaver himself opened the front door and said good-bye to his companion on the doorstep. When he had gone Mr Cleaver came upstairs; he went into what I had learnt was his bedroom. I hurried to the apartment half of which was mine, then I hurried down again, bearing in a piece of tissue paper the body of the snake which had sprung at me from among those Maréchal Niel roses. I went into the conservatory; I cut four roses; the French window which opened into the room in which the two men had been sitting was open. I passed through it. On a table in the centre I placed those roses with the snake in full sight on the top of them, and I left it there.

It was perhaps half an hour afterwards when a bell sounded in the kitchen, which I was informed came from Mr Cleaver's study, and it was my duty to attend to it. I started to do my duty with my heart beating a little faster than it is wont to do. I knocked at the door, a voice bade me enter. I went in. Mr Harold Cleaver was dressed for dinner; in his black suit he seemed fairer than ever. It needed but a moment's glance to see that he was in a state of agitation. A paper was lying on the table in the centre of the room; I wondered if what I had placed there was underneath it.

'Who are you?' he asked.

'I am the new house-parlourmaid, Eliza Saunders.'

'Indeed? Come a little farther into the room, Eliza Saunders, I should like to have a look at you.'

I hesitated. He had his hand on an oblong box. I moved a little farther into the room; we eyed each other. He spoke again.

'Come a little closer, I can't quite see you.'

I knew better. I vaguely wondered why he kept his hand upon that oblong box, as if it contained something precious. I was not afraid of him; the sight of him seemed to serve as a tonic, to brace me up. He might not know it, but I knew that his hour had come. I went right forward and I lifted the paper off the table. As I had expected, the four roses and the snake were underneath.

'Do you know anything of these?' I asked.

'You are Judith Lee!' he cried. 'Of all the sluts—'

'And you,' I told him—I was less afraid than ever—'are the coward who tried this morning to kill me with the same weapon with which you murdered Mr and Mrs Le Blanc. Here the weapon is, I have brought it back to you.'

I pointed to the snake. He never took his eyes off my face.

'So you know, do you?'

'I didn't know when I saw you on the boat coming from Ryde, but you told me this morning when you sent this.' Again I pointed to the snake.

'Did I? That's how you put it, is it? And now what are you going to do, or what do you think you're going to do?'

'They know at Scotland Yard that I am here, and on what errand. When I put those roses on the table I sent them a message by your telephone to come here at once. In a very few minutes the officers of the law will be here; they'll deal with you; they are the only sort of people who can.'

'Are they? Will they? When they come—if they come—they'll find you dead.'

'I think not.'

'And I am sure. Can't you see murder in my eyes? You see so many things, can't you see that? You hell-cat! The man who rids the earth of you will perform a service to humanity. You are everybody's enemy. By getting rid of you I shall prove myself to be everybody's friend. I have tried once and failed. I shan't fail again, this time I'm going to do it.'

'I tell you again that I think not.'

'Don't you? Then I'll show you, if there's time.'

He lifted his arm off the oblong box; the lid flew off; a dreadful-looking head sprang out of it, attached to a sinuous body. A huge snake, as if it had been specially trained, made a rush at me across the table. I had a revolver in the pocket of my apron. As the reptile raised its head, opened its jaws, showed its hideous fangs, I struck it with the weapon. Exactly what I did to it I do not know, I only know that I struck it. It whirled right round. In his eagerness Mr Cleaver leaned over the table as if to urge it on. As it wheeled the creature seemed to come right against his face. The man gave a strange cry; with both his hands he gripped the reptile by the throat. The serpent seemed to fight the man; it was like a nightmare. I did not know what to do. I dared not fire, I dared do nothing. My eye caught sight of a metal rod which was in a corner of the room. I rushed to it. I hurried back, the rod in my hand, and with all my force I struck the snake. As it seemed in that same instant the man fell to the ground, and the snake, limp, lifeless, broken-backed, fell with him.

Mr Harold Cleaver was dead. The cobra had struck him again and again when once would have been sufficient. The death which he had meant for me was his.

I telephoned to Dr George Evans, who arrived almost as soon as Inspector Ellis from Scotland Yard. A medical man was already there. There was no necessity for him to declare the cause of death, it was self-evident. Dr Evans informed us that that particular cobra was almost as dangerous a plaything as that other specimen of the *Viperidæ*. It had once belonged to him. Acceding to his reiterated requests, he had sold it to Cleaver on the understanding that he was going to destroy it and stuff it, and dispose of it in the ordinary way of business.

For what seemed to me to be obvious reasons, nothing was ever made public. We had no positive proof, but there was a very strong presumption that Mr Harold Cleaver had killed the Le Blancs. He had what probably appeared to him to be sufficient motives. Old Le Blanc was by way of being a usurer; Cleaver owed him a considerable sum; he was pressing for payment; Cleaver was in no position to pay. Cleaver knew that both the Le Blancs had made wills leaving all they possessed to their daughter. He had made surreptitious love to Freda Le Blanc, who, a simple-minded girl, had in a way encouraged him. After a fashion they were engaged—in secret. It was old Le Blanc's discovery of the engagement which had caused him to put pressure on Cleaver, and to send his daughter away to friends in France, which action on his part brought about Cleaver's opportunity.

No doubt he stole the doctor's snake, which was of so small a size that it was easy to carry in his pocket; no doubt that with it in his pocket he gained entry to The Elms; no doubt he used it to slay both the husband and the wife; he thought that with the father and mother both dead—safely dead—he would be able to marry their daughter and sole heiress, and all that they possessed would be his.

Freda Le Blanc went with her fortune to France—to her relatives. I do not think she has any suspicion of how her parents came to die. The shock of her lover's death had been a great blow to her. She had no notion that it had been his intention to kill me.

The entire episode was still another illustration of the power which conscience has. If, on the Ryde boat, a suddenly startled conscience had not caused him to behave in a fashion which caught my attention, if the same pricking conscience had not prompted him to send me that message of death, I should not have been aware even of his existence. It would scarcely be speaking figuratively if one said that his conscience slew him.

The Magic Casket

R. Austin Freeman

Richard Austin Freeman (1862–1943) tackled fiction in a very different way from Richard Marsh. He eschewed sensation, even in a story like this, with potentially lurid ingredients, and concentrated instead on scrupulously accurate detective work. Raymond Chandler called Freeman 'a wonderful performer. He has no equal in his genre.... In spite of the immense leisure of his writing he accomplished an even suspense which is quite unexpected. The apparatus of his writing makes for dullness, but he is not dull. There is even a gaslight charm about his Victorian love affairs.'

Freeman was born in London, and his best work featured the hero of this story, Dr John Evelyn Thorndyke of 5A King's Bench Walk in the Inner Temple. Thorndyke practised medical jurisprudence, which in Freeman's words 'deals with the human body in its relation to all kinds of legal problem', but he could turn his hand to all kinds of scientific detection. Freeman, like many admirers of Poe and Conan Doyle, borrowed the idea of having a great detective's cases related by an admiring sidekick. The narrator here is his regular 'Watson', Christopher Jervis.

◇◇◇

It was in the near neighbourhood of King's Road, Chelsea, that chance, aided by Thorndyke's sharp and observant eyes, introduced us to the dramatic story of the Magic Casket. Not that there was anything strikingly dramatic in the opening phase of the affair, nor even in the story of the casket itself. It was Thorndyke who added the dramatic touch, and most of the magic, too; and I record the affair principally as an illustration of his extraordinary capacity for producing odd items of out-of-the-way knowledge and instantly applying them in the most unexpected manner.

Eight o'clock had struck on a misty November night when we turned out of the main road, and, leaving behind the glare of the shop windows, plunged into the maze of dark and narrow streets to the north. The abrupt change impressed us both, and Thorndyke proceeded to moralize on it in his pleasant, reflective fashion.

'London is an inexhaustible place,' he mused. 'Its variety is infinite. A minute ago we walked in a glare of light, jostled by a multitude. And now look at this little street. It is as dim as a tunnel, and we have got it absolutely to ourselves. Anything might happen in a place like this.'

Suddenly he stopped. We were, at the moment, passing a small church or chapel, the west door of which was enclosed in an open porch; and as my observant friend stepped into the latter and stooped, I perceived, in the deep shadow against the wall, the object which had evidently caught his eye.

'What is it?' I asked, following him in.

'It is a handbag,' he replied; 'and the question is, what is it doing here?'

He tried the church door, which was obviously locked, and coming out, looked at the windows.

'There are no lights in the church,' said he; 'the place is

locked up, and there is nobody in sight. Apparently the bag is derelict. Shall we have a look at it?'

Without waiting for an answer, he picked it up and brought it out into the mitigated darkness of the street, where we proceeded to inspect it. But at the first glance it told its own tale; for it had evidently been locked, and it bore unmistakable traces of having been forced open.

'It isn't empty,' said Thorndyke. 'I think we had better see what is in it. Just catch hold while I get a light.'

He handed me the bag while he felt in his pocket for the tiny electric lamp which he made a habit of carrying—and an excellent habit it is. I held the mouth of the bag open while he illuminated the interior, which we then saw to be occupied by several objects neatly wrapped in brown paper. One of these Thorndyke lifted out, and untying the string and removing the paper, displayed a Chinese stoneware jar. Attached to it was a label, bearing the stamp of the Victoria and Albert Museum, on which was written:

'Miss Mabel Bonney,
168 Willow Walk, Fulham Road, W.'

'That tells us all that we want to know,' said Thorndyke, re-wrapping the jar and tenderly replacing it in the bag. 'We can't do wrong in delivering the things to their owner, especially as the bag itself is evidently her property, too,' and he pointed to the gilt initials, 'M. B.", stamped on the morocco.

It took us but a few minutes to reach the Fulham Road, but we then had to walk nearly a mile along that thoroughfare before we arrived at Willow Walk—to which an obliging shopkeeper had directed us; and, naturally, No. 168 was at the farther end.

As we turned into the quiet street we almost collided with two men, who were walking at a rapid pace, but both looking back over their shoulders. I noticed that they were both

Japanese—well-dressed, gentlemanly-looking men—but I gave them little attention, being interested, rather, in what they were looking at. This was a taxi-cab which was dimly visible by the light of a street lamp at the farther end of the 'Walk,' and from which four persons had just alighted. Two of these had hurried ahead to knock at a door, while the other two walked very slowly across the pavement and up the steps to the threshold. Almost immediately the door was opened; two of the shadowy figures entered, and the other two returned slowly to the cab; and as we came nearer, I could see that these latter were policemen in uniform. I had just time to note this fact when they both got into the cab and were forthwith spirited away.

'Looks like a street accident of some kind,' I remarked; and then, as I glanced at the number of the house we were passing, I added: 'Now, I wonder if that house happens to be—yes, by Jove! it is. It is 168! Things have been happening, and this bag of ours is one of the dramatis personæ.'

The response to our knock was by no means prompt. I was, in fact, in the act of raising my hand to the knocker to repeat the summons when the door opened and revealed an elderly servant-maid, who regarded us inquiringly, and, as I thought, with something approaching alarm.

'Does Miss Mabel Bonney live here?' Thorndyke asked.

'Yes, sir,' was the reply; 'but I am afraid you can't see her just now, unless it is something urgent. She is rather upset, and particularly engaged at present.'

'There is no occasion whatever to disturb her,' said Thorndyke. 'We have merely called to restore this bag, which seemed to have been lost;' and with this he held it out towards her. She grasped it eagerly, with a cry of surprise, and as the mouth fell open, she peered into it.

'Why,' she exclaimed, 'they don't seem to have taken anything, after all. Where did you find it, sir?'

'In the porch of a church in Spelton Street,' Thorndyke replied, and was turning away when the servant said earnestly:

'Would you kindly give me your name and address, sir? Miss Bonney will wish to write and thank you.'

'There is really no need,' said he; but she interrupted anxiously:

'If you would be so kind, sir. Miss Bonney will be so vexed if she is unable to thank you; and besides, she may want to ask you some questions about it.'

'That is true,' said Thorndyke (who was restrained only by good manners from asking one or two questions, himself). He produced his card-case, and having handed one of his cards to the maid, wished her 'good evening' and retired.

'That bag had evidently been pinched,' I remarked, as we walked back towards the Fulham Road.

'Evidently,' he agreed, and was about to enlarge on the matter when our attention was attracted to a taxi, which was approaching from the direction of the main road. A man's head was thrust out of the window, and as the vehicle passed a street lamp, I observed that the head appertained to an elderly gentleman with very white hair and a very fresh-coloured face.

'Did you see who that was?' Thorndyke asked.

'It looked like old Brodribb,' I replied.

'It did; very much. I wonder where he is off to.'

He turned and followed, with a speculative eye, the receding taxi, which presently swept alongside the kerb and stopped, apparently opposite the house from which we had just come. As the vehicle came to rest, the door flew open and the passenger shot out like an elderly, but agile, Jack-in-the-box, and bounced up the steps.

'That is Brodribb's knock, sure enough,' said I, as the old-fashioned flourish reverberated up the quiet street. 'I have heard it too often on our own knocker to mistake it. But we had better not let him see us watching him.'

As we went once more on our way, I took a sly glance, now and again, at my friend, noting with a certain malicious enjoyment his profoundly cogitative air. I knew quite well what was happening in his mind; for his mind reacted to observed facts in an invariable manner. And here was a group of related facts: the bag, stolen, but deposited intact; the museum label; the injured or sick person—probably Miss Bonney, herself—brought home under police escort; and the arrival, post-haste, of the old lawyer; a significant group of facts. And there was Thorndyke, under my amused and attentive observation, fitting them together in various combinations to see what general conclusion emerged. Apparently my own mental state was equally clear to him, for he remarked, presently, as if replying to an unspoken comment:

'Well, I expect we shall know all about it before many days have passed if Brodribb sees my card, as he most probably will. Here comes an omnibus that will suit us. Shall we hop on?'

He stood at the kerb and raised his stick; and as the accommodation on the omnibus was such that our seats were separated, there was no opportunity to pursue the subject further, even if there had been anything to discuss.

But Thorndyke's prediction was justified sooner than I had expected. For we had not long finished our supper; and had not yet closed the 'oak,' when there was heard a mighty flourish on the knocker of our inner door.

'Brodribb, by Jingo!' I exclaimed, and hurried across the room to let him in.

'No, Jervis,' he said as I invited him to enter, 'I am not coming in. Don't want to disturb you at this time of night.

I've just called to make an appointment for to-morrow with a client.'

'Is the client's name Bonney?' I asked.

He started and gazed at me in astonishment. 'Gad, Jervis!' he exclaimed, 'you are getting as bad as Thorndyke. How the deuce did you know that she was my client?'

'Never mind how I know. It is our business to know everything in these chambers. But if your appointment concerns Miss Mabel Bonney, for the Lord's sake come in and give Thorndyke a chance of a night's rest. At present, he is on broken bottles, as Mr Bumble would express it.'

On this persuasion, Mr Brodribb entered, nothing loath—very much the reverse, in fact—and having bestowed a jovial greeting on Thorndyke, glanced approvingly round the room.

'Ha!' said he, 'you look very cosy. If you are really sure I am not—'

I cut him short by propelling him gently towards the fire, beside which I deposited him in an easy chair, while Thorndyke pressed the electric bell which rang up in the laboratory.

'Well,' said Brodribb, spreading himself out comfortably before the fire like a handsome old Tom-cat, 'if you are going to let me give you a few particulars—but perhaps you would rather that I should not talk shop.'

'Now you know perfectly well, Brodribb,' said Thorndyke, 'that 'shop' is the breath of life to us all. Let us have those particulars.'

Brodribb sighed contentedly and placed his toes on the fender (and at this moment the door opened softly and Polton looked into the room. He took a single, understanding glance at our visitor and withdrew, shutting the door without a sound.)

'I am glad,' pursued Brodribb, 'to have this opportunity of a preliminary chat, because there are certain things that one can say better when the client is not present; and I am deeply interested in Miss Bonney's affairs. The crisis in those affairs which has brought me here is of quite recent date—in fact, it dates from this evening. But I know your partiality for having events related in their proper sequence, so I will leave to-day's happenings for the moment and tell you the story—the whole of which is material to the case—from the beginning.'

Here there was a slight interruption, due to Polton's noiseless entry with a tray on which was a decanter, a biscuit box, and three port glasses. This he deposited on a small table, which he placed within convenient reach of our guest. Then, with a glance of altruistic satisfaction at our old friend, he stole out like a benevolent ghost.

'Dear, dear!' exclaimed Brodribb, beaming on the decanter, 'this is really too bad. You ought not to indulge me in this way.'

'My dear Brodribb,' replied Thorndyke, 'you are a bene-factor to us. You give us a pretext for taking a glass of port. We can't drink alone, you know.'

'I should, if I had a cellar like yours,' chuckled Brodribb, sniffing ecstatically at his glass. He took a sip, with his eyes closed, savoured it solemnly, shook his head, and set the glass down on the table.

'To return to our case,' he resumed; 'Miss Bonney is the daughter of a solicitor, Harold Bonney—you may remember him. He had offices in Bedford Row; and there, one morning, a client came to him and asked him to take care of some property while he, the said client, ran over to Paris, where he had some urgent business. The property in question was a collection of pearls of most unusual size and value, forming a great necklace, which had been unstrung for the sake of portability. It is not clear where they came from, but as the transaction occurred soon after the Russian Revolution, we may make a guess. At any rate, there they were, packed loosely in a leather bag, the string of which was sealed with the owner's seal.

'Bonney seems to have been rather casual about the affair. He gave the client a receipt for the bag, stating the nature of the contents, which he had not seen, and deposited it, in the client's presence, in the safe in his private office. Perhaps he intended to take it to the bank or transfer it to his strong-room, but it is evident that he did neither; for his managing clerk, who kept the second key of the strong-room—without which the room could not be opened—knew nothing of the transaction. When he went home at about seven o'clock, he left Bonney hard at work in his office, and there is no doubt that the pearls were still in the safe.

'That night, at about a quarter to nine, it happened that a couple of C.I.D. officers were walking up Bedford Row when they saw three men come out of one of the houses. Two of them turned up towards Theobald's Road, but the third came south, towards them. As he passed them, they both recognized him as a Japanese named Uyenishi, who was believed to be a member of a cosmopolitan gang and whom the police were keeping under observation. Naturally, their suspicions were aroused. The first two men had hurried round the corner and were out of sight; and when they turned to look after Uyenishi, he had mended his pace considerably and was looking back at them. Thereupon one of the officers, named Barker, decided to follow the Jap, while the other, Holt, reconnoitred the premises.

'Now, as soon as Barker turned, the Japanese broke into a run. It was just such a night as this: dark and slightly foggy. In order to keep his man in sight, Barker had to run, too; and he found that he had a sprinter to deal with. From the bottom of Bedford Row, Uyenishi darted across and shot down Hand Court like a lamplighter. Barker followed, but at the Holborn end his man was nowhere to be seen. However, he presently learned from a man at a shop door that the fugitive had run past and turned up Brownlow Street, so off he went again in pursuit. But when he got to the top of the street, back in Bedford Row, he was done. There was no sign of the man, and no one about from whom he could make inquiries. All he could do was to cross the road and walk up Bedford Row to see if Holt had made any discoveries.

'As he was trying to identify the house, his colleague came out on to the doorstep and beckoned him in; and this was the story that he told. He had recognized the house by the big lamp-standard; and as the place was all dark, he had gone into the entry and tried the office door. Finding it unlocked, he had entered the clerks' office, lit the gas, and tried the door of the private office, but found it locked. He knocked at it, but getting no answer, had a good look round the clerks' office; and there, presently, on the floor in a dark corner, he found a key. This he tried in the door of the private office, and finding that it fitted, turned it and opened the door. As he did so, the light from the outer office fell on the body of a man lying on the floor just inside.

'A moment's inspection showed that the man had been murdered—first knocked on the head and then finished with a knife. Examination of the pockets showed that the dead man was Harold Bonney, and also that no robbery from the person seemed to have been committed. Nor was there any sign of any other kind of robbery. Nothing seemed to have been disturbed, and the safe had not been broken into, though that was not very conclusive, as the safe key was in the dead man's pocket. However, a murder had been committed, and obviously Uyenishi was either the murderer or an accessory; so Holt had, at once, rung up Scotland Yard on the office telephone, giving all the particulars.

'I may say at once that Uyenishi disappeared completely and at once. He never went to his lodgings at Limehouse, for the police were there before he could have arrived. A lively hue and cry was kept up. Photographs of the wanted man were posted outside every police-station, and a watch was set at all the ports. But he was never found. He must have got away at once on some outward-bound tramp from the Thames. And there we will leave him for the moment.

'At first it was thought that nothing had been stolen, since the managing clerk could not discover that anything was missing. But a few days later the client returned from Paris, and presenting his receipt, asked for his pearls. But the pearls had vanished. Clearly they had been the object of the crime. The robbers must have known about them and traced them to the office. Of course the safe had been opened with its own key, which was then replaced in the dead man's pocket.

'Now, I was poor Bonney's executor, and in that capacity I denied his liability in respect of the pearls on the ground that he was a gratuitous bailee—there being no evidence that any consideration had been demanded—and that being murdered cannot be construed as negligence. But Miss Mabel, who was practically the sole legatee, insisted on accepting liability. She said that the pearls could have been secured in the bank or the strong-room, and that she was morally, if not legally, liable for their loss; and she insisted on handing to the owner the full amount at which he valued them. It was a wildly foolish proceeding, for he would certainly have accepted half the sum. But still, I take my hat off to a person—man or woman—who can accept poverty in preference to a broken covenant"; and here Brodribb, being in fact, that sort of person himself, had to be consoled with a replenished glass.

'And mind you,' he resumed, 'when I speak of poverty, I wish to be taken literally. The estimated value of those pearls was fifty thousand pounds—if you can imagine anyone out of Bedlam giving such a sum for a parcel of trash like that; and when poor Mabel Bonney had paid it, she was left with the prospect of having to spread her butter mighty thin for the rest of her life. As a matter of fact, she has had to sell one after another of her little treasures to pay just her current expenses, and I'm hanged if I can see how she is going to carry on when she has sold the last of them. But there, I mustn't take up your time with her private troubles. Let us return to our muttons.

'First, as to the pearls. They were never traced, and it seems probable that they were never disposed of. For, you see, pearls are different from any other kind of gems. You can cut up a big diamond, but you can't cut up a big pearl. And the great value of this necklace was due not only to the size, the perfect shape and 'orient' of the separate pearls, but to the fact that the whole set was perfectly matched. To break up the necklace was to destroy a good part of its value.

'And now as to our friend Uyenishi. He disappeared, as I have said; but he reappeared at Los Angeles, in custody of the police, charged with robbery and murder. He was taken red-handed and was duly convicted and sentenced to death; but for some reason—or more probably, for no reason, as we should think—the sentence was commuted to imprisonment for life. Under these circumstances, the English police naturally took no action, especially as they really had no evidence against him.

'Now Uyenishi was, by trade, a metal-worker; a maker of those pretty trifles that are so dear to the artistic Japanese, and when he was in prison he was allowed to set up a little workshop and practise his trade on a small scale. Among other things that he made was a little casket in the form of a seated figure, which he said he wanted to give to his brother as a keepsake. I don't know whether any permission was granted for him to make this gift, but that is of no consequence; for Uyenishi got influenza and was carried off in a few days by pneumonia; and the prison authorities learned that his brother had been killed, a week or two previously, in a shooting affair at San Francisco. So the casket remained on their hands.

'About this time, Miss Bonney was invited to accompany an American lady on a visit to California, and accepted gratefully. While she was there she paid a visit to the prison to inquire whether Uyenishi had ever made any kind of statement concerning the missing pearls. Here she heard of Uyenishi's recent death; and the governor of the prison, as he could not give her any information, handed over to her the casket as a sort of memento. This transaction came to the knowledge of the press, and—well, you know what the Californian press is like. There were 'some comments,' as they would say, and quite an assortment of Japanese, of shady antecedents, applied at the prison to have the casket 'restored' to them as Uyenishi's heirs. Then Miss Bonney's rooms at the hotel were raided by burglars—but the casket was in the hotel strong-room—and Miss Bonney and her hostess were shadowed by various undesirables in such a disturbing fashion that the two ladies became alarmed and secretly made their way to New York. But there another burglary occurred, with the same unsuccessful result, and the shadowing began again. Finally, Miss Bonney, feeling that her presence was a danger to her friend, decided to return to England, and managed to get on board the ship without letting her departure be known in advance.

'But even in England she has not been left in peace. She has had an uncomfortable feeling of being watched and attended, and has seemed to be constantly meeting Japanese men in the streets, especially in the vicinity of her house. Of course, all the fuss is about this infernal casket; and when she told me what was happening, I promptly popped the thing in my pocket and took it to my office, where I stowed it in the strong-room. And there, of course, it ought to have remained. But it didn't. One day Miss Bonney told me that she was sending some small things to a loan exhibition of oriental works of art at the South Kensington Museum, and she wished to include the casket. I urged her strongly to do nothing of the kind, but she persisted; and the end of it was that we went to the museum together, with her pottery and stuff in a handbag and the casket in my pocket.

'It was a most imprudent thing to do, for there the beastly casket was, for several months, exposed in a glass case for anyone to see, with her name on the label; and what was worse, full particulars of the origin of the thing. However, nothing happened while it was there—the museum is not an easy place to steal from—and all went well until it was time to remove the things after the close of the exhibition. Now, to-day was the appointed day, and, as on the previous occasion, she and I went to the museum together. But the unfortunate thing is that we didn't come away together. Her other exhibits were all pottery, and these were dealt with first, so that she had her handbag packed and was ready to go before they had begun on the metalwork cases. As we were not going the same way, it didn't seem necessary for her to wait; so she went off with her bag and I stayed behind until the casket was released, when I put it in my pocket and went home, where I locked the thing up again in the strong-room.

'It was about seven when I got home. A little after eight I heard the telephone ring down in the office, and down I went, cursing the untimely ringer, who turned out to be a policeman at St. George's Hospital. He said he had found Miss Bonney lying unconscious in the street and had taken her to the hospital, where she had been detained for a while, but she was now recovered and he was taking her home. She would like me, if possible, to go and see her at once. Well, of course, I set off forthwith and got to her house a few minutes after her arrival, and just after you had left.

'She was a good deal upset, so I didn't worry her with many questions, but she gave me a short account of her misadventure, which amounted to this: She had started to walk home from the museum along the Brompton Road, and she was passing down a quiet street between that and Fulham Road when she heard soft footsteps behind her. The next moment, a scarf or shawl was thrown over her head and drawn tightly round her neck. At the same moment, the bag was snatched from her hand. That is all that she remembers, for she was half-suffocated and so terrified that she fainted, and knew no more until she found herself in a cab with two policemen, who were taking her to the hospital.

'Now it is obvious that her assailants were in search of that damned casket, for the bag had been broken open and searched, but nothing taken or damaged; which suggests the Japanese again, for a British thief would have smashed the crockery. I found your card there, and I put it to Miss Bonney that we had better ask you to help us—I told her all about you—and she agreed emphatically. So that is why I am here, drinking your port and robbing you of your night's rest.'

'And what do you want me to do?' Thorndyke asked.

'Whatever you think best,' was the cheerful reply. 'In the first place, this nuisance must be put a stop to—this shadowing and hanging about. But apart from that, you must see that there is something queer about this accursed casket. The beastly thing is of no intrinsic value. The museum man turned up his nose at it. But it evidently has some extrinsic value, and no small value either. If it is good enough for these devils to follow it all the way from the States, as they seem to have done, it is good enough for us to try to find out what its value is. That is where you come in. I propose to bring Miss Bonney to see you to-morrow, and I will bring the infernal casket, too. Then you will ask her a few questions, take a look at the casket—through the microscope, if necessary—and tell us all about it in your usual necromantic way.'

Thorndyke laughed as he refilled our friend's glass. 'If faith will move mountains, Brodribb,' said he, 'you ought to have been a civil engineer. But it is certainly a rather intriguing problem.'

'Ha!' exclaimed the old solicitor; 'then it's all right. I've known you a good many years, but I've never known you to be stumped; and you are not going to be stumped now. What time shall I bring her? Afternoon or evening would suit her best.'

'Very well,' replied Thorndyke; 'bring her to tea—say, five o'clock. How will that do?'

'Excellently; and here's good luck to the adventure.' He drained his glass, and the decanter being now empty, he rose, shook our hands warmly, and took his departure in high spirits.

It was with a very lively interest that I looked forward to the prospective visit. Like Thorndyke, I found the case rather intriguing. For it was quite clear, as our shrewd old friend had said, that there was something more than met the eye in the matter of this casket. Hence, on the following afternoon, when, on the stroke of five, footsteps became audible on our stairs, I awaited the arrival of our new client with keen curiosity, both as to herself and her mysterious property.

To tell the truth, the lady was better worth looking at than the casket. At the first glance, I was strongly prepossessed in her favour, and so, I think, was Thorndyke. Not that she was a beauty, though comely enough. But she was an example of a type that seems to be growing rarer; quiet, gentle, soft-spoken, and a lady to her finger-tips; a little sad-faced and care-worn, with a streak or two of white in her prettily-disposed black hair, though she could not have been much over thirty-five. Altogether a very gracious and winning personality.

When we had been presented to her by Brodribb—who treated her as if she had been a royal personage—and had enthroned her in the most comfortable easy-chair, we inquired as to her health, and were duly thanked for the salvage of the bag. Then Polton brought in the tray, with an air that seemed to demand an escort of choristers; the tea was poured out, and the informal proceedings began.

She had not, however, much to tell; for she had not seen her assailants, and the essential facts of the case had been fully presented in Brodribb's excellent summary. After a very few questions, therefore, we came to the next stage; which was introduced by Brodribb's taking from his pocket a small parcel which he proceeded to open.

'There,' said he, 'that is the *fons et origo mali*. Not much to look at, I think you will agree.' He set the object down on the table and glared at it malevolently, while Thorndyke and I regarded it with a more impersonal interest. It was not much to look at. Just an ordinary Japanese casket in the form of a squat, shapeless figure with a silly little grinning face, of which the head and shoulders opened on a hinge; a pleasant enough object, with its quiet, warm colouring, but certainly not a masterpiece of art.

Thorndyke picked it up and turned it over slowly for a preliminary inspection; then he went on to examine it detail by detail, watched closely, in his turn, by Brodribb and me. Slowly and methodically, his eye—fortified by a watchmaker's eyeglass—travelled over every part of the exterior. Then he opened it, and having examined the inside of the lid, scrutinized the bottom from within, long and attentively. Finally, he turned the casket upside down and examined the bottom from without, giving to it the longest and most rigorous inspection of all—which puzzled me somewhat, for the bottom was absolutely plain. At length, he passed the casket and the eyeglass to me without comment.

'Well,' said Brodribb, 'what is the verdict?'

'It is of no value as a work of art,' replied Thorndyke. 'The body and lid are just castings of common white metal—an antimony alloy, I should say. The bronze colour is lacquer.'

'So the museum man remarked,' said Brodribb.

'But,' continued Thorndyke, 'there is one very odd thing about it. The only piece of fine metal in it is in the part which matters least. The bottom is a separate plate of the alloy known to the Japanese as Shakudo—an alloy of copper and gold.'

'Yes,' said Brodribb, 'the museum man noted that, too, and couldn't make out why it had been put there.'

'Then,' Thorndyke continued, 'there is another anomalous feature; the inside of the bottom is covered with elaborate decoration—just the place where decoration is most inappropriate, since it would be covered up by the contents of the casket. And, again, this decoration is etched; not engraved or chased. But etching is a very unusual process for this purpose, if it is ever used at all by Japanese metal-workers. My impression is that it is not; for it is most unsuitable for decorative purposes. That is all that I observe, so far.'

'And what do you infer from your observations?' Brodribb asked.

'I should like to think the matter over,' was the reply. 'There is an obvious anomaly, which must have some significance. But I won't embark on speculative opinions at this stage. I should like, however, to take one or two photographs of the casket, for reference; but that will occupy some time. You will hardly want to wait so long.'

'No,' said Brodribb. 'But Miss Bonney is coming with me to my office to go over some documents and discuss a little business. When we have finished, I will come back and fetch the confounded thing.'

'There is no need for that,' replied Thorndyke. 'As soon as I have done what is necessary, I will bring it up to your place.'

To this arrangement Brodribb agreed readily, and he and his client prepared to depart. I rose, too, and as I happened to have a call to make in Old Square, Lincoln's Inn, I asked permission to walk with them.

As we came out into King's Bench Walk I noticed a smallish, gentlemanly-looking man who had just passed our entry and now turned in at the one next door; and by the light of the lamp in the entry he looked to me like a Japanese. I thought Miss Bonney had observed him, too, but she made no remark, and neither did I. But, passing up Inner Temple Lane, we nearly overtook two other men, who—though I got but a back view of them and the light was feeble enough—aroused my suspicions by their neat, small figures. As we approached, they quickened their pace, and one of them looked back over his shoulder; and then my suspicions were confirmed, for it was an unmistakable Japanese face that looked round at us. Miss Bonney saw that I had observed the men, for she remarked, as they turned sharply at the Cloisters and entered Pump Court:

'You see, I am still haunted by Japanese.'

'I noticed them,' said Brodribb. 'They are probably law students. But we may as well be companionable;' and with this, he, too, headed for Pump Court.

We followed our oriental friends across the Lane into Fountain Court, and through that and Devereux Court out to Temple Bar, where we parted from them; they turning westward and we crossing to Bell Yard, up which we walked, entering New Square by the Carey Street gate. At Brodribb's doorway we halted and looked back, but no one was in sight. I accordingly went my way, promising to return anon to hear Thorndyke's report, and the lawyer and his client disappeared through the portal.

My business occupied me longer than I had expected, but nevertheless, when I arrived at Brodribb's premises—where he lived in chambers over his office—Thorndyke had not yet made his appearance. A quarter of an hour later, however, we heard his brisk step on the stairs, and as Brodribb threw the door open, he entered and produced the casket from his pocket.

'Well,' said Brodribb, taking it from him and locking it, for the time being, in a drawer, 'has the oracle spoken; and if so, what did he say?'

'Oracles,' replied Thorndyke, 'have a way of being more concise than explicit. Before I attempt to interpret the message, I should like to view the scene of the escape; to see if there was any intelligible reason why this man, Uyenishi, should have returned up Brownlow Street into what must have been the danger zone. I think that is a material question.'

'Then,' said Brodribb, with evident eagerness, 'let us all walk up and have a look at the confounded place. It is quite close by.'

We all agreed instantly, two of us, at least, being on the tip-toe of expectation. For Thorndyke, who habitually understated his results, had virtually admitted that the casket had told him something; and as we walked up the Square to the gate in Lincoln's Inn Fields, I watched him furtively, trying to gather from his impassive face a hint as to what the something amounted to, and wondering how the movements of the fugitive bore on the solution of the mystery.

Brodribb was similarly occupied, and as we crossed from Great Turnstile and took our way up Brownlow Street, I could see that his excitement was approaching bursting-point.

At the top of the street Thorndyke paused and looked up and down the rather dismal thoroughfare which forms a continuation of Bedford Row and bears its name. Then he crossed to the paved island surrounding the pump which stands in the middle of the road, and from thence surveyed the entrances to Brownlow Street and Hand Court; and then he turned and looked thoughtfully at the pump.

'A quaint old survivor, this,' he remarked, tapping the iron shell with his knuckles. 'There is a similar one, you may remember, in Queen Square, and another at Aldgate. But that is still in use.'

'Yes,' Brodribb assented, almost dancing with impatience and inwardly damning the pump, as I could see, 'I've noticed it.'

'I suppose,' Thorndyke proceeded, in a reflective tone, 'they had to remove the handle. But it was rather a pity.'

'Perhaps it was,' growled Brodribb, whose complexion was rapidly developing affinities to that of a pickled cabbage, 'but what the d—'

Here he broke off short and glared silently at Thorndyke, who had raised his arm and squeezed his hand into the opening once occupied by the handle. He groped in the interior with an expression of placid interest, and presently reported: 'The barrel is still there, and so, apparently, is the plunger—' (Here I heard Brodribb mutter huskily, 'Damn the barrel and the plunger too!') 'but my hand is rather large for the exploration. Would you, Miss Bonney, mind slipping your hand in and telling me if I am right?'

We all gazed at Thorndyke in dismay, but in a moment Miss Bonney recovered from her astonishment, and with a deprecating smile, half shy, half amused, she slipped off

her glove, and reaching up—it was rather high for her—
inserted her hand into the narrow slit. Brodribb glared at
her and gobbled like a turkey-cock, and I watched her with
a sudden suspicion that something was going to happen.
Nor was I mistaken. For, as I looked, the shy, puzzled smile
faded from her face and was succeeded by an expression of
incredulous astonishment. Slowly she withdrew her hand,
and as it came out of the slit it dragged something after it.
I started forward, and by the light of the lamp above the
pump I could see that the object was a leather bag secured
by a string from which hung a broken seal.

'It can't be!' she gasped as, with trembling fingers, she
untied the string. Then, as she peered into the open mouth,
she uttered a little cry.

'It is! It is! It is the necklace!'

Brodribb was speechless with amazement. So was I; and
I was still gazing open-mouthed at the bag in Miss Bonney's
hands when I felt Thorndyke touch my arm. I turned quickly
and found him offering me an automatic pistol.

'Stand by, Jervis,' he said quietly, looking towards Gray's
Inn.

I looked in the same direction, and then perceived three
men stealing round the corner from Jockey's Fields. Brodribb saw them, too, and snatching the bag of pearls from
his client's hands, buttoned it into his breast pocket and
placed himself before its owner, grasping his stick with a
war-like air. The three men filed along the pavement until
they were opposite us, when they turned simultaneously
and bore down on the pump, each man, as I noticed, holding his right hand behind him. In a moment, Thorndyke's
hand, grasping a pistol, flew up—as did mine, also—and
he called out sharply:

'Stop! If any man moves a hand, I fire.'

The challenge brought them up short, evidently unprepared for this kind of reception. What would have happened next it is impossible to guess. But at this moment a police whistle sounded and two constables ran out from Hand Court. The whistle was instantly echoed from the direction of Warwick Court, whence two more constabulary figures appeared through the postern gate of Gray's Inn. Our three attendants hesitated but for an instant. Then, with one accord, they turned tail and flew like the wind round into Jockey's Fields, with the whole posse of constables close on their heels.

'Remarkable coincidence,' said Brodribb, 'that those policemen should happen to be on the look-out. Or isn't it a coincidence?'

'I telephoned to the station superintendent before I started,' replied Thorndyke, 'warning him of a possible breach of the peace at this spot.'

Brodribb chuckled. 'You're a wonderful man, Thorndyke. You think of everything. I wonder if the police will catch those fellows.'

'It is no concern of ours,' replied Thorndyke. 'We've got the pearls, and that finishes the business. There will be no more shadowing, in any case.'

Miss Bonney heaved a comfortable little sigh and glanced gratefully at Thorndyke. 'You can have no idea what a relief that is!' she exclaimed; 'to say nothing of the treasure-trove.'

We waited some time, but as neither the fugitives nor the constables reappeared, we presently made our way back down Brownlow Street. And there it was that Brodribb had an inspiration.

'I'll tell you what,' said he. 'I will just pop these things in my strong-room—they will be perfectly safe there until the bank opens to-morrow—and then we'll go and have a nice little dinner. I'll pay the piper.'

'Indeed you won't!' exclaimed Miss Bonney. 'This is my thanksgiving festival, and the benevolent wizard shall be the guest of the evening.'

'Very well, my dear,' agreed Brodribb. 'I will pay and charge it to the estate. But I stipulate that the benevolent wizard shall tell us exactly what the oracle said. That is essential to the preservation of my sanity.'

'You shall have his *ipsissima verba*,' Thorndyke promised; and the resolution was carried, *nem. con.*

An hour and a half later we were seated around a table in a private room of a café to which Mr Brodribb had conducted us. I may not divulge its whereabouts, though I may, perhaps, hint that we approached it by way of Wardour Street. At any rate, we had dined, even to the fulfilment of Brodribb's ideal, and coffee and liqueurs furnished a sort of gastronomic doxology. Brodribb had lighted a cigar and Thorndyke had produced a vicious-looking little black cheroot, which he regarded fondly and then returned to its abiding-place as unsuited to the present company.

'Now,' said Brodribb, watching Thorndyke fill his pipe (as understudy of the cheroot aforesaid), 'we are waiting to hear the words of the oracle.'

'You shall hear them,' Thorndyke replied. 'There were only five of them. But first, there are certain introductory matters to be disposed of. The solution of this problem is based on two well-known physical facts, one metallurgical and the other optical.'

'Ha!' said Brodribb. 'But you must temper the wind to the shorn lamb, you know, Thorndyke. Miss Bonney and I are not scientists.'

'I will put the matter quite simply, but you must have the facts. The first relates to the properties of malleable metals—excepting iron and steel—and especially of copper and its alloys. If a plate of such metal or alloy—say, bronze, for instance—is made red-hot and quenched in water, it becomes quite soft and flexible—the reverse of what happens in the case of iron. Now, if such a plate of softened metal be placed on a steel anvil and hammered, it becomes extremely hard and brittle.'

'I follow that,' said Brodribb.

'Then see what follows. If, instead of hammering the soft plate, you put on it the edge of a blunt chisel and strike on that chisel a sharp blow, you produce an indented line. Now the plate remains soft; but the metal forming the indented line has been hammered and has become hard. There is now a line of hard metal on the soft plate. Is that clear?'

'Perfectly,' replied Brodribb; and Thorndyke accordingly continued:

'The second fact is this: If a beam of light falls on a polished surface which reflects it, and if that surface is turned through a given angle, the beam of light is deflected through double that angle.'

'H'm!' grunted Brodribb. 'Yes. No doubt. I hope we are not going to get into any deeper waters, Thorndyke.'

'We are not,' replied the latter, smiling urbanely. 'We are now going to consider the application of these facts. Have you ever seen a Japanese magic mirror?'

'Never; nor even heard of such a thing.'

'They are bronze mirrors, just like the ancient Greek or Etruscan mirrors—which are probably 'magic' mirrors, too. A typical specimen consists of a circular or oval plate of bronze, highly polished on the face and decorated on the back with chased ornament—commonly a dragon or some such device—and furnished with a handle. The ornament is, as I have said, chased; that is to say, it is executed in indented lines made with chasing tools, which are, in effect, small chisels, more or less blunt, which are struck with a chasing-hammer.

'Now these mirrors have a very singular property. Although the face is perfectly plain, as a mirror should be, yet, if a beam of sunlight is caught on it and reflected, say, on to a white wall, the round or oval patch of light on the wall is not a plain light patch. It shows quite clearly the ornament on the back of the mirror.'

'But how extraordinary!' exclaimed Miss Bonney. 'It sounds quite incredible.'

'It does,' Thorndyke agreed. 'And yet the explanation is quite simple. Professor Sylvanus Thompson pointed it out years ago. It is based on the facts which I have just stated to you. The artist who makes one of these mirrors begins, naturally, by annealing the metal until it is quite soft. Then he chases the design on the back, and this design then shows slightly on the face. But he now grinds the face perfectly flat with fine emery and water so that the traces of the design are completely obliterated. Finally, he polishes the face with rouge on a soft buff.

'But now observe that wherever the chasing-tool has made a line, the metal is hardened right through, so that the design is in hard metal on a soft matrix. But the hardened metal resists the wear of the polishing buff more than the soft metal does. The result is that the act of polishing causes the design to appear in faint relief on the face. Its projection is infinitesimal—less than the hundred-thousandth of an inch—and totally invisible to the eye. But, minute as it is, owing to the optical law which I mentioned—which, in effect, doubles the projection—it is enough to influence the reflection of light. As a consequence, every chased line appears on the patch of light as a dark line with a bright border, and so the whole design is visible. I think that is quite clear.'

'Perfectly clear,' Miss Bonney and Brodribb agreed.

'But now,' pursued Thorndyke, 'before we come to the casket, there is a very curious corollary which I must mention. Supposing our artist, having finished the mirror, should proceed with a scraper to erase the design from the back; and on the blank, scraped surface to etch a new design. The process of etching does not harden the metal, so the new design does not appear on the reflection. But the old design would. For although it was invisible on the face and had been erased from the back, it would still exist in the substance of the metal and continue to influence the reflection. The odd result would be that the design which would be visible in the patch of light on the wall would be a different one from that on the back of the mirror.

'No doubt, you see what I am leading up to. But I will take the investigation of the casket as it actually occurred. It was obvious, at once, that the value of the thing was extrinsic. It had no intrinsic value, either in material or workmanship. What could that value be? The clear suggestion was that the casket was the vehicle of some secret message or information. It had been made by Uyenishi, who had almost certainly had possession of the missing pearls, and who had been so closely pursued that he never had an opportunity to communicate with his confederates. It was to be given to a man who was almost certainly one of those confederates; and, since the pearls had never been traced, there was a distinct probability that the (presumed) message referred to some hiding-place in which Uyenishi had concealed them during his flight, and where they were probably still hidden.

'With these considerations in my mind, I examined the casket, and this was what I found. The thing, itself, was a common white-metal casting, made presentable by means of lacquer. But the white metal bottom had been cut out and replaced by a plate of fine bronze—Shakudo. The inside of this was covered with an etched design, which immediately aroused my suspicions. Turning it over, I saw that the outside of the bottom was not only smooth and polished; it was a true mirror. It gave a perfectly undistorted reflection of my face. At once, I suspected that the mirror held the secret; that the message, whatever it was, had been chased on the back, had then been scraped away and an etched design worked on it to hide the traces of the scraper.

'As soon as you were gone, I took the casket up to the laboratory and threw a strong beam of parallel light from a condenser on the bottom, catching the reflection on a sheet of white paper. The result was just what I had expected. On the bright oval patch on the paper could be seen the shadowy, but quite distinct, forms of five words in the Japanese character.

'I was in somewhat of a dilemma, for I have no knowledge of Japanese, whereas the circumstances were such as to make it rather unsafe to employ a translator. However, as I do just know the Japanese characters and possess a Japanese dictionary, I determined to make an attempt to fudge out the words myself. If I failed I could then look for a discreet translator.

'However, it proved to be easier than I had expected, for the words were detached; they did not form a sentence, and so involved no questions of grammar. I spelt out the first word and then looked it up in the dictionary. The translation was 'pearls.' This looked hopeful, and I went on to the next, of which the translation was 'pump.' The third word floored me. It seemed to be 'jokkis,' or 'jokkish,' but there was no such word in the dictionary; so I turned to the next word, hoping that it would explain its predecessor. And it did. The fourth word was 'fields,' and the last word was evidently 'London.' So the entire group read: 'Pearls, Pump, Jokkis, Fields, London.'

'Now, there is no pump, so far as I know, in Jockey's Fields, but there is one in Bedford Row close to the corner of the Fields, and exactly opposite the end of Brownlow Street. And by Mr Brodribb's account, Uyenishi, in his flight, ran down Hand Court and returned up Brownlow Street, as if he were making for the pump. As the latter is disused and the handle-hole is high up, well out of the way of children, it offers quite a good temporary hiding-place, and I had no doubt that the bag of pearls had been poked into it and was probably there still. I was tempted to go at once and explore; but I was anxious that the discovery should be made by Miss Bonney, herself, and I did not dare to make a preliminary exploration for fear of being shadowed. If I had found the treasure I should have had to take it and give it to her; which would have been a flat ending to the adventure. So I had to dissemble and be the occasion of much smothered objurgation on the part of my friend, Brodribb. And that is the whole story of my interview with the oracle.'

Our mantelpiece is becoming a veritable museum of trophies of victory, the gifts of grateful clients. Among them is a squat, shapeless figure of a Japanese gentleman of the old school, with a silly, grinning little face—The Magic Casket. But its possession is no longer a menace. Its sting has been drawn; its magic is exploded; its secret is exposed, and its glory departed.

The Holloway Flat Tragedy

Ernest Bramah

Ernest Brammah Smith (1868–1942), who wrote as Ernest Bramah, was a reclusive writer who achieved literary fame with three distinct types of fiction. His tales about Kai Lung, an itinerant Chinese story-teller, enjoyed a considerable vogue, while his dystopian novel What Might Have Been *was a distant influence on George Orwell's* Nineteen Eighty-Four. *Turning to crime fiction in 1914, he created Max Carrados, perhaps the genre's most effectively realised blind detective.*

Carrados is a wealthy and urbane fellow, and his other gifts make up for his lack of sight. He too has his own 'Watson', in this case Louis Carlyle, who set up as a private investigator after being struck off the solicitors' Roll. This story couples a neat puzzle with a reminder that there is nothing new about buy-to-let property investment in London.

A good many years ago, when chance brought Max Carrados and Louis Carlyle together again and they renewed the friendship of their youth, the blind man's first inquiry had been a jesting, 'Do you unearth many murders, Louis?' and the private detective's reply a wholly serious, 'No; our business lies mostly on the conventional lines among defalcation and divorce.' Since that day Carlyle's business had increased beyond the fondest dreams of its creator, but 'defalcation and divorce' still constituted the bulwarks of his prosperity. Yet from time to time a more sensational happening or a more romantic course raised a case above the commonplace, but none, it is safe to say, ever rivalled in public interest the remarkable crime which was destined to become labelled in the current Press as 'The Holloway Flat Tragedy.'

It was Mr Carlyle's rule to see all callers who sought his aid, for the very nature of their business precluded clients from willingly unbosoming themselves to members of his office staff. Afterwards, they might accept the discreet attention of tactful subordinates, but for the first impression Carlyle well knew the value of his sympathetic handshake, his crisply reassuring voice, his—if need be—humanly condoning eye, and his impeccably prosperous person and surroundings. Men and women, guilty and innocent alike, pouring out their stories felt that at last they were really 'understood', and, to give Louis Carlyle his due, the deduction was generally fully justified.

To the quiet Bampton Street establishment one September afternoon there came a new client who gave the name of Poleash and wished to see Mr Carlyle in person. There was, as usual, no difficulty about that, and, looking up from his desk, Louis registered the impression of an inconspicuous man, somewhere in the thirties. He used spectacles, wore a moustache, and his clothes were a lounge suit of dark material, cut on the simple lines affected by the prudent man who reflects that he may be wearing that selfsame garment two or three seasons hence. There was a slight air of untidiness—or rather, perhaps, an absence of spruceness in any detail—about his general appearance, and the experienced observer put him down as a middle-class worker in any of the clerical, lower professional, or non-manual walks of life.

'Now, Mr Poleash, sit down and tell me what I can do for you,' said Carlyle when they had shaken hands—a rite to which the astute gentleman attached no slight importance and invariably offered. 'Some trouble or little difficulty, I suppose, umph? But first let me get your name right and have your address for reference. You can rely on this, Mr Poleash'—the inclination of Mr Carlyle's head and the arrest of his lifted pen were undeniably impressive—'every word you utter is strictly confidential.'

'Oh, that'll be all right, I'm sure,' said the visitor carelessly. 'It is rather out-of-the-way all the same, and at first—'

'The name?' insinuated Mr Carlyle persuasively.

'Albert Henry Poleash: P-o-l-e-a-s-h—twelve Meridon House, Sturgrove Road, Holloway.'

'Thank you. Now, if you will.'

'Of course I could tell you in a dozen words, but I expect you'd need to know the circumstances, so perhaps I may as well begin where I think you'll understand it best from.'

'By all means,' assented Mr Carlyle heartily; 'by all means. In your own words and exactly as it occurs to you. I'm entirely at your service, so don't feel hurried. Do you care—' The production of a plain gold case completed the inquiry.

'To begin with,' said Mr Poleash, after contributing a match to their common purpose, 'I may say that I'm a married man, living with my wife at that address—a smallish flat which suits us very well as we have no children. Neither of us has any near relations either, and we keep ourselves pretty much to ourselves. Our only servant is a daily woman, who seems able to do everything that we require.'

'One moment, if you please,' interposed Mr Carlyle briskly. 'I don't want you to do anything but tell your story in your own way, Mr Poleash, but if you would indicate by a single word the nature of the event that concerns us it would enable me to judge which points are likely to be most vital to our purpose. Theft—divorce—blackmail —'

'No—murder,' replied Mr Poleash with literal directness.

'Murder!' exclaimed the startled professional. 'Do you mean that a murder has been committed?'

'No, not yet. I am coming to that. For ordinary purposes I generally describe myself as a rent-collector, but that is because official Jacks-in-office seem to have a morbid suspicion of anyone who is obviously not a millionaire calling himself independent. As a matter of fact, I have quite enough private income to serve my purpose. Most of it comes from small house property scattered about London. I see to the management of this myself and personally collect the rents. It takes a few days a week, gives me an interest, keeps me in exercise, and pays as well as anything else I could be doing in the time.'

'Quite so,' encouraged the listener.

'That's always there,' went on Mr Poleash, continuing his leisurely narrative with no indication of needing any encouragement, 'but now and then I take up other work if it suits me—certain kinds of special canvassing; sometimes research. I don't want to slave making more money than we have the need of, and I don't want ever to find that we haven't enough money for anything we may require.'

'Ideal,' contributed Mr Carlyle. 'You are a true philosopher.'

'My wife also has no need to be dependent on anyone either,' continued Mr Poleash, without paying the least attention to the suave compliment. 'As a costume designer and fashion artist she is fully qualified to earn her living, and in fact up to a couple of years ago she did work of that kind regularly. Then she had a long illness that made a great change in her. This brings me to one of the considerations that affect whatever I may wish to do: the illness left her a nervous wreck—jumpy, excitable, not altogether reasonable.'

'Neurasthenia,' was Mr Carlyle's seasonable comment. 'The symptom of the age.'

'Very likely. It doesn't affect me—at least it doesn't affect me directly. Living in the same house with Mrs Poleash, it's bound to affect me, because I have to consider how every blessed thing I do will affect her. And just lately something very lively indeed has come along.

'There is a girl in a shop that I got friendly with—no, I don't want you to put her name down yet. It began a year or eighteen months....But I don't suppose that matters. The only thing I really think that I'm to blame about is that I never told her I was married. At first there was no reason why I should; afterwards—well, there was a certain amount of reason why I shouldn't. Anyhow, I suppose that it was bound to come out sooner or later, and it did, a few weeks ago. She said, quite nicely, that she thought we ought to get married as things were, and then, of course, I had to explain that we couldn't.

'I really hadn't the ghost of an idea that she'd take it so terribly to heart as she did. There's nothing of the Don Juan about me, as you can see at a glance. The thing had simply come about—one step leading to another. But she fainted clean away, and when she came to again she was like a solid block of ice to everything I said. And then to cap matters who should appear at that moment but a fellow she'd been half engaged to before I came along. She'd frequently spoken about this man—his jealousy and temper and so on—and begged me never to let him pick a quarrel with me. 'Peter' was the only name I ever heard him called by, but he was a foreign-looking fellow—an Italian, I think.'

'"Pietro", perhaps?' suggested Mr Carlyle.

'No; 'Peter' she called him. 'Please take me back home, Peter,' was all she said, and off they went together without a word from either to me. Whenever I've seen her since it's been the same. 'Will I please leave her as there is nothing to be said?' and I've been trying to think of all manner of arrangements to put things right.'

'The only arrangement that would seem likely to do that is the one that's out of your power to make,' said Mr Carlyle.

'I suppose so. However, this Peter evidently had a different idea. This is what happened two nights ago. I woke up in the dark—it was about three o'clock I found afterwards—with one of those feelings you get that you've forgotten to do something. It was a letter that I should have posted: it was important that it got delivered some time the next day—the same day by then—and there it was in my breast pocket. I knew if I left it that I should never be up in time for the first morning dispatch, so I determined to slip out then and make sure of it.

'It would only be a matter of twenty minutes or so. There is a pillar-box nearer, but that isn't cleared early. I pulled on a few things and prepared to tiptoe out when a fresh thought struck me.

'Mrs Poleash is a very uncertain sleeper nowadays, and if she is disturbed it's ten to one if she gets off again, and for that reason we use different rooms. I knew better than wake her up to tell her I was going out, but at the same time there was just the possibility that she might wake and, hearing some noise, look in at my door to see if I was all right. If she found me gone she would nearly have a fit. On the spur of the moment I pushed the bolster down the bed and rucked up my dressing gown—it was lying about—above it. In the poor light it served very well for a sleeping man, and I knew that she would not disturb me.

'In less time than I'd given myself I had done my business and was back again at the building. I was entering—my hand was on the knob of the outer door in fact—when the door was pulled sharply open from the other side and another man and I came face to face on the step. We both fell back a bit, I think, but the next moment he had pushed past me and was hurrying down the street. There was just enough light from the lamp across the way for me to be certain of him; it was Peter, and I'm pretty sure that he was equally sharp in recognizing me.

'Of course I went up the stairs in double quick time after that. The door of the flat was as I had left it—simply on the handle as I had put up the latch catch, never dreaming of anyone coming along in that time—and all was quiet and undisturbed inside. But one thing was different in my room, although it took me a few minutes to discover it. There was a clean cut through my dressing gown, through the sheet, through the bolster. Someone, Mr Carlyle, had driven a knife well home before he discovered his mistake.'

'But that was plain evidence of an attempt to murder,' declared Mr Carlyle feelingly—he disliked crimes of violence from every point of view. 'Your business is obviously to inform the police.'

'No,' replied the visitor slowly, 'no. Of course I thought of that, but I soon had to let it slide. What would it mean? Visits, inquiries, cross-examinations, explanations. Everything must come out. After a sufficient exhibition of nerves-torm Mrs Poleash would set about getting a divorce and I should have to go through that. Then I suppose I should have to marry the other one, and, when all's said and done, that's the last thing I really want. In any case, my home would be broken up and my whole life spoiled. No, if it comes to that I might just as well be dead.'

'Then what do you propose doing, may I ask? Calmly wait to be assassinated?'

'That's exactly what I came to see you about. You know my position, my difficulty. I understand that you are a man of wide experience. Putting aside the police and certain publicity, what should you advise?'

'Well, well,' admitted the expert, 'it's rather a formidable handicap, but we will do the best for you that is to be done. Can you indicate exactly what you want?'

'I can easily indicate exactly what I don't want. I don't want to be murdered or molested and I don't want Mrs Poleash to get wind of what's been going on.'

'Why not go away for a time? Meanwhile we could find out who your man is and keep him under observation.'

'I might do that—unless Kitty took it into her head that she didn't want to go, and then, of course, I couldn't leave her alone in the flat just now. After Tuesday night's business—this is what concerns me most—should you think it likely that the fellow would come again or not?'

Mr Carlyle pondered wisely. The longer he took over an opinion, he had discovered—providing he kept up the right expression—the greater weight attached to his pronouncement.

'No,' he replied with due authority. 'I should say not—not in anything like the same way. Of course he will naturally assume that you will now take due precautions—probably imagine that the police are after him. What sort of fastenings have you to your doors and windows?'

'Nothing out of the way. They are old flats and not in very good repair. The outer door is never kept locked, night or day. The front door of our flat has a handle, a latch lock, and a mortice lock. During the day it is simply kept on the latch; at night we fasten the other lock, but do not secure the latch, so that the woman can let herself in when she comes—she has one set of keys, I another, and Mrs Poleash the third.'

'But when you were out on Tuesday night there was no lock fastened, I understand?'

'That is so. Simply the handle to turn. I purposely fastened the latch lock out of action as I found at the door that I hadn't the keys with me and I didn't want to go back to the room again.'

'And the inner doors?'

'They have locks, but few now work—either the key is lost or the lock broken. We never trouble about them—except Kitty's room. She has scrupulously locked that at night, since she has had burglars among other nerve fancies.'

Mr Carlyle shook his head.

'You ought at the very least to have the locks put right at once. Practically all windows are fitted with catches that a child can push back with a table-knife.'

'That's all very well, but, you see, if I get a locksmith in I shall have to make up some cock-and-bull story about house-breaking to Mrs Poleash, and that will set her off. And, anyway, we are on the third storey up.'

'If you are going to consider your wife's nerves at every turn, my dear sir,' remarked Mr Carlyle with some contempt, from the security of his single state, 'you will begin to find yourself in rather a tight fix, I am afraid. How are you going to account for the cut linen, for instance?'

'Oh, I've arranged all that,' replied Mr Poleash, nodding sagaciously. 'My dressing gown she will never notice. The sheet and bolster case—it was a hot night so there was only a single sheet fortunately—I have hidden away in a drawer for the present and put others in their place. I shall buy another of each and burn or lose these soon—Kitty doesn't keep a very close check on things. The bolster itself I can sew up well enough before it's noticed.'

'You may be able to keep it up,' was Mr Carlyle's dubious admission. 'At all events,' he continued, 'as I understand it, you want me to advise you on the lines of taking no direct action against the man you call Peter and at the same time adopting no precautions that would strike Mrs Poleash as being unusual?'

'Nothing that would suggest burglars or murder to her just now,' assented Poleash. 'Yes; that's about what it comes to. You may be able to give me a useful tip or two. If not—well, I know it's a tough proposition and I don't grudge the outlay.'

'At least let us see,' replied the professional man, never failing on the side of lack of self-confidence. 'Now as regards—'

It redounds to Louis Carlyle's credit as an inquiry agent that in an exacting world no serious voice ever accused him of taking unearned money; for so long as there was anything to be learned he plied his novel client with questions, explored surmises and bestowed advice. Even when they had come to the end of useful conversation and the prolific notebook had been closed Carlyle lingered on the topic.

'It's an abnormal situation, Mr Poleash, and full of professional interest. I shall keep it in mind, you may be sure, and if anything further occurs to me, why, I will let you know.'

'Please don't write on any account,' begged Mr Poleash with sudden earnestness. 'In fact, I'd ask you to put a line to that effect across my address. You see, I'm liable to be out at any post time, and if my wife should happen to get curious about a strange letter, why, that, in the language of the kerb, would blow the gaff.'

'I see,' assented Mr Carlyle. 'Very well; it shall be just as you like.'

'And if I can settle with you now,' continued Poleash; 'for of course I don't want to have an account sent. Then some day—say next week—I might look in to report and to hear if you have anything further to suggest.'

'You might, in the meanwhile, consider the most practical course—that of having your man kept under observation.'

'I will,' promised the other. 'But so far I'm all in favour of letting sleeping dogs lie.'

Not unnaturally Mr Carlyle had heard that line before and had countered it.

'True, but it is as well to know when they wake up again,' he replied. With just the necessary touch of dignity and graciousness he named and received the single guinea at which he assessed the interview and began to conduct Mr Poleash towards the door—not the one by which he had entered from the waiting-room but another leading directly down into the street. 'Have you lost something?'

'Only my hat and things—I left them in your ante-room.' He held up his gloved left hand as though it required a word of explanation. 'I keep this on because I am short of a finger, and I've noticed that some people don't like to see it.'

'We'll go out that way instead then—it's all the same,' remarked Carlyle, as he crossed to the other door.

Two later callers were sitting in the waiting-room, and at the sight of them Mr Carlyle's somewhat cherubic face at once assumed an expression of the heartiest welcome. But beyond an unusually mellifluent 'Good afternoon!' he said nothing until his departing client was out of hearing. Names were not paraded in those precincts. With a muttered apology Mr Poleash recovered his belongings from among the illustrated papers and hurried away.

'And why in the world have you been waiting here, Max, instead of sending in to me?' demanded the hospitable Carlyle with a show of indignation.

'Business,' replied Mr Carrados tersely. '*Your* business, understand. Your chief minion was eager to blow a message

through to you but 'No,' I said, 'we'll take our proper turn".
Why should I interrupt the Bogus Company Promoter's
confession or cut short the Guilty Husband's plea?'

'Joking apart, that fellow who just went brought a very
remarkable story,' said Mr Carlyle. 'I should be glad to know
what you would have had to say to him when we have time to
go into it.' (Do not be too ready to condemn the gentleman
as an arrant humbug and this a gross breach of confidence:
Max Carrados had been appointed Honorary Consultant
to the firm, so that what would have otherwise been grave
indiscretions were strictly business discussions.)

'In the meantime the suggestion is that you haven't
taken a half-day off lately and that Monday morning is a
convenient time.'

'Generous man! What is happening on Monday morning then?'

'Something rather surprising in wireless at the Imperial
Salon—ten to twelve-thirty. I know it's the sort of thing
you'll be interested in, and I have two tickets and want
someone fairly intelligent to go with.'

'An ideal chain of circumstances,' rippled Mr Carlyle. 'I
shall endeavour to earn the price of my seat.'

'I am sure you will succeed,' retorted Carrados. 'By the
way, it's free.'

To a strain of this intellectual horseplay the arrangements
for their meeting were made, and that having been the only
reason for the call, Mr Carrados departed under Parkinson's
watchful escort. In due course the wireless demonstration
took place, but (although an invention then for the first
time shown bore no small part in one of the blind man's
subsequent cases) it is unnecessary to accompany them inside
the hall, for with the enigma centring in Mr Poleash that
event had no connexion. It is only touched upon as bringing
Carrados and his friend together at that hour, for as they

walked along Pall Mall after lunching Mr Carlyle suddenly gave a whistle of misgiving and surprise and stopped a hurrying newsboy.

'Holloway Flat Tragedy,' he read from the bill as he investigated sundry pockets for the exact coin. 'By gad, if that should happen to be—'

'Poleash! My God, it is!' he exclaimed as soon as his eye had found the paragraph concerned—a mere inch in the 'Stop Press' news. 'Poor beggar! Tshk! Tshk!'—his clicking tongue expressed disapproval and regret. 'He ought to have known better after what had happened. It was madness. I wonder what he actually did—

'Your remarkable caller of last Thursday, Louis?'

'Yes; but how do you come to know?'

'A trifling indiscretion on his part. With a carelessness that must be rare among your clients I should say, Mr Poleash dropped one of his cards under the table in your writing-room, where the conscientious Parkinson discovered it.'

'Well, the unfortunate chap doesn't need cards now. Listen, Max.

NORTH LONDON TRAGEDY

> Early this morning a charwoman going to a flat in Meridon House, Holloway, made a gruesome discovery. Becoming suspicious at the untouched milk and newspapers, she looked into a bedroom and there found the occupier, a Mr Poleash, dead in bed. He had received shocking injuries, and everything points to deliberate murder. Mrs Poleash is understood to be away on a holiday in Devonshire.

'Of course Scotland Yard takes it up now, but I must put my information at their service. They're devilish lucky, too.

I can practically hand over the miscreant to them and they will scoop the credit.'

'I was to hear about that,' Carrados reminded him. 'Suppose we walk across to Scotland Yard, and you can tell me on the way.'

At the corner of Derby Street they encountered two men who had just turned out of the Yard. The elder had the appearance of being a shrewd farmer, showing his likely son the sights of London and keeping a wideawake eye for its notorious pitfalls. To pursue appearances a step farther they might even have been calling to recover the impressive umbrella that the senior carried.

'Beedel,' dropped Mr Carlyle beneath his breath, but his friend was already smiling recognition.

'The very man,' said Carrados genially. 'I'll wager you can tell us something about the Poleash arrangements, inspector.'

The two plain-clothes men exchanged amused glances.

'I can tell you this much, Mr Carrados,' replied Inspector Beedel, in unusually good spirits, 'my nephew George here is going to do the work and I'm going to look after the bouquets at the finish. We're on our way there now.'

'Couldn't be better,' said the blind man. 'Perhaps you wouldn't mind us going up there with you?'

'Very pleased,' replied Beedel. 'We were making for the station.'

'You may as well help to fill our taxi,' suggested Carrados. 'Mr Carlyle may have something to tell you on the way.'

On the whole Mr Carlyle would have preferred to make his disclosure to headquarters, but the convenience of the arrangement was not to be denied, and with a keen appreciation of the astonishing piece of luck Beedel and George heard the story of the inquiry agent's client.

'It looks like being simply a matter of finding this girl, if the conditions up there bear out his tale,' remarked George, between satisfaction at so veritable a clue and a doubt whether he would not have preferred a more complicated case. 'Did you happen to get her name and address, sir?'

'No,' admitted Mr Carlyle with a slight aloofness, 'it did not arise. Poleash was naturally reluctant to bring in the lady more than he need and I did not press him.'

'Makes no odds,' conceded George generously. 'Shop-girl—kept company with a foreigner—known as Peter. Even without anything else there ought to be no difficulty in finding her.'

Sturgrove Road was not deserted, and there was a rapid concentration about the door of Meridon House 'to see the 'tecs arrive.' On the whole, public opinion was disappointed in their appearance, but the action of George in looking up at the frontage of the building and then glancing sharply right and left along the road was favourably commented on. The policeman stationed at the outer door admitted them at once.

A sergeant and a constable of the local division were in possession of No. 12, and the scared daily woman, temporarily sustained by their impression of absolute immobility, was waiting in the kitchen to indicate whatever was required. Greetings on a slightly technical plane passed between the four members of the force.

'Mrs Poleash has been sent for, I suppose?' asked Mr Carlyle.

'We telephoned from our office to Torquay some hours ago,' replied the sergeant. 'They'll send an officer to the place she's staying at and break it to her as well as possible. That's the course we usually follow.' He took out a weighty presentation watch and considered it. 'Torquay. I don't suppose she could be here yet.'

'Not even if she was in first go,' amplified his subordinate.

'Well,' suggested George. 'Suppose we look round?'

The bedroom was the first spot visited. There was nothing unusual to be seen, apart from the outline of the bed, its secret now hidden beneath a decorous covering—nothing beyond the rather untidy details of the occupant's daily round. All these would in due course receive a careful scrutiny, but at the moment one point drew every eye.

'Hold one another's hands,' advised the sergeant, as he prepared to turn down the sheet. The hovering charwoman gave a scream and fled.

'That's a wild beast been at work,' said Inspector Beedel, coolly drawing nearer to appreciate the details.

'My word, yes!' agreed George, following a little reluctantly.

'Shocking! Shocking!' Mr Carlyle made no pretence about turning away.

'Killed at the first blow,' continued the sergeant, indicating, 'though it's not the only one. Then his face slashed about like a fancy loaf till his own mother wouldn't know him. Something dreadful, isn't it? Finger gone? Oh, that's an old affair. What're you to make of it all?'

'Revenge—revenge and rage and sheer blood-thirstiness,' summed up Mr Carlyle. 'Was anything taken?'

'Nothing disturbed so far as we can see, and the old party there'—a comprehensive nod in the direction of the absent charlady—'says that all the things she knows of seem to be right.'

'What time do they put it at?' asked Beedel.

'Dr Meadows has been here. Midnight Saturday to early Sunday morning, he said. That agrees with the people at the flat opposite hearing the door locked at about ten on Saturday night and the Sunday morning milk and paper not being touched.'

'Milk-can on the doorstep all day, I suppose?' suggested someone.

'Yes; people opposite noticed it, but thought nothing of it. They knew Mrs Poleash was going away on Saturday and thought that he might have gone with her. Mrs Jones, she doesn't come on Sundays, so nothing was found out till this morning.'

'May as well hear what she has to say now,' said Beedel. 'No need to keep her about that I know of.'

'Just one minute, please, if you don't mind,' put in Mr Carlyle, not so much asking anyone's permission as directing the affair. The sight of a wardrobe had reminded him of the dead man's story, and he was now handling the clothes that hung there with keen anticipation. 'There is something that I really came especially to see. This is his dressing gown, and, yes, by Jupiter, it's here!'

He pointed to a clean cut through the material as they gathered round him.

'What's that?' inquired the sergeant, looking from one face to another.

'Previous attempt,' replied Beedel shortly.

'There ought to be a sheet and a bolster case somewhere about,' continued the eager gentleman, now thoroughly intrigued, and under the impulse of his zeal drawers and cupboards were opened and their contents gingerly displaced.

'Something of the sort here among the shirts,' announced George.

'Have them out then. Not likely to be any others put away there.' The hidden things were unfolded and displayed and here also the tragic evidence lay clear before them.

'By gad, you know, I half thought he might have dreamt it until this came,' confided Mr Carlyle to the room at large. 'Tshk! Tshk! How on earth the fellow could have gone—' He remembered the quiet figure lying within earshot and finished with a tolerant shrug.

'Let's get on,' said Beedel. These details could very well have waited had been his thought all along.

'I'll fold the things,' volunteered Mr Carrados. All the others had satisfied their curiosity by glance or scrutiny and he was free to take his time. He took up the loose bundle in his arms and with the strange impulse towards light that so often moved him he turned away from them and sought the window.

'Now, missis, come along and tell us all about it,' called out the young constable.

'No,' interposed the inspector kindly, 'the poor creature's upset enough already without bringing her in here again. Stay where you are, Mrs Jones, we're coming there,' he announced from the door, and they filed along the skimpy passage into the dingy kitchen. 'Now can you just tell us quietly what you know about this bad business?'

Mrs Jones's testimony, given on the frequently expressed understanding that she was quite prepared to be struck dead at any point of it if she deviated from the strictest line of truth, did not disclose any new feature, while its frequent references to the lives and opinions of friends not concerned in the progress of the drama threatened now and then to stifle the narrative with a surfeit of pronouns. But she was listened to with patience and complimented on her nerve. Mrs Jones sadly shook her antique black bonnet and disclaimed the quality.

'I could do nothing but stand and scream,' she confessed wistfully, referring to the first dreadful moment at the bedroom door, 'I stood and screamed three times before I could get myself away. The poor gentleman! What harm was he, for to be done in like that!'

There was a string of questions from one or another of the company before she was finally dismissed—generally from Beedel or George with Mr Carlyle's courteously assertive voice intervening once or twice: the Poleashes had few visitors that she had ever seen—she was only there from eight to six—and she had never known of anyone staying with them; no one had knocked at the door for anything on Saturday; she had not noticed anyone whom she could call to mind as 'a foreigner' loitering about or at the door recently (a foreign family lived at No. 5, but they were well spoken of); neither Mr nor Mrs Poleash had talked to her of anything uncommon of late—the gentleman was mostly out and 'she' wasn't one of the friendly sort; the couple seemed to get on together 'as well as most', and she had never heard a 'real' quarrel; Mrs Poleash had gone off for a week (she understood) about noon on Saturday, and Mr Poleash had accompanied her to Paddington (as he had mentioned on his return for tea); she had last seen him at about five o'clock on Saturday, when she left, a little earlier than usual; she knew nothing of the ashes in the kitchen grate, not having had a fire there for weeks past; the picture post card (passed round) from Mrs Poleash, announcing her arrival at Torquay, she had found on the hall floor together with the Sunday paper; she was to go on just the same while Mrs Poleash was away, coming daily to 'do up', and so on; it was a regular arrangement 'week in and week out'.

'That seems to be about all,' summed up Inspector Beedel, looking round. 'We have your address, Mrs Jones, and you're sure to hear from us about something pretty soon.'

'Before you go,' said a matter-of-fact voice from the door, 'do you happen to remember what you were doing last Thursday afternoon?' It was the first question that Mr Carrados had put, and they had scarcely noticed whether he had re-joined them yet or not.

'Last Thursday afternoon?' repeated Mrs Jones helplessly. 'Oh, Lor', sir, my head's in that whirl—'

'Yes, but it isn't so difficult if you think—early closing day, you know.'

This stimulus proved effective and the charwoman remembered. She had something special to remember by. On Thursday morning Mrs Poleash has passed on to her a single ticket for that afternoon's performance at the Parkhurst Theatre, and told her that she could go after she had washed up the dinner things.

'So that you were not here at all on Thursday afternoon? Just one more thing, Mrs Jones. Sooner or later a photograph of your master will be wanted. Is there one anywhere about?'

'The only one I know of stands on the sideboard in the little room. There may be others put away, but not being what you might call curious sir—'

'I'm sure you're not,' agreed Carrados. 'Now, as you go you shall point it out to us so that there can be no mistake.'

'You couldn't make no mistake because there's only that and one of her stands there,' explained Mrs Jones, but she proceeded to comply. 'There it—'

'Yes?' said the blind man, close upon her.

'I'm sorry, sir, indeed. I must have made a mistake—'

'I don't think you made any mistake,' he urged. 'I don't think you really think so either.'

'I'm that mithered I don't rightly know what to think,' she declared. 'That isn't him.'

'Is it the frame? No, don't touch it—that might be unlucky, you know—but you can remember that.'

'It's the frame, right enough. I ought to know, the times I've dusted it.'

'Then the photograph has been changed: there's nothing unlikely in that. When was the last time that you noticed the other one there?'

Quite recently, it would seem, but taking refuge behind her whirling head Mrs Jones held out against precision. It might have been Friday or it might have been Saturday. Carrados forbore to press her more exactly, and she departed, sustained by the advice of Authority that she should have nothing to say to nobody, under the excuse, if need be, that she had answered enough questions already for one day.

'While we are here,' said the sergeant—they were still in the 'little room', the only one that looked out on the front—'you might as well see where he got in.' He went to the window and indicated certain marks on the wood- and stone-work. 'We found the lower sash still a few inches up when we came.'

'Went the same way as he came, I suppose?' suggested George.

'Must have done. All the keys are accounted for, and Mrs Jones found the front door locked as usual. And why not; why shouldn't he? There's the balcony, and you hardly have to lean out to see the stairway window not a yard away. Why, it's as easy as ring-a-roses. Might have been made for it.'

'Tshk! Tshk!' fumed Mr Carlyle unhappily. 'After what I said. And not one of the locks has been seen to.'

'Locks?' echoed the young policeman, appearing that moment at the door. 'Why, here is a chap with tools, says he's come to repair and fit the locks!'

'Well, if this isn't the fair *nefus ultra*!' articulated the sergeant. 'However, show him in, lad.'

The locksmith, looking scarcely less alarmed than if he had fallen into a den of thieves, had a very short and simple tale to tell. His shop was in the Seven Sisters Road, and on Friday afternoon a gentleman had called there and arranged with him to come on Monday and repair some locks. He had given the name of Poleash and that address. The man knew nothing of what had taken place and had come as fixed.

'It's a pity you didn't happen to make it Saturday, Mr Hipwaite,' said Inspector Beedel, as he took a note of this new evidence. 'It might—I don't say it would, but it might—have prevented murder being done.'

'But that's the very thing I was not to do,' declared Hipwaite, with some warmth. '"Don't come on Saturday because the wife is very nervous, and if she thinks burglars are about she'll have a fit," he said—those very words. "She'll be away on Monday, and then by the time she comes back she mayn't notice." Was I likely to come on Saturday?'

Plainly he was not. 'That's all right,' it was conceded, 'but there's nothing in your line doing today.' So Mr Hipwaite departed, more than half persuaded that he had been hardly used and not in the least mollified by being concerned in so notable a tragedy.

'Before I go,' resumed the sergeant, leading the way back to the kitchen, 'there's one other thing I must hand over. You heard what Mrs Jones said about the fire—that there hadn't been one for weeks as they always used the stove?'

'That's what I asked her,' George reminded him. 'Someone has had a fire here.'

'Correct,' continued the officer imperturbably. 'It's also what I asked her a couple of hours before you came. Someone's had a fire here. Who and what for? Well, I've had the cinders out to see and now I'll make over to you what there was.'

'Glove fasteners,' commented the inspector. 'All the metal there was about them. Millions of the pattern, I suppose.'

'Burned his gloves after the job—they must have been in a fair mess,' said George. '"Audubon Frères" they're stamped—foreign make.'

'That reminds me—there's one thing more.' It was produced from the sergeant's pocket-book, a folded fragment of paper, charred along its edge. 'It's from the hearth; evidently a bit that fell out when the fire was made. Foreign newspaper, you will see; Italian it looks to me.'

Mr Carlyle, Inspector Beedel, and George exchanged appreciative glances. Upon this atmosphere of quiet satisfaction there fell something almost like a chuckle.

'Did anyone happen to notice if he had written '*Si parla Italiano*' in red on the wall over the bed?' inquired the guileless voice.

The young constable, chancing to be the nearest person to the door, rose to this mendacious suggestion by offering to go and see. The others stared at the blind man in various stages of uncertainty.

'No, no,' called out Mr Carlyle feelingly. 'There is no need to look, thank you. When you know Mr Carrados as well as I do you will understand that although there is always something in what he says it is not always the something you think it is. Now, Max, pray enlighten the company. Why should the murderer write 'Italian spoken' over the bed?'

'Obviously to make sure that you shouldn't miss it,' replied Mr Carrados.

'Well,' remarked the sergeant, demonstrating one or two simple exercises in physical drill as a suitable preparation, 'I may as well be going. I don't understand Italian myself. Nor Dutch either,' he added cryptically.

Mr Carlyle also had nothing more to stay for. 'If you have done here, Max—' he began, and turned only to find that Carrados was no longer there.

'Your friend has just gone to the front room, sir,' said the constable, catching the words as he passed. 'Funny to see a blind man getting about so—' But a sudden crash of glass from the direction referred to cut short the impending compliment.

It was, as Carrados explained, entirely his own preposterous fault. Nothing but curiosity about the size of the room had impelled him to touch the walls, and the picture, having a weak cord or an insecure nail…had it not brought something else down in its fall?

'Only the two frames from the sideboard, so far as I can see,' replied Carlyle. 'All the glass is shattered. But I don't suppose that Mrs Poleash will be in a condition to worry about trifles. Jolly good thing you aren't hurt, that's all.'

'Of course I should like to replace the damage,' said the delinquent.

Inspector Beedel said nothing, but as he looked on he recalled one or two other mischances in the past, and being of an introspective nature he continued to massage his chin thoughtfully.

> > >

Three days later the inquest on the body of Albert Henry Poleash was opened. It was of the merest formal description, proof of identity and a bare statement of the cause of death being the only evidence put forward. An adjournment for a week was then declared.

At the resumed inquiry the story of Poleash's death was taken forward, and the newspaper reader for the first time was encouraged to see in it the promise of a first-class popular sensation. Louis Carlyle related the episode of his unexpected client. Corroboration of that wildly romantic story was forthcoming from many sides. Mr Hipwaite carried the drama two days later by describing the dead man's visit to his shop, the order to repair the locks, and his own futile journey to the flat. Mrs Jones, skilfully piloted among dates and details, was in evidence as the discoverer of the body. Two doctors—a private practitioner called hurriedly in at the first alarm and the divisional surgeon—agreed on all essential points, and the police efficiently bridged the narration at one stage and another and contrived to present a faithful survey of the tragedy.

But the most arresting figure of the day, though her evidence was of very slight account and mainly negative, was the unhappy widow. As she moved into the witness-box, a wan, graceful creature in her unaccustomed, but, it may be said, not unattractive crêpe, a rustle of compassion stirred the court and Mr Carlyle, who had come prejudiced against her, as an automatic reflex of his client's fate, chirruped sympathy.

Mrs Poleash gave her testimony in a low voice, not particularly attractive in its tone, and she looked straight before her with eyes neither downcast nor wandering. Her name, she said, was Katherine Poleash, her age twenty-nine. She knew nothing of the tragedy, having been in Torquay at the time. She had gone there on the Saturday afternoon, her husband seeing her off from Paddington. Their relationship was perfectly friendly, but not demonstrative. Her husband was a considerate but rather reserved man with no especial interests. Up to two years ago she had been accustomed to earn her own living, but a nervous break-down had interfered with her capacity for work. It was on account of that illness that she had generally occupied a separate bedroom; it had left her nervous in many ways, but she was surprised to hear that she should have been described as exacting or ill-tempered.

'"Not wholly reasonable and excitable" were the precise terms used, I think,' put in Mr Carlyle gallantly.

'It's much the same,' she replied apathetically.

Continuing, she had no knowledge at all of any intrigue between her husband and a shop-girl, such as had been referred to, nor had she ever heard of the man Peter, either by name or as an Italian. She could not suggest in what quarter of London the shop in question was likely to be as the deceased was accustomed to go about a good deal. The police already had a list of the various properties he owned. At the conclusion of her evidence Mrs Poleash seemed to be on the point of fainting and had to be assisted out.

There was nothing to be gained by a further adjournment. The cause of death—the real issue before that court—was reasonably clear. The jury brought in a verdict of 'Wilful Murder against Some Person or Persons Unknown.' Before the reporters left the police asked that the Press should circulate a request for anyone having knowledge of a shop-assistant who had been friendly with a foreigner known as Peter or Pietro, or with a man answering to Mr Poleash's description, to communicate with them either at New Scotland Yard or to any local station. The Press promised to comply and offered to publish photographs of Mr Poleash as a means towards that end, only to learn that no photograph possessing identification value could be found. So began the memorable paper-chase for an extremely nebulous shop-assistant and a foreigner whose description began and ended with the sobriquet 'Peter the Italian'.

⟩⟩⟩

'I was wondering if you or Inspector Beedel would come round one day to see me,' said Mr Carrados as George was shown into the study at The Turrets. Two full weeks had elapsed since the conclusion of the inquest and the news-paper value of the Holloway Flat Tragedy had sunk from a column opposite the leader page to a six-line fill-up beneath 'Home and General'. 'Your uncle used often to drop in to entertain me with the progress of his cases.'

'That wasn't his way of looking at it, Mr Carrados. He used to say that when it came to seeing through a brick wall you were—well, hell!'

'Curious,' remarked Mr Carrados. 'I don't remember ever hearing Inspector Beedel make use of that precise expression.'

George went a trifle red and laughed to demonstrate his self-possession.

'Well, perhaps I dropped a word of my own in by accident,' he said. 'But that was what he meant—in a complimentary sense, of course. As a matter of fact, it was on his advice that I ventured to trouble you now.'

'Not 'trouble",' protested the blind man, ever responsive to the least touch of diffidence. 'That's another word the inspector wouldn't use about me, I'm sure.'

'You're very kind,' said George, accepting a cigarette, 'and as I had to come this way to see another—oh, my Lord, another!—shop-girl, why, I thought—'

'Ah; how is the case going?'

'It's no go, Mr Carrados. We've seen thousands of shop-girls and hundreds of Italian Peters. I'm beginning to think,' said the visitor, watching Mr Carrados's face as he propounded the astonishing heresy, 'that there is no such person.'

'Yes?' replied Carrados unmoved. 'It is always as well to look beyond the obvious, isn't it? What does the inspector say?'

'He says, 'I should like to know what Mr Carrados really meant by 'Italian spoken', and what he really did when he smashed that picture".'

Carrados laughed his appreciation as he seemed actually to watch the blue smoke curling upwards.

'How easy it is to give a straightforward answer when a plain question is asked,' he replied. 'By '*Si parla Italiano*' I ventured to insinuate my own private opinion that there was no Italian Peter; when I broke the picture I tried to obtain some definite evidence of someone there was.'

George waited in the hope of this theme developing, but his host seemed to consider that he had said all that was necessary, and it is difficult to lead on a man into disclosures when you cannot fix him with your eye.

'Poleash may have been mistaken himself,' he continued tentatively; 'or he may have purposely misled Mr Carlyle on details, with the idea of getting his advice but not entirely trusting him to the full extent.'

'He may,' admitted the placid smoker.

'One thing I can't understand is however the man set about keeping company with a girl without spending more on her than he seems to have done. We found a small pocket diary that he entered his current expenses in, and there isn't a single item for chocolates, flowers, theatres, or anything of that sort.'

'A diary?'

'Oh, he didn't keep a diary; only entered cash, and rents received, and so on. Here it is, if you care to—examine it.'

'Thank you, I should. I wonder what our friend Carlyle charged for the consultation?'

'I don't remember seeing that,' admitted George, referring to the pages. 'Thursday, the 3rd, wasn't it? No, curiously enough, that doesn't appear....I wonder if he never put down any of these what you might call questionable items for fear of Mrs Poleash seeing?'

'Not unnaturally,' agreed Carrados. 'You found nothing else of interest then—no addresses or new names?'

'Nothing at all. Oh, that page you've got is only his memorandum of sizes and numbers and so on.'

'Yes; quite a useful habit, isn't it?' The long, vibrant fingers touched off line after line without a pause or stumble. 'When he made this handy list Albert Henry Poleash little thought—Boots, size 9; hat, size 7 1/8; collars, size 16; gloves, size 8 3/4; watch, No. 31903; weight, 11st. 8lbs. There we have the man: *Ex pede Herculem*, as the motto has it—only in this case of course the hat and gloves are more useful.'

'Very true, sir,' said George, whose instinct was to keep a knowing front on all occasions.

When Parkinson was summoned to the room some time later he found his master there alone. Every light was blazing on, and, sitting at his desk, Mr Carrados confronted a single sheet of paper. With his trained acuteness for the minutiae of every new condition, Parkinson immediately took mental photographs of the sheet of paper with its slim written column, of the position and appearance of the chair George had used, of the number and placing of cigarette ends and matches, of all the details connected with the tray and contents, and of a few other matters. It was his routine.

'Close the door and come in,' said Carrados. 'I want you to carry your mind back about four weeks to the last occasion when we called at Mr Carlyle's office together. As we sat in the waiting-room I asked you if the things left there belonged to anyone we knew.'

'I remember the circumstances perfectly, sir.'

'I want the articles described. The gloves?'

'There was only one glove—that for the right hand. It was a dark grey *suède*, moderately used, and not of the best cut. The fastening was a press button stamped 'Audubon Frères". The only marking inside the glove was the size, 7 1/2.'

Carrados made a note on the sheet before him. 'The hat?' he said. 'What size was that?'

'The size of hat, printed on an octagonal white ticket, was 6 3/4, sir.'

'Excellent, so far. When the caller passed through you saw him for a moment. Apart from clothes, which do not matter just now, was there any physical peculiarity that would identify him?'

'He had a small dark mole beneath the left eye. The lobe of his right ear was appreciably less than the other. The nail of the middle finger of the right hand was corrugated from an injury at some time.'

Carrados made a final note on the paper before him.

'Very good indeed, Parkinson,' he remarked. 'That is all I wanted.'

〉〉〉

A month passed and nothing happened. Occasionally a newspaper, pressed for a subject, commented on the disquieting frequency with which undetected murder could be done, and among other instances mentioned the Holloway Flat Tragedy and deplored the ease with which Peter the Italian had remained at large. The name by that time struck the reader as distantly familiar.

Then one evening early in November Beedel rang Mr Carrados up. The blind man happened to take the call himself, and at the first words he knew that the dull, patient shadowing of weeks was about to fructify.

'Yes, Inspector Beedel himself, sir,' said the voice at the other end. 'I'm speaking from Beak Street. The two you know of have just gone to the Restaurant X in Warsaw Street. The lady has booked two seats at the Alhambra for tonight, so we expect them to be there for the best part of an hour.'

'I'll come at once,' replied Carrados. 'What about Carlyle?'

'He's been notified. Back entrance in Boulton Court,' said the inspector. 'I'm off there now myself.'

It was the first time that the two the blind man 'knew of' had met since the watch was set, and their correspondence had been singularly innocuous. Yet not a breath of suspicion had been raised, and the same elaborate care that had prompted Mr Carrados to bring down a picture to cover the abstraction of a small square of glass had been maintained throughout.

'Nice private little room upstairs, saire,' insinuated the proprietor as 'the two' looked round. He guessed that they shunned publicity, and he was right, although not entirely so. With a curt nod the man led the way up the narrow stairway to the equivocal little den on the first floor. The general room below had not been crowded, but this one was wholly empty.

'Quite like old times,' said the woman with an unmusical laugh as she threw off her cloak—there was little indication of the sorrowing widow now, 'I thought we had better fight shy of the 'Toledo' for the future.'

''M yes,' replied her companion slowly, looking dubiously about him—he no longer wore glasses or moustache, nor was his left hand, the glove now removed, deficient of a finger. 'The only thing is whether it isn't too soon for us to be about together at all.'

'Pha!' she snapped expressively. 'They've gone to sleep again. There isn't a thing—no not a single detail—gone wrong. The most that could happen would be a raid here to look for Peter the Italian!'

'For God's sake don't keep on that,' he urged in a low voice. 'Your husband was a brute to you by what you say, and I'm not sorry now it's done, but I want to forget it all. You had your way: I've done everything you planned. Now you are free and decently well off and as soon as it's safe we can really marry—if you still will.'

'If I still will,' she repeated, looking at him meaningly. 'Do you know, Dick, I think it may become desirable sooner even than I thought.'

'Sssh!' he warned; 'here comes someone. You order, Kitty—you always have done! Anything will suit me.' He turned to arrange his overcoat across an empty chair and reassured his hand among the contents of the nearest pocket.

Downstairs, in his nondescript living-room, the proprietor of the Restaurant X was being very quickly and efficiently made to understand just so much of the situation as turned on his immediate and complete acceptance of it. In the presence of authority so vigorously expressed the stout gentleman bowed profusely, lowered his voice, and from time to time placed a knowing finger on his lips in agreement.

'Hallo,' said the man called 'Dick' as a different attendant brought a dish. 'Where has our other waiter got to?'

'Party of regular customers as always has him just come in,' explained the new one. ''Ope you don't mind, sir.'

'Not a brass button.'

'It's all right, inspector,' reported the 'waiter'. 'He has the three marks you said—mole, ear, nail.'

'Certain of the woman?'

'Mrs Poleash, sure as snow.'

'Any reference to it?'

'Don't think so while I'm about. Drama just now. Has his little gun handy.'

'Take this in now. Leave the door open and see if you can make him talk up....If you two gentlemen will step just across there I think you'll be able to hear.'

Carrados smiled as he proceeded to comply.

'I have already heard,' he said. 'It is the voice of the man who called on Mr Carlyle on September the third.'

'I think it is the voice,' admitted Mr Carlyle when he had tiptoed back again. 'I really think so, but after two months I should not be prepared to swear.'

'He is the man,' repeated Carrados deliberately.

Inspector Beedel, clinking something quietly in his pocket, nodded to his waiter.

'Morgan follows you in with the coffee,' he said. 'Put it down on the table, Morgan, and stand beside the woman. Call me as soon as you have him.'

It was the sweet that the first waiter was to take, and with it there was a sauce. It was not exactly overturned, but there was an awkward movement and a few drops were splashed. With a clumsy apology the waiter, napkin in hand, leaned across the customer to remove a spot that marked his coat-sleeve.

'Here!' exclaimed the startled man. 'What the devil are you up to?'

It was too late. Speech was the only thing left to him then. His wrists were already held in a trained, relentless grasp; he was pressed helplessly back into his chair at the first movement of resistance. Kitty Poleash rose from her seat with a dreadful coldness round her heart, felt a hand upon her shoulder, cast one fearful glance round, and sank down upon her chair again. Before another word was spoken Inspector Beedel had appeared, and the grip of bone and muscle on the straining wrists was changed to one of steel. Less than thirty seconds bridged the whole astonishing transformation.

'Richard Crispinge, you are charged with the murder of this woman's husband. Katherine Poleash, you are held as an accessory.' The usual caution followed. 'Get a taxi to the back entance, Morgan.'

Half a dozen emotions met on Crispinge's face as he shot a glance at his companion and then faced the accuser again.

'You're crazy,' he panted, still labouring from the effort. 'I've never even seen the man.'

'I shouldn't say anything now, if I were you,' advised Beedel, on a quite human note. 'You may find out later that we know more than you might think.'

What followed could not have been charged against human foresight, for at a later stage it was shown that a certain cable failed and in a trice one side of Warsaw Street was involved in darkness. What happened in that darkness—where they had severally stood before and after—who moved or spoke—whose hand was raised—were all matters of dispute, but suddenly the black was stabbed by a streak of red, a little crack—scarcely more than the sharp bursting of a paper bag—nearly caught up to it, and almost slowly to the awaiting ears came the sound of strain and the long crash of falling glass and china.

'A lamp from down there!' snapped Beedel's sorely-tried voice, as the ray of an electric torch whirled like a pygmy searchlight and then centred on a tumbled thing lying beyond the table. 'Look alive!'

'They say there is gas somewhere,' announced Mr Carlyle, striking a match as he ran in. 'Ah, here it is.'

No need to ask then what had happened, though how it had happened could never be set quite finally at rest; for if Kitty Poleash was standing now, whereas before she had sat, the weapon lay beyond her reach close to the shackled hands. A curious apathy seemed to fall upon the room as though the tang of the drifting wisp of smoke dulled their alertness, and when the woman moved slowly towards her lover Beedel merely picked the pistol up and waited. With a terrible calmness she knelt by the huddled form and raised the inert head.

'Good-bye, my dear,' she said quietly, kissing the dead lips for the last time; 'it's over.' And with a strange tragic fitness she added, in the words of another fatal schemer, 'We fail!'

She seemed to be the only one who had any business there; Beedel was abstracted; Carlyle and Carrados felt like spectators walking on a stage when the play is over. In the street below the summoned taxi throbbed unheeded; they were waiting for another equipage now. When that had moved off with its burden Kitty Poleash would follow her captors submissively, like a dog without a home.

'It isn't a feather in our caps to have a man slip away like that,' remarked the inspector moodily as the two joined him for a word before they left; 'but, of course, as far as they are both concerned, it's the very best that could have happened.'

'In what way do you mean the best?' demanded Mr Carlyle with a professional keenness for the explicit.

'Why, look at what will happen now. He's saved all the trouble and thought of being hanged, which it was bound to be in the end, and has got it over without a moment's worry. She will get the full benefit of it as well, because her counsel will now be able to pile it all up against the fellow and claim that he exercised an irresistible influence over her. Personally, I should say that it's twelve of one and thirteen of the other, and I don't know that she isn't the thirteen, but she is about as likely to be hanged as I am to be made superintendent tomorrow.'

⟩⟩⟩

'Max,' said Mr Carlyle, as they sat smoking together the same night, 'when you think of the elaboration of that plot it was appalling.'

'Curious,' replied Carrados thoughtfully. 'To me it seems absolutely simple and inevitable. Perhaps that is because I should have done it—fundamentally, that is—just the same way myself.'

'And got caught the same way?'

'There were mistakes made. If you decide to kill a man you must do it either secretly or openly. If you do it secretly and it comes to light you are done for. If you do it openly there is the chance of putting another appearance on the crime.

'These two—Crispinge and Mrs Poleash—knew that in the ordinary way the killing of the husband would immediately attract suspicion to the wife. Under that fierce scrutiny it could not long be hidden that the woman had a lover, and the disclosure would be fatal. Indeed, if Poleash had lived, that fact must shortly have come to light, and it was the sordid determination to secure his income for themselves before he discovered the intrigue and divorced his wife that sealed his fate and forced an early issue.

'If you intend to commit a murder, Louis, and know that suspicion will automatically fall on you, what is the first thing that you would wish to effect? Obviously that it should fall on someone else more strongly. But as the arrest of that someone else would upset the plan, you would naturally make his identity such that he would have the best chance of remaining at large. The most difficult person to find is one who does not exist.

'There you have the whole strategy of the sorry business. Everything hinged on that, and when you once possess that clue you not only see why everything happened as it did but you can confidently forecast exactly what will happen. To go on believing that you had talked with the real Poleash it was necessary that you should never actually see the man as he was. Hence the disfigurement. What assailant would act in that way? Only one maddened by a jealous fury. The Southern people are popularly the most jealous and revengeful, so we must have a native of Italy or Spain, and the Italian is the more credible of the two. Similarly, Mr Hipwaite is brought in to add another touch of corroboration to your tale. But why Mr Hipwaite from a mile away? There is a locksmith quite near at hand; I made it my business to call on him, and I learned that, as I expected, he knew Poleash by sight. Plainly he would never have served the purpose.'

'Perhaps I ought to have been more sceptical of the fellow's tale,' conceded Mr Carlyle; 'but, you know, Max, I have a dozen fresh people call on me every month with queer stories, and it's not once in a million times that this would happen. I, at any rate, saw nothing to rouse suspicion. You say he made mistakes?'

'Crispinge, among divers other things he's failed in, has been an actor, and with Mrs Poleash's coaching on facts there is no doubt that he carried the part all right. Being wise after the event, we may say that he overstressed the need of secrecy.

The idea of the previous attack, designed, of course, to throw irrefutable evidence into the scales, was too pronounced. Something slighter would have served better. Personally, I think it was excess of caution to send Mrs Jones out on the Thursday afternoon. She could have been relied upon to be too 'mithered' for her recollections to carry any weight. It was necessary to destroy the only reliable photograph of Poleash, but the risk ought to have been taken of burning it before she went off to establish her unassailable alibi, and not leaving it for her accomplice to do. In the event, by handling the frame after he had burned his gloves, Crispinge furnished us with the solitary finger-print that linked up his identity.'

'He had been convicted then?'

'Blackmail, six years ago, and other things before. A mixture of weakness and violence, he has always gravitated towards women for support. But the great mistake—the vital oversight—the alarm signal to my perceptions—'

'Yes?'

'Well, I should really hardly like to mention it to anyone but you. The sheet and the bolster-case that so convincingly turned up to clinch your client's tale once and for all demolished it. They had never been on Poleash's bed, believe me, Louis. What a natural thing for the woman to take them from her own, and yet how fatal! I sensed that damning fact as soon as I had them in my hands, and in a trice the whole fabric of deception, so ingeniously contrived, came down in ruins. Nothing—nothing—could ever retrieve that simple, deadly blunder.'

The Magician of
Cannon Street

J. S. Fletcher

Joseph Smith Fletcher (1863–1935) was a Yorkshireman who moved to London and carved a successful career as a journalist and author. He wrote historical books before turning successfully to crime. Some of his crime fiction was set in Yorkshire, but his most famous mysteries, The Middle Temple Murder *(which was admired by President Woodrow Wilson) and* The Charing Cross Mystery *both benefited from London settings.*

Fletcher's focus was on producing lively entertainments rather than the elaborate puzzles of whodunit, whydunit or howdunit favoured by the likes of Agatha Christie, Dorothy L. Sayers and Anthony Berkeley. He created a number of detectives, including Paul Campenhaye, a master of disguise and keen observer of humankind who features in a collection of stories with settings in London and Yorkshire, Paul Campenhaye, Specialist in Criminology. *It is an obscure book, but it deserves to be better known.*

❯❯❯

My reason for going down to Cannon Street at all that morning was not connected in any way with crimes and mysteries—I had no idea of either in my mind when I stepped out of the Underground at the Mansion House Station. I was on a much pleasanter errand than the solving of problems arising from crimes; the fact was, that, having matrimony in view, I was busy in reconstructing and remodelling a beautiful old Jacobean house which I had just bought, away out in a Surrey village, and I had been recommended by my architect to visit a man in Budge Row who had some good scheme or idea about patent flooring. I had meant to have a leisurely half-hour's chat with him, but as luck would have it, I was not in Budge Row for the space of five minutes, and I went out of it, not only in a state of hurried precipitation, but also in one of considerable surprise. And in spite of the hurry and the surprise I had wit enough to gather that I was in for an affair.

It was raining that morning—a November morning. I thought as I turned into Budge Row from Cannon Street that the City (a quarter of the town rarely visited by me) looked infinitely miserable under rain. There was slop on the roofs, and slop in the streets; it was one of those days on which the sight of an umbrella suggests thoughts of infinite wretchedness, and men turn up the collars of their coats out of sheer sympathy with the weather. In the narrow confines of Budge Row there were few people about; it a little surprised me, therefore, to see at the corner one of those individuals who are known as 'gazers,' which term, I may explain to the uninitiated, means those street merchants who stand in the gutters supporting small trays on which are set out cheap mechanical toys, usually sold at the price of a penny. This particular gazer rather attracted my attention; he was a tall, well-built fellow, arrayed in a multiplicity of old, odd-coloured garments, finished off by a tattered waterproof cape;

he was lame of one leg, and supported himself by a crutch; there was a scar that looked very like an old sword-cut, on one cheek, and his right eye was obsessed by a black patch. On his tray he displayed a number of small metal tigers: you pressed a spring and the tiger's eyes glared and his tail waved; it seemed to me that the sudden lighting-up of the yellow eyes was the only sign of warmth in that wind-swept street. The vendor cried at intervals in a hoarse, fog-spoilt voice:

'The real Royal Indian Tiger from Bengal! One penny!' And as I passed him he muttered thickly: 'Buy a tiger, captain—just the same as your honour's shot in the jungle—all alive, captain!'

I suppose it flatters every civilian to be accused of relationship with the Army; anyhow, having one handy in my ticket pocket, I dropped a shilling on the gazer's tray as I walked by. He picked it up, spat on it, and thanked me with an eloquent look which was almost a wink, and fell to crying his wares still more raucously and loudly.

Where the ancient church of Saint Anthony, patron saint of the good grocers of London, once stood in Budge Row, shrining the bones of many estimable citizens who in their time were aldermen and sheriffs of our proud city, there are now certain of those modern abominations called chambers, wherein a man may as easily lose himself as a mouse might in entering a thickly-populated rabbit-warren. The man I wanted to see had his place of business in one of these barrack-like buildings, and my first proceeding, on discovering the set of chambers which I wanted, was to read the names on the list of tenants that was posted up at the door. This occupied some time; there appeared to be some dozens of floors and scores of separate offices. And, as I stood in the entry, my hands behind me, reading steadily down one side of the list, preparatory to going methodically up the other, I felt something thrust into my fingers, and turning sharply round, saw an urchin throw me a backward grin as he darted into the street and vanished in a neighbouring entry.

I glanced at what this impudent gamin had thrust into my hand. A scrap of paper—creased, damp. Nevertheless, I opened it, on principle, having long before made it a strict rule of life to attend to the smallest details in a day's adventures. There were words hastily scribbled on that bit of paper; they ran thus:

'For God's sake, Campenhaye, get out of that doorway and away from this street, *quick!* But come, see me at my rooms at four o'clock, and if you still have him, bring that clerk of yours with you. Now scoot—and look neither right nor left.—Tregarthen.'

I obeyed this command to the letter: I did not even wait to fold up the paper. Crushing it in my hand, I shot hurriedly out of the doorway, up the street, and into a taxi-cab which happened to be passing. Not until I was west of St. Paul's did I begin to ask myself what had really happened.

Tregarthen!—I had not seen Tregarthen for three years—not since soon after the affair of the Taplin mystery. He and I, working independently of the police, had tried to find Mendoba, the murderer of Dr Francis Taplin; like the police, we had failed to do so. Then I had turned to other matters, and Tregarthen had gone away somewhere and I had not heard of him since; he was always a strangely mysterious person, and so I had not been surprised at his silence. But here he was in London again—and I knew his peculiar hand-writing well enough—and yet I had not seen him at any of his usual haunts—which were also mine—nor heard of his return.

'This is an affair!' I informed myself. 'Tregarthen is back. Tregarthen is up to something. Tregarthen is watching somebody. That somebody has something to do with those chambers in Budge Row. Perhaps if I had looked up I should have seen Tregarthen's striking face confronting me from one of the opposite windows. However, I have done as I was told. Now, Tregarthen wants to see me. Also, which is possibly more important—he wants to see Killingley. I think—I am disposed to think—that this means that Tregarthen will be glad of a little professional assistance.'

I found that astute young gentleman, my clerk Killingley, improving his knowledge of men and things by a studious reading of the *Sporting Times*. I introduced the matter in hand to him at once.

'Killingley, you remember Mr Tregarthen?'

Killingley's sharp eyes gleamed intelligent affirmation.

'Case of Taplin and Mendoba,' he replied. 'Yes, sir.'

'Mr Tregarthen is back in town. He wants to see me at his rooms in the Albany at four o'clock.'

Killingley laid one hand on my diary; the other on his fountain-pen.

'Also,' I added, 'he desires to see you.'

'Same time and place, sir?' asked Killingley, making notes.

'Same time and place,' I answered. 'We'll go together.'

So, four o'clock found my clerk and myself in Tregarthen's eminently comfortable parlour in his excellent rooms. He had not come in, but every-thing betokened his immediate arrival. There was a bright, warm fire; there was tea laid out for three; there was a soft-footed man-servant ready to do service whenever he was wanted. And suddenly there was a sound of footsteps in the little hall, and the door opened and Tregarthen entered, and stripping off a big ulster presented to my astonished eyes the face and figure—minus the eye-patch and the crutch—of the tiger-selling gazer of Budge Row.

I was for the moment too much surprised to speak, for it had never entered my head that Tregarthen was the man to whom I had given a shilling, much less that it was from that man that the note came. And Tregarthen saw my surprise, and laughed as he went across to a sideboard and helped himself to a stiff glass of whiskey.

'Ugh!' he exclaimed, shivering a little. 'That's about the coldest job I ever took on, Campenhaye. I'm chilled through. Well, and how are you? But wait until I've got these rags off and changed into something clean, and then we'll talk. I've had a stiff day of it—and I don't know that I've done much good, either. But perhaps you and Killingley can help.'

Then, leaving us still mystified, he disappeared, to come back in ten minutes in a comfortable tweed suit, brisk and bustling.

'Now, we'll talk, over a cup of tea,' he said, as his man brought in a steaming kettle. 'Well, how've you been going on and what's doing, eh?'

'A more fitting topic will be—what are you doing?' I answered. 'Why this disguise? Why expose yourself to the whistling winds and sorry sleet of Budge Row, on as vile a day as ever I remember? Also—which is somewhat pertinent—why hurry me away from my business there?'

Tregarthen helped himself to hot buttered muffin and took a generous mouthful.

'I don't know what your business was,' he said, nonchalantly; 'but I'm jolly well certain it wasn't as important as mine—which your distinguished presence in that place might have interfered with. You're known, my boy—you're known!'

'To about one person in each twenty-five thousand of the numerous millions in this city,' I retorted. 'And that's a high estimate.'

'You're known well enough to, at any rate, one man who might have gone in and out of that entry in which you were standing,' he said calmly. 'And I didn't want that man to see you there.'

'And who's he, pray?' I asked.

Tregarthen took a hearty gulp of tea and looked over the rim of his cup at Killingley and myself with eyes that seemed to be sizing us up.

'You remember the Francis Taplin case?' he said suddenly. 'Yes, well, it's Mendoba that I'm after.'

'What—again?' I exclaimed.

'Again? Well, now, I've been after him ever since, and for a long time before that,' replied Tregarthen. 'But call it again, if you like. Certainly, it's a new trail.'

'And Mendoba's here in London?' I asked, greatly surprised.

'I believe he's in Budge Row,' he answered. 'But—so far, I haven't seen him. And—I want to see him. Yes—I want to see that man pretty badly, Campenhaye. So—you and Killingley must help me.'

I glanced at Killingley, who was steadily devoting himself to tea and plum cake, and keeping his eyes fixed on our host.

'All right,' I said. 'But before Killingley and I start out to help people, we like to know what it's all about. Eh?'

'I'm going to tell you,' answered Tregarthen. 'That's what I got you here for—I don't know that you'll be much use, Campenhaye, but I believe Killingley might be. You're known—he isn't.'

'Don't be too sure of that,' I said. 'Killingley is a person of importance. Half the swell crooks in town know him.'

'But Mendoba doesn't, and he knows Mendoba,' said Tregarthen quickly.

Killingley cleared his jaws of plum cake.

'Excuse me, sir,' he said. 'I saw Mr Mendoba with a beard and a wig. If you consult your memory you will find that Mr Mendoba left wig and beard behind him in the railway carriage at Charing Cross after he had blown out Dr Taplin's brains.'

'That's so,' agreed Tregarthen. 'All the same, I think you'll be useful—I remember you. Well, you see it's this way, Campenhaye. I've just come back from the States. Never mind, just now, what my business there was—I may tell you about it when we've more leisure. But suffice it to say that while I was in New York I rendered a highly important service to a well-known business man who had the grace to be properly grateful. And, one night, having dined me very, very well at the Knickerbocker Club, he not only grew still more grateful but extremely confidential.'

'"Look here," said he, 'I guess you know a good many of the secrets of the secret side of London life?'

'"Some," said I. 'But not all by a long way.'

'"I guess not," he said with a wink. 'And I daresay I know one or two that you don't know—just as you'll know a good many that I never even heard of.'

'"I should think so," said I. For I knew, d'you see, Campenhaye, that he was on this side a good deal and knew his way about. 'Yes,' I said, 'that's more than likely both ways.'

'"D'you ever go in for a flutter in stocks?' he asked, eyeing me keenly.

'"I have done so when I'd money that I wasn't particular about losing,' I answered.

'"All the same, you'd rather it came back to you with more sticking to it?' he remarked.

'"Naturally,' I replied. 'I should.'

'We were in a quiet corner, and there was no one near, but he edged himself closer, looking round as men do when they've something remarkably confidential to tell you.

'"Did you ever hear of the Magician of Cannon Street?' said he, with another keen look.

'"Never,' I answered. 'Who's he?'

'He laughed at that.

'"Heaven knows!' he replied. 'Re-incarnation of Confucius or Socrates, or of old Abe Lincoln—anyhow, he's a wise man, magic or no magic.'

'"And what does he do?' I asked.

'"Ah! that's it!' he said. 'I guess you're aware that most of the big bugs in the money world are uncommonly superstitious?'

'"No, I didn't, but I knew that sportsmen—that is to say, racing-men—are,' I answered.

'"Same thing,' said he. 'Well, sir, it's a fact that this fellow who's known as the Magician of Cannon Street to a very, very select coterie of moneyed men who love to speculate, is a swell hand at telling his clients what their luck's likely to be. That's a fact—I've proved it.'

'"What does he exactly do?' I asked. 'Gaze into crystals, or consult the stars, or read your palm, or what?'

'"No hanky-panky,' he answered. 'It's all done without ornament. Supposing you're thinking of doing this, that, or the other, you go to him and tell him your schemes. He tells you whether you're to go in or not. That's all.'

'"And do you mean to say that the chap's always right?' I exclaimed. 'If he is, it's a big order.'

'"No, he isn't always right,' he answered. 'But he's a winner five times out of six—or, maybe, nine times out of ten. You see,' he added, poking his finger into my ribs, 'you see, I've tried him, and I know some other men who've also tried him.'

'Well, now, I know, Campenhaye, as I daresay you know, that there is this sort of thing going on in town here. I know of two remarkably astute city financiers who never undertake any serious deal until they've consulted some sybil or siren who hangs out in mysteriously lighted and heavily scented rooms off New Bond Street; but I'd never heard of this Cannon Street prophet, and I said so again.

"'Just so,' said my New York friend. 'I knew you hadn't—he deals with a very, very select coterie. Now, look here, as you've done me a real good turn, I'll do you one. I'll give you an introduction to this man—and if ever you're thinking of doing anything important go to him for advice—and for a tip.'

"'Oh!' I said. 'So he gives tips, does he? A sharp observer of the markets, eh?'

"'Put it at that,' said he. 'But you take my introduction—you'll never regret it.'

'Well, I never refuse anything on principle—and I said I was much obliged to him, and what was this magician's name, and where did he sit in his particular cave or cell, or whatever it was?

"'There's no hanky-panky,' he answered. 'No magic circles, and no yellow robes, and no fool's caps—all's plain business. The address is Contango Chambers, Budge Row, Cannon Street, London, England, and the man's name is plain Mister Morton. And—here's the letter of introduction.'

'And with that he furtively slipped into my hand a ring, once more looking round as if to make sure that he wasn't observed. And, humouring him, though I didn't see that it was in any way necessary, I, too, stole a furtive glance at what he had given me. And I saw then, Campenhaye, my boy, that what he really had given me was a clue to the whereabouts of our precious friend, Mendoba!'

Killingley and I were by this time too much interested to be ready with words, and Tregarthen smiled triumphantly, and went on:

'To Mendoba!' he repeated. 'The very man I wanted! Now, then, what was this clue? You won't remember, Campenhaye, because you only saw him twice, that Mendoba wore a very curious ring—a signet ring, on the shield of which was a device which I have never seen before. But here's the ring which my New York friend presented to me—to save explanations, I may as well say that it is, in reality, a duplicate of that worn by Mendoba. There are, I found out, a certain number of these duplicates in existence, and each forms a passport to the presence of the Magician of Cannon Street.'

I took the ring which Tregarthen handed to me, and Killingley and I carefully examined it. It was a plain gold ring, having on its upper rim a circular shield on which was deeply engraved a curious arabesque device. Tregarthen indicated that with the tip of his finger.

'I told you,' he said, 'that Mendoba has Spanish, Moorish, and Arab blood in him—I believe that this device has something to do with his family. Anyway, I'll stake all I've got that this is an exact duplicate of the ring which Mendoba wore when I knew him. And I believe that the Magician of Cannon Street is—Mendoba.'

'Well?' I said, not yet quite sure of what Tregarthen was after. 'And what then?'

'I only landed at Plymouth yesterday morning,' he continued. 'Naturally, I wanted to find out all I could about my man as soon as possible. I knew that it would be of no use to present myself at Budge Row, because I should have had to go in the attire and semblance of a man of probity and standing, and this sword-cut on my cheek would instantly have been recognised by Mendoba—if Mendoba is the Magician. So I adopted the disguise in which you saw me—it's one that I've found very useful more than once in the city—old, crippled soldier, you know, and the black patch over the eye partly hides and also draws attention away from the scar. I went down there early this morning; my object was to keep a strict watch on the entrance to Contango Chambers in the hope of seeing Mendoba enter or leave. Well, I saw you, Campenhaye, and drove you off, for I knew that Mendoba would recognise you at once if he caught half a glimpse of you. Also, I saw one or two famous financial magnates who were doubtless on their way to consult the Magician. But I never saw Mendoba—that is, I never saw anybody whom I should have believed to be Mendoba. And there's where a difficulty comes in. For you see, Campenhaye, I never saw Mendoba except when he wore that disguise of grey wig and beard which he discarded in the railway carriage at Charing Cross after he'd blown out Francis Taplin's brains. Eh?'

'Just so,' I said. 'How would you know Mendoba if you saw him?'

'I'd know enough to be certain if I could have him in this room or in his room for two minutes,' he answered. 'But now, here's the point. Somebody's got to gain access to the Magician. I can't—neither can you. But—what about Killingley? You told me, Campenhaye, that Killingley is an adept in the art of making up. Why not disguise him as—'

But I had been thinking pretty hard while Tregarthen was speaking. And now I interrupted him.

'No,' I said. 'Give me the ring, and I'll see this magician chap myself. I, too, am an adept at disguise—I taught Killingley all he knows. I'll engage that Mendoba doesn't know me—unless he's an extraordinarily clever man and a very cute observer. Remember, he scarcely ever saw me at that gambling-hell of his, and, when he did, it was in a half-light.'

Tregarthen hesitated.

'Mendoba is remarkably cute,' he said, 'and as to his ability, I reckon he's one of the most able men I've ever had to do with. I was amazed when he so far lost his head as to revenge himself on Taplin as he did—I suppose his southern blood got the better of him. But, do you really think that you'd better tackle the job, seeing that he has seen you? It's my impression that if Mendoba ever took stock of anybody he'd remember their every eyelash for fifty years.'

'I'll engage that I could present myself to you this very evening and that you wouldn't know me,' I answered. 'You can trust me, if you like.'

And Killingley spoke for the first time.

'Leave it to the guv'nor, sir,' he said. 'I fancy myself a bit in that line, but he's far beyond me.'

Tregarthen handed over the ring again.

'All right,' he said. 'Now, then, let's settle the details.'

When Tregarthen and I had fixed matters up, my duty was a very simple one. I was to present myself, made up according to my own liking, at Contango Chambers next morning at eleven o'clock, and to exhibit the ring as credentials, and to ask for Mr Morton. Tregarthen carefully posted me as to what I was to do and say on being admitted to the presence of the Magician of Cannon Street: the rest was left to me. As to Tregarthen himself, he was to resume his rôle of gazer; Killingley was to act as I judged best.

And so all that being settled, Killingley and I left our host and walked away together, and as we stepped out of the Albany into Piccadilly I asked my companion what he thought of this adventure. For Killingley was a great hand at thinking, and he had been unusually silent during the recent conversation.

'What I think, sir,' he answered, 'is, that this man, if he is Mendoba, will be a stiff customer to tackle.'

'That goes without saying, Killingley,' I said. 'He will.'

'You'll go armed, of course?' he continued.

'I shall.'

'All the same,' he went on, 'I don't believe much in that, sir. A revolver isn't much use nowadays—it's clumsy and out of date. I think I had better keep an eye on you. How do you propose to go, sir?'

We discussed that point. The result of our discussion was that after an early dinner Killingley and I spent the first part of the evening in concocting and arranging my disguise. And as I am a great believer in details and in rehearsal, I made myself up with infinite care and precision as a middle-aged man of an eminently but quietly and unobtrusively prosperous appearance, slightly inclined to stoutness (I am normally spare, not to say slender), slightly grizzled as to moustache and hair (I am normally clean-shaven, and my hair is of distinctly raven hue), and much bronzed as if from close acquaintance with the southern sun. When all was finished and I was clothed in the fine linen and purple of a moneyed magnate (I always possess a very considerable and exhaustive wardrobe in order to be prepared to cope with any emergency), Killingley uttered words of admiration.

'You were right in saying that Mr Tregarthen wouldn't know you, sir,' he exclaimed. 'He wouldn't.'

'Just to test things, we'll give him the chance,' I said. 'He'll be at the Odeon Club to-night. I'll drive round there, and send in my name as a former American acquaintance.'

From a heap which lay in a bowl on my desk I picked out an old visiting-card that bore the name Colonel Charlton P. Lysters, and armed with it, drove round to the Odeon. There were two or three other men in the visitors' waiting-room; when Tregarthen entered, turning Colonel Lyster's card on his fingers, he stared helplessly at each. I stepped forward with outstretched hand.

'I guess you've forgotten me, Mr Tregarthen,' I said. 'We met way back in ninety-five, in Denver.'

He was plainly nonplussed, and he took my hand with a very limp response to my vigorous shake.

'I—I really don't remember,' he said, staring at me steadily and scrutinisingly. 'I can't recall—'

'Let me jog your memory,' I said, and I took him by the arm and led him a little aside. 'But only,' I continued, relapsing into my natural voice, 'only to the extent of reminding you that Killingley and I drank tea with you this afternoon.'

Tregarthen started back, staring still more.

'Good God!' he exclaimed. 'Well, that's fine, old chap. You'll keep that up in the morning?'

'Of course,' I replied. 'But—we'll have to rely on more than this, I reckon.'

'Well, if the man's Mendoba, he'll not recognise you, anyway,' he said. 'And that's the main thing, at first.'

It was not a man, Mendoba, or Morton, or any other, that I encountered when I walked into a quietly but well-furnished little outer office in Contango Chambers next morning. I gained a general impression of a bright fire shining on a thick and warm-coloured Turkey carpet, of an easy-chair or two, a good picture or so, and of a young lady who sat at an elegant desk which was *not* furnished with a typewriting machine. She was stylishly attired; she had nothing of the usual girl clerk in her appearance; but her eyes, bright and penetrating, sized me up shrewdly as she advanced to the pretence for a counter which fenced me off from her and the rest of the room. She looked an enquiry.

'Mr Morton?' I said.

And, following out instructions, I gave the young lady a look as enquiring as her own, and at the same time laid my ungloved left hand on the little counter and thus exhibited the curiously marked signet ring.

The Magician's unconventional janitor slightly inclined her head. Without verbal reply she turned and vanished through a door on the left of the room. Without delay she reappeared, silently admitted me within the counter, and opened another door on the right.

'Mr Morton will come to you in a few moments,' she said as she motioned me to enter. 'Please be seated.'

Then she closed the door upon me and left me alone. I looked round. The room was a tiny apartment; a small table in the middle of the floor was furnished with a plain morocco writing-pad, a gold-mounted inkstand, a bundle of quill pens, all new; on either side of the table were set two elbow-chairs. The walls were panelled in dark wood, unrelieved by any picture or ornament; the floor was covered by a thick carpet in which one's feet sank with a sense of luxury; the one window of the place was filled with old painted glass. The place was an ideal cabinet in which to discuss extremely confidential business. And it was soundproof. I was close to the heart of the city, just above one of its busiest thorough-fares along which rolled a perpetual tide of heavy traffic. But I could not hear a sound; the silence in that small room was deeper than any silence I ever knew; its deepness seemed to be accentuated by the gentle murmur of a fire which burnt brightly in the grate behind me.

I sat down in one of the elbow-chairs (there were but two seats in the room) and waited. The silence became, if possible, deeper; the murmur of the fire grew monotonous. And I suddenly conceived the idea that I was being watched.

That feeling of being alone, in a strange place, and of being silently looked at, inspected, taken stock of, from some coign of vantage of which one knows nothing, is one of the most trying experiences, one of the most severe nerve-tests, which a human being can go through. It makes you feel that you are at somebody's or at something's mercy. You cannot move a finger or wink an eye without the consciousness that it is being seen and noted by a watchful observer who is stationed you know not where. It is an uncanny, a weird feeling—like all such feelings, it grows upon you. In this case the feeling grew upon me. I suppose I am naturally highly-strung; certainly my nerves began to feel the strain of sitting there under this conviction. In cases where I am face to face with either danger or difficulty they come readily to the scratch and are as strong as iron and dependable as steel; if any man stared at me I should give him as long and as steady a stare as he gave me. But to sit alone, feeling until you reached the point of absolute certainty that *an eye* is on you, and that you do not know where that eye is—this is enough to disconcert even the strongest nerved man, and in this instance it disconcerted me. For the effect of such a feeling is to force you to a state of absolute quietude lest you should betray something in your face or your attitude, and that is wearing. And in this case I did not care to think that I was being watched at all.

I kept quiet, my eyes fixed on the morocco writing-case. I was thinking. I was endeavouring to summon up some notion of what I expected Mendoba (if this was the man) to be like. I had only seen him twice, and for a mere moment on each occasion, at the gambling-hell; he then presented himself as a tall, well-built man, a very little inclined to stoutness, with grey hair, a full grey beard, who wore slightly smoked spectacles. But I knew that he had discarded beard and wig in the train at Charing Cross when he shot Francis Taplin. What was he like then, when they were removed? I had nothing to go by but his height and figure, and they—

The door suddenly opened, and as suddenly closed. I turned to see a young gentleman, irreproachably garbed after the fashion of that aristocracy of the City which is particular in matters of raiment. And as I looked at him, gaining a general impression of his personality and appearance, a curious doubt and feeling of difficulty fell on me. Could this Mr Morton—if the young gentleman was Mr Morton—be one and the same person with the Mendoba of the gambling-hell?

I took a closer look at him as he came forward. He was tall and of a spare but athletic figure, which was well set off

by his beautifully cut and shaped morning coat. He was a
handsome young man—my first glance at him had showed
me an olive-complexioned skin; black, smooth hair, scrupulously arranged; a pair of black, penetrating eyes. Those
eyes fixed themselves upon me as we exchanged bows. He
waved a slim, white hand in the direction of the chair from
which I had risen at his entrance.

'Mr Morton?' I said interrogatively.

He bowed again; again motioned me to my chair, and
taking that on the other side of the table, leaned his elbows
upon it, put his fingers together, rested his chin upon their
tips, and continued to regard me with attention. Something in his eyes disconcerted me; they were so steady, so
penetrating, so very cold and inflexible (these, I think, are
the terms I should use), that I began to feel uncomfortable.
Only once did they move from my face; that was to glance
for the fraction of a second at the ring on my finger. After
that they never left mine. And—whether I would or no—I
was *compelled* to keep mine upon them. I say compelled
deliberately—there is no other word for it.

There was a momentary silence, after my *vis-à-vis* had
taken his seat. Then he said—using a formal tone:

'You wish to consult me?'

'Under advice,' I answered. 'The advice of the man from
whom I procured this.'

I was about to say 'ring,' but he waved a finger carelessly.

'Just so. My preliminary fee, as he no doubt informed
you, is five hundred guineas in cash. Afterwards, you pay me
ten per cent. on the profit of the deal which you propose to
make—that is, if I advise you to make it.'

I had been coached for all this, and I drew out the amount
of money for which he asked. I handed him five one-hundred
pound Bank of England notes and five five-pound notes,
and he placed them on the morocco writing-case.

'What do you wish me to advise you about?' he asked.

I was prepared for that, too. But I wanted to fence with him a little. And for that I was also prepared. All the same, I began to wish that he would not stare at me so persistently with those coal-black eyes!

'You are famous for a remarkable gift of insight?' I remarked, with what was doubtless a feeble attempt at a smile.

'I possess a gift of insight, coupled with some financial knowledge,' he replied.

'A remarkably astute and deep-seated knowledge,' I said.

'Call it so, if you will. You wish to engage in some financial operation?'

'I do. That is why I am here.'

'Of a considerable nature, of course? Otherwise you would certainly not be here. What is it?'

'What it is,' I said, 'will be best explained by my asking you a simple question. What place will Russia occupy as a political and financial power two years hence?'

He inclined his head slightly, but his eyes were still fixed on mine, and I was unpleasantly conscious of their power.

'Two years hence,' he answered quietly, 'Russia will be at war with Japan. And Russia will be beaten. Does that answer your question?'

Now, as events proved, he was right in this prophecy. I do not pretend to know how he came to prognosticate matters so successfully; I only know that what he foretold came to pass within the time specified. But at that time I personally knew of no reason why Russia and Japan should so soon go to war, so I displayed a little incredulity.

'You are sure of that?' I asked.

'I never say anything unless I am sure of it,' he answered. 'What I say in this matter, will be.'

I made pretence of hesitation.

'This is a big question to me,' I said. 'I had the intention of making most important investments in Russia, which would be seriously prejudiced in the event of that country going to war within the next six years, especially if, as you prophesy, she suffered defeat. Is it within your province to give me ground for your expectations?'

'Most certainly,' he answered. His eyes appeared to draw my own more compellingly than ever. Their expression deepened to one of intense concentration: unconsciously I edged my elbow-chair nearer to the table. 'Most certainly,' he repeated. 'Now, attend to me.'

What I am going to state or confess may sound incredible to all people save those who understand and have seen something of the effects of suggestive influence. But it is the plain truth—and like all plain truths it can be put into a very few words.

And the plain truth is this: I have no knowledge whatever of what further took place between me and the young man of the remarkable eyes. From the moment that he told me to attend to him until another moment of which I am presently going to speak, my mind was a blank.

Whether a man can be rightly called unconscious who walks, talks, eats, transacts business, has conversation, rational and coherent, with other folk, and who is not aware that he has done any of these things, is a question which I shall leave the experts to decide. It is quite certain that before noon of one day and eight o'clock of the next I walked, talked, ate and drank, smoked and behaved myself as a rational man does, and was quite unaware of the fact. I have since conversed with several people who met me during that period; they all agreed that they saw nothing in me that was not absolutely normal and ordinary.

But the truth is that I passed out of one state of consciousness about noon on one day, seated in that snug room in

Contango Chambers in Budge Row, and woke up to another state of equal—perhaps sharper, more alert—consciousness at eight o'clock the next morning in a bedroom of the Royal York Hotel at Brighton.

It was a beautiful, sharp, winter morning; the clear light that flooded my bedroom awoke me. I opened my eyes....

There are few things in the ordinary way of life that can frighten a man so much as waking suddenly in a strange room wherein he certainly does not expect to find himself. I was frightened. I shut my eyes as soon as I had opened them. But in that momentary opening I had seen that I was in the bedroom of an hotel, and I had remembered the interview of yesterday. Again I heard the compelling voice of the man with the equally compelling eyes.

'Attend to me!'

But—what since then?

I sprang out of bed, and made for the window I jerked up the blinds and looked out. Instantly I recognised the Old Steine. The tramcars were running on the road beneath; early birds were walking across the gardens. So I was in Brighton. But—how did I come there?

I turned from the window, and looked around me. It was quite evident that when I left town I had known what I was doing. There was a suit-case, there were toilet articles, duly set out; a winter dressing-gown lay ready to hand. And—yes, of course, this was the room which I usually occupied when I visited Brighton, as I often did. But—once more—how did I come to be in it?

I remember everything of my recent doings up to the point where the Magician of Cannon Street bade me attend to him: after that I remembered nothing. And, naturally, the only word I could think of, the conventional word, often meaningless, but by no means so in my case, sprang to my lips:

'Hypnotised!'

That, of course, must be the explanation—I was a victim to hypnotic suggestion. The man of Contango Chambers had driven my own will clean away from me with those devilish eyes of his and had substituted impulses of his own for his own purpose. What purpose? Obviously to get me out of the way, while he got himself out of the way. And so, there were precious hours—twenty of them—lost, and—where was he?

I have always prided myself on being pretty smart about tackling emergencies and difficulties. I recognised that the only thing to do in this case was to get a quick move on in the direction of London. I glanced at my watch and saw that it was precisely five minutes past eight. Now, I know that Killingley never presented himself at my office until ten o'clock, and it was accordingly useless to telephone to him there; I also knew that there was no telephone at the cottage at Hampstead where he lived with his mother and sister. Well, I would endeavour to be in town before half the morning had passed, and I started to take measures. I summoned a certain man-servant, and gave him sharp orders.

'Send me some coffee, and some hot toast here at once,' I said. 'Order for me the best and quickest motor-car you can get in Brighton, with a thoroughly good chauffeur. Let him be round here with the car as quickly as he can. There's only one word for it—hurry!'

The man knew me and my ways, and he shot off in a way that satisfied me. I dressed as rapidly as ever I had performed that operation in my life, swallowed the toast and the coffee, and was down in the hall and ready for the car within twenty minutes of giving my orders.

'Car'll be here in a minute, sir,' said my factotum.

Turning to the office to pay my bill, I caught sight of a pile of morning papers which had just come in. I picked one up mechanically, and opening it, ran my eye over the headlines of the middle pages. And then, for the second time that morning, I jumped with amazement. For there, in great, staring black letters I read:

THE MURDER OF DR. TAPLIN
REMARKABLE ARREST IN LONDON

'Car, sir!' said a voice behind me.

I forgot that the newspaper was the property of the hotel. I have confused recollections that I crumpled it up in my hand, leaped into, or was bundled into, the automobile, that I gave the chauffeur a peremptory command, and that Brighton faded away behind me.

The car was speeding away northwards between Batham and Pangdean before I woke to the fact that I was holding the newspaper crushed up in my hand. Then I spread its creases out and read what appeared beneath those staring headlines. There was not much to be read, but what there was made me think harder than before.

'The murder of Dr Francis Taplin, of Wimpole Street, which took place at Charing Cross Railway Station two years ago, under highly sensational circumstances, the murderer killing his victim and making his escape just as a boat train was about to start, was recalled yesterday afternoon, when the police, acting on information, quietly effected at Charing Cross the arrest of a man who is alleged to have committed the crime.

'The man in question had booked a ticket for Paris, and had already taken his seat in a first-class smoking compartment. when he was arrested by plain-clothes officers, who acted in such swift and unobtrusive fashion that their prisoner was removed from both train and station without any excitement or commotion being aroused.

'Great reticence is being shown by the police authorities, but it is understood that they derived their information from private sources, and that they have full confidence that they not only hold the murderer of Dr Francis Taplin, but that the prisoner is also a person who was wanted at the time of the murder in connection with the keeping of a private gaming-house in the West End, and who effected a clever escape when it was raided by the police. It is rumoured that he is a foreigner of great ability who is an adept at skilfully disguising himself, and that he has of late been engaged in various questionable transactions in the City. He is expected to be brought up at Bow Street at noon to-day.'

I dropped the newspaper on the opposite seat as I leaned back in the swiftly-speeding car.

'That's Killingley!' I said. 'Killingley's done the trick. But how?'

We turned into Jermyn Street well before eleven o'clock. I dashed straight upstairs to my office—to find Killingley and Tregarthen closeted together. And I saw at one glance that neither had been to bed. Further, I saw that Killingley was in a state of high concern; he so far lost his usual sang-froid, indeed, as to rush forward, and shake my hand violently. After which he relapsed into his usual normal condition.

'If one may ask a plain question, Campenhaye,' said Tregarthen, who had watched this little scene with amused eyes, 'we should like to know where you come from? Killingley and I have spent most of our time since yesterday afternoon in searching high and low for you.'

'I have just come from Brighton,' I answered. 'But—as to how I got to Brighton, frankly, I don't know. But—you may laugh, if you like—I believe that magician chap put me under hypnotic suggestion.'

Tregarthen, however, did not laugh. He turned to Killingley.

'Tell him,' he said. 'It will perhaps make things clear.'

'There's not such a lot to tell you, sir,' responded Killingley, turning to me. 'You know that, as we had arranged, I kept a watch on the hall door of those chambers in Budge Row. I saw you enter. About half an hour later I saw you come out. You came out in company with a tall, dark young gentlemen. And when I saw him, I was certain we'd got Mendoba.'

'You were!' I exclaimed. 'Why?'

'Because, sir, when I watched Taplin's house in Wimpole Street that night of the murder I saw Mendoba, and you will remember, though he was then disguised in his grey beard and wig and smoked glasses,' answered Killingley. 'True, sir, I only saw him for a minute or so, but I noticed a certain peculiarity which I didn't forget. He has a curious action of his left leg, something like a mild case of string-halt in a horse, sir.'

'Good for you, Killingley,' said I. 'Well?'

'Well, sir, and so had this man who came out of Contango Chambers with you. But after I had seen that, I gave my attention to you.'

'Why to me?'

'Because you appeared to be on such friendly terms with him. You walked together down the street, passed Mr Tregarthen, there, to whom you threw a shilling, and then turned up towards the Mansion House—you were arm in arm by that time, and more friendly than ever. You went across to Lombard Street, and there the two of you went into your bank, sir.'

Like a flash my hand went to my breast-pocket to find a cheque-book which I always carried there. Killingley smiled.

'It's all right, sir,' he said. 'You cashed a pretty heavy cheque there, and you evidently handed over the proceeds to Mendoba; but we found them on him, and they're safe. But let me go on, sir. I waited safely outside. The man—and he

is Mendoba, or that's one of his names—came out alone—
you didn't re-appear. Then I remembered that there are two
entrances to that bank, and I thought that you must have left
by the other. Then—what was I to do? I decided to follow
the man—I felt sure that he didn't know me: at any rate, I
couldn't think of any reason why he should. And so I kept
him in view. And he didn't go back to that office. Instead,
he set off west. He rode to some chambers in Mayfair—I
followed him. I followed him later to Charing Cross, where
he went in company of a handbag and a rug. I was close
behind him when he booked for Paris. But, meantime, I'd
managed to send to the Yard, and as he set out for the 2.20
I had him taken. And—that's all, sir,' concluded Killingley,
'and I'm glad you're safe.'

'But, is he our man?' I said, turning to Tregarthen. 'Is
he—Mendoba?'

'He's my man,' answered Tregarthen grimly. 'I've seen
him. Oh! he's the man we knew as Mendoba right enough.
We'll go along to Bow Street presently, and you shall have
another look at him—under safe conditions. I say, Campenhaye, that's an unfortunate accomplishment of yours. I didn't
know you were subject to influence.'

'Neither did I,' I growled. 'However, you know I'm retiring. But this Mendoba—'

Just then a sharp rap came at the outer door, and Killingley, going to open it, admitted a New Scotland Yard man
who was very well known to us. He smiled sardonically when
he saw Tregarthen and myself.

'Well, there's an end of that,' he said. 'There'll be little
more to hear about that chap, I'm thinking.'

'You don't mean to say he's escaped?' exclaimed
Tregarthen.

'Escaped hanging,' said the other coolly. 'He's dead—
suicide. They think he'd concealed something in a hollow

tooth—it's a favourite dodge with some of the dare-devil lot. Did it an hour ago. They want you, Mr Tregarthen—they think you might clear something up. Can you come now?'

And Tregarthen went, and Killingley and I went with him. But there was little that he could clear up, and we have never known to this day what the real identity of the man was, who, but for that fatal twist of character which inclined him to crime, might have been a Napoleon to whom no Waterloo need have come!

The Stealer of Marble

Edgar Wallace

Richard Horatio Edgar Wallace (1875–1932) was born in Greenwich, the illegitimate son of two actors. From impoverished beginnings, he rose to become a celebrity, the world's most popular thriller writer. The Four Just Men *(1905) was his first book, and he also enjoyed immense success with* Sanders of the River, *published six years later. Shortly before the end of his life, he became a Hollywood script doctor, and worked on the screenplay of* King Kong.

Much of Edgar Wallace's best work drew on his knowledge and understanding of London and Londoners. The vivacity of his story-telling compensated, by and large, for his slapdash emphasis on quantity of writing rather than quality. This story comes from The Mind of Mr J. G. Reeder, *the first in a series featuring a mild-mannered public servant with a talent for solving crime. In 1969, the Reeder stories were brought to television, with Hugh Burden in the lead role.*

⟩⟩⟩

Margaret Belman's chiefest claim to Mr Reeder's notice was that she lived in the Brockley Road, some few doors from his own establishment. He did not know her name, being wholly incurious about law-abiding folk, but he was aware that she was pretty, that her complexion was that pink and white which is seldom seen away from a magazine cover. She dressed well, and there was one thing that he noted about her more than any other, it was that she walked and carried herself with a certain grace that was especially pleasing to a man of aesthetic predilections.

He had, on occasions, walked behind her and before her, and had ridden on the same street car with her to Westminster Bridge. She invariably descended at the corner of the Embankment, and was as invariably met by a good-looking young man and walked away with him. The presence of that young man was a source of passive satisfaction to Mr Reeder, for no particular reason, unless it was that he had a tidy mind, and preferred a rose when it had a background of fern and grew uneasy at the sight of a saucerless cup.

It did not occur to him that he was an object of interest and curiosity to Miss Belman.

'That was Mr Reeder—he has something to do with the police, I think,' she said.

'Mr J. G. Reeder?'

Roy Master looked back with interest at the middle-aged man scampering fearfully across the road, his unusual hat on the back of his head, his umbrella over his shoulder like a cavalryman's sword.

'Good Lord! I never dreamt he was like that.'

'Who is he?' she asked, distracted from her own problem.

'Reeder? He's in the Public Prosecutor's Department, a sort of a detective—there was a case the other week where he gave evidence. He used to be with the Bank of England—'

Suddenly she stopped, and he looked at her in surprise.

'What's the matter?' he asked.

'I don't want you to go any farther, Roy,' she said. 'Mr Telfer saw me with you yesterday, and he's quite unpleasant about it.'

'Telfer?' said the young man indignantly. 'That little worm! What did he say?'

'Nothing very much,' she replied, but from her tone he gathered that the 'nothing very much' had been a little disturbing.

'I am leaving Telfers,' she said unexpectedly. 'It is a good job, and I shall never get another like it—I mean, so far as the pay is concerned.'

Roy Master did not attempt to conceal his satisfaction.

'I'm jolly glad,' he said vigorously. 'I can't imagine how you've endured that boudoir atmosphere so long. What did he say?' he asked again, and, before she could answer: 'Anyway, Telfers are shaky. There are all sorts of queer rumours about them in the City.'

'But I thought it was a very rich corporation!' she said in astonishment.

He shook his head.

'It was—but they have been doing lunatic things—what can you expect when a half-witted weakling like Sidney Telfer is at the head of affairs? They underwrote three concerns last year that no brokerage business would have touched with a barge-pole, and they had to take up the shares. One was a lost treasure company to raise a Spanish galleon that sank three hundred years ago! But what really did happen yesterday morning?'

'I will tell you tonight,' she said, and made her hasty adieux.

Mr Sidney Telfer had arrived when she went into a room which, in its luxurious appointments, its soft carpet and dainty etceteras, was not wholly undeserving of Roy Master's description.

The head of Telfers Consolidated seldom visited his main office on Threadneedle Street. The atmosphere of the place, he said, depressed him; it was all so horrid and sordid and rough. The founder of the firm, his grandfather, had died ten years before Sidney had been born, leaving the business to a son, a chronic invalid, who had died a few weeks after Sidney first saw the light. In the hands of trustees the business had flourished, despite the spasmodic interferences of his eccentric mother, whose peculiarities culminated in a will which relieved him of most of that restraint which is wisely laid upon a boy of sixteen.

The room, with its stained-glass windows and luxurious furnishing, fitted Mr Telfer perfectly, for he was exquisitely arrayed. He was tall and so painfully thin that the abnormal smallness of his head was not at first apparent. As the girl came into the room he was sniffing delicately at a fine cambric handkerchief, and she thought that he was paler than she had ever seen him—and more repellent.

He followed her movements with a dull stare, and she had placed his letters on his table before he spoke.

'I say, Miss Belman, you won't mention a word about what I said to you last night?'

'Mr Telfer,' she answered quietly, 'I am hardly likely to discuss such a matter.'

'I'd marry you and all that, only…clause in my mother's will,' he said disjointedly. 'That could be got over—in time.'

She stood by the table, her hands resting on the edge.

'I would not marry you, Mr Telfer, even if there were no clause in your mother's will; the suggestion that I should run away with you to America—'

'South America,' he corrected her gravely. 'Not the United States; there was never any suggestion of the United States.'

She could have smiled, for she was not as angry with this rather vacant young man as his startling proposition entitled her to be.

'The point is,' he went on anxiously, 'you'll keep it to yourself? I've been worried dreadfully all night. I told you to send me a note saying what you thought of my idea—well, don't!'

This time she did smile, but before she could answer him he went on, speaking rapidly in a high treble that sometimes rose to a falsetto squeak:

'You're a perfectly beautiful girl, and I'm crazy about you, but…there's a tragedy in my life…really. Perfectly ghastly tragedy. An' everything's at sixes an' sevens. If I'd had any sense I'd have brought in a feller to look after things. I'm beginning to see that now.'

For the second time in twenty-four hours this young man, who had almost been tongue-tied and had never deigned to notice her, had poured forth a torrent of confidences, and in one had, with frantic insistence, set forth a plan which had amazed and shocked her. Abruptly he finished, wiped his weak eyes, and in his normal voice:

'Get Billingham on the phone; I want him.'

She wondered, as her busy fingers flew over the keys of her typewriter, to what extent his agitation and wild eloquence was due to the rumoured 'shakiness' of Telfers Consolidated.

Mr Billingham came, a sober little man, bald and taciturn, and went in his secretive way into his employer's room. There was no hint in his appearance or his manner that he contemplated a great crime. He was stout to a point of podginess; apart from his habitual frown, his round face, unlined by the years, was marked by an expression of benevolence.

Yet Mr Stephen Billingham, managing director of the Telfer Consolidated Trust, went into the office of the London and Central Bank late that afternoon and, presenting a bearer cheque for one hundred and fifty thousand pounds, which was duly honoured, was driven to the Credit Lilloise. He had telephoned particulars of his errand, and there were waiting for him seventeen packets, each containing a million francs, and a smaller packet of a hundred and forty-six *mille* notes. The franc stood at 74.55 and he received the eighteen packages in exchange for a cheque on the Credit Lilloise for £80,000 and the 150 thousand-pound notes which he had drawn on the London and Central.

Of Billingham's movements thenceforth little was known. He was seen by an acquaintance driving through Cheapside in a taxicab which was traced as far as Charing Cross—and there he disappeared. Neither the airways nor the waterways had known him, the police theory being that he had left by an evening train that had carried an excursion party via Havre to Paris.

'This is the biggest steal we have had in years,' said the Assistant Director of Public Prosecutions. 'If you can slip in sideways on the inquiry, Mr Reeder, I should be glad. Don't step on the toes of the City police—they are quite amiable people where murder is concerned, but a little touchy where money is in question. Go along and see Sidney Telfer.'

Fortunately, the prostrated Sidney was discoverable outside the City area. Mr Reeder went into the outer office and saw a familiar face.

'Pardon me, I think I know you, young lady,' he said, and she smiled as she opened the little wooden gate to admit him.

'You are Mr Reeder—we live in the same road,' she said, and then quickly: 'Have you come about Mr Billingham?'

'Yes.' His voice was hushed, as though he were speaking of a dead friend. 'I wanted to see Mr Telfer, but perhaps you could give me a little information.'

The only news she had was that Sidney Telfer had been in the office since seven o'clock and was at the moment in such a state of collapse that she had sent for the doctor.

'I doubt if he is in a condition to see you,' she said.

'I will take all responsibility,' said Mr Reeder soothingly. 'Is Mr Telfer—er—a friend of yours, Miss—?'

'Belman is my name.' He had seen the quick flush that came to her cheek: it could mean one of two things. 'No, I am an employee, that is all.'

Her tone told him all he wanted to know. Mr J. G. Reeder was something of an authority on office friendships.

'Bothered you a little, has he?' he murmured, and she shot a suspicious look at him. What did he know, and what bearing had Mr Telfer's mad proposal on the present disaster? She was entirely in the dark as to the true state of affairs; it was, she felt, a moment for frankness.

'Wanted you to run away! Dear me!' Mr Reeder was shocked. 'He is married?'

'Oh, no—he's not married,' said the girl shortly. 'Poor man, I'm sorry for him now. I'm afraid that the loss is a very heavy one—who would suspect Mr Billingham?'

'Ah! who indeed!' sighed the lugubrious Reeder, and took off his glasses to wipe them; almost she suspected tears. 'I think I will go in now—that is the door?'

Sidney jerked up his face and glared at the intruder. He had been sitting with his head on his arms for the greater part of an hour.

'I say…what do you want?' he asked feebly. 'I say…I can't see anybody…Public Prosecutor's Department?' He almost screamed the words. 'What's the use of prosecuting him if you don't get the money back?'

Mr Reeder let him work down before he began to ply his very judicious questions.

'I don't know much about it,' said the despondent young man. 'I'm only a sort of figurehead. Billingham brought the cheques for me to sign and I signed 'em. I never gave him instructions; he got his orders. I don't know very much about it. He told me, actually told me, that the business was in a bad way—half a million or something was wanted by next week....Oh, my God! And then he took the whole of our cash.'

Sidney Telfer sobbed his woe into his sleeve like a child. Mr Reeder waited before he asked a question in his gentlest manner.

'No, I wasn't here: I went down to Brighton for the weekend. And the police dug me out of bed at four in the morning. We're bankrupt. I'll have to sell my car and resign from my club—one has to resign when one is bankrupt.'

There was little more to learn from the broken man, and Mr Reeder returned to his chief with a report that added nothing to the sum of knowledge. In a week the theft of Mr Billingham passed from scare lines to paragraphs in most of the papers—Billingham had made a perfect getaway.

In the bright lexicon of Mr J. G. Reeder there was no such word as holiday. Even the Public Prosecutor's office has its slack time, when juniors and sub-officials and even the Director himself can go away on vacation, leaving the office open and a subordinate in charge. But to Mr J. G. Reeder the very idea of wasting time was repugnant, and it was his practice to brighten the dull patches of occupation by finding a seat in a magistrate's court and listening, absorbed, to cases which bored even the court reporter.

John Smith, charged with being drunk and using insulting language to Police Officer Thomas Brown; Mary Jane Haggitt, charged with obstructing the police in the execution of their duty; Henry Robinson, arraigned for being a suspected person, having in his possession housebreaking tools, to wit, one cold chisel and a screw-driver; Arthur Moses, charged with driving a motor car to the common danger—all these were fascinating figures of romance and legend to the lean man who sat between the Press and railed dock, his square-crowned hat by his side, his umbrella gripped between his knees, and on his melancholy face an expression of startled wonder.

On one raw and foggy morning, Mr Reeder, self-released from his duties, chose the Marylebone Police Court for his recreation. Two drunks, a shop theft and an embezzlement had claimed his rapt attention, when Mrs Jackson was escorted to the dock and a rubicund policeman stepped to the witness stand, and, swearing by his Deity that he would tell the truth and nothing but the truth, related his peculiar story.

'PC Perryman, No. 9717 L Division,' he introduced himself conventionally. 'I was on duty in the Edgeware Road early this morning at 2.30 a.m. when I saw the prisoner carrying a large suitcase. On seeing me she turned round and walked rapidly in the opposite direction. Her movements being suspicious, I followed and, overtaking her, asked her whose property she was carrying. She told me it was her own and that she was going to catch a train. She said that the case contained her clothes. As the case was a valuable one of crocodile leather I asked her to show me the inside. She refused. She also refused to give me her name and address and I asked her to accompany me to the station.'

There followed a detective-sergeant.

'I saw the prisoner at the station and in her presence opened the case. It contained a considerable quantity of small stone chips—'

'Stone chips?' interrupted the incredulous magistrate. 'You mean small pieces of stone—what kind of stone?'

'Marble, your worship. She said that she wanted to make a little path in her garden and that she had taken them from the yard of a monumental mason in the Euston Road. She made a frank statement to the effect that she had broken open a gate into the yard and filled the suitcase without the mason's knowledge.'

The magistrate leant back in his chair and scrutinised the charge sheet with a frown.

'There is no address against her name,' he said.

'She gave an address, but it was false, your worship—she refuses to offer any further information.'

Mr J. G. Reeder had screwed round in his seat and was staring open-mouthed at the prisoner. She was tall, broad-shouldered and stoutly built. The hand that rested on the rail of the dock was twice the size of any woman's hand he had ever seen. The face was modelled largely, but though there was something in her appearance which was almost repellent, she was handsome in her large way. Deep-set brown eyes, a nose that was large and masterful, a well-shaped mouth and two chins—these in profile were not attractive to one who had his views on beauty in women, but Mr J. G. Reeder, being a fair man, admitted that she was a fine-looking woman. When she spoke it was in a voice as deep as a man's, sonorous and powerful.

'I admit it was a fool thing to do. But the idea occurred to me just as I was going to bed and I acted on the impulse of the moment. I could well afford to buy the stone—I had over fifty pounds in my pocketbook when I was arrested.'

'Is that true?' and, when the officer answered, the magistrate turned his suspicious eyes to the woman. 'You are giving us a lot of trouble because you will not tell your name and address. I can understand that you do not wish your friends to know of your stupid theft, but unless you give me the information, I shall be compelled to remand you in custody for a week.'

She was well, if plainly, dressed. On one large finger flashed a diamond which Mr Reeder mentally priced in the region of two hundred pounds. 'Mrs Jackson' was shaking her head as he looked.

'I can't give you my address,' she said, and the magistrate nodded curtly.

'Remanded for inquiry,' he said, and added, as she walked out of the dock: 'I should like a report from the prison doctor on the state of her mind.'

Mr J. G. Reeder rose quickly from his chair and followed the woman and the officer in charge of the case through the little door that leads to the cells.

'Mrs Jackson' had disappeared by the time he reached the corridor, but the detective-sergeant was stooping over the large and handsome suitcase that he had shown in court and was now laying on a form.

Most of the outdoor men of the CID knew Mr J. G. Reeder, and Sergeant Mills grinned a cheerful welcome.

'What do you think of that one, Mr Reeder? It is certainly a new line on me! Never heard of a tombstone artist being burgled before.'

He opened the top of the case, and Mr Reeder ran his fingers through the marble chips.

'The case and the loot weighs over a hundred pounds,' said the officer. 'She must have the strength of a navvy to carry it. The poor officer who carried it to the station was hot and melting when he arrived.'

Mr J. G. was inspecting the case. It was a handsome article, the hinges and locks being of oxidised silver. No maker's name was visible on the inside, or owner's initials on its glossy lid. The lining had once been of silk, but now hung in shreds and was white with marble dust.

'Yes,' said Mr Reeder absently, 'very interesting—most interesting. Is it permissible to ask whether, when she was searched, any—er—document—?' The sergeant shook his head. 'Or unusual possession?'

'Only these.'

By the side of the case was a pair of large gloves. These also were soiled, and their surfaces cut in a hundred places.

'These have been used frequently for the same purpose,' murmured Mr J. G. 'She evidently makes—er—a collection of marble shavings. Nothing in her pocket-book?'

'Only the banknotes: they have the stamp of the Central Bank on their backs. We should be able to trace 'em easily.'

Mr Reeder returned to his office and, locking the door, produced a worn pack of cards from a drawer and played patience—which was his method of thinking intensively. Late in the afternoon his telephone bell rang, and he recognised the voice of Sergeant Mills.

'Can I come along and see you? Yes, it is about the banknotes.'

Ten minutes later the sergeant presented himself.

'The notes were issued three months ago to Mr Telfer,' said the officer without preliminary, 'and they were given by him to his housekeeper, Mrs Welford.'

'Oh, indeed?' said Mr Reeder softly, and added, after reflection: 'Dear me!'

He pulled hard at his lip.

'And is 'Mrs Jackson' that lady?' he asked.

'Yes. Telfer—poor little devil—nearly went mad when I told him she was under remand—dashed up to Holloway in a taxi to identify her. The magistrate has granted bail, and she'll be bound over tomorrow. Telfer was bleating like a child—said she was mad. Gosh! that fellow is scared of her—when I took him into the waiting-room at Holloway Prison she gave him one look and he wilted. By the way, we have had a hint about Billingham that may interest you. Do you know that he and Telfer's secretary were very good friends?'

'Really?' Mr Reeder was indeed interested. 'Very good friends? Well, well!'

'The Yard has put Miss Belman under general observation: there may be nothing to it, but in cases like Billingham's it is very often a matter of *cherchez la femme*!'

Mr Reeder had given his lip a rest and was now gently massaging his nose.

'Dear me!' he said. 'That is a French expression, is it not?'

He was not in court when the marble stealer was sternly admonished by the magistrate and discharged. All that interested Mr J. G. Reeder was to learn that the woman had paid the mason and had carried away her marble chips in triumph to the pretty little detached residence in the Outer Circle of Regent's Park. He had spent the morning at Somerset House, examining copies of wills and the like; his afternoon he gave up to the tracing of Mrs Rebecca Alamby Mary Welford.

She was the relict of Professor John Welford of the University of Edinburgh, and had been left a widow after two years of marriage. She had then entered the service of Mrs Telfer, the mother of Sidney, and had sole charge of the boy from his fourth year. When Mrs Telfer died she had made the woman sole guardian of her youthful charge. So that Rebecca Welford had been by turns nurse and guardian, and was now in control of the young man's establishment.

The house occupied Mr Reeder's attention to a considerable degree. It was a red-brick modern dwelling consisting of two floors and having a frontage on the Circle and a side road. Behind and beside the house was a large garden which, at this season of the year, was bare of flowers. They were probably in snug quarters for the winter, for there was a long greenhouse behind the garden.

He was leaning over the wooden palings, eyeing the grounds through the screen of box hedge that overlapped the fence with a melancholy stare, when he saw a door open and the big woman come out. She was bare-armed and wore an apron. In one hand she carried a dust box, which she emptied into a concealed ashbin, in the other was a long broom.

Mr Reeder moved swiftly out of sight. Presently the door slammed and he peeped again. There was no evidence of a marble path. All the walks were of rolled gravel.

He went to a neighbouring telephone booth, and called his office.

'I may be away all day,' he said.

There was no sign of Mr Sidney Telfer, though the detective knew that he was in the house.

Telfer's Trust was in the hands of the liquidators, and the first meeting of creditors had been called. Sidney had, by all accounts, been confined to his bed, and from that safe refuge had written a note to his secretary asking that 'all papers relating to my private affairs' should be burnt. He had scrawled a postscript: 'Can I possibly see you on business before I go?' The word 'go' had been scratched out and 'retire' substituted. Mr Reeder had seen that letter—indeed, all correspondence between Sidney and the office came to him by arrangement with the liquidators. And that was partly why Mr J. G. Reeder was so interested in 904, The Circle.

It was dusk when a big car drew up at the gate of the house. Before the driver could descend from his seat, the door of 904 opened, and Sidney Telfer almost ran out. He carried a suitcase in each hand, and Mr Reeder recognised that nearest him as the grip in which the housekeeper had carried the stolen marble.

Reaching over, the chauffeur opened the door of the machine and, flinging in the bags, Sidney followed hastily. The door closed, and the car went out of sight round the curve of the Circle.

Mr Reeder crossed the road and took up a position very near the front gate, waiting.

Dusk came and the veil of a Regent's Park fog. The house was in darkness, no flash of light except a faint glimmer that burnt in the hall, no sound. The woman was still there—Mrs Sidney Telfer, nurse, companion, guardian and wife. Mrs Sidney Telfer, the hidden director of Telfers Consolidated, a masterful woman who, not content with marrying a weakling twenty years her junior, had applied her masterful but ill-equipped mind to the domination of a business she did not understand, and which she was destined to plunge into ruin. Mr Reeder had made good use of his time at the Records Office: a copy of the marriage certificate was almost as easy to secure as a copy of the will.

He glanced round anxiously. The fog was clearing, which was exactly what he did not wish it to do, for he had certain acts to perform which required as thick a cloaking as possible.

And then a surprising thing happened. A cab came slowly along the road and stopped at the gate.

'I think this is the place, miss,' said the cabman, and a girl stepped down to the pavement.

It was Miss Margaret Belman.

Reeder waited until she had paid the fare and the cab had gone, and then, as she walked towards the gate, he stepped from the shadow.

'Oh!—Mr Reeder, how you frightened me!' she gasped. 'I am going to see Mr Telfer—he is dangerously ill—no, it was his housekeeper who wrote asking me to come at seven.'

'Did she now! Well, I will ring the bell for you.'

She told him that that was unnecessary—she had the key which had come with the note.

'She is alone in the house with Mr Telfer, who refuses to allow a trained nurse near him,' said Margaret, 'and—'

'Will you be good enough to lower your voice, young lady?' urged Mr Reeder in an impressive whisper. 'Forgive the impertinence, but if our friend is ill—'

She was at first startled by his urgency.

'He couldn't hear me,' she said, but spoke in a lower tone.

'He may—sick people are very sensitive to the human voice. Tell me, how did this letter come?'

'From Mr Telfer? By district messenger an hour ago.'

Nobody had been to the house or left it—except Sidney. And Sidney, in his blind fear, would carry out any instructions which his wife gave to him.

'And did it contain a passage like this?' Mr Reeder considered a moment. '"Bring this letter with you"?'

'No,' said the girl in surprise, 'but Mrs Welford telephoned just before the letter arrived and told me to wait for it. And she asked me to bring the letter with me because she didn't wish Mr Telfer's private correspondence to be left lying around. But why do you ask me this, Mr Reeder—is anything wrong?'

He did not answer immediately. Pushing open the gate, he walked noiselessly along the grass plot that ran parallel with the path.

'Open the door, I will come in with you,' he whispered and, when she hesitated: 'Do as I tell you, please.'

The hand that put the key into the lock trembled, but at last the key turned and the door swung open. A small nightlight burnt on the table of the wide panelled hall. On the left, near the foot of the stairs, only the lower steps of which were visible, Reeder saw a narrow door which stood open, and, taking a step forward, saw that it was a tiny telephone-room.

And then a voice spoke from the upper landing, a deep, booming voice that he knew.

'Is that Miss Belman?'

Margaret, her heart beating faster, went to the foot of the stairs and looked up.

'Yes, Mrs Welford.'

'You brought the letter with you?'

'Yes.'

Mr Reeder crept along the wall until he could have touched the girl.

'Good,' said the deep voice. 'Will you call the doctor—Circle 743—and tell him that Mr Telfer has had a relapse—you will find the booth in the hall: shut the door behind you, the bell worries him.'

Margaret looked at the detective and he nodded.

The woman upstairs wished to gain time for something—what?

The girl passed him: he heard the thud of the padded door close, and there was a click that made him spin round. The first thing he noticed was that there was no handle to the door, the second that the keyhole was covered by a steel disc, which he discovered later was felt lined. He heard the girl speaking faintly, and put his ear to the keyhole.

'The instrument is disconnected—I can't open the door.'

Without a second's hesitation, he flew up the stairs, umbrella in hand, and as he reached the landing he heard a door close with a crash. Instantly he located the sound. It came from a room on the left immediately over the hall. The door was locked.

'Open this door,' he commanded, and there came to him the sound of a deep laugh.

Mr Reeder tugged at the stout handle of his umbrella. There was a flicker of steel as he dropped the lower end, and in his hand appeared six inches of knife blade.

The first stab at the panel sliced through the thin wood as though it were paper. In a second there was a jagged gap through which the black muzzle of an automatic was thrust.

'Put down that jug or I will blow your features into comparative chaos!' said Mr Reeder pedantically.

The room was brightly lit, and he could see plainly. Mrs Welford stood by the side of a big square funnel, the narrow end of which ran into the floor. In her hand was a huge enamelled iron jug, and ranged about her were six others. In one corner of the room was a wide circular tank, and beyond, at half its height, depended a large copper pipe.

The woman's face turned to him was blank, expressionless.

'He wanted to run away with her,' she said simply, 'and after all I have done for him!'

'Open the door.'

Mrs Welford set down the jug and ran her huge hand across her forehead.

'Sidney is my own darling,' she said. 'I've nursed him, and taught him, and there was a million—all in gold—in the ship. But they robbed him.'

She was talking of one of the ill-fated enterprises of Telfers Consolidated Trust—that sunken treasure ship to recover which the money of the company had been poured out like water. And she was mad. He had guessed the weakness of this domineering woman from the first.

'Open the door; we will talk it over. I'm perfectly sure that the treasure ship scheme was a sound one.'

'Are you?' she asked eagerly, and the next minute the door was open and Mr J. G. Reeder was in that room of death.

'First of all, let me have the key of the telephone-room— you are quite wrong about that young lady: she is my wife.'

The woman stared at him blankly.

'Your wife?' A slow smile transfigured the face. 'Why—I was silly. Here is the key.'

He persuaded her to come downstairs with him, and when the frightened girl was released, he whispered a few words to her, and she flew out of the house.

'Shall we go into the drawing-room?' he asked, and Mrs Welford led the way.

'And now will you tell me how you knew—about the jugs?' he asked gently.

She was sitting on the edge of a sofa, her hands clasped on her knees, her deep-set eyes staring at the carpet.

'John—that was my first husband—told me. He was a professor of chemistry and natural science, and also about the electric furnace. It is so easy to make if you have power—we use nothing but electricity in this house for heating and everything. And then I saw my poor darling being ruined through me, and I found how much money there was in the bank, and I told Billingham to draw it and bring it to me without Sidney knowing. He came here in the evening. I sent Sidney away—to Brighton, I think. I did everything—put the new lock on the telephone box and fixed the shaft from the roof to the little room—it was easy to disperse everything with all the doors open and an electric fan working on the floor—'

She was telling him about the improvised furnace in the greenhouse when the police arrived with the divisional surgeon, and she went away with them, weeping because there would be nobody to press Sidney's ties or put out his shirts.

Mr Reeder took the inspector up to the little room and showed him its contents.

'This funnel leads to the telephone box—' he began.

'But the jugs are empty,' interrupted the officer.

Mr J. G. Reeder struck a match and, waiting until it burnt freely, lowered it into the jug. Half an inch lower than the rim the light went out.

'Carbon monoxide,' he said, 'which is made by steeping marble chips in hydrochloric acid—you will find the mixture in the tank. The gas is colourless and odourless—and heavy. You can pour it out of a jug like water. She could have bought the marble, but was afraid of arousing suspicion. Billingham was killed that way. She got him to go to the telephone box, probably closed the door on him herself, and then killed him painlessly.'

'What did she do with the body?' asked the horrified officer.

'Come out into the hothouse,' said Mr Reeder, 'and pray do not expect to see horrors: an electric furnace will dissolve a diamond to its original elements.'

Mr Reeder went home that night in a state of mental perturbation, and for an hour paced the floor of his large study in Brockley Road.

Over and over in his mind he turned one vital problem: did he owe an apology to Margaret Belman for saying that she was his wife?

The Tea Leaf

Robert Eustace and Edgar Jepson

Robert Eustace was the pen name of a doctor, Robert Eustace Barton (1871–1943), who specialised in detective stories written in collaboration. Towards the end of the Victorian era, he supplied scientific know-how for popular stories co-written with L. T. Meade, but his major achievement was to suggest an original and ambitious concept for a crime story to Dorothy L. Sayers; the result was a highly unusual novel, The Documents in the Case.

Eustace also worked sporadically with Edgar Jepson (1863– 1938), a novelist and translator who spent much of his adult life in London. Both men were founder members of the Detection Club, an accolade that Jepson in particular probably owed to their joint masterpiece, 'The Tea Leaf'. This is a classic example of the 'impossible crime' story, a form of puzzle which has remained popular since the earliest days of the detective genre.

›››

Arthur Kelstern and Hugh Willoughton met in the Turkish bath in Duke Street, St. James's, and rather more than a year later in that Turkish bath they parted. Both of them were bad-tempered men, Kelstern cantankerous and Willoughton violent. It was, indeed, difficult to decide which was the worse-tempered; and when I found that they had suddenly become friends, I gave that friendship three months. It lasted nearly a year.

When they did quarrel they quarrelled about Kelstern's daughter Ruth. Willoughton fell in love with her and she with him, and they became engaged to be married. Six months later, in spite of the fact that they were plainly very much in love with one another, the engagement was broken off. Neither of them gave any reason for breaking it off. My belief was that Willoughton had given Ruth a taste of his infernal temper and got as good as he gave.

Not that Ruth was at all a Kelstern to look at. Like the members of most of the old Lincolnshire families, descendants of the Vikings and the followers of Canute, one Kelstern is very like another Kelstern, fair-haired, clear-skinned, with light blue eyes and a good bridge to the nose. But Ruth had taken after her mother; she was dark, with a straight nose, dark-brown eyes of the kind often described as liquid, dark-brown hair, and as kissable lips as ever I saw. She was a proud, self-sufficing, high-spirited girl, with a temper of her own. She needed it to live with that cantankerous old brute Kelstern. Oddly enough, in spite of the fact that he always would try to bully her, she was fond of him; and I will say for him that he was very fond of her. Probably she was the only creature in the world of whom he was really fond. He was an expert in the application of scientific discoveries to industry; and she worked with him in his laboratory. He paid her five hundred a year, so that she must have been uncommonly good.

He took the breaking off of the engagement very hard indeed. He would have it that Willoughton had jilted her. Ruth took it hard, too; her warm colouring lost some of its warmth; her lips grew less kissable and set in a thinner line. Willoughton's temper grew worse than ever; he was like a bear with a perpetually sore head. I tried to feel my way with both him and Ruth with a view to help to bring about a reconciliation. To put it mildly, I was rebuffed. Willoughton swore at me; Ruth flared up and told me not to meddle in matters that didn't concern me. Nevertheless, my strong impression was that they were missing one another badly and would have been glad enough to come together again if their stupid vanity could have let them.

Kelstern did his best to keep Ruth furious with Willoughton. One night I told him—it was no business of mine; but I never did give a tinker's curse for his temper—that he was a fool to meddle and had much better leave them alone. It made him furious, of course; he would have it that Willoughton was a dirty hound and a low blackguard—at least those were about the mildest things he said of him. Given his temper and the provocation, nothing less could be expected. Moreover, he was looking a very sick man and depressed.

He took immense trouble to injure Willoughton. At his clubs, the Athenaeum, the Devonshire, and the Savile, he would display considerable ingenuity in bringing the conversation round to him; then he would declare that he was a scoundrel of the meanest type. Of course, it did Willoughton harm, though not nearly as much as Kelstern desired, for Willoughton knew his job as few engineers knew it; and it is very hard indeed to do much harm to a man who really knows his job. People have to have him. But of course it did him some harm; and Willoughton knew that Kelstern was doing it. I came across two men who told me that they had given him a friendly hint. That did not improve *his* temper.

An expert in the construction of those ferro-concrete buildings which are rising up all over London, he was as distinguished in his sphere as Kelstern in his. They were alike not only in the matters of brains and bad temper; but I think that their minds worked in very much the same way. At any rate, both of them seemed determined not to change their ordinary course of life because of the breaking off of that engagement.

It had been the habit of both of them to have a Turkish bath, at the baths in Duke Street, at four in the afternoon on the second and last Tuesday in every month. To that habit they stuck. The fact that they must meet on those Tuesdays did not cause either of them to change his hour of taking his Turkish bath by the twenty minutes which would have given them no more than a passing glimpse of one another. They continued to take it, as they always had, simultaneously. Thick-skinned? They were thick-skinned. Neither of them pretended that he did not see the other; he scowled at him; and he scowled at him most of the time. I know this, for sometimes I had a Turkish bath myself at that hour.

It was about three months after the breaking off of the engagement that they met for the last time at that Turkish bath, and there parted for good.

Kelstern had been looking ill for about six weeks; there was a greyness and a drawn look to his face; and he was losing weight. On the second Tuesday in October he arrived at the bath punctually at four, bringing with him, as was his habit, a thermos flask full of a very delicate China tea. If he thought that he was not perspiring freely enough he would drink it in the hottest room; if he did perspire freely enough, he would drink it after his bath. Willoughton arrived about two minutes later. Kelstern finished undressing and went into the bath a couple of minutes before Willoughton. They stayed in the hot room about the same time; Kelstern went into the hottest room about a minute after Willoughton. Before he went into it he sent for his thermos flask, which he had left in the dressing-room, and took it into the hottest room with him.

As it happened, they were the only two people in the hottest room; and they had not been in it two minutes before the four men in the hot room heard them quarrelling. They heard Kelstern call Willoughton a dirty hound and a low blackguard, among other things, and declare he would do him in yet. Willoughton told him to go to the devil twice. Kelstern went on abusing him, and presently Willoughton fairly shouted: 'Oh, shut up, you old fool! Or I'll make you!'

Kelstern did not shut up. About two minutes later Willoughton came out of the hottest room, scowling, walked through the hot room into the shampooing room, and put himself into the hands of one of the shampooers. Two or three minutes after that a man of the name of Helston went into the hottest room and fairly yelled. Kelstern was lying back on a couch, with the blood still flowing from a wound over his heart.

There was a devil of a hullabaloo. The police were called in; Willoughton was arrested. Of course he lost his temper and, protesting furiously that he had had nothing whatever to do with the crime, abused the police. That did not incline them to believe him.

After examining the room and the dead body the detective-inspector in charge of the case came to the conclusion that Kelstern had been stabbed as he was drinking his tea. The thermos flask lay on the floor and some of the tea had evidently been spilt, for some tea-leaves—the tea in the flask must have been carelessly strained off the leaves by the maid who filled it—lay on the floor about the mouth of the empty flask. It looked as if the murderer had taken advantage of Kelstern's drinking his tea to stab him while the flask rather blocked his vision and prevented him from seeing what he would be at.

The case would have been quite plain sailing but for the fact that they could not find the weapon. It had been easy enough for Willoughton to take it into the bath in the towel in which he was draped. But how had he got rid of it? Where had he hidden it? A Turkish bath is no place to hide anything in. It is as bare as an empty barn—if anything barer; and Willoughton had been in the barest part of it. The police searched every part of it—not that there was much point in doing that, for Willoughton had come out of the hottest room and gone through the hot room into the shampooers' room. When Helston started shouting 'Murder!' he had rushed back with the shampooers to the hottest room and there he had stayed. Since it was obvious that he had committed the murder, the shampooers and the bathers had kept their eyes on him. They were all of them certain that he had not left them to go to the dressing-room; they would not have allowed him to do so.

It was obvious that he must have carried the weapon into the bath, hidden in the folds of the towel in which he was draped, and brought it away in the folds of that towel. He had laid the towel down beside the couch on which he was being shampooed; and there it still lay when they came to look for it, untouched, with no weapon in it, with no traces of blood on it. There was not much in the fact that it was not stained with blood, since Willoughton could have wiped the knife, or dagger, or whatever weapon he used, on the couch on which Kelstern lay. There were no marks of any such wiping on the couch; but the blood, flowing from the wound, might have covered them up. But why was the weapon not in the towel?

There was no finding that weapon.

Then the doctors who made the autopsy came to the conclusion that the wound had been inflicted by a circular, pointed weapon nearly three-quarters of an inch in diameter.

It had penetrated rather more than three inches, and, supposing that its handle was only four inches long, it must have been a sizable weapon, quite impossible to overlook. The doctors also discovered a further proof of the theory that Kelstern had been drinking tea when he was stabbed. Half-way down the wound they found two halves of a tea-leaf which had evidently fallen on to Kelstern's body, been driven into the wound, and cut in half by the weapon. Also they discovered that Kelstern was suffering from cancer. This fact was not published in the papers; I heard it at the Devonshire.

Willoughton was brought before the magistrates, and to most people's surprise did not reserve his defence. He went into the witness-box and swore that he had never touched Kelstern, that he had never had anything to touch him with, that he had never taken any weapon into the Turkish bath and so had had no weapon to hide, that he had never even seen any such weapon as the doctors described. He was committed for trial.

The papers were full of the crime; every one was discussing it; and the question which occupied every one's mind was: where had Willoughton hidden the weapon? People wrote to the papers to suggest that he had ingeniously put it in some place under everybody's eyes and that it had been overlooked because it was so obvious. Others suggested that, circular and pointed, it must be very like a thick lead-pencil, that it was a thick lead-pencil; and that was why the police had overlooked it in their search. The police had not overlooked any thick lead-pencil; there had been no thick lead-pencil to overlook. They hunted England through—Willoughton did a lot of motoring—to discover the man who had sold him this curious and uncommon weapon. They did not find the man who had sold it to him; they did not find a man who sold such weapons at all. They came to the conclusion that

Kelstern had been murdered with a piece of steel, or iron, rod filed to a point like a pencil.

In spite of the fact that only Willoughton *could* have murdered Kelstern, I could not believe that he had done it. The fact that Kelstern was doing his best to injure him professionally and socially was by no means a strong enough motive. Willoughton was far too intelligent a man not to be very well aware that people do not take much notice of statements to the discredit of a man whom they need to do a job for them; and for the social injury he would care very little. Besides, he might very well injure, or even kill, a man in one of his tantrums; but his was not the kind of bad temper that plans a cold-blooded murder; and if ever a murder had been deliberately planned, Kelstern's had.

I was as close a friend as Willoughton had, and I went to visit him in prison. He seemed rather touched by my doing so, and grateful. I learnt that I was the only person who had done so. He was subdued and seemed much gentler. It might last. He discussed the murder readily enough, and naturally with a harassed air. He said quite frankly that he did not expect me, in the circumstances, to believe that he had not committed it; but he had not, and he could not for the life of him conceive who had. I did believe that he had not committed it; there was something in his way of discussing it that wholly convinced me. I told him that I was quite sure that he had not killed Kelstern; and he looked at me as if he did not believe the assurance. But again he looked grateful.

Ruth was grieving for her father; but Willoughton's very dangerous plight to some degree distracted her mind from her loss. A woman can quarrel with a man bitterly without desiring to see him hanged; and Willoughton's chance of escaping hanging was not at all a good one. But she would not believe for a moment that he had murdered her father.

'No; there's nothing in it—nothing whatever,' she said firmly. 'If dad had murdered Hugh I could have understood it. He had reasons—or at any rate he had persuaded himself that he had. But whatever reason had Hugh for murdering dad? It's all nonsense to suppose that he'd mind dad's trying all he knew to injure him as much as that. All kinds of people are going about trying to injure other people in that way, but they don't really injure them very much; and Hugh knows that quite well.'

'Of course they don't; and Hugh wouldn't really believe that your father was injuring him much,' I said. 'But you're forgetting his infernal temper.'

'No, I'm not,' she protested. 'He might kill a man in one of his rages on the spur of the moment. But this wasn't the spur of the moment. Whoever did it had worked the whole thing out and came along with the weapon ready.'

I had to admit that that was reasonable enough. But who had done it? I pointed out to her that the police had made careful inquiries about every one in the bath at the time, the shampooers and the people taking their baths, but they found no evidence whatever that any one of them had at any time had any relations, except that of shampooer, with her father.

'Either it was one of them, or somebody else who just did it and got right away, or there's a catch somewhere,' she said, frowning thoughtfully.

'I can't see how there can possibly have been any one in the bath, except the people who are known to have been there,' said I. 'In fact, there can't have been.'

Then the Crown subpoenaed her as a witness for the prosecution. It seemed rather unnecessary and even a bit queer, for it could have found plenty of evidence of bad blood between the two men without dragging her into it. Plainly it was bent on doing all it knew to prove motive enough.

Ruth worked her brain so hard trying to get to the bottom of the business that there came a deep vertical wrinkle just above her right eyebrow that stayed there.

On the morning of the trial I called for her after breakfast to drive her down to the New Bailey. She was pale and looked as if she had had a poor night's rest, and, naturally enough, she seemed to be suffering from an excitement she found hard to control. It was not like her to show any excitement she might be feeling.

She said in an excited voice: 'I think I've got it!' and would say no more.

We had, of course, been in close touch with Willoughton's solicitor, Hamley; and he had kept seats for us just behind him. He wished to have Ruth to hand to consult should some point turn up on which she could throw light, since she knew more than any one about the relations between Willoughton and her father. I had timed our arrival very well; the jury had just been sworn in. Of course, the court was full of women, the wives of peers and bookmakers and politicians, most of them overdressed and over-scented.

Then the judge came in; and with his coming the atmosphere of the court became charged with that sense of anxious strain peculiar to trials for murder. It was rather like the atmosphere of a sick-room in a case of fatal illness, but worse.

Willoughton came into the dock looking under the weather and very much subdued. But he was certainly looking dignified, and he said that he was not guilty in a steady enough voice.

Greatorex, the leading counsel for the Crown, opened the case for the prosecution. There was no suggestion in his speech that the police had discovered any new fact. He begged the jury not to lay too much stress on the fact that the weapon had not been found. He had to, of course.

Then Helston gave evidence of finding that Kelstern had been stabbed, and he and the other three men who had been with him in the hot room gave evidence of the quarrel they had overheard between Willoughton and the dead man, and that Willoughton came out of the hottest room scowling and obviously furious. One of them, a fussy old gentleman of the name of Underwood, declared that it was the bitterest quarrel he had ever heard. None of the four of them could throw any light on the matter of whether Willoughton was carrying the missing weapon in the folds of the towel in which he was draped; all of them were sure that he had nothing in his hands.

The medical evidence came next. In cross-examining the doctors who had made the autopsy, Hazeldean, Willoughton's counsel, established the fact quite definitely that the missing weapon was of a fair size; that its rounded blade must have been over half an inch in diameter and between three and four inches long. They were of the opinion that to drive a blade of that thickness into the heart a handle of at least four inches in length would be necessary to give a firm enough grip. They agreed that it might very well have been a piece of a steel, or iron, rod sharpened like a pencil. At any rate, it was certainly a sizable weapon, not one to be hidden quickly or to disappear wholly in a Turkish bath. Hazeldean could not shake their evidence about the tea-leaf; they were confident that it had been driven into the wound and cut in half by the blade of the missing weapon, and that went to show that the wound had been inflicted while Kelstern was drinking his tea.

Detective-Inspector Brackett, who was in charge of the case, was cross-examined at great length about his search for the missing weapon. He made it quite clear that it was nowhere in that Turkish bath, neither in the hot rooms, nor the shampooing room, nor the dressing-rooms, nor the vestibule, nor the office. He had had the plunge bath emptied; he had searched the roofs, though it was practically certain that the skylight above the hot room, not the hottest, had been shut at the time of the crime. In re-examination he scouted the idea of Willoughton's having had an accomplice who had carried away the weapon for him. He had gone into that matter most carefully.

The shampooer stated that Willoughton came to him scowling so savagely that he wondered what had put him into such a bad temper. In cross-examining him, Arbuthnot, Hazeldean's junior, made it clearer than ever that, unless Willoughton had already hidden the weapon in the bare hottest room, it was hidden in the towel. Then he drew from the shampooer the definite statement that Willoughton had set down the towel beside the couch on which he was shampooed; that he had hurried back to the hot rooms in front of the shampooer; that the shampooer had come back from the hot rooms, leaving Willoughton still in them discussing the crime, to find the towel lying just as Willoughton had set it down, with no weapon in it and no trace of blood on it.

Since the inspector had disposed of the possibility that an accomplice had slipped in, taken the weapon from the towel, and slipped out of the bath with it, this evidence really made it clear that the weapon had never left the hottest room.

Then the prosecution called evidence of the bad terms on which Kelstern and Willoughton had been. Three well-known and influential men told the jury about Kelstern's efforts to prejudice Willoughton in their eyes and the damaging statements he had made about him. One of them had felt it to be his duty to tell Willoughton about this; and Willoughton had been very angry. Arbuthnot, in cross-examining, elicited the fact that any damaging statement that Kelstern made about any one was considerably discounted by the fact that every one knew him to be in the highest degree cantankerous.

I noticed that during the end of the cross-examination of the shampooer and during this evidence Ruth had been fidgeting and turning to look impatiently at the entrance to the court, as if she were expecting someone. Then, just as she was summoned to the witness-box, there came in a tall, stooping, grey-headed, grey-bearded man of about sixty, carrying a brown-paper parcel. His face was familiar to me, but I could not place him. He caught her eye and nodded to her. She breathed a sharp sigh of relief, and bent over and handed a letter she had in her hand to Willoughton's solicitor and pointed out the grey-bearded man to him. Then she went quietly to the witness-box.

Hamley read the letter and at once bent over and handed it to Hazeldean and spoke to him. I caught a note of excitement in his hushed voice. Hazeldean read the letter and appeared to grow excited too. Hamley slipped out of his seat and went to the grey-bearded man, who was still standing just inside the door of the porch, and began to talk to him earnestly.

Greatorex began to examine Ruth; and naturally I turned my attention to her. His examination was directed also to show on what bad terms Kelstern and Willoughton had been. Ruth was called on to tell the jury some of Kelstern's actual threats. Then he questioned Ruth about her own relations with Willoughton and the breaking off of the engagement and its infuriating effect on her father. She admitted that he had been very bitter about it, and had told her that he was resolved to do his best to do Willoughton in. I thought that she went out of her way to emphasize this resolve of Kelstern's. It seemed to me likely to prejudice the jury still more against Willoughton, making them sympathize with a father's righteous indignation, and making yet more obvious that he was a dangerous enemy. Yet she would not admit that her father was right in believing that Willoughton had jilted her.

Hazeldean rose to cross-examine Ruth with a wholly confident air. He drew from her the fact that her father had been on excellent terms with Willoughton until the breaking off of the engagement.

Then Hazeldean asked: 'Is it a fact that since the breaking off of your engagement the prisoner has more than once begged you to forgive him and renew it?'

'Four times,' said Ruth.

'And you refused?'

'Yes,' said Ruth. She looked at Willoughton queerly and added: 'He wanted a lesson.'

The judge asked: 'Did you intend, then, to forgive him ultimately?'

Ruth hesitated; then she rather evaded a direct answer; she scowled frankly at Willoughton, and said: 'Oh, well, there was no hurry. He would always marry me if I changed my mind and wanted to.'

'And did your father know this?' asked the judge.

'No. I didn't tell him. I was angry with Mr Willoughton,' Ruth replied.

There was a pause. Then Hazeldean started on a fresh line.

In sympathetic accents he asked: 'Is it a fact that your father was suffering from cancer in a painful form?'

'It was beginning to grow very painful,' said Ruth sadly.

'Did he make a will and put all his affairs in order a few days before he died?'

'Three days,' said Ruth.

'Did he ever express an intention of committing suicide?'

'He said that he would stick it out for a little while and then end it all,' said Ruth. She paused and added: '*And that is what he did do.*'

One might almost say that the court started. I think that every one in it moved a little, so that there was a kind of rustling murmur.

'Will you tell the court your reasons for that statement?' said Hazeldean.

Ruth seemed to pull herself together—she was looking very tired—then she began in a quiet, even voice: 'I never believed for a moment that Mr Willoughton murdered my father. If my father had murdered Mr Willoughton it would have been a different matter. Of course, like everybody else, I puzzled over the weapon; what it was and where it had got to. I did not believe that it was a pointed piece of a half-inch steel rod. If anybody had come to the Turkish bath meaning to murder my father and hide the weapon, they wouldn't have used one so big and so difficult to hide, when a hat-pin would have done just as well and could be hidden much more easily. But what puzzled me most was the tea-leaf in the wound. All the other tea-leaves that came out of the flask were lying on the floor. Inspector Brackett told me they were. And I couldn't believe that one tea-leaf had fallen on to my father at the very place above his heart at which the point of the weapon had penetrated the skin and got driven in by it. It was too much of a coincidence for me to swallow. But I got no nearer understanding it than any one else.'

She paused to ask if she might have a glass of water, for she had been up all night and was very tired. It was brought to her.

Then she went on in the same quiet voice: 'Of course, I remembered that dad had talked of putting an end to it; but no one with a wound like that could get up and hide the weapon. So it was impossible that he had committed suicide. Then, the night before last, I dreamt that I went into the laboratory and saw a piece of steel rod, pointed, lying on the table at which my father used to work.'

'Dreams!' murmured Greatorex, a trifle pettishly, as if he was not pleased with the way things were going.

'I didn't think much of the dream, of course,' Ruth went on. 'I had been puzzling about it all so hard for so long that it was only natural to dream about it. But after breakfast I had a sudden feeling that the secret was in the laboratory if I could only find it. I did not attach any importance to the feeling; but it went on growing stronger; and after lunch I went to the laboratory and began to hunt.

'I looked through all the drawers and could find nothing. Then I went round the room looking at everything and into everything, instruments and retorts and tubes and so on. Then I went into the middle of the floor and looked slowly round the room pretty hard. Against the wall, near the door, lying ready to be taken away, was a gas cylinder. I rolled it over to see what gas had been in it and found no label on it.'

She paused to look round the court as if claiming its best attention; then she went on: 'Now that was very queer, because every gas cylinder must have a label on it—so many gases are dangerous. I turned on the tap of the cylinder and nothing came out of it. It was quite empty. Then I went to the book in which all the things which come in are entered, and found that ten days before dad died he had had a cylinder of CO_2 and seven pounds of ice. Also he had had seven pounds of ice every day till the day of his death. It was the ice and the CO_2 together that gave me the idea. CO_2, carbon dioxide, has a very low freezing-point—eighty degrees centigrade—and as it comes out of the cylinder and mixes with the air it turns into very fine snow; and that snow, if you compress it, makes the hardest and toughest ice possible. It flashed on me that dad could have collected this snow and forced it into a mould and made a weapon that would not only inflict that wound but would evaporate very quickly! Indeed, in that heat you'd have to see the wound inflicted to know what had done it.'

She paused again to look round the court at about as rapt a lot of faces as any narrator could desire. Then she went on: 'I knew that that was what he had done. I knew it for certain. Carbon dioxide ice would make a hard, tough dagger, and it would evaporate quickly in the hottest room of a Turkish bath and leave no smell because it is scentless. So there wouldn't be any weapon. And it explained the tea-leaf, too. Dad had made a carbon dioxide dagger perhaps a week before he used it, perhaps only a day. And he had put it into the thermos flask as soon as he had made it. The thermos flask keeps out the heat as well as the cold, you know. But to make sure that it couldn't melt at all, he kept the flask in ice till he was ready to use the dagger. It's the only way you can explain that tea-leaf. It came out of the flask sticking to the point of the dagger and was driven into the wound!'

She paused again, and one might almost say that the court heaved a deep sigh of relief.

'But why didn't you go straight to the police with this theory?' asked the judge.

'But that wouldn't have been any good,' she protested quickly. 'It was no use my knowing it myself; I had to make other people believe it; I had to find evidence. I began to hunt for it. I felt in my bones that there was some. What I wanted was the mould in which dad compressed the carbon dioxide snow and made the dagger. I found it!'

She uttered the words in a tone of triumph and smiled at Willoughton; then she went on: 'At least, I found bits of it. In the box into which we used to throw odds and ends, scraps of material, damaged instruments, and broken test-tubes, I found some pieces of vulcanite; and I saw at once that they were bits of a vulcanite container. I took some wax and rolled it into a rod about the right size, and then I pieced the container together on the outside of it—at least most of it—there are some small pieces missing. It took me nearly all night. But I found the most important bit—*the pointed end.*'

She dipped her hand into her handbag and drew out a black object about nine inches long and three-quarters of an inch thick, and held it up for every one to see.

Someone, without thinking, began to clap; and there came a storm of applause that drowned the voice of the clerk calling for order.

When the applause died down, Hazeldean, who never misses the right moment, said: 'I have no more questions to ask the witness, my lord,' and sat down.

That action seemed to clinch it in my eyes, and I have no doubt it clinched it in the eyes of the jury.

The judge leant forward and said to Ruth in a rather shocked voice: 'Do you expect the jury to believe that a well-known man like your father died in the act of deliberately setting a trap to hang the prisoner?'

Ruth looked at him, shrugged her shoulders, and said, with a calm acceptance of the facts of human nature one would expect to find only in a much older woman: 'Oh, well, daddy was like that. And he certainly believed he had very good reasons for killing Mr Willoughton.'

There was that in her tone and manner which made it absolutely certain that Kelstern was not only like that, but that he had acted according to his nature.

Greatorex did not re-examine Ruth; he conferred with Hazeldean. Then Hazeldean rose to open the case for the defence. He said that he would not waste the time of the court, and that, in view of the fact that Miss Kelstern had solved the problem of her father's death, he would only call one witness, Professor Mozley.

The grey-headed, grey-bearded, stooping man, who had come to the court so late, went into the witness-box. Of course his face had been familiar to me; I had seen his portrait in the newspapers a dozen times. He still carried the brown-paper parcel.

In answer to Hazeldean's questions he stated that it was possible, not even difficult, to make a weapon of carbon dioxide hard enough and tough enough and sharp enough to inflict such a wound as that which had caused Kelstern's death. The method of making it was to fold a piece of chamois leather into a bag, hold that bag with the left hand, protected by a glove, over the nozzle of a cylinder containing liquid carbon dioxide, and open the valve with the right hand. Carbon dioxide evaporates so quickly that its freezing-point, eighty degrees centigrade, is soon reached; and it solidifies in the chamois-leather bag as a deposit of carbon dioxide snow. Then turn off the gas, spoon that snow into a vulcanite container of the required thickness, and ram it down with a vulcanite plunger into a rod of the required hardness. He added that it was advisable to pack the container in ice while filling it and ramming down the snow. Then put the rod into a thermos flask; and keep it till it is needed.

'And you have made such a rod?' said Hazeldean.

'Yes,' said the professor, cutting the string of the brown-paper parcel. 'When Miss Kelstern hauled me out of bed at half-past seven this morning to tell me her discoveries, I perceived at once that she had found the solution of the problem of her father's death, which had puzzled me considerably. I had breakfast quickly and got to work to make such a weapon myself for the satisfaction of the court. Here it is.'

He drew a thermos flask from the brown paper, unscrewed the top of it, and inverted it. There dropped into his gloved hand a white rod, with a faint sparkle to it, about eight inches long. He held it out for the jury to see, and said:

'This carbon dioxide ice is the hardest and toughest ice we know of; and I have no doubt that Mr Kelstern killed himself with a similar rod. The difference between the rod he used and this is that his rod was pointed. I had no pointed vulcanite container; but the container that Miss Kelstern pieced together is pointed. Doubtless Mr Kelstern had it specially made, probably by Messrs. Hawkins and Spender.'

He dropped the rod back into the thermos flask and screwed on the top.

Hazeldean sat down, Greatorex rose.

'With regard to the point of the rod, Professor Mozley, would it remain sharp long enough to pierce the skin in that heat?' he asked.

'In my opinion it would,' said the professor. 'I have been considering that point, and bearing in mind the facts that Mr Kelstern would from his avocation be very deft with his hands, and being a scientific man would know exactly what to do, he would have the rod out of the flask and the point in position in very little more than a second—perhaps less. He would, I think, hold it in his left hand and drive it home by striking the butt of it hard with his right. The whole thing would not take him two seconds. Besides, if the point of the weapon had melted the tea-leaf would have fallen off it.'

'Thank you,' said Greatorex, and turned and conferred with the Crown solicitors.

Then he said: 'We do not propose to proceed with the case, my lord.'

The foreman of the jury rose quickly and said: 'And the jury doesn't want to hear anything more, my lord. We're quite satisfied that the prisoner isn't guilty.'

'Very good,' said the judge, and he put the question formally to the jury, who returned a verdict of 'Not guilty.' He discharged Willoughton.

I came out of the court with Ruth and we waited for Willoughton.

Presently he came out of the door and stopped and shook himself. Then he saw Ruth and came to her. They did not greet one another. She just slipped her hand through his arm; and they walked out of the New Bailey together.

We made a good deal of noise, cheering them.

The Hands of Mr Ottermole

Thomas Burke

Thomas Burke (1886–1945) was a Londoner whose work was distinguished by an understanding of and insight into working-class life in the capital. Limehouse Nights, *a collection of stories published during the First World War, garnered much praise, not least from H. G. Wells and Arnold Bennett, and led to Burke being described as 'the laureate of London's Chinatown'.*

Burke's stock-in-trade was melodrama, and not all of his work has stood the test of time. 'The Hands of Mr Ottermole', however, has long been recognised as an outstanding example of the short crime story. It makes powerful use of a Ripper-type series of killings, adding the bonus of a clever twist at the end. The American mystery writer Ellery Queen (a pen name for Manfred Lee and Frederic Dannay) went so far as to say of it: 'No finer crime story has ever been written, period'.

'Murder (said old Quong)—oblige me by passing my pipe—murder is one of the simplest things in the world to do. Killing a man is a much simpler matter than killing a duck. Not always so safe, perhaps, but simpler. But to certain gifted people it is both simple and entirely safe. Many minds of finer complexion than my own have discolored themselves in seeking to name the identity of the author of those wholesale murders which took place last year. Who that man or woman really was, I know no more than you do, but I have a theory of the person it could have been; and if you are not pressed for time I will elaborate that theory into a little tale.'

As I had the rest of that evening and the whole of the next day for dalliance in my ivory tower, I desired that he would tell me the story; and, having reckoned up his cash register and closed the ivory gate, he told me—between then and the dawn—his story of the Mallon End murders. Paraphrased and condensed, it came out something like this.

At six o'clock of a January evening Mr Whybrow was walking home through the cobweb alleys of London's East End. He had left the golden clamor of the great High Street to which the tram had brought him from the river and his daily work, and was now in the chessboard of byways that is called Mallon End. None of the rush and gleam of the High Street trickled into these byways a few paces south—a flood tide of life, foaming and beating. Here—only slow shuffling figures and muffled pulses. He was in the sink of London, the last refuge of European vagrants.

As though in tune with the street's spirit, he too walked slowly, with head down. It seemed that he was pondering some pressing trouble, but he was not. He had no trouble. He was walking slowly because he had been on his feet all day; and he was bent in abstraction because he was wondering whether the Missis would have herrings for his tea, or haddock; and he was trying to decide which would be the more tasty on a night like this. A wretched night it was, of damp and mist, and the mist wandered into his throat and his eyes, and the damp had settled on pavement and roadway, and where the sparse lamplight fell it sent up a greasy sparkle that chilled one to look at. By contrast it made his speculations more agreeable, and made him ready for that tea—whether herring or haddock. His eye turned from the glum bricks that made his horizon, and went forward half a mile. He saw a gas-lit kitchen, a flamy fire, and a spread tea table. There was toast in the hearth and a singing kettle on the side and a piquant effusion of herrings, or maybe of haddock, or perhaps sausages. The vision gave his aching feet a throb of energy. He shook imperceptible damp from his shoulders, and hastened toward its reality.

But Mr Whybrow wasn't going to get any tea that evening—or any other evening. Mr Whybrow was going to die. Somewhere within a hundred yards of him, another man was walking: a man much like Mr Whybrow and much like any other man, but without the only quality that enables mankind to live peaceably together and not as madmen in a jungle. A man with a dead heart eating into itself and bringing forth the foul organisms that arise from death and corruption. And that thing in man's shape, on a whim or a settled idea—one cannot know—had said within himself that Mr Whybrow should never taste another herring. Not that Mr Whybrow had injured him. Not that he had any dislike of Mr Whybrow. Indeed, he knew nothing of him save as a familiar figure about the streets. But, moved by a force that had taken possession of his empty cells, he had picked on Mr Whybrow with that blind choice that makes us pick one restaurant table that has nothing to mark it from four or five other tables, or one apple from a dish of half-a-dozen equal apples; or that drives nature to send a cyclone upon one corner of this planet and destroy five hundred lives in that corner, and leave another five hundred in the same corner unharmed. So this man had picked on Mr Whybrow as he might have picked on you or me, had we been within his daily observation; and even now he was creeping through the blue-toned streets, nursing his large white hands, moving ever closer to Mr Whybrow's tea table, and so closer to Mr Whybrow himself.

He wasn't, this man, a bad man. Indeed, he had many of the social and amiable qualities, and passed as a respectable man, as most successful criminals do. But the thought had come into his moldering mind that he would like to murder somebody, and as he held no fear of God or man, he was going to do it, and would then go home to *his* tea. I don't say that flippantly, but as a statement of fact. Strange as it may seem to the humane, murderers must and do sit down to meals after a murder. There is no reason why they shouldn't, and many reasons why they should. For one thing, they need to keep their physical and mental vitality at full beat for the business of covering their crime. For another, the strain of their effort makes them hungry, and satisfaction at the accomplishment of a desired thing brings a feeling of relaxation toward human pleasures. It is accepted among non-murderers that the murderer is always overcome by fear for his safety and horror at his act; but this type is rare. His own safety is, of course, his immediate concern, but vanity is a marked quality of most murderers, and that, together with the thrill of conquest, makes him confident that he can secure it; and when he has restored his strength with food, he goes about securing it as a young hostess goes about the arranging of her first big dinner—a little anxious, but no more. Criminologists and detectives tell us that *every* murderer, however intelligent or cunning, always makes one slip in his tactics—one little slip that brings the affair home to him. But that is only half-true. It is true only of the murderers who are caught. Scores of murderers are not caught: therefore, scores of murderers do not make any mistake at all. This man didn't.

As for horror or remorse, prison chaplains, doctors, and lawyers have told us that of murderers they have interviewed under condemnation and the shadow of death, only one here and there has expressed any contrition for his act or shown any sign of mental misery. Most of them display only exasperation at having been caught when so many have gone undiscovered, or indignation at being condemned for a perfectly reasonable act. However normal and humane they may have been before the murder, they are utterly without conscience after it. For what is conscience? Simply a polite nickname for superstition, which is a polite nickname for fear. Those who associate remorse with murder are, no doubt, basing their ideas on the world-legend of the remorse of Cain, or are projecting their own frail minds into the mind of the murderer, and getting false reactions. Peaceable folk cannot hope to make contact with this mind, for they are not merely different in mental type from the murderer; they are different in their personal chemistry and construction. Some men can and do kill—not one man, but two or three—and go calmly about their daily affairs. Other men could not, under the most agonizing provocation, bring themselves even to wound. It is men of this sort who imagine the murderer in torments of remorse and fear of the law, whereas he is actually sitting down to his tea.

The man with the large white hands was as ready for his tea as Mr Whybrow was, but he had something to do before he went to it. When he had done that something, and made no mistake about it, he would be even more ready for it, and would go to it as comfortably as he went to it the day before, when his hands were stainless.

◇◇◇

Walk on, then, Mr Whybrow, walk on; and as you walk, look your last upon the familiar features of your nightly journey. Follow your jack-o'-lantern tea table. Look well upon its warmth and color and kindness; feed your eyes with it and tease your nose with its gentle domestic odors, for you will never sit down to it. Within ten minutes' pacing of you, a pursuing phantom has spoken in his heart, and you are doomed. There you go—you and phantom—two nebulous dabs of mortality moving through green air along pavements of powder-blue, the one to kill, the other to be killed. Walk on. Don't annoy your burning feet by hurrying, for the more slowly you walk, the longer you will breathe the green air of this January dusk, and see the dreamy lamplight and the little shops, and hear the agreeable commerce of the London crowd and the haunting pathos of the street organ. These things are dear to you, Mr Whybrow. You don't know it now, but in fifteen minutes you will have two seconds in which to realize how inexpressibly dear they are.

Walk on, then, across this crazy chessboard. You are in Lagos Street now, among the tents of the wanderers of Eastern Europe. A minute or so, and you are in Loyal Lane, among the lodging houses that shelter the useless and the beaten of London's camp followers. The lane holds the smell of them, and its soft darkness seems heavy with the wail of the futile. But you are not sensitive to impalpable things, and you plod through it, unseeing, as you do every evening, and come to Blean Street, and plod through that. From basement to sky rise the tenements of an alien colony. Their windows slot the ebony of their walls with lemon. Behind those windows, strange life is moving, dressed with forms that are not of London or of England, yet, in essence, the same agreeable life that you have been living, and tonight will live no more. From high above you comes a voice crooning *The Song of Katta*. Through a window you see a family keeping a religious rite. Through another you see a woman pouring out tea for her husband. You see a man mending a pair of boots; a mother bathing her baby. You have seen all these things before, and never noticed them. You do not notice them now, but if you knew that you were never going to see them again, you would notice them. You never *will* see them again, not because your life has run its natural course, but because a man whom you have often passed in the street has at his own solitary pleasure decided to usurp the awful authority of nature, and destroy you. So perhaps it's as well that you don't notice them, for your part in them is ended. No more for you these pretty moments of our earthly travail: only one moment of terror, and then a plunging darkness.

Closer to you this shadow of massacre moves, and now he is twenty yards behind you. You can hear his footfall, but you do not turn your head. You are familiar with footfalls. You are in London, in the easy security of your daily territory, and footfalls behind you, your instinct tells you, are no more than a message of human company.

But can't you hear something in those footfalls—something that goes with a widdershins beat? Something that says: *Look out, look out. Beware, beware.* Can't you hear the very syllables of *murd-er-er, murd-er-er?* No; there is nothing in footfalls. They are neutral. The foot of villainy falls with the same quiet note as the foot of honesty. But those footfalls, Mr Whybrow, are bearing on to you a pair of hands, and there *is* something in hands. Behind you that pair of hands is even now stretching its muscles in preparation for your end. Every minute of your days, you have been seeing human hands. Have you ever realized the sheer horror of hands—those appendages that are a symbol of our moments of trust and affection and salutation? Have you thought of the sickening potentialities that lie within the scope of that five-tentacled member? No, you never have; for all the human hands that you have seen have been stretched to you in kindness or fellowship. Yet, though the eyes can hate and the lips can sting, it is only that dangling member that can gather the accumulated essence of evil and electrify it into currents of destruction. Satan may enter into man by many doors, but in the hands alone can he find the servants of his will.

Another minute, Mr Whybrow, and you will know all about the horror of human hands.

You are nearly home now. You have turned into your street—Caspar Street—and you are in the center of the chessboard. You can see the front window of your little four-roomed house. The street is dark, and its three lamps give only a smut of light that is more confusing than darkness. It is dark—empty, too. Nobody about; no lights in the front parlors of the houses, for the families are at tea in their kitchens; and only a random glow in a few upper rooms occupied by lodgers. Nobody about but you and your following companion, and you don't notice him. You see him so often that he is never seen. Even if you turned your head and saw him, you would only say 'Good evening' to him, and walk on. A suggestion that he was a possible murderer would not even make you laugh. It would be too silly.

And now you are at your gate. And now you have found your door key. And now you are in, and hanging up your hat and coat. The Missis has just called a greeting from the kitchen, whose smell is an echo of that greeting (herrings!), and you have answered it, when the door shakes under a sharp knock.

Go away, Mr Whybrow. Go away from that door. Don't touch it. Get right away from it. Get out of the house. Run with the Missis to the back garden, and over the fence. Or call the neighbors. But don't touch that door. Don't, Mr Whybrow, don't open....

Mr Whybrow opened the door.

⟨⟩⟨⟩⟨⟩

That was the beginning of what became known as London's Strangling Horrors. Horrors they were called because they were something more than murders: they were motiveless, and there was an air of black magic about them. Each murder was committed at a time when the street where the bodies were found was empty of any perceptible or possible murderer. There would be an empty alley. There would be a policeman at its end. He would turn his back on the empty alley for less than a minute. Then he would look round and run into the night with news of another strangling. And in any direction he looked, nobody to be seen and no report to be had of anybody being seen. Or he would be on duty in a long-quiet street, and suddenly be called to a house of dead people whom a few seconds earlier he had seen alive. And, again, whichever way he looked nobody to be seen; and although police whistles put an immediate cordon around the area and searched all houses, no possible murderer to be found.

The first news of the murder of Mr and Mrs Whybrow was brought by the station sergeant. He had been walking through Caspar Street on his way to the station for duty, when he noticed the open door of No. 98. Glancing in, he saw by the gaslight of the passage a motionless body on the floor. After a second look he blew his whistle; and when the constables answered him, he took one to join him in search of the house, and sent others to watch all neighboring streets and make inquiries at adjoining houses. But neither in the house nor in the streets was anything found to indicate the murderer. Neighbors on either side, and opposite, were questioned, but they had seen nobody about, and had heard nothing. One had heard Mr Whybrow come home—the scrape of his latchkey in the door was so regular an evening sound, he said, that you could set your watch by it for half-past six—but he had heard nothing more than the sound of the opening door until the sergeant's whistle. Nobody had been seen to enter the house or leave it, by front or back, and the necks of the dead people carried no fingerprints or other traces. A nephew was called in to go over the house, but he could find nothing missing; and anyway his uncle possessed nothing worth stealing The little money in the house was untouched, and there were no signs of any disturbance of the property, or even of struggle. No signs of anything but brutal and wanton murder.

Mr Whybrow was known to neighbors and workmates as a quiet, likable, home-loving man; such a man as could not have any enemies. But, then, murdered men seldom have. A relentless enemy who hates a man to the point of wanting to hurt him seldom wants to murder him, since to do that puts him beyond suffering. So the police were left with an impossible situation: no clue to the murderer and no motive for the murders, only that they had been done.

The first news of the affair sent a tremor through London generally, and an electric thrill through all Mallon End. Here was a murder of two inoffensive people, not for gain and not for revenge; and the murderer, to whom, apparently, killing was a casual impulse, was at large. He had left no traces, and provided he had no companions, there seemed no reason why he should not remain at large. Any clearheaded man who stands alone and has no fear of God or man, can, if he chooses, hold a city, even a nation, in subjection; but your everyday criminal is seldom clearheaded and dislikes being lonely. He needs, if not the support of confederates, at least somebody to talk to; his vanity needs the satisfaction of perceiving at first hand the effect of his work. For this he will frequent bars and coffee shops and other public places. Then, sooner or later, in a glow of comradeship, he will utter the one word too much; and the nark, who is everywhere, has an easy job.

But though the doss-houses and saloons and other places were 'combed' and set with watches, and it was made known by whispers that good money and protection were assured to those with information, nothing attaching to the Whybrow case could be found. The murderer clearly had no friends and kept no company. Known men of this type were called up and questioned, but each was able to give a good account of himself; and in a few days the police were at a dead end. Against the constant public gibe that the thing had been done almost under their noses, they became restive, and for four days each man of the force was working his daily beat under a strain. On the fifth day they became still more restive.

It was the season of annual teas and entertainments for the children of the Sunday Schools; and on an evening of fog, when London was a world of groping phantoms, a small girl, in the bravery of best Sunday frock and shoes, shining face and new-washed hair, set out from Logan Passage for St. Michael's Parish Hall. She never got there. She was not actually dead until half-past six, but she was as good as dead from the moment she left her mother's door. Somebody like a man, pacing the street from which the passage led, saw her come out; and from that moment she was dead. Through the fog somebody's large white hands reached after her, and in fifteen minutes they were about her.

At half-past six a whistle screamed trouble, and those answering it found the body of little Nellie Vrinoff in a warehouse entry in Minnow Street. The sergeant was first among them, and he posted his men to useful points, ordering them here and there in the tart tones of repressed rage, and berating the officer whose beat the street was. 'I saw you, Magson, at the end of the lane. What were you up to there? You were there ten minutes before you turned.' Magson began an explanation about keeping an eye on a suspicious-looking character at that end, but the sergeant cut him short: 'Suspicious characters be damned. You don't want to look for suspicious characters. You want to look for *murderers*. Messing about…and then this happens right where you ought to be. Now think what they'll say.'

With the speed of ill news came the crowd, pale and perturbed; and on the story that the unknown monster had appeared again, and this time to a child, their faces streaked the fog with spots of hate and horror. But then came the ambulance and more police, and swiftly they broke up the crowd; and as it broke, the sergeant's thought was thickened into words, and from all sides came low murmurs of 'Right under their noses.' Later inquiries showed that four people of the district, above suspicion, had passed that entry at intervals of seconds before the murder, and seen nothing and heard nothing. None of them had passed the child alive or seen her dead. None of them had seen anybody in the street except themselves. Again the police were left with no motive and with no clue.

And now the district, as you will remember, was given over, not to panic, for the London public never yields to that, but to apprehension and dismay. If these things were happening in their familiar streets, then anything might happen. Wherever people met—in the streets, the markets, and the shops—they debated the one topic. Women took to bolting their windows and doors at the first fall of dusk. They kept their children closely under their eye. They did their shopping before dark, and watched anxiously—while pretending they weren't watching—for the return of their husbands from work. Under the cockney's semi-humorous resignation to disaster, they hid an hourly foreboding. By the whim of one man with a pair of hands, the structure and tenor of their daily life were shaken, as they always can be shaken by any man contemptuous of humanity and fearless of its laws. They began to realize that the pillars that supported the peaceable society in which they lived were mere straws that anybody could snap; that laws were powerful only so long as they were obeyed; that the police were potent only so long as they were feared. By the power of his hands this one man had made a whole community do something new: he had made it think, and left it gasping at the obvious.

And then, while it was yet gasping under his first two strokes, he made his third. Conscious of the horror that his hands had created, and hungry as an actor who has once tasted the thrill of the multitude, he made fresh advertisement of his presence; and on Wednesday morning, three days after the murder of the child, the papers carried to the breakfast tables of England the story of a still more shocking outrage.

At 9.32 on Tuesday night a constable was on duty in Jarnigan Road, and at that time spoke to a fellow officer named Petersen at the top of Clemming Street. He had seen this officer walk down that street. He could swear that the street was empty at that time, except for a lame bootblack whom he knew by sight, and who passed him and entered a tenement on the side opposite that on which his fellow officer was walking. He had the habit, as all constables had just then, of looking constantly behind him and around him, whichever way he was walking, and he was certain that the street was empty. He passed his sergeant at 9.33, saluted him, and answered his inquiry for anything seen. He reported that he had seen nothing, and passed on. His beat ended at a short distance from Clemming Street, and having paced it, he turned and came again at 9.34 to the top of the street. He had scarcely reached it before he heard the hoarse voice of the sergeant: 'Gregory! You there? Quick. Here's another. My God, it's Petersen! Garroted. Quick, call 'em up!'

That was the third of the Strangling Horrors, of which there were to be a fourth and a fifth; and the five horrors were to pass into the unknown and unknowable. That is, unknown as far as authority and the public were concerned. The identity of the murderer *was* known, but to two men only. One was the murderer himself; the other was a young journalist.

This young man, who was covering the affairs for his paper, the *Daily Torch*, was no smarter than the other zealous newspapermen who were hanging about these byways in the hope of a sudden story. But he was patient, and he hung a little closer to the case than the other fellows, and by continually staring at it he at last raised the figure of the murderer like a genie from the stones on which he had stood to do his murders.

After the first few days the men had given up any attempt at exclusive stories, for there were none to be had. They met regularly at the police station, and what little information there was they shared. The officials were agreeable to them, but no more. The sergeant discussed with them the details of each murder; suggested possible explanations of the man's methods; recalled from the past those cases that had some similarity; and on the matter of motive reminded them of the motiveless Neil Cream and the wanton John Williams, and hinted that work was being done which would soon bring the business to an end; but about that work he would not say a word. The Inspector, too, was gracefully garrulous on the thesis of Murder, but whenever one of the party edged the talk toward what was being done in this immediate matter, he glided past it. Whatever the officials knew, they were not giving it to newspapermen. The business had fallen heavily upon them, and only by a capture made by their own efforts could they rehabilitate themselves in official and public esteem. Scotland Yard, of course, was at work, and had all the station's material; but the station's hope was that they themselves would have the honor of settling the affair; and however useful the cooperation of the press might be in other cases, they did not want to risk a defeat by a premature disclosure of their theories and plans.

So the sergeant talked at large, and propounded one interesting theory after another, all of which the newspapermen had thought of themselves.

The young man soon gave up these morning lectures on the philosophy of crime, and took to wandering about the streets and making bright stories out of the effect of the murders on the normal life of the people. A melancholy job made more melancholy by the district. The littered roadways, the crestfallen houses, the bleared windows—all held the acid misery that evokes no sympathy: the misery of the frustrated poet. The misery was the creation of the aliens, who were living in this makeshift fashion because they had no settled homes, and would neither take the trouble to make a home where they *could* settle, nor get on with their wandering.

There was little to be picked up. All he saw and heard were indignant faces, and wild conjectures of the murderer's identity and of the secret of his trick of appearing and disappearing unseen. Since a policeman himself had fallen a victim, denunciations of the force had ceased, and the unknown was now invested with a cloak of legend. Men eyed other men as though thinking: It might be *him*. It might be *him*. They were no longer looking for a man who had the air of a Madame Tussaud murderer; they were looking for a man, or perhaps some harridan woman, who had done these particular murders. Their thoughts ran mainly on the foreign set. Such ruffianism could scarcely belong to England, nor could the bewildering cleverness of the thing. So they turned to Rumanian gypsies and Turkish carpet-sellers. There, clearly, would be found the 'warm' spot. These Eastern fellows—they knew all sorts of tricks, and they had no real religion—nothing to hold them within bounds. Sailors returning from those parts had told tales of conjurors who made themselves invisible; and there were tales of Egyptian and Arab potions that were used for abysmally queer purposes. Perhaps it *was* possible to them; you never knew. They were so slick and cunning, and they had such gliding movements; no Englishman could melt away as they could. Almost certainly the murderer would be found to be one of that sort—with some dark trick of his own—and just because they were sure that he *was* a magician, they felt that it was useless to look for him. He was a power, able to hold them in subjection and to hold himself untouchable. Superstition, which so easily cracks the frail shell of reason, had got into them. He could do anything he chose; he would never be discovered. These two points they settled, and they went about the streets in a mood of resentful fatalism.

They talked of their ideas to the journalist in half-tones, looking right and left, as though *HE* might overhear them and visit them. And though all the district was thinking of him and ready to pounce upon him, yet, so strongly had he worked upon them, that if any man in the street—say, a small man of commonplace features and form—had cried '*I* am the Monster!' would their stifled fury have broken into flood and have borne him down and engulfed him? Or would they not suddenly have seen something unearthly in that everyday face and figure, something unearthly in his everyday boots, something unearthly about his hat, something that marked him as one whom none of their weapons could alarm or pierce? And would they not momentarily have fallen back from this devil, as the devil fell back from the cross made by the sword of Faust, and so have given him time to escape? I do not know; but so fixed was their belief in his invincibility that it is at least likely that they would have made this hesitation, had such an occasion arisen. But it never did. Today this commonplace fellow, his murder lust glutted, is still seen and observed among them as he was seen and observed all the time; but because nobody then dreamt, or now dreams, that he was what he was, they observed him then, and observe him now, as people observe a lamppost.

Almost was their belief in his invincibility justified; for, five days after the murder of the policeman Petersen, when the experience and inspiration of the whole detective force of London were turned toward his identification and capture, he made his fourth and fifth strokes.

At nine o'clock that evening, the young newspaperman, who hung about every night until his paper was away, was strolling along Richards Lane. Richards Lane is a narrow street, partly a stall-market, and partly residential. The young man was in the residential section, which carries on one side small working-class cottages, and on the other the wall of a railway goods-yard. The great wall hung a blanket of shadow over the lane, and the shadow and the cadaverous outline of the now deserted market stalls gave it the appearance of a living lane that had been turned to frost in the moment between breath and death. The very lamps, that elsewhere were nimbuses of gold, had here the rigidity of gems. The journalist, feeling this message of frozen eternity, was telling himself that he was tired of the whole thing, when in one stroke the frost was broken. In the moment between one pace and another, silence and darkness were racked by a high scream and through the scream a voice: 'Help! help! *He's here!'*

Before he could think what movement to make, the lane came to life. As though its invisible populace had been waiting on that cry, the door of every cottage was flung open, and from them and from the alleys poured shadowy figures bent in question-mark form. For a second or so they stood as rigid as the lamps; then a police whistle gave them direction, and the flock of shadows sloped up the street.

The journalist followed them, and others followed him. From the main street and from surrounding streets they came, some risen from unfinished suppers, some disturbed in their ease of slippers and shirtsleeves, some stumbling on infirm limbs, and some upright and armed with pokers or the tools of their trade. Here and there above the wavering cloud of heads moved the bold helmets of policemen. In one dim mass they surged upon a cottage whose doorway was marked by the sergeant and two constables; and voices of those behind urged them on with 'Get in! Find him! Run round the back! Over the wall!' And those in front cried, 'Keep back! Keep back!'

And now the fury of a mob held in thrall by unknown peril broke loose. He was here—on the spot. Surely this time he *could not* escape. All minds were bent upon the cottage; all energies thrust toward its doors and windows and roof; all thought was turned upon one unknown man and his extermination. So that no one man saw any other man. No man saw the narrow, packed lane and the mass of struggling shadows, and all forgot to look among themselves for the monster who never lingered upon his victims. All forgot, indeed, that they, by their mass crusade of vengeance, were affording him the perfect hiding place. They saw only the house, and they heard only the rending of woodwork and the smash of glass at back and front, and the police giving orders or crying with the chase; and they pressed on.

But they found no murderer. All they found was news of murder and a glimpse of the ambulance, and for their fury there was no other object than the police themselves, who fought against this hampering of their work.

The journalist managed to struggle through to the cottage door, and to get the story from the constable stationed there. The cottage was the home of a pensioned sailor and his wife and daughter. They had been at supper, and at first it appeared that some noxious gas had smitten all three in mid-action. The daughter lay dead on the hearth rug, with a piece of bread and butter in her hand. The father had fallen sideways from his chair, leaving on his plate a filled spoon of rice pudding. The mother lay half under the table, her lap filled with the pieces of a broken cup and splashes of cocoa. But in three seconds the idea of gas was dismissed. One glance at their necks showed that this was the Strangler again; and the police stood and looked at the room and momentarily shared the fatalism of the public. They were helpless.

This was his fourth visit, making seven murders in all. He was to do, as you know, one more—and to do it that night; and then he was to pass into history as the unknown London horror, and return to the decent life that he had always led, remembering little of what he had done and worried not at all by the memory. Why did he stop? Impossible to say. Why did he begin? Impossible again. It just happened like that; and if he thinks at all of those days and nights, I surmise that he thinks of them as we think of foolish or dirty little sins that we committed in childhood. We say that they were not really sins because we were not then consciously ourselves: we had not come to realization; and we look back at that foolish little creature that we once were and forgive him because he didn't know. So, I think, with this man.

There are plenty like him. Eugene Aram, after the murder of Daniel Clarke, lived a quiet, contented life for fourteen years, unhaunted by his crime and unshaken in his self-esteem. Dr Crippen murdered his wife, and then lived pleasantly with his mistress in the house under whose floor he had buried the wife. Constance Kent, found Not Guilty of the murder of her young brother, led a peaceful life for five years before she confessed. George Joseph Smith and William Palmer lived amiably among their fellows untroubled by fear or by remorse for their poisonings and drownings. Charles Peace, at the time he made his one unfortunate essay, had settled down into a respectable citizen with an interest in antiques. It happened that, after a lapse of time, these men were discovered; but more murderers than we guess are living decent lives today, and will die in decency, undiscovered and unsuspected. As this man will.

But he had a narrow escape, and it was perhaps this narrow escape that brought him to a stop. The escape was due to an error of judgment on the part of the journalist.

As soon as he had the full story of the affair, which took some time, he spent fifteen minutes on the telephone, sending the story through, and at the end of the fifteen minutes, when the stimulus of the business had left him, he felt physically tired and mentally disheveled. He was not yet free to go home; the paper would not go away for another hour; so he turned into a bar for a drink and some sandwiches.

It was then, when he had dismissed the whole business from his mind and was looking about the bar and admiring the landlord's taste in watch chains and his air of domination, and was thinking that the landlord of a well-conducted tavern had a more comfortable life than a newspaperman, that his mind received from nowhere a spark of light. He was not thinking about the Strangling Horrors; his mind was on his sandwich. As a public-house sandwich, it was a curiosity. The bread had been thinly cut, it was buttered, and the ham was not two months stale; it was ham as it should be. His mind turned to the inventor of this refreshment, the Earl of Sandwich, and then to George the Fourth, and then to the Georges, and to the legend of that George who was worried to know how the apple got into the apple dumpling. He wondered whether George would have been equally puzzled to know how the ham got into the ham sandwich, and how long it would have been before it occurred to him that the ham could not have got there unless somebody had put it there. He got up to order another sandwich, and in that moment a little active corner of his mind settled the affair. If there was ham in his sandwich, somebody must have put it there. If seven people had been murdered, somebody must have been there to murder them. There was no aeroplane or automobile that would go into a man's pocket; therefore, that somebody must have escaped either by running away or standing still; and again therefore—

He was visualizing the front-page story that his paper would carry if his theory was correct, and if—a matter of conjecture—his editor had the necessary nerve to make a bold stroke, when a cry of 'Time, gentlemen, please! All out!' reminded him of the hour. He got up and went out into a world of mist, broken by the ragged discs of roadside puddles and the streaming lightning of motor buses. He was certain that he had *the* story, but even if it was proved, he was doubtful whether the policy of his paper would permit him to print it. It had one great fault. It was truth, but it was impossible truth. It rocked the foundations of everything that newspaper readers believed and that newspaper editors helped them to believe. They might believe that Turkish carpet-sellers had the gift of making themselves invisible. They would not believe this.

As it happened, they were not asked to, for the story was never written. As his paper had by now gone away, and as he was nourished by his refreshment and stimulated by his theory, he thought he might put in an extra half hour by testing that theory. So he began to look about for the man he had in mind—a man with white hair and large white hands; otherwise an everyday figure whom nobody would look twice at. He wanted to spring his idea on this man without warning, and he was going to place himself within reach of a man armored in legends of dreadfulness and grue. This might appear to be an act of supreme courage—that one man, with no hope of immediate outside support, should place himself at the mercy of one who was holding a whole parish in terror. But it wasn't. He didn't think about the risk. He didn't think about his duty to his employers or loyalty to his paper. He was moved simply by an instinct to follow a story to its end.

He walked slowly from the tavern and crossed into Fingal Street, making for Deever Market, where he had hope of finding his man. But his journey was shortened. At the corner of Lotus Street he saw him—or a man who looked like him. This street was poorly lit, and he could see little of the man: but he *could* see white hands. For some twenty paces he stalked him; then drew level with him; and at a point where the arch of a railway crossed the street, he saw that this was his man. He approached him with the current conversational phrase of the district: 'Well, seen anything of the murderer?' The man stopped to look sharply at him; then, satisfied that the journalist was not the murderer, said:

'Eh? No, nor's anybody else, curse it. Doubt if they ever will.'

'I don't know. I've been thinking about them, and I've got an idea.'

'So?'

'Yes. Came to me all of a sudden. Quarter of an hour ago. And I'd felt that we'd all been blind. It's been staring us in the face.'

The man turned again to look at him, and the look and the movement held suspicion of this man who seemed to know so much. 'Oh? Has it? Well, if you're so sure, why not give us the benefit of it?'

'I'm going to.' They walked level, and were nearly at the end of the little street where it meets Deever Market when the journalist turned casually to the man. He put a finger on his arm. 'Yes, it seems to me quite simple now. But there's still one point I don't understand. One little thing I'd like to clear up. I mean the motive. Now, as man to man, tell me, Sergeant Ottermole, just *why* did you kill all those inoffensive people?'

The sergeant stopped, and the journalist stopped. There was just enough light from the sky, which held the reflected light of the continent of London, to give him a sight of the sergeant's face, and the sergeant's face was turned to him with a wide smile of such urbanity and charm that the journalist's eyes were frozen as they met it. The smile stayed for some seconds. Then said the sergeant, 'Well, to tell you the truth, Mister Newspaperman, I don't know. I really don't know. In fact, I've been worried about it myself. But I've got an idea—just like you. Everybody knows that we can't control the workings of our minds. Don't they? Ideas come into our minds without asking. But everybody's supposed to be able to control his body. Why? Eh? We get our minds from lord-knows-where—from people who were dead hundreds of years before we were born. Mayn't we get our bodies in the same way? Our faces—our legs—our heads—they aren't completely ours. We don't make 'em. They come to us. And couldn't ideas come into our bodies like ideas come into our minds? Eh? Can't ideas live in nerve and muscle as well as in brain? Couldn't it be that parts of our bodies aren't really us, and couldn't ideas come into those parts all of a sudden, like ideas come into…into'—he shot his arms out, showing the great white-gloved hands and hairy wrists; shot them out so swiftly to the journalist's throat that his eyes never saw them—'into *my hands!*'

The Little House

H. C. Bailey

Henry Christopher Bailey (1878–1961) worked for many years as a journalist for the Daily Telegraph. *Like J. S. Fletcher, he wrote historical fiction before concentrating on crime. His principal detective was Reggie Fortune, a doctor associated with the Home Office, who appeared in many short stories as well as in novels. Reggie became one of the most popular detectives of the 'Golden Age of Murder' between the two world wars, but Bailey's star has fallen since then, and his stylistic quirks mean that his work is nowadays an acquired taste. Nevertheless, he remains an interesting and unorthodox writer.*

For all his amiability, Reggie is tough-minded, as Bailey made clear: 'A cruel crime is to him the work of a pestilential creature, and he sees his duty in dealing with such cases as that of a doctor in treating illness. The cause must be discovered and extirpated. There is no more mercy for the cruel criminal than for the germs of disease.' Bailey's hatred of cruelty—especially the mistreatment of children—is evident time and again in his detective fiction, and this story is a striking example.

〉〉〉

Mrs Pemberton always calls it providential. She is not the only one. But when he hears her say so Mr Fortune looks at her with a certain envy. It is one of the few cases which have frightened him.

The hand of providence, Mrs Pemberton is convinced, sent her to Mr Fortune: and she only just caught him. He was, with reluctance, leaving his fire to go to Scotland Yard about the man who died in Kensington Gardens when her card was brought to him. 'I was to tell you Mrs Warnham sent her, sir,' the parlourmaid explained.

Mr Fortune went down to receive a little old lady dressed like Queen Victoria. She had a rosy round face and a lot of white hair. Her manner was not royal but very feminine. 'Mr Fortune! How good of you to help me! Mrs Warnham said you would.' She clasped his hands. 'You were so beautiful with her.'

'Mrs Warnham is too kind—'

'You saved her dear boy's life.'

'I hope it's nothing like that,' said Mr Fortune anxiously.

Mrs Pemberton wiped her eyes and the white lilac on her black bonnet shook. 'No, indeed. My darling Vivian is quite well. But she has lost her kitten, Mr Fortune!'

Mr Fortune controlled his emotions. 'I'm so sorry. I'm afraid kittens aren't much in my way.'

Her nice face looked distress. 'I know. That's what I said to Mrs Warnham. I told her you wouldn't want to be bothered with it, you would only laugh at me, like the police.'

'But I'm not laughing,' said Reggie.

'Please don't.' Her nice voice was anxious. 'She said I was to go and tell you I was really troubled and you would listen.'

'She was quite right.'

'I am dreadfully troubled.' She wrung her little hands. 'You see, it's the strange way it went and the people next door are so peculiar and I know the police don't take it seriously. The officer was quite civil and attentive, but he smiled, you know, Mr Fortune, he just smiled at me.'

'I know,' said Reggie. 'They do smile. I've felt it myself.'

'Don't they,' Mrs Pemberton sighed. 'Mrs Warnham said you would understand.'

'Yes. Yes. She's very kind. Perhaps if you began at the beginning.'

Mrs Pemberton had difficulty over that. Her nice mind worked on the theory that everybody knew all about her. The facts when patiently extracted and put in order by Reggie took this shape. She was a widow, her only son was a general commanding in India. She lived in Elector's Gate, one of those streets of big Victorian houses by the park. Her granddaughter Vivian, aged six, had lately come to live with her and brought a grey Persian kitten. With care and pains a garden had been persuaded to bloom behind the house. There Vivian and her kitten were playing when the kitten went over the wall. Vivian scrambled up high enough to look over and saw it in the paved yard of the house next door, saw a little girl run out of that house, snatch up the kitten and run in again. Vivian called to her and was not answered. Vivian came weeping to Mrs Pemberton. Mrs Pemberton put on her bonnet and called at the house next door. She was told that nobody had been out at the back, no kitten had come in, they had no kitten, her granddaughter must have made a mistake. They were not at all nice about it.

'Who are they?' said Reggie.

It was Miss Cabot. Miss Cabot and her father lived there. She did not really know them, only to bow to. But they had been there quite a long while, a dozen years or more, very quiet people, perfect neighbours, never the least trouble till this dreadful thing. But of course Mrs Pemberton couldn't let them take Vivian's kitten. She went to the police station and complained. And the police wouldn't take it seriously at all.

Mr Fortune, with her innocent blue eyes upon him, contrived to do that. It has been remarked by the envious that he has great success with old ladies. Mrs Pemberton went away murmuring that he had been so kind. He was left wondering how long she would think so. It did not seem to him a case over which the police would be persuaded to lose much sleep. But it had points which occupied his mind as he drove down to Scotland Yard.

He was late for his appointment. 'Ye gentlemen of England who sit at home at ease!' the Chief of the Criminal Investigation Department rebuked him. 'This luncheon habit is growing on you, Fortune!' He pointed an accusing finger at Reggie's girth.

'It wasn't lunch,' said Reggie with indignation. 'I've had a most difficult and interestin' case.'

Lomas sat up. 'Difficult, was it? Come along then. Avery's full of ideas about it. What was the cause of death?'

Reggie stared at him. Reggie looked at Inspector Avery and murmured: 'How are you?' Reggie stared again at Lomas. 'Cause of death? Oh, ah. You mean the man found in Kensington Gardens.'

'That is what I'm talking about,' said Lomas with some bitterness. 'That happens to be what we're here for.'

'Nothing in it. He died from exposure.'

'Exposure, sir?' Inspector Avery was disappointed. 'Just being out on a spring night?'

'Takin' the winds of March,' Reggie shrugged. 'He wasn't a good life. Badly nourished. Rotten heart. Nothing much good about him. Drug habits—and other errors. Who was he?'

'In the foreign restaurant business, sir. Lots of money. Quite a big man in his own line. Why he should go and lie down in the gardens to die beats me.'

Reggie shrugged again. 'He just got there and got no farther. No vitality in him. He'd go out at a breath.'

'You said something about drugs, sir?'

'Oh, he wasn't drugged when he died. Probably he had run out of his dope and life wasn't worth living. And the night frost finished him.'

Lomas lay back. 'That clears him up, Avery. You can go home to tea.'

But Inspector Avery was not satisfied. 'Mr Fortune was worried about something, sir?'

'Yes, yes. Most interesting case. Is Elector's Gate in your division?'

'That's right, sir.'

'What do you know about Mrs Pemberton's Persian kitten?'

Lomas put up his eyeglass. 'My dear fellow!' he protested.

Inspector Avery also felt a shock to his dignity. 'They don't come to me about kittens, sir.'

'They come to me,' said Reggie sadly. 'It wasn't you that smiled, then?'

'Sir?'

'Mrs Pemberton says she went to the station and they only smiled. Quite sweet but smiling. It hurts her.'

'I do remember hearing talk of it,' Inspector Avery admitted. 'The lady was so pathetic. But they did the usual, sir, sent a sergeant round to the house where the kitten was supposed to have gone in. The lady there said they hadn't got it. Her little niece did try to catch it, but it got away. We couldn't do any more.'

Reggie lit a cigar. '"Her little niece did try to catch it,"' he repeated slowly. 'Now that's very interesting.' He gazed at the puzzled inspector through smoke.

'It might be if I knew anything about it,' Lomas grumbled. 'Why this devotion to kittens, Reginald?'

So Reggie told him the story Mrs Pemberton had told.

'Very, very sad,' Lomas sighed. 'But kittens will be cats. What do you want me to do? Leave a card with deep sympathy and regret?'

Reggie shook his head. 'Not one of our good listeners,' he said sadly. 'Didn't you notice anything? You're not taking this seriously, Lomas. When Mrs Pemberton called about the kitten, Miss Cabot said no one had been out at the back. When the police called, she said her little niece did try to catch it.'

Lomas put up his eyeglass. 'Aha! The case looks black indeed!' said he. 'Miss Cabot didn't know about the little niece at first and found out afterwards. A deep, dark woman, Fortune,' and he smiled.

'Yes. A facetious force, the police force,' Reggie nodded. 'That's what annoyed Mrs Pemberton. And now do you mind thinking? A dear old lady calls very distressed and says Miss Cabot's little girl has caught her kitten and Miss Cabot says there wasn't any little girl and bundles her out. Why so curt? Because there was a little girl and there was a kitten.' He turned on Inspector Avery. 'Did your sergeant see the little girl?'

'No, sir. No occasion. He saw Miss Cabot, who was quite definite the kitten got away.'

'Yes. Marked anxiety to know nothing about the kitten. Elusive little girl.'

'My dear Reginald!' Lomas protested. 'There're a dozen obvious explanations. The woman doesn't like cats. The little girl is a naughty little girl. The woman doesn't want to be bothered.'

'No. She doesn't want to be bothered. That's what struck me.'

'I fear your dear Mrs Pemberton is a little fussy, Reginald.'

'That isn't your complaint, Lomas,' Reggie said sharply. 'Well, well. Sorry I don't interest you.' He nodded to Avery and went out.

Avery looked at Lomas with some concern. 'That's all right,' Lomas laughed. 'Wonderful fellow. But he will see things that aren't there.'

'I wish he'd been more interested in that death in the Gardens,' said Avery sadly.

'Too ordinary, my dear fellow, too ordinary for Mr Fortune.'

'This kitten business rather put me off.' Avery was thoughtful. 'I suppose we did ought to have seen the little girl.'

'Good gad!' said Lomas. 'You run along home and have a nice quiet night. I don't want my inspectors seeing things.'

But Inspector Avery did not go home. He had a conscience. He went back to the police station of his division. Mr Fortune is not at Scotland Yard thought to resemble the prim little inspector. But he also has an active conscience. He went to Elector's Gate.

It is maintained by Superintendent Bell and others of his devoted admirers that he has a queer power of divining the people behind facts, a sort of sixth sense. At this he would jeer. His own account of himself is that he is so ordinary anything which isn't ordinary disturbs him. From the first he felt the vanishing of the kitten was queer. But the only credit he takes for the case, which they call one of his best, is that he brought to it a perfectly open mind. The rest was merely obedience to the rule of scientific inquiry, that one ought to try everything.

What there was to try in Elector's Gate, he had no notion. He left his car by the park and strolled down that majestically Victorian street. The range of stucco fronts was broken on one side by an opening which led to a dead wall. In this recess two little red brick houses faced each other, neat and prim, hiding behind the solemn mansions of the rest of Elector's

Gate. At one corner of the opening stood Mrs Pemberton's house. Then Miss Cabot's next door—Miss Cabot's was that little house behind it in the recess. Reggie rubbed his chin. So Miss Cabot did not live in the way suggested by an address in Elector's Gate. Quite a small place, a one or two servant house. Nice and quiet too. No traffic. No neighbours on one side. Retiring folk, the Cabots.

Reggie rang Mrs Pemberton's bell. He had hardly been shown into her dowdy comfortable drawing-room when she hurried in crying: 'Dear Mr Fortune! But how good of you! Have you found out anything?'

'No. I came to see what I could find here.'

'Oh, but I'm so glad! Such a queer thing has happened. Let me show you.' She led him away into a little sitting-room and took from a drawer in the writing-table a piece of coarse blue paper. 'Look! When I came back from you that was lying in the garden.'

Reggie laid it on the table. It was a queer shape, it had a rough black line round the edges.

'You see! It's meant for a kitten!'

'Yes. It's meant for a kitten,' said Reggie gravely. 'Somebody drew a kitten on packing paper—with a piece of coal—and then tore the paper along the line—so as to make a paper kitten. Somebody who's not very old.' He shivered a little. 'Has your little granddaughter seen it?'

'No, Vivian was out when we found it. She has gone to a party. I was rather glad, you know. It seemed meant to tease her.'

Reggie folded the paper and put it in his pocket-book. His round face was pale and angry.

'Oh, did you want to talk to her about it?' Mrs Pemberton fluttered.

'I don't want anyone to talk to her about it.'

'I'm so glad. Vivian is only six, you see, and—'

'And nobody but Vivian has ever seen the little girl next door?'

'Why no. I never thought of it like that. No, indeed. We didn't know there was a little girl. Oh, but Mr Fortune, I'm sure there was if Vivian said so.'

'Did Vivian notice what she was like?'

'Poor child she was so distressed,' Mrs Pemberton apologized for her. 'She said it was a nasty, dirty little girl. Children will talk like that, you know, when they're upset. It doesn't mean anything.'

Reggie did not answer. He walked to the window. Mrs Pemberton's garden was a pleasant place of crazy paving and rock plants. The little house next door had a bare, paved yard.

'Oh, wouldn't you like to go out?' Mrs Pemberton cried. 'I could show you just where the paper fell.'

'No, I won't go out.' Reggie turned away. 'Good-bye, Mrs Pemberton. Don't let anyone talk to anybody. Don't let anybody know who I am. Don't let Vivian think about the business.'

'Mr Fortune! You mean there's something dreadful?'

'The worst of it for Vivian is that she's lost a kitten. There's nothing else to trouble you.'

'But you're troubled about something.'

'Yes, that's what I'm for,' said Mr Fortune. 'Good-bye.'

It was an hour which Lomas is wont to give to his club. He was before the smoking-room fire, he was pronouncing the doom of the last new play, when Reggie looked round the door, caught his eye and vanished. Lomas went after him at leisure. He was in the hall, tapping an impatient foot. 'My dear fellow, what's the matter? Has the kitten had foul play?'

'Come on,' said Reggie.

Lomas came on with his usual studied jauntiness, to be thrust into a car and driven away at Reggie's side. 'Why this stealthy haste, Reginald?' he protested. 'Why thus abduct my blameless youth? Miserable man, where are you taking me?'

Mr Fortune was not amused. 'We're going to Avery's damned police station,' he said. He spread out on his knee the blue paper. 'That's why.'

'Good gad!' Lomas groaned. 'A kitten! An infant's effort at creating a kitten. Oh, my dear Reginald!'

'Yes. An infant's effort at creating a kitten,' Reggie repeated. 'Exactly that. That's what frightened me. It was flung over into Mrs Pemberton's garden this afternoon.'

'Tut, tut. Not quite nice. Designed, I fear, to harrow the feelings of the bereaved.'

Reggie drew a long breath. 'Do you mind not being funny?' he said in a low voice. 'I'm scared.'

'My dear fellow! Oh, my dear fellow! What on earth for?'

'For the child who made that.' Reggie put it away again. 'My God, don't you feel it? There's something devilish in that little house.'

Lomas was shaken. Strong language is very rare on the lips of Reggie Fortune. 'I can't say I feel anything,' he said slowly. 'What do you want to do?'

'See Avery about the people. Here we are.'

Inspector Avery was still at the station. Inspector Avery showed no surprise at seeing them. 'I told you to go home, young fellow,' said Lomas.

'Yes, sir. I know. I was a bit worried about that kitten case.'

'Oh, you were, were you? Mr Fortune's got it very bad.'

Avery's keen face turned to Reggie. 'About the little girl, sir?' he said eagerly.

'Yes, yes. What do you know about the little girl?'

'Nobody knows anything. That's just it. It don't look right to my mind.'

'No. It isn't right,' said Reggie. 'Send two men to watch the house.'

'I've put one there, sir.'

'The deuce you have!' Lomas exclaimed.

'Good. But we'll have two, please. One to follow if the child's taken away. One to stand by whatever happens. The constable on the beat must keep in touch with them.'

'Right, sir. Just a moment.' Avery went out with visible satisfaction to give the orders.

'You won't mind me, will you?' said the Chief of the Criminal Investigation Department with some bitterness. 'But aren't you going rather fast, Fortune?'

'No. We're going far too slow.'

'I can't let you commit the police to anything, you know.'

'I know. You like a crime finished before you begin. Mr Lomas, his theory of police work. Well, I've committed you to watching a suspected house. Ever heard of that being done before?'

Lomas, however, kept his temper. 'You can have it watched, if it amuses you. But there's no reasonable ground for suspicion.'

'Oh my aunt!' Reggie murmured.

Avery bustled in. 'I've got that done, sir. Now is there anything else?'

'Yes, I'm not satisfied there's anything in it,' said Lomas sharply. 'What have you got against these people, Avery?'

'Mr Lomas touches the spot,' Reggie nodded. 'Who are these people, Avery?'

'Ah, that's what I'd like to know,' said Inspector Avery with relish. 'Very retiring people, sir. Kind of secluded.'

'Retiring be hanged,' Lomas cried. 'You've nothing against them but this stuff about a kitten and a girl.'

'Pretty queer stuff, isn't it, sir? Girl is seen taking a kitten, owner of the kitten is told nobody there saw it, we're told the girl did see it, like I said. But there's more to it than that.

Nobody round there knew there was a little girl in that house, nobody's ever seen her, nobody's heard of her.'

'Why should they?'

'Ever lived next door to a house with a child, Lomas?' said Reggie wearily. 'You notice it. But Mrs Pemberton lives next door and she didn't know there was a child in that house.'

'Nobody knew. They won't hardly believe it,' said Avery. 'How the deuce can you tell?'

Avery smiled. 'The men get to know the servants in their beats, sir. I've had some inquiries made. That house, there's Miss Cabot, handsome lady not so young as she was, and her father and an old married couple o' servants very stand-offish. Been there a dozen years, living very quiet, never any guests and as for a child—well, the servants in Elector's Gate laugh at it. If there is a child, they keep her in the cupboard, one of 'em said. But there is, Miss Cabot owned up to her.'

'There was a child,' said Reggie gravely, and took out the blue paper kitten.

Inspector Avery gasped at it. 'Kind of uncanny, sir.' He puzzled over it. 'I don't know what to make of it, sir.'

'There was a child in that little house wanted to create a kitten. She only had packing paper, she only had a bit of coal to draw with, she had no scissors to cut it out. This was the best she could do. She wanted to tell that other child next door something about her kitten. She threw this over the wall.'

'I don't like it, sir.'

'What's it all come to?' Lomas cried. 'There's a lonely child playing tricks.'

Reggie turned on him. 'There's a child in that little house living a queer life. And the only paper she can get hold of came off a parcel. It happened to be a parcel of scientific apparatus.'

'Are you sure about that, sir?' Avery cried eagerly.

'This is the sort of stuff they always use for glass.' Reggie fingered it. 'Look at the scrap of a label: 'ette & Co.' That's Burette's. First-class firm. What are the Cabots doing in that little house that they want glass from Burette's and keep a child shut up and squalid and miserable?'

'Squalid?' Lomas took up the word.

'The Pemberton child saw her. She was dirty.'

'The house is kept as clean as a pin, they say,' Avery frowned.

'Yes. Quite clean. And the hidden child is nasty and dirty.'

'And they're at some scientific work. Do you think they're doing experiments on the child, sir?'

'I don't know. I don't know anything. But I'm frightened.'

'We've got 'em all right, whatever their game is,' Avery said fiercely.

'And the child?' Reggie murmured.

Lomas stood up. 'You win,' he said. 'Sorry, Reginald. My error. Well, I haven't wasted much time. We'll go through with it now. First points to work on, who are the Cabots and what is it that Burette's send them? They're to be watched wherever they go, Avery—and their servants. I'll put Bell on to the case to-night. Report to him. We can deal with Burette's in half an hour in the morning. Anything else, Reginald?'

'Yes. You might find out if anybody lost a little girl some time ago.'

Lomas shrugged. 'We can look up the records. Rather an off-chance, isn't it? Whoever she is, they'd get hold of her quietly, these quiet people.'

'Oh, it isn't ordinary kidnapping,' Reggie said wearily. 'I say, Avery, for God's sake don't let the Cabots know they're being watched. They might do the child in to-night.'

'Good Lord, sir! No, I don't think it. If they know they're watched they'd know they couldn't get away with a murder.'

'We might not be able to prove murder. He's a man of science, Mr Cabot is. Warn your men to be careful.'

'We can't have a search-warrant on this evidence,' Lomas frowned. 'We can't do anything to-night. Begad, I'll have somebody get into the house in the morning.'

'Yes, I'm going,' said Reggie.

'My dear fellow!'

'You want a doctor to see that child.'

That night lives in the memory of Mr Fortune. He could not sleep. It is a condition otherwise unknown to him. He drove early to Scotland Yard and found Superintendent Bell fresh and hearty from a night watch.

'You've got something, Mr Fortune. They're queer folk, these Cabots. Where do you think they went last night? Night club, if you please. The Doodah Club. Yes, the old man and the woman living in that quiet style, they go off to the Doodah which is about as hot as we've got. Well, as soon as I heard they were there, I sent round one of the night club experts. He knew the Cabots by sight right enough. They're pretty regular at the Doodah. He made out that Cabot is known there as Smithson and runs some sort of an accountant's business in Soho. Nothing on our books against him. But we're looking into Smithson & Co., of course.'

'Yes. Have you found anything about a lost child?'

Bell shook his head. 'We've got no record of any to fit this little girl. Not many children get lost nowadays. I'm still looking about. But it's a bit of a long shot, sir.'

'I know. And Burette's?'

'Harland's on that, sir. We'll know all about their end of the business before lunch.'

'Now who's going with me to the house? I want some fellow with a nerve and lots of chat.'

Superintendent Bell looked at him with solicitude. 'Are you set on going yourself, sir? If you don't mind my saying so—'

'I do,' Reggie smiled.

'Well, I knew you would,' Bell sighed. 'You can't do better than Avery, sir. He's a little bull-terrier.'

'Yes. I thought that myself. But is he chatty?'

'He can keep it up. He's a politician.'

'Oh my aunt!' said Reggie.

Some time later two men in the uniform of the inspectors of the Metropolitan Water Board strolled into Elector's Gate. A street sweeper asked one of them for a match and over his cigarette remarked: 'All out but the woman servant. Cabot and Miss Cabot went off together. The manservant's gone to the pub.'

The water inspectors strolled on. 'That's a bit of luck, sir,' said Avery.

'No. That's Bell making a fuss down at Smithson & Co. I thought he would draw 'em. Your fellows said the manservant was in the pub till it closed. I thought he'd be on the doorstep when it opened—if master was out of the way. Now then. Lots of patter, please.'

Avery rang the tradesmen's bell of the little house. After some minutes the side door opened to display a gaunt woman in black who scowled. Avery was sorry to trouble her, but they were going over the water fittings. She objected. Avery was very sorry, regular inspection, must go through with it, the law was the law. 'Constable over there, mum, go and ask him if you like.' They were admitted. 'All the taps, please, then the run of the pipes, then the cistern. All fittings. Now then, where's the main?' He listened professionally. 'Ah, I thought so. Just have a look at the scullery, mate. Now, mum, upstairs if you please.' He swept her on before him, still talking about water and the law.

Reggie went into the kitchen, crossed to the scullery and turned on taps so that a noise of splashing water arose and came back to the kitchen. He called out, 'Taps running, mate,' and was answered: 'Right-o! Stand by the main,' and heard Avery in continuous eloquence and the servant grumbling. He went swiftly from room to room, such rooms as upholsterers furnish to their own taste, and saw no child's gear nor any mark that a child would make. He could hear Avery moving about upstairs arguing about the lead of pipes and having doors opened. Avery was not missing anything. 'Hallo, mate!' Avery called. 'Try the main tap. Now up to the cistern if you please, mum.' Talking, he climbed.

Reggie stood in the hall. There was a cupboard under the stairs. He opened that, saw darkness and in darkness the gleam of eyes. He went in. 'My dear,' he said gently. 'What's your name?'

There was no answer but panting breath.

He switched on an electric torch and saw a little girl cowering in the corner. Her face was pinched and dirty, she seemed to have no body so she was huddled shrinking from him.

'I'm friends,' said Reggie and reached for her hand. 'It's all right.' His fingers moved along the lean bare arm, about her neck. 'Where's the kitten?'

Her face shook. 'It died. It did. It's in the dust,' she gasped.

'I'm friends,' Reggie said again. 'Wait: just wait. It's all right.'

He shut off the torch and slipped out of the cupboard. The feet of Avery were heavy on the stair.

'I say, mate. Waste pipes at the back,' Reggie called.

'Have a look at 'em, Bill. Have a look at 'em,' said Avery and held the gaunt woman in conversation in the hall.

Reggie went out to the paved yard. While he watched the scullery window his arm slid into the dustbin and brought out a bass basket. He buttoned that into his jacket and came back calling, 'That's all right, mate. Shall I shut off the taps?'

'Shut 'em off, Bill. Come on. Good day, mum. Sorry to trouble you. Duty is duty.'

The gaunt woman grumbling about a lot of fuss and nonsense slammed the door on them.

A chauffeur came out of the bonnet of his car as they passed him. 'Watch it. Watch it,' Avery muttered and hurried on. It was hard work to keep up with Reggie.

He made for a post office and telling Avery to get a taxi shut himself into the telephone box. 'Superintendent Bell? Fortune speaking. What have you got about the Cabots? Somebody interviewing them at the Smithson & Co. Office? Let him keep 'em busy. Child in the house in danger of foul play. Yes. Death. Instant danger. I want a search-warrant quick. Right. At my house.' He joined Avery in the taxi and they drove away.

'No sign of the child, sir,' Avery began. 'But there was—'

'I saw the child,' said Reggie. 'She's still alive. I got the kitten too. He isn't.' The bass basket was produced and from it the stiff cold body of a Persian kitten.

'Dead, eh? Looks all right too. Did it die natural, sir?'

Reggie pointed to the eyes. 'No. Not natural. There isn't much natural in that house.' He shivered.

'What did they want to kill it for?'

'What do they want to keep the child in a dark cupboard for?'

'Had her there when we came, I reckon.'

'Yes. She's out sometimes. But she's used to the dark.'

'The devils,' said Avery heartily. 'But what is the game, sir? Scientific experiments? There was a room I couldn't get into. The woman said the master had the key. But I made out it had water laid on.'

'Yes. Laboratories have.' The taxi turned into Wimpole Street and stopped. 'You go on to the Yard and see Bell. I've got to look into the kitten.' But he went first to the telephone and talked to his hospital and asked for a certain nurse.

He was in his own clothes again, he was eating lunch without appetite when Bell came. 'Got the warrant?' He started up. 'Good. Where are the Cabots?'

'I couldn't say for the moment, sir. Our fellows had orders to keep 'em talking as long as they could. But there wasn't anything much to go on. That business looks all right. They do accountants' work for the foreign restaurants.'

'The man who died in Kensington Gardens,' Reggie murmured.

'Good Lord, sir!' Bell stared. 'He was in the restaurant trade, sure enough. And he was a drug fiend, you said.'

'Come on, come on. I want to get back to that child before the Cabots.'

But as soon as the car was moving Bell returned to his point. 'About the drugs, sir. What did you make of the house this morning? Avery said there was a room might be a laboratory. Burette's say they've been supplying Mr Cabot with laboratory glass ware for years.'

'Yes. I think we shall find a laboratory. The kitten has been drugged. The little girl has been drugged.'

'What's their game, sir? Some kind of scientific experiments with drugs?'

Reggie shuddered. 'They've been making experiments. Not for science. For the devil. They killed the kitten because she liked it. And she made her paper kitten to tell the other little girl it was gone. Silly, isn't it?' He laughed nervously. 'This car's damned slow, Bell.'

'We're almost there, sir.'

'Almost! Nice word, almost! My God!'

'Steady, sir, steady.' Bell laid an anxious hand on his arm. 'I want you, you know. I'll ask for the child first.'

The car swung into Elector's Gate and stopped just short of the recess in which the little house stood. As Bell sprang out a large man on the pavement met him. 'Both of 'em drove straight here from the office, sir. Only just gone in.'

Bell strode on to the house and rang and rang again. It was some while before the door moved. Then it opened only a little way and a man's flabby face with watery eyes looked round it. 'I am a police officer. I have a warrant to enter this house.' Bell pushed the door back and went in with Reggie and on their heels two large men followed. Silent and adroit they took the manservant and put him into the street where careful hands received him, and shut the door.

Bell stood still in the hall listening. There was a murmur of voices in one of the rooms. Its door opened. The gaunt woman came out. 'Well?' she said defiantly. 'Who may you be?'

The large men swept her aside. Bell and Reggie went into the room.

Two people were in it. A plump old man, neatly professional in his clothes, with a large brown face under his white hair, the face of a clever fellow who enjoyed his life, a woman darker than he, black-haired, black-browed, a woman on a large scale who might have been handsome before she was full-blown. She looked at them with gleaming eyes, and the lines were deep about her big mouth. She laughed, a shrill sound that began suddenly and suddenly ended.

'What is all this, gentlemen?' the man said.

'Mr and Miss Cabot, alias Smithson?' Bell inquired.

'My name is Cabot and this is my daughter. The name of my firm is Smithson & Co. But you have the advantage of me.'

'I am Superintendent Bell. I have a warrant to search your house.'

'Very good of the police to take this interest in me. May I ask why?'

'I want the child you have here.'

Mr Cabot looked at his daughter. 'Oh, our poor little darling,' he said slowly.

'What's her name?' Bell snapped.

'I beg your pardon?' Mr Cabot suddenly became aware of him. 'Her name? Why Grace of course.'

'Grace of course?'

'Grace Cabot, sir. I see that you don't know our family tragedy. My poor son's child is mentally defective. Practically imbecile. It has—'

'Since she came here or before?'

Mr Cabot licked his lips. 'I see that you have picked up some scandal. She was—'

'Where is she?'

'Oh, I'll find her for you,' Miss Cabot cried.

But Reggie was at the door first. He went before her into the hall. Miss Cabot followed him and calling 'Grace, Grace,' ran upstairs.

A moment he stood, then pointed and one of the large men went heavily after her. Reggie moved to the cupboard under the stairs and unlocked it and looked into the dark. 'I'm friends,' he said very gently. 'Come, dear. I'm friends,' And above Miss Cabot's shrill voice called 'Grace! Grace!'

He could see something faintly white. He heard a moan. 'It's all over now,' he said. 'All right now. Friends, just friends.'

'Grace! Grace!' the shrill voice came nearer.

'No, no, no,' the child sobbed in the dark.

Reggie went in, groped for her and gathered her into his arms. She was very frail. 'My dear,' he whispered. She was carried out into the light, shaking, trying to hide into her dirty dress.

Miss Cabot ran down the stairs, 'So you've found the dear creature!' she cried. Her arms shot out.

Reggie swung on his heel, offering her a solid shoulder. 'Hold her wrist,' he said.

The large man behind her had both arms in a grip that brought a scream out of her. A syringe fell tinkling to the floor. And Miss Cabot began to swear.

'Take the child out of this,' Reggie said fiercely. 'Take her to my place.' But she nestled up against him and moaned. 'All right. All right. Get the woman off.' Handcuffs snapped upon Miss Cabot's wrists while she bit and struggled and blasphemed. She was thrust out to the ready hands in the street.

'A beauty, she is,' one of the large men muttered.

And then silence came down upon the house. The child felt it, raised her wan starved face from Reggie's shoulder. 'Is she gone?' she murmured, looked about her, saw nothing but those solid, comfortable men and listened again to the silence. 'Weally, weally gone?'

'Really gone. She'll never hurt you any more,' Reggie said. 'There's only friends for you now. You're coming home with me. Nice home. But just wait a minute. This man will hold you quite safe.' He persuaded her to go to the arms of one of the detectives. 'Take her out into the air at the back. I shan't be long, dear.'

He picked up the syringe carefully, he turned into the room where Bell watched Cabot. The old man stood by the window looking out. His face was yellow. But he had control of his nerves and his voice. 'Perhaps you will tell me what all this means, superintendent?' he was saying.

'You'll hear what it means all right,' Bell growled.

'I see my daughter arrested—'

'Yes. She didn't like it, did she?' Reggie spoke to hurt.

The old man swung round. 'Who is this person, pray?'

'That's Mr Fortune.'

'Oh, the great Mr Fortune! Why trouble him with our poor affairs?'

'A pleasure,' said Reggie.

'So happy to interest you! And will you be good enough to tell me why you have arrested my daughter?'

'We've found a child in your house who has been tortured.'

'I suppose she told you so,' the old man chuckled. 'Good evidence you have found, Mr Fortune. The child's an imbecile.'

'We shan't use her evidence,' said Reggie. 'You won't torture her any more, Mr Cabot.'

The old man grinned. 'Is the child dead, sir?' Bell cried.

Reggie did not answer for a moment. He was watching the old man's face. 'No,' he said slowly. 'Oh no. Miss Cabot tried to kill her just now. But it didn't happen.'

The old man was breathing hard. 'A poor story, isn't it?' he sneered. 'You won't make much of it in court, Mr Fortune. Is that all, pray?'

'No. I should like to see your laboratory.'

'My laboratory? Oh, that's too kind of you! A very humble little place where I play with chemical experiments. Do you really want to see it?'

'We're going to see it,' said Bell.

'But I shall be delighted to show you.'

Bell looked at Reggie who nodded. The old man went upstairs between them. He unlocked a door and they came into a room fitted with a long bench and shelves and sink and much chemical apparatus. Reggie moved to and fro looking at the array of bottles, opening cupboards. There were many things which interested him.

'Ah, do you like that?' The old man came forward as he lingered by an arrangement of flasks and glass tube. 'It's a method of my own.' He became technical, skilled fingers moved demonstrating. 'And here,'—he turned away and opened a drawer and bent over it,—'here you see—'

'Yes. I see,' said Reggie and caught the hand that was going to his mouth.

Bell took the old man in his solid grip. The hand was opened and produced a white pellet.

'Not that way, Mr Cabot,' said Reggie. 'Not yet.'

'You go where your daughter's gone,' said Bell and called to the detective in the hall.

'I shall have some things to think of, gentlemen,' the old man grinned as he was led away.

'You will. And plenty of time to think. In this world and the next,' said Bell fiercely.

The old man laughed.

Reggie and Bell looked at each other and Reggie shivered and 'Thank God,' he said. He went to the window and leaned out to see the child with the big detective in the free air below.

'What was it the old scoundrel was doing here, sir? Kind of vivisecting the child?'

'Oh no, no. The little girl was a side line. He was making narcotic drugs—dope. Very neat plant.'

'Turning out dope? He's been doing that for years?'

'Yes, yes. Prosperous industry.'

'But why the child? For testing the drugs?'

'No. He wouldn't need her for tests. No. They drugged her for fun. You haven't got to the child's story yet. Lots of work to do yet.'

'What did you want me to work on, sir?'

'Go over this place. Go over the Cabot's past. Go and look for somebody that's lost a child. Good-bye.'

The big detective in the yard, nursing the little girl with awkward gentleness, grinned embarrassment at Reggie. 'I'm not much of a hand at this, sir. But she don't seem to like me to put her down.'

'No. Nice to have somebody to hold on to, isn't it, shrimp?' Reggie touched her cheek. 'Come and hold on to me.' He held out his arms. For the first time he saw something like a smile on that pinched face. She swayed towards him. 'Come along. We're going to a pretty house and a kind jolly lady and everybody there is waiting to love you.'

She was wrapped in a rug in Superintendent Bell's car, she sat on Reggie's knee watching the trees in the park rush by, the busy, gay streets. Suddenly she clutched at him. 'Is it weal?' she cried. 'Weally weal?'

'Yes. It's all real now,' Reggie said and put his hand over hers. 'Jolly things, real things.'

When the car stopped at his house, his parlourmaid had the door open before he reached it and watched him carry the child in with benign amusement which yielded to pity. 'Shall I take her, sir?' she said eagerly.

'She's all right, thanks. Has Nurse Cary come?'

'Here I am, Mr Fortune,' a small buxom woman ran down the stairs. 'Well!' She looked at the child. 'I'm going to like you ever so much. Please like me.'

It was difficult not to like those pretty pink and white cheeks, that kind voice. Again something like a smile came on the pinched, wan face.

'Oh, my dear,' said Nurse Cary with tears in her voice and her eyes. She gave a glance at Mr Fortune.

'Yes. I know,' he said quickly.

'I'm going to make you so beautifully cosy,' said Nurse Cary. 'You just come and try.' She took the child to her comfortable bosom.

Upstairs in the bathroom filthy clothes were stripped from the starved little body. But it was marked with something worse than dirt, punctured marks on the arms and here and there a rash. Nurse Cary looked at Mr Fortune.

'Yes, I know,' he said softly. 'They've been giving her drugs.'

'But why?'

'For fun.'

'Devils,' said Nurse Cary under her breath.

'Yes. I think so,' said Mr Fortune. He was handling the filthy clothes. They had been good honest stuff once. He looked close, made out a bit of tape with a name in stitched letters—Rose Harford. He turned to the child lying in the steaming water, Nurse Cary's hands busy upon her. 'Well, isn't it jolly, Rose?'

'So you're Rose, are you?' Nurse Cary smiled. 'My little Rose.'

'Mummy's Wose,' the child murmured.

Mr Fortune went out. The telephone called to Scotland Yard. 'Is that Lomas? Fortune speaking. The child is Rose Harford. There's a mother—or was. Get on to it.'

The small Rose in golden pyjamas was among many pillows watching Mr Fortune and Nurse Cary set out a farm on her bed. They were being very funny about the hens, but she did not laugh, she watched with grave, tranquil eyes and sometimes stroked her beautiful pyjamas. Mr Fortune was called away.

At Scotland Yard he found a conference, Lomas, Bell, Avery. 'My dear fellow! How's the patient?'

'She'll come through with luck. But it's a long job. They've made a vile mess of her.'

'Hanging's too good for that pair,' Bell sighed. 'And we can't even hang 'em.'

'No, no. I hope not. They'll feel what they get, quite a lot, the family Cabot.'

'They've done enough to be hanged more than once,' said Avery fiercely. 'You remember that fellow who died in Kensington Gardens, Mr Fortune? He used to get his drugs from Smithson & Co.'

'Yes. You were right about him, Avery. I ought to have seen there was something to work on there.'

Avery laughed. 'You're the one that's been right, sir. Do you remember how we made fun of you about the kitten? If you hadn't taken that up, the Cabots would be playing at hell now quite happy and comfortable.'

'Don't recall my awful past, Avery,' Lomas said. 'It's not respectful. My dear Reginald, you're a disturbing fellow. You're sapping the foundations of the criminal courts of this country.'

'No flowers, by request,' Reggie murmured.

'You don't work by evidence, like a reasonable man.'

'My only aunt!' Reggie was annoyed. 'I use nothing but evidence. That's why I don't get on with lawyers and policemen. I believe evidence, Lomas, old thing. That's what bothers you.'

'You do bother me. And now will you kindly tell me the whole history of the Cabot affair.'

'Quite clear, isn't it? Cabot was a skilled chemist. The trouble in the dope trade is always to get supplies. He solved that by getting raw materials and making the stuff. He found his customers at the night clubs and the restaurants he was in touch with through the Smithson & Co. accountant business. He distributed probably by post from Smithson & Co.'

'That's right, sir,' Bell nodded. 'We've got on the track of that now. Big trade he did. Lots of poor fools he must have sent to the devil.'

'Very neat, Reginald,' Lomas smiled. 'You omit to explain the little girl.'

'Oh, that's revenge. Revenge on somebody. Probably her father and mother.'

'Did you get that out of the child?' said Lomas quickly.

'No. The child mustn't be asked anything about the past. Haven't you got that clear? No evidence from her. She mustn't come into court.'

'My dear fellow, we don't want her. There's two of you to swear to attempted murder and your medical evidence. That's all right. I only wanted to know how you arrived at the mother.'

'Have you found her at last?'

'Three months ago George and Rose Harford were convicted of dealing in drugs. The man is a young accountant, the woman an actress. They lived in a Bloomsbury flat and often went to one of the Soho restaurants. A waiter there gave information that the woman had been offering drugs. They were arrested. Dope was found in the pockets of the man's coat and the woman's cloak. More dope in their flat. A clear case and they were both convicted. Some time after they were in prison the woman complained that she had heard nothing of her daughter, whom another actress in the flats had promised to look after. Well, the prison people had inquiries made for her. It took time. The actress had gone on tour. When they found her, her story was that Mrs Harford's sister had called and taken the child away. The prison authorities told Mrs Harford and she said she had no sister extant. So at last it worked round to us.'

'Yes. At last. And you've had the mother in jail three months— wondering.'

'Wondering if there was a God,' said Bell solemnly.

'Well—it's a black business,' Lomas shrugged. 'See your way, Reginald?'

'Oh, I suppose the Cabot woman wanted George Harford herself. When he married, she looked for a chance to make the wife suffer. She bided her time. And sent father and mother to prison and took the child and tortured her. Patient woman.'

'The Harfords have been out of England. The man had a job for his firm in France. They hadn't been back long before this happened to them.'

'What evidence have you got?'

'That drunken dog of a manservant wants to turn King's evidence. He says he was under the thumb of his wife—'

'I dare say he was. Have you seen her? Born brute.'

'His story is that his wife was turned on to plant the dope in the Harford flat. The waiter put the stuff in their coat pockets while they were at dinner. We can't lay our hands on the waiter. Several people have vanished since the Cabots were taken. George Harford says he knew Miss Cabot at a night club, never knew her well, just danced with her. His wife had never seen her. Both of them always declared they knew nothing of the dope.'

'Yes. Gross miscarriage of justice, Lomas.'

'Clear case,' Lomas shrugged. 'Nobody's fault.'

'Yes. That's very gratifying. Great consolation for the Harfords. Cheering for the child.'

'We'll do all we can, of course. Put 'em right before the world, set 'em on their feet again and all that. An unfortunate affair. Shakes confidence in police work.'

Mr Fortune stared at him. Mr Fortune drew a long breath. 'Yes. That is one way of looking at it,' he murmured.

'Thank God for the kitten, sir,' Bell said.

Mr Fortune turned large grave eyes on him. 'Yes, that's another,' he said.

'I'd call it all providential,' Bell said earnestly. 'Just providential.'

Wonder grew in Mr Fortune's eyes. 'Providential!' he said. 'Well, well.'

The Silver Mask

Hugh Walpole

Sir Hugh Seymour Walpole (1884–1941) enjoyed immense success as a writer, earning a knighthood and considerable wealth along the way, but he began to fall out of critical favour before his early death. At the height of his fame, he divided his time between the Lake District (setting for his popular family saga The Herries Chronicles*) and London. In the mid-1930s he spent time in Hollywood, where he wrote the screenplay for George Cukor's film of* David Copperfield. *Today, his work is strangely underappreciated.*

Walpole is not commonly thought of as a crime writer, but many of his finest stories display a macabre imagination, and his subject matter sometimes veered towards crime. He was a founder member of the Detection Club, and contributed to the Club's first 'round robin' detective story, Behind the Screen, *which was broadcast by the BBC in 1930. His posthumous novel* The Killer and the Slain *is a chilling masterpiece of psychological suspense.*

〉〉〉

Miss Sonia Herries, coming home from a dinner-party at the Westons', heard a voice at her elbow.

'If you please—only a moment—'

She had walked from the Westons' flat because it was only three streets away, and now she was only a few steps from her door, but it was late, there was no one about and the King's Road rattle was muffled and dim.

'I am afraid I can't—' she began. It was cold and the wind nipped her cheeks.

'If you would only—' he went on.

She turned and saw one of the handsomest young men possible. He was the handsome young man of all romantic stories, tall, dark, pale, slim, distinguished—oh! everything!—and he was wearing a shabby blue suit and shivering with the cold just as he should have been.

'I'm afraid I can't—' she repeated, beginning to move on.

'Oh, I know,' he interrupted quickly. 'Everyone says the same and quite naturally. I should if our positions were reversed. But I *must* go on with it. I *can't* go back to my wife and baby with simply nothing. We have no fire, no food, nothing except the ceiling we are under. It is my fault, all of it. I don't want your pity, but I have to attack your comfort.'

He trembled. He shivered as though he were going to fall. Involuntarily she put out her hand to steady him. She touched his arm and felt it quiver under the thin sleeve.

'It's all right...' he murmured. 'I'm hungry...I can't help it.'

She had had an excellent dinner. She had drunk perhaps just enough to lead to recklessness—in any case, before she realised it, she was ushering him in, through her dark blue painted door. A crazy thing to do! Nor was it as though she were too young to know any better, for she was fifty if she was a day and, although sturdy of body and as strong as a horse (except for a little unsteadiness of the heart), intelligent enough to be thin, neurotic and abnormal; but she was none of these.

Although intelligent she suffered dreadfully from impulsive kindness. All her life she had done so. The mistakes that she had made—and there had been quite a few—had all arisen from the triumph of her heart over her brain. She knew it—how well she knew it!—and all her friends were for ever dinning it into her. When she reached her fiftieth birthday she said to herself—'Well, now at last I'm too old to be foolish any more.' And here she was, helping an entirely unknown young man into her house at dead of night, and he in all probability the worst sort of criminal.

Very soon he was sitting on her rose-coloured sofa, eating sandwiches and drinking a whisky and soda. He seemed to be entirely overcome by the beauty of her possessions. 'If he's acting he's doing it very well,' she thought to herself. But he had taste and he had knowledge. He knew that the Utrillo was an early one, the only period of importance in that master's work, he knew that the two old men talking under a window belonged to Sickert's 'Middle Italian', he recognised the Dobson head and the wonderful green bronze Elk of Carl Mules.

'You are an artist,' she said. 'You paint?'

'No, I am a pimp, a thief, a what you like—anything bad,' he answered fiercely. 'And now I must go,' he added, springing up from the sofa.

He seemed most certainly invigorated. She could scarcely believe that he was the same young man who only half an hour before had had to lean on her arm for support. And he was a gentleman. Of that there could be no sort of question. And he was astoundingly beautiful in the spirit of a hundred years ago, a young Byron, a young Shelley, not a young Ramon Novarro or a young Ronald Colman.

Well, it was better that he should go, and she did hope (for his own sake rather than hers) that he would not demand money and threaten a scene. After all, with her snow-white hair, firm broad chin, firm broad body, she did not look like someone who could be threatened. He had not apparently the slightest intention of threatening her. He moved towards the door.

'Oh!' he murmured with a little gasp of wonder. He had stopped before one of the loveliest things that she had—a mask in silver of a clown's face, the clown smiling, gay, joyful, not hinting at perpetual sadness as all clowns are traditionally supposed to do. It was one of the most successful efforts of the famous Sorat, greatest living master of masks.

'Yes. Isn't that lovely?' she said. 'It was one of Sorat's earliest things, and still, I think, one of his best.'

'Silver is the right material for that clown,' he said.

'Yes, I think so too,' she agreed. She realised that she had asked him nothing about his troubles, about his poor wife and baby, about his past history. It was better perhaps like this.

'You have saved my life,' he said to her in the hall. She had in her hand a pound note.

'Well,' she answered cheerfully, 'I was a fool to risk a strange man in my house at this time of night—or so my friends would tell me. But such an old woman like me—where's the risk?'

'I could have cut your throat,' he said quite seriously.

'So you could,' she admitted. 'But with horrid consequences to yourself.'

'Oh no,' he said. 'Not in these days. The police are never able to catch anybody.'

'Well, good night. Do take this. It can get you some warmth at least.'

He took the pound. 'Thanks,' he said carelessly. Then at the door he remarked: 'That mask. The loveliest thing I ever saw.'

When the door had closed and she went back into the sitting-room she sighed:

'What a good-looking young man!' Then she saw that her most beautiful white jade cigarette-case was gone. It had been lying on the little table by the sofa. She had seen it just before she went into the pantry to cut the sandwiches. He had stolen it. She looked everywhere. No, undoubtedly he had stolen it.

'What a good-looking young man!' she thought as she went up to bed.

Sonia Herries was a woman of her time in that outwardly she was cynical and destructive while inwardly she was a creature longing for affection and appreciation. For though she had white hair and was fifty she was outwardly active, young, could do with little sleep and less food, could dance and drink cocktails and play bridge to the end of all time. Inwardly she cared for neither cocktails nor bridge. She was above all things maternal and she had a weak heart, not only a spiritual weak heart but also a physical one. When she suffered, must take her drops, lie down and rest, she allowed no one to see her. Like all the other women of her period and manner of life she had a courage worthy of a better cause.

She was a heroine for no reason at all.

But, beyond everything else, she was maternal. Twice at least she would have married had she loved enough, but the man she had really loved had not loved her (that was twenty-five years ago), so she had pretended to despise matrimony. Had she had a child her nature would have been fulfilled; as she had not had that good fortune she had been maternal (with outward cynical indifference) to numbers of people who had made use of her, sometimes laughed at her, never deeply cared for her. She was named 'a jolly good sort', and was always 'just outside' the real life of her friends. Her Herries relations, Rockages and Cards and Newmarks, used her to take odd places at table, to fill up spare rooms at house-parties, to make purchases for them in London, to talk to when things went wrong with them or people abused them. She was a very lonely woman.

She saw her young thief for the second time a fortnight later. She saw him because he came to her house one evening when she was dressing for dinner.

'A young man at the door,' said her maid Rose.

'A young man? Who?' But she knew.

'I don't know, Miss Sonia. He won't give his name.'

She came down and found him in the hall, the cigarette-case in his hand. He was wearing a decent suit of clothes, but he still looked hungry, haggard, desperate and incredibly handsome. She took him into the room where they had been before. He gave her the cigarette-case. 'I pawned it,' he said, his eyes on the silver mask.

'What a disgraceful thing to do!' she said. 'And what are you going to steal next?'

'My wife made some money last week,' he said. 'That will see us through for a while.'

'Do you never do any work?' she asked him.

'I paint,' he answered. 'But no one will touch my pictures. They are not modern enough.'

'You must show me some of your pictures,' she said, and realised how weak she was. It was not his good looks that gave him his power over her, but something both helpless and defiant, like a wicked child who hates his mother but is always coming to her for help.

'I have some here,' he said, went into the hall, and returned with several canvases. He displayed them. They were very bad—sugary landscapes and sentimental figures.

'They are very bad,' she said.

'I know they are. You must understand that my aesthetic taste is very fine. I appreciate only the best things in art, like your cigarette-case, that mask there, the Utrillo. But I can paint nothing but these. It is very exasperating.' He smiled at her.

'Won't you buy one?' he asked her.

'Oh, but I don't want one,' she answered. 'I should have to hide it.' She was aware that in ten minutes her guests would be here.

'Oh, do buy one.'

'No, but of course not—'

'Yes, please.' He came nearer and looked up into her broad kindly face like a beseeching child.

'Well…how much are they?'

'This is twenty pounds. This twenty-five—'

'But how absurd! They are not worth anything at all.'

'They may be one day. You never know with modern pictures.'

'I am quite sure about these.'

'Please buy one. That one with the cows is not so bad.'

She sat down and wrote a cheque.

'I'm a perfect fool. Take this, and understand I never want to see you again. Never! You will never be admitted. It is no use speaking to me in the street. If you bother me I shall tell the police.'

He took the cheque with quiet satisfaction, held out his hand and pressed hers a little.

'Hang that in the right light and it will not be so bad—'

'You want new boots,' she said. 'Those are terrible.'

'I shall be able to get some now,' he said and went away.

All that evening while she listened to the hard and crackling ironies of her friends she thought of the young man. She did not know his name. The only thing that she knew about him was that by his own confession he was a scoundrel and had at his mercy a poor young wife and a starving child. The picture that she formed of these three haunted her. It had been, in a way, honest of him to return the cigarette-case. Ah, but he knew, of course, that did he not return it he could never have seen her again. He had discovered at once that she was a splendid source of supply, and now that she had bought one of his wretched pictures— Nevertheless he could not be altogether bad. No one who cared so passionately for beautiful things could be quite worthless. The way that he had gone straight to the silver mask as soon as he entered the room and gazed at it as though with his very soul! And, sitting at her dinner-table, uttering the most cynical sentiments, she was all softness as she gazed across to the wall upon whose pale surface the silver mask was hanging. There was, she thought, a certain look of the young man in that jolly shining surface. But where? The clown's cheek was fat, his mouth broad, his lips thick—and yet, and yet—

For the next few days as she went about London she looked in spite of herself at the passers-by to see whether he might not be there. One thing she soon discovered, that he was very much more handsome than anyone else whom she saw. But it was not for his handsomeness that he haunted her. It was because he wanted her to be kind to him, and because she wanted—oh, so terribly—to be kind to someone!

The silver mask, she had the fancy, was gradually changing, the rotundity thinning, some new light coming into the empty eyes. It was most certainly a beautiful thing.

Then, as unexpectedly as on the other occasions, he appeared again. One night as she, back from a theatre, smoking one last cigarette, was preparing to climb the stairs to bed, there was a knock on the door. Everyone of course rang the bell—no one attempted the old-fashioned knocker shaped like an owl that she had bought, one idle day, in an old curiosity shop. The knock made her sure that it was he. Rose had gone to bed so she went herself to the door. There he was—and with him a young girl and a baby. They all came into the sitting-room and stood awkwardly by the fire. It was at that moment when she saw them in a group by the fire that she felt her first sharp pang of fear. She knew suddenly how weak she was—she seemed to be turned to water at sight of them, she, Sonia Herries, fifty years of age, independent and strong, save for that little flutter of the heart—yes, turned to water! She was afraid as though someone had whispered a warning in her ear.

The girl was striking, with red hair and a white face, a thin graceful little thing. The baby, wrapped in a shawl, was soaked in sleep. She gave them drinks and the remainder of the sandwiches that had been put there for herself. The young man looked at her with his charming smile.

'We haven't come to cadge anything this time,' he said. 'But I wanted you to see my wife and I wanted her to see some of your lovely things.'

'Well,' she said sharply. 'You can only stay a minute or two. It's late. I'm off to bed. Besides, I told you not to come here again.'

'Ada made me,' he said, nodding at the girl. 'She was so anxious to see you.'

The girl never said a word but only stared sulkily in front of her.

'All right. But you must go soon. By the way, you've never told me your name.'

'Henry Abbott, and that's Ada, and the baby's called Henry too.'

'All right. How have you been getting on since I saw you?'

'Oh, fine! Living on the fat of the land.' But he soon fell into silence and the girl never said a word. After an intolerable pause Sonia Herries suggested that they should go. They didn't move. Half an hour later she insisted. They got up. But, standing by the door, Henry Abbott jerked his head towards the writing-desk.

'Who writes your letters for you?'

'Nobody. I write them myself.'

'You ought to have somebody. Save a lot of trouble. I'll do them for you.'

'Oh no, thank you. That would never do. Well, goodnight, goodnight—'

'Of course I'll do them for you. And you needn't pay me anything either. Fill up my time.'

'Nonsense…goodnight, goodnight.' She closed the door on them. She could not sleep. She lay there thinking of him. She was moved, partly by a maternal tenderness for them that warmed her body (the girl and the baby had looked so helpless sitting there), partly by a shiver of apprehension that chilled her veins. Well, she hoped that she would never see them again. Or did she? Would she not tomorrow, as she walked down Sloane Street, stare at everyone to see whether by chance that was he?

Three mornings later he arrived. It was a wet morning and she had decided to devote it to the settling of accounts. She was sitting there at her table when Rose showed him in.

'I've come to do your letters,' he said.

'I should think not,' she said sharply. 'Now, Henry Abbott, out you go. I've had enough—'

'Oh no, you haven't,' he said, and sat down at her desk.

She would be ashamed for ever, but half an hour later she was seated in the corner of the sofa telling him what to write. She hated to confess it to herself, but she liked to see him sitting there. He was company for her, and to whatever depths he might by now have sunk, he was most certainly a gentleman. He behaved very well that morning; he wrote an excellent hand. He seemed to know just what to say.

A week later she said, laughing, to Amy Weston: 'My dear, would you believe it? I've had to take on a secretary. A very good-looking young man—but you needn't look down your nose. You know that good-looking young men are nothing to *me*—and he does save me endless bother.'

For three weeks he behaved very well, arriving punctually, offering her no insults, doing as she suggested about everything. In the fourth week, about a quarter to one on a day, his wife arrived. On this occasion she looked astonishingly young, sixteen perhaps. She wore a simple grey cotton dress. Her red bobbed hair was strikingly vibrant about her pale face.

The young man already knew that Miss Herries was lunching alone. He had seen the table laid for one with its simple appurtenances. It seemed to be very difficult not to ask them to remain. She did, although she did not wish to. The meal was not a success. The two of them together were tiresome, for the man said little when his wife was there, and the woman said nothing at all. Also, the pair of them were in a way sinister.

She sent them away after luncheon. They departed without protest. But as she walked, engaged on her shopping that afternoon, she decided that she must rid herself of them, once and for all. It was true that it had been rather agreeable having him there; his smile, his wicked humorous remarks, the suggestion that he was a kind of malevolent gamin who preyed on the world in general but spared her because he liked her—all this had attracted her—but what really alarmed her was that during all these weeks he had made no request for money, made indeed no request for anything. He must be piling up a fine account, must have some plan in his head with which one morning he would balefully startle her! For a moment there in the bright sunlight, with the purr of the traffic, the rustle of the trees about her, she

saw herself in surprising colour. She was behaving with a
weakness that was astonishing. Her stout, thick-set, resolute
body, her cheery rosy face, her strong white hair—all these
disappeared, and in their place, there almost clinging for
support to the park railings, was a timorous little old woman
with frightened eyes and trembling knees. What was there
to be afraid of? She had done nothing wrong. There were
the police at hand. She had never been a coward before.
She went home, however, with an odd impulse to leave her
comfortable little house in Walpole Street and hide herself
somewhere, somewhere that no one could discover.

That evening they appeared again, husband, wife and
baby. She had settled herself down for a cosy evening with
a book and an 'early to bed'. There came the knock on the
door.

On this occasion she was most certainly firm with them.
When they were gathered in a little group she got up and
addressed them.

'Here is five pounds,' she said, 'and this is the end. If one
of you shows his or her face inside this door again I call the
police. Now go.'

The girl gave a little gasp and fell in a dead faint at her
feet. It was a perfectly genuine faint. Rose was summoned.
Everything possible was done.

'She has simply not had enough to eat,' said Henry
Abbott. In the end (so determined and resolved was the
faint) Ada Abbott was put to bed in the spare room and a
doctor was summoned. After examining her he said that she
needed rest and nourishment. This was perhaps the critical
moment of the whole affair. Had Sonia Herries been at this
crisis properly resolute and bundled the Abbott family, faint
and all, into the cold unsympathising street, she might at this
moment be a hale and hearty old woman enjoying bridge
with her friends. It was, however, just here that her maternal

temperament was too strong for her. The poor young thing lay exhausted, her eyes closed, her cheeks almost the colour of her pillow. The baby (surely the quietest baby ever known) lay in a cot beside the bed. Henry Abbott wrote letters to dictation downstairs. Once Sonia Herries, glancing up at the silver mask, was struck by the grin on the clown's face. It seemed to her now a thin sharp grin—almost derisive.

Three days after Ada Abbott's collapse there arrived her aunt and her uncle, Mr and Mrs Edwards. Mr Edwards was a large red-faced man with a hearty manner and a bright waistcoat. He looked like a publican. Mrs Edwards was a thin sharp-nosed woman with a bass voice. She was very, very thin, and wore a large old-fashioned brooch on her flat but emotional chest. They sat side by side on the sofa and explained that they had come to enquire after Ada, their favourite niece. Mrs Edwards cried, Mr Edwards was friendly and familiar. Unfortunately Mrs Weston and a friend came and called just then. They did not stay very long. They were frankly amazed at the Edwards couple and deeply startled by Henry Abbott's familiarity. Sonia Herries could see that they drew the very worst conclusions.

A week later Ada Abbott was still in bed in the upstairs room. It seemed to be impossible to move her. The Edwardses were constant visitors. On one occasion they brought Mr and Mrs Harper and their girl Agnes. They were profusely apologetic, but Miss Herries would understand that 'with the interest they took in Ada it was impossible to stay passive'. They all crowded into the spare bedroom and gazed at the pale figure with the closed eyes sympathetically.

Then two things happened together. Rose gave notice and Mrs Weston came and had a frank talk with her friend. She began with that most sinister opening: 'I think you ought to know, dear, what everyone is saying—' What everyone was saying was that Sonia Herries was living with a young ruffian from the streets, young enough to be her son.

'You must get rid of them all and at once,' said Mrs Weston, 'or you won't have a friend left in London, darling.'

Left to herself, Sonia Herries did what she had not done for years, she burst into tears. What had happened to her? Not only had her will and determination gone but she felt most unwell. Her heart was bad again; she could not sleep; the house, too, was tumbling to pieces. There was dust over everything. How was she ever to replace Rose? She was living in some horrible nightmare. This dreadful handsome young man seemed to have some authority over her. Yet he did not threaten her. All he did was to smile. Nor was she in the very least in love with him. This must come to an end or she would be lost.

Two days later, at tea-time, her opportunity arrived. Mr and Mrs Edwards had called to see how Ada was; Ada was downstairs at last, very weak and pale. Henry Abbott was there, also the baby. Sonia Herries, although she was feeling dreadfully unwell, addressed them all with vigour. She especially addressed the sharp-nosed Mrs Edwards.

'You must understand,' she said. 'I don't want to be unkind, but I have my own life to consider. I am a very busy woman, and this has all been forced on me. I don't want to seem brutal. I'm glad to have been of some assistance to you, but I think Mrs Abbott is well enough to go home now—and I wish you all good night.'

'I am sure,' said Mrs Edwards, looking up at her from the sofa, 'that you've been kindness itself, Miss Herries. Ada recognises it, I'm sure. But to move her now would be to kill her, that's all. Any movement and she'll drop at your feet.'

'We have nowhere to go,' said Henry Abbott.

'But Mrs Edwards—' began Miss Herries, her anger rising.

'We have only two rooms,' said Mrs Edwards quietly. 'I'm sorry, but just now, what with my husband coughing all night—'

'Oh, but this is monstrous!' Miss Herries cried. 'I have had enough of this. I have been generous to a degree—'

'What about my pay,' said Henry, 'for all these weeks?'

'Pay! Why, of course—' Miss Herries began. Then she stopped. She realised several things. She realised that she was alone in the house, the cook having departed that afternoon. She realised that none of them had moved. She realised that her 'things'—the Sickert, the Utrillo, the sofa—were alive with apprehension. She was fearfully frightened of their silence, their immobility. She moved towards her desk, and her heart turned, squeezed itself dry, shot through her body the most dreadful agony.

'Please,' she gasped. 'In the drawer—the little green bottle—oh, quick! Please, please!'

The last thing of which she was aware was the quiet handsome features of Henry Abbott bending over her.

When, a week later, Mrs Weston called, the girl, Ada Abbott, opened the door to her.

'I came to enquire for Miss Herries,' she said. 'I haven't seen her about. I have telephoned several times and received no answer.'

'Miss Herries is very ill.'

'Oh, I'm so sorry. Can I not see her?'

Ada Abbott's quiet gentle tones were reassuring her. 'The doctor does not wish her to see anyone at present. May I have your address? I will let you know as soon as she is well enough.'

Mrs Weston went away. She recounted the event. 'Poor Sonia, she's pretty bad. They seem to be looking after her. As soon as she's better we'll go and see her.'

The London life moves swiftly. Sonia Herries had never been of very great importance to anyone. Herries relations enquired. They received a very polite note assuring them that so soon as she was better—

Sonia Herries was in bed, but not in her own room. She was in the little attic bedroom but lately occupied by Rose the maid. She lay at first in a strange apathy. She was ill. She slept and woke and slept again. Ada Abbott, sometimes Mrs Edwards, sometimes a woman she did not know, attended to her. They were all very kind. Did she need a doctor? No, of course she did not need a doctor, they assured her. They would see that she had everything that she wanted.

Then life began to flow back into her. Why was she in this room? Where were her friends? What was this horrible food that they were bringing her? What were they doing here, these women?

She had a terrible scene with Ada Abbott. She tried to get out of bed. The girl restrained her—and easily, for all the strength seemed to have gone from her bones. She protested, she was as furious as her weakness allowed her, then she cried. She cried most bitterly. Next day she was alone and she crawled out of bed; the door was locked; she beat on it. There was no sound but her beating. Her heart was beginning again that terrible strangled throb. She crept back into bed. She lay there, weakly, feebly crying. When Ada arrived with some bread, some soup, some water, she demanded that the door should be unlocked, that she should get up, have her bath, come downstairs to her own room.

'You are not well enough,' Ada said gently.

'Of course I am well enough. When I get out I will have you put in prison for this—'

'Please don't get excited. It is so bad for your heart.'

Mrs Edwards and Ada washed her. She had not enough to eat. She was always hungry.

Summer had come. Mrs Weston went to Etretat. Every-one was out of town.

'What's happened to Sonia Herries?' Mabel Newmark wrote to Agatha Benson. 'I haven't seen her for ages....'

But no one had time to enquire. There were so many things to do. Sonia was a good sort, but she had been nobody's business....

Once Henry Abbott paid her a visit. 'I am so sorry that you are not better,' he said smiling. 'We are doing everything we can for you. It is lucky we were around when you were so ill. You had better sign these papers. Someone must look after your affairs until you are better. You will be downstairs in a week or two.'

Looking at him with wide-open terrified eyes, Sonia Herries signed the papers.

The first rains of autumn lashed the streets. In the sitting-room the gramophone was turned on. Ada and young Mr Jackson, Maggie Trent and stout Harry Bennett were dancing. All the furniture was flung against the walls. Mr Edwards drank his beer; Mrs Edwards was toasting her toes before the fire.

Henry Abbott came in. He had just sold the Utrillo. His arrival was greeted with cheers.

He took the silver mask from the wall and went upstairs. He climbed to the top of the house, entered, switched on the naked light.

'Oh! Who—What—?' A voice of terror came from the bed.

'It's all right,' he said soothingly. 'Ada will be bringing your tea in a minute.'

He had a hammer and nail and hung the silver mask on the speckled, mottled wall-paper where Miss Herries could see it.

'I know you're fond of it,' he said. 'I thought you'd like it to look at.'

She made no reply. She only stared.

'You'll want something to look at,' he went on. 'You're too ill, I'm afraid, ever to leave this room again. So it'll be nice for you. Something to look at.'

He went out, gently closing the door behind him.

Wind in the East

Henry Wade

Henry Wade was the name under which a member of the landed gentry Sir Henry Lancelot Aubrey-Fletcher (1887–1969) wrote detective fiction of high calibre. In the early stages of his literary career, Wade was influenced by the work of the Irishman Freeman Wills Crofts, and novels such as The Duke of York's Steps *were accomplished but conventional.*

Several of Wade's best books featured an ambitious Scotland Yard man, Inspector John Poole. As his confidence grew, Wade took more risks with his writing, experimenting with different types of crime fiction. Mist on the Saltings *(1933) offers a poignant study in character,* Heir Presumptive *(1935) wittily anticipates the popular film* Kind Hearts and Coronets, *and* Lonely Magdalen *(1940) is a superb example of the police procedural. His short stories are almost equally varied and appealing.*

›››

'Got such a thing as tuppence on you, Poole?' inquired Superintendent Flackett. 'No, not for me—your bus fare to Lordship Lane Police Station. From there an intelligent constable will guide you through devious ways to No. 157, Baldwin Terrace, the residence of Messrs. Reginald and Herbert Gainly. In No. 157 you will find an open scullery window, an empty and mutilated safe, a bloodstained jemmy, and an elderly gentleman with his head caved in. Bring to bear upon this astounding mystery all your trained intelligence, your matchless powers of deduction—and report the result to me before tea. Your country needs you. Go.'

Inspector John Poole cursed the unimaginativeness of the South London criminal. Six weeks ago he had been transferred from 'Central,' at Scotland Yard, to the Southern Area (Headquarters, Camberwell), with the idea of broadening his experience; during that time he had had to deal with no fewer than three cases of the type described by his chief, and he was sick of them. The station-sergeant, Horridge, who, as he heard from his guide, was already on the spot, could, with his local knowledge, deal with this case as well, if not better than himself. Still, duty was duty.

Baldwin Terrace was a gloomy row of semi-detached houses in the network of 'desirably-residential' streets that lie between Dulwich Park and Peckham Rye. In front of No. 157 the usual group of morbid idlers was standing, feasting their imagination upon blank walls and the blanker face of a sentinel policeman. To him, Poole showed his 'authority,' learning in return that 'the sergeant' was in the kitchen, the 'corp.' in the living-room just to the left of the front door.

Declining P.C. Lorerley's offer of a personal introduction to the latter, Poole made his way through into the back regions, and soon unearthed Sergeant Horridge, who was combining pleasure with duty by drinking a bowl of steaming tea, evidently provided by the elderly dame he was questioning. Introductions being effected, the detective was soon in possession of the facts as far as Sergeant Horridge had ascertained them.

At 7 a.m. that morning, Mrs Gubb—the lady who came in daily to 'do' for the brothers Gainly—had, after getting the kitchen fire lighted, gone into the living-room to tidy up. There, crumpled up in an arm-chair by the fire, she had found the body of one of her employers—the younger, Mr Herbert Gainly; a terrible gash in the top of the head was enough in itself, without the added testimony of glazed eyes and ice-cold flesh, to show that the unfortunate man was dead.

Mrs Gubb had at once summoned a passer-by, and sent him in search of doctor and police—there was no telephone in the house; she had then gone up and awakened Mr Reginald. Gainly, the elder brother. Police-constable Lorerley had arrived before Mr Reginald had dressed and come down, and had taken charge of the situation, rightly excluding everybody from the room until the arrival of Dr Blonahay, who had made a superficial examination of the body, pronounced life extinct, and departed.

'Right,' said Poole, rising to his feet. 'That'll do to go on with. Now we'll have a look at the room.'

Sergeant Horridge led the way back into the front hall and, opening the door already indicated by P.C. Lorerley, ushered Poole into the living-room. Without even glancing at the body, the detective turned to his subordinate.

'Where's the brother?' he asked.

'In the parlour, sir—across the passage. Proper stew he's in—gutless little rotter, I should call him—not worth half of Mrs Gubb.'

'Talked to him?'

'Not much, sir—thought I might as well leave that for the specialists.' Sergeant Horridge, who had quickly realised his superior officer to be human, grinned at his little joke.

'Who are these Gainlys, anyway?'

'Stationers, sir, in Lewisham High Road—nice little business, I believe—but it's out of my area. I've never met either of the brothers before, sir, but I've heard a fair amount about them. It's a case of the fat kine and the lean, sir; morally and physically too, from what I've seen to-day. Mr Herbert the younger, was the strong man of the show, the brains and the brawn, too, from all accounts. Mr Reginald the elder, was a shadow of his brother—small in body and small in character—played second fiddle all along—in the shop and at home. That reminds me, sir; he's panting to be off to the shop—there's only a boy to mind it; at least, he's half-panting to go, and half afraid to move out of the parlour.'

'Well, he'll have to wait till I've been through him,' said Poole. 'Now, let's have a look round.'

Standing with his back to the door, Poole took a mental photograph of the room, as it appeared to anyone entering from the hall. On his left was the bow-window looking on to Baldwin Terrace; opposite him was the outer wall of the 'detached' side of the house, with a window looking on to the small space that earned it that distinction; on his right was the fireplace, in the wall that evidently backed on to the kitchen; behind him was the fourth wall, containing the door into the hall.

On the far side of the fireplace—the left, as Poole looked at it—pushed up close against the wall, was a small, timid-looking arm-chair; obviously, this was the chair allotted to Reginald, the meek elder brother. Almost directly in front of the fire—just enough to the right to be in a direct line between the fire and the door—was a large, leather arm-chair, dominating the whole room, as its accustomed occupant had dominated the life of the Gainly family.

The dominion of Herbert Gainly, however, was no longer of this world; over the back of the chair Poole could just see the top of a man's head, clotted with blood.

Poole stepped round to the front of the chair and gazed down at the dead man. Someone—the doctor probably—had closed the eyes, allowing himself that much of 'interference' with the exact *status quo* on which the police set such store; by that much he had reduced the horror of the dead man's appearance and Poole was able to realise that in life Herbert Gainly must have been a fine-looking man—tall, rather heavy perhaps, with large head, firm jaw, and well-shaped nose—all eloquent of the character to which his very chair bore witness. A small black moustache was the only feature of the man which was not in the major key—it gave just a touch of meanness to the whole; Poole wished that he had seen the eyes in life—for there alone does the soul of a man lie open to those who know how to read. Now, death had laid his hand upon them too long—their secret was hidden.

On Gainly's lap lay an open book—Dreiser's *The Financier*—its pages defiled by stains of blood.

Standing straight in front of the chair, the detective gazed down at the dead man.

'What do you think, Horridge?' he said. 'Did he move before he was hit? Did he half rise, or look round, or did he get it as he was reading?'

'Never moved, I should say, sir. Look at that book still on his lap and open. Blow's right on top of his head—shade to the right, as it would be if it was a right-handed man—and runs straight from back to front; if he'd turned, it would have caught him across the head.'

Poole nodded.

'I agree. He had no warning—never heard a sound. Now, what was it done for? Money, hate, love—one of the three.'

'Money, sir; that safe in the corner.'

'Yes, I noticed that—and a bunch of keys in the lock. Did he keep money there?'

'Couldn't say, sir; I didn't question the brother on that—thought I might put my foot in it.'

'Right, I'll tackle him presently. Now about who did it; any sign of an entry?'

'Oh, yes, sir; that's clear enough—window forced by the back door.'

'Show me.'

Sergeant Horridge led the way out into the hall and through the swing-door into the back regions; stopping by the back door, he pointed to the window at one side of it.

'That's the way in, sir; you'll see the catch has been forced—scratches on it—it's pretty stiff. On the wall outside you see marks on the brickwork, apparently where the man kicked his way up on to the ledge.' Poole confirmed these phenomena.

'No finger-prints anywhere, I suppose?'

'None that I've found, sir.'

'Nor footmarks on these asphalt paths, of course. What about the back door itself—was that locked?'

'Locked, sir, when Mrs Gubb came this morning. She takes the key with her when she goes and lets herself in in the morning.'

'So it's not bolted or chained inside?'

'I suppose not, sir.'

'The assumption, then, is that the man went out by the way he came in, raising the window behind him?'

'That's it, sir.'

'If he ever went out at all—or came in,' muttered Poole to himself. 'Now then, the brother—in the parlour, you said?'

Reginald Gainly was sitting on a stiff, straight-backed chair in the Victorian parlour when Poole entered the room. He had apparently been sitting there, doing nothing, not even reading, but waiting—waiting for the ordeal that was before him.

As he rose to his feet on the detective's entry, Poole saw that he was a bigger man than Horridge's description had led him to expect. Certainly he was thin and feeble-looking, with a pronounced stoop, but he was probably little less tall than his brother. His hair was thin and grey, his face white, with a harassed, worn expression that might be caused by the anxiety of the occasion, but was quite possibly habitual. He was clean-shaven—except that he had evidently not used his razor that morning—and his mouth revealed a set of miserable teeth.

Poole could, from his short glimpses of the two brothers, even though one was dead, visualise their joint lives—the ascendancy of the younger over his feeble elder.

'Good-morning, sir,' he said. 'I'm Detective-Inspector Poole. I've been instructed to investigate the circumstances of your brother's death. I'm very sorry to disturb you, but it's my duty to ask you one or two questions. I'll make it as little painful to you as I can.'

Gainly gave a nervous assent, and motioned Poole to a chair, resuming his own when the detective was seated.

'When did you last see your brother alive, sir?'

'Last night, officer, at about eleven o'clock. I usually retire about that time; my brother sits up rather later, often till twelve. Sometimes I hear him come up to bed, but not always, and I noticed nothing unusual last night—nothing at all. My room is right at the top of the house—I like to be high up—and I shouldn't be likely to hear anything. I'm a sound sleeper—Mrs Gubb will tell you that she often has a job to wake me in the morning—so I heard nothing at all—not a sound. I—I might have saved his life, perhaps, if I'd heard anything—but I'm not very strong.'

The man spoke in a quick, nervous manner, the words and sentences tumbling over each other. Poole got the impression that he had been rehearsing this speech during

the time that he had been waiting, and that now it splut-
tered out, almost too quickly to be intelligible. It was
perhaps natural that a man of this temperament should
be nervous in such an emergency, but Poole determined
to discover whether there was any deeper reason for his
condition.

'Was your brother in the habit of keeping money in that
safe, Mr Gainly?' asked the detective.

'Oh, yes; oh, yes, he was, I think.'

'But you are not sure?'

'Oh, yes, quite sure; certainly he did.'

'In what form?'

'Notes—and a certain amount of silver.'

'Banknotes or Treasury notes?'

The question appeared to take Gainly by surprise; he
hesitated before answering.

'Both, I think,' he said at last.

'You have actually seen him put money in the safe?'

'Yes; from time to time I have.'

'Then you have seen whether he put in banknotes or
Treasury notes?'

'I—I don't think I've noticed particularly. My impression is both.'

'You couldn't say what denomination—£5, £10, £100?'

'Oh, no, I couldn't say that.'

'A banknote, of course would be more difficult to dispose
of than a Treasury note—for the murderer, I mean?'

'Oh, yes, I suppose it would.'

'Perhaps that was why he left the banknotes.'

For a second, an expression of astonishment appeared
on Reginald Gainly's face; it quickly faded, however, to one
of mild surprise.

'Did he?' he said. 'How very surprising.'

'I mean that that would be an explanation if we were to find banknotes still in the safe,' explained the detective ingenuously. 'I haven't looked yet.'

Gainly shifted uncomfortably in his chair, but made no comment.

'Have you any idea of the amount of money in the safe?'

'None at all,' Gainly said shortly.

'Your brother never told you?'

'No.'

'Do you suppose that this money that he kept in the safe was money from the business?'

'I don't know—at least, not directly, of course. He always banked the takings from the business.'

'It is a flourishing business, isn't it?'

'Fairly; not very. But I don't know a great deal about it; my brother attended to all that. I only acted as his assistant in the shop—he gave me a salary. I am not very strong; my health has always been poor, and I found the strain of controlling the business too great. I handed the control over to my brother; he managed everything. I really know nothing about money matters. My wants are very few and simple.'

Again the quick, tumbling sentences, as if the speaker was anxious to disengage himself from the necessity of further explanation. Poole thought that it might be good policy to relax pressure now and re-apply it later, perhaps at some less guarded moment. He gave Reginald Gainly leave to depart to his shop and called Sergeant Horridge into the living-room.

'Experiment, Horridge,' he said. 'I want to find out what chance there was of Herbert Gainly hearing this chap get in; presumably it was dead of night and no other noise going on—traffic or anything. A break-in generally makes some noise, but Gainly seems to have heard nothing at all.'

'He probably wore rubbers, sir.'

'He had leather soles, anyhow, if he made those marks on the wall. But it's that window-catch I'm thinking of; it's a stiff one. First of all we'll try with the doors open; the swing door into the hall and the living-room door. I'll sit by the fire next to Herbert—you force the catch.'

With the doors open, the sound was very distinct—a sharp snap that must have caught the ear of the man in the living-room, however deeply immersed in his book. Even with the swing door shut, the sound was audible, but with the living-room door shut as well there was no sound.

'Now, Horridge,' said Poole, 'we'll do a full dress rehearsal. You go outside, climb up, snap the catch, open the window, get in, creep along, through the swing door, open this door, creep up and hit me on the top of the head with the hatchet. By the way, you haven't found the weapon, I suppose?'

'No, sir; nothing for certain—nothing with blood on it.'

'I didn't think you would. Well, off you go, and be as quiet as ever you know how.'

Poole had pulled Reginald Gainly's chair out from the wall and put it close up against his brother's, so that he had his back as much to the door as the dead man had—he did not want to move the body yet. He now sank comfortably down into it and as far as possible immersed his attention in a copy of the *Statist*, which he had found on the table. He had read several paragraphs of a summary of the past year's balance of trade, and in spite of himself was becoming interested in it, when a picture on the wall on his left suddenly lifted and flapped back against the wall with a loud clatter. Involuntarily Poole whisked round. There in the half-open doorway crouched Sergeant Horridge, a rolled-up paper in his hand and a positively murderous expression on his face.

'By Jove, that picture made me jump!' said Poole. 'Why did it do that, I wonder?'

'When I opened the door, I expect, sir. Pictures do do that sometimes if there's a draught.'

'Lucky for the murderer it didn't do it last night,' said Poole. 'I wonder what governs it?'

'Wind, I expect, sir.'

The detective stared at the eccentric picture.

'Go and fetch Mrs Gubb, Horridge,' he said.

In a minute the sergeant was back, accompanied by Mrs Gubb, the good lady thrilled at the prospect of further consultation.

'Were the windows shut like this when you came in this morning?'

'Oh, yes, sir; yes. I haven't touched nothing in 'ere.'

Poole nodded.

'Just come and stand by me a minute, Mrs Gubb; I want to see if you notice anything. Again, Horridge.'

Mrs Gubb approached the detective—and the body— with a look of awe, amounting almost to terror.

'It ain't goin' to move, sir, is it—the corp. ain't?'

Poole laughed.

'No, no; nothing to be frightened of. Just listen.'

Her nerves tensely strung in expectation of some horror— in spite of the detective's assurance—Mrs Gubb stood, her eyes glued upon the door. Slowly it opened, and instantly the picture flapped out upon the opposite wall. Mrs Gubb took no notice of it, but remained staring at the door with horrified fascination, which changed to mingled relief and disappointment when nothing more thrilling than the solid police-sergeant appeared. She looked questioningly at Poole.

'Didn't you notice it?' asked the latter, surprised.

'What, sir; the door?'

'No, no, the picture.'

'Oh, that! That ain't nothing. That often does that.'

'But when, Mrs Gubb, when? What makes it do it?'

'When the wind's in the east, sir.'

'Always?'

'Yes, sir, always when the wind's there—like it 'as been these last two days. The picture's 'ung wrong, Mr 'Erbert always used to say—rest 'is soul. The ring's nearly 'alf-way down the back, and that makes it 'ang forward mor'n it should. When the door opens, the wind seems to get be'ind it and make it jump—when it's in the east, that is.'

Poole looked at his subordinate.

'This is vital, Horridge,' he said. 'The wind's certainly been in the east for two days as far as I know, but we must be sure. Get on to the Meteorological Office and find out if it dropped in the night at all—if so, how much and what time. By the way, what did the doctor say about time of death?'

'He thought some time between ten and one, sir; wouldn't be more exact.'

'Wise man; now then, off to the telephone, quick.'

While Sergeant Horridge was away, Poole examined the safe. It was a simple affair, with a plain lock; only the key—not a memorised arrangement of letters—was required to open it. Poole wondered that a shrewd business man should keep his money in such an unburglar-proof affair. It was not large, containing only some ledgers and two small steel drawers.

The drawers were empty, but on pulling one right out, Poole found a crumpled ten shilling note at the back of the aperture. He examined it carefully, but could gain no clue from it. He was running his eye over the ledgers when Sergeant Horridge returned.

'Wind steady E. by N.E. all night, sir; exactly where it is now,' he reported.

Poole nodded slowly.

'That settles it,' he said, 'as far as I'm concerned. Either that door was never opened last night, or it was opened by someone whom Herbert Gainly took no notice of—and that could only be his brother. Personally, I'm inclined to think that Reginald did it as he was—apparently—going to bed. I as good as caught him out when I talked to him this morning—a point about banknotes being left in the safe—and I'd very little doubt about it after that. But that's quite a different thing to proving it. That picture business would be no use in court. We shall have to scratch our brains, Horridge.'

'What about motive, sir?'

'Money; what more d'you want? As a matter of fact, there's plenty of motive without that; psychological motive— that again is no use for a jury—inferiority complex; 'minority lobby' all his life to his successful younger brother, and all the rest of it.'

'But what's he done with the money, sir?'

'Hidden it, no doubt. We must go over this house with a pocket-comb. But he had plenty of time last night to take it any distance away and hide it.'

'But what'll he do with it, sir? If it's banknotes, they can be traced if he tries to cash them.'

'He said there were Treasury notes as well—though, of course, his evidence is of no value. You can't trace Treasury notes.'

'But, sir, those two little drawers wouldn't hold enough Treasury notes to make it worth while killing his brother.'

Poole's jaw dropped. He looked at the safe in silence.

'Good point, Horridge,' he said at last. 'Damn good point. Damn good point.'

He rose from his chair and walked about the room. After five minutes of this, he turned to the inwardly-gratified sergeant.

'Here, we must get rid of this thing,' he said, irritably, pointing to the body of Herbert Gainly. 'I don't want it any more; I know all about how it was done. Ring D.H.Q. and get an ambulance sent. I must think out this money business; I'll be in the parlour, or whatever he calls his plush and plaster room.'

Poole did not at once set himself to the task of thinking out the 'money business.' Instead, he took himself upstairs to the top floor, where Reginald Gainly's bedroom was located. It was a bare, characterless apartment; not exactly uncomfortable, but comfortless—a thin carpet, narrow brass bed, two or three dull pictures, no easy-chair, a fireplace that had obviously not had a fire in it for months. Although he knew that there was no chance of finding the money in it, Poole searched it thoroughly; he found neither money nor any sort of clue.

Descending to the next floor, he transferred his attention to the dead man's room—quite another affair—as comfortable as a bachelor's room can be.

'More motive,' he said to himself grimly.

One of the first things to catch his attention was an unframed photograph, perched on the mantelpiece, of the dead man himself. He was looking at it, and wondering why Herbert Gainly displayed his own photograph in a room which no one else was likely to enter, when Mrs Gubb appeared in the doorway.

'Speakin' likeness, ain't it, sir?' she said gloomily. 'Lucky thing now that 'e 'ad it done. Mr Reginald persuaded 'im to; said that now 'e was on the Guardians 'e was a public man an' ought to be pictured. Mr 'Erbert, 'e pretended to think it was nonsense, but 'e 'ad it done, and when it *was* done, 'e wasn't 'alf proud of it. Speakin' likeness, ain't it, sir?'

As Poole did not feel that he was in a position to judge of this, he replaced the photograph, and, shepherding Mrs Gubb out of the room, continued his search. Nothing of significance rewarded him. Mr Herbert Gainly had a well-stocked wardrobe and evidently enjoyed life; no doubt his success in business enabled him to do so.

Poole decided that he ought to consult Superintendent Flackett before further cross-examining Reginald Gainly. Leaving Sergeant Horridge in charge, therefore, with a promise to send a search party to help him go over the house, he returned to headquarters, taking the Gainly ledgers with him. Superintendent Flackett was out, and Poole, sitting down to examine them, soon became deeply absorbed.

After half an hour he put on his hat and took the books round to the Inspector of Taxes, whom he happened to know. Expert scrutiny of the books soon revealed what Poole had dimly divined; in order to defraud the revenue authorities, Gainly had kept an elaborate set of duplicate accounts, one for the benefit of the Inspector of Taxes, one showing the true state of affairs. Stock had been bought from a variety of wholesale houses, but only about two-thirds of these transactions appeared in the 'official' accounts; to balance this, only two-thirds of the sales were shown. A visit to Gainly's bank revealed the fact that his account there tallied with the 'official' accounts; as all cheques paid to him by purchasers would have to go through the bank, it was clear that the one-third sales not shown in the 'official' accounts were cash transactions.

The Gainlys' business was largely of a cash nature, and it was clear that Herbert had been in the habit of not banking the bulk of his till, but disposing of it in some other way. Some of it would probably be required to pay for the wholesale purchases which did not appear in the 'official' accounts—but where was the rest? The house-safe was clearly not big enough to hold the very large amount which Gainly, as his 'private' accounts showed, had accumulated. If it was neither in his bank nor his safe, where…? the answer flashed to Poole's mind—a safe-deposit!

After an hour's thought Poole felt that he had the details of the crime clear. Reginald Gainly must have known of the secret hoard and determined to get it for himself, at the same time revenging himself for all the slights he had suffered at his brother's hand. He had rifled the house-safe to lay a false clue; what he wanted was the key of the safe-deposit. How he had hoped to get the money was not clear, as he would have to fetch it in person and sign his brother's name. He must have been ignorant of the duplicated accounts or he would not have left the incriminating ledgers in the safe.

The next move was to have every safe-deposit in London searched. It was almost certain that Gainly would have hired the compartment in an assumed name; the only way to trace it was by issuing a description of him, and to support this it was decided to supply each officer making the search with a copy of the photograph Poole had seen in the dead man's room. On the following morning, therefore, Poole repaired to Baldwin Terrace and, assuming from the absence of the 'watcher' that Reginald Gainly himself was not at home— being presumably at his office—presented himself to Mrs Gubb. Explaining that he wished to make a further examination of the dead man's belongings, the detective betook himself to the comfortable bedroom on the first floor. The photograph was gone.

Smothering his annoyance, Poole summoned Mrs Gubb and demanded an explanation.

'Oh, the likeness, sir?' said the 'daily lady.' 'Mr Reginald's got that now—in 'is bedroom.'

Poole ran up to the top floor; there on the mantelpiece of the depressing bedroom, leaning against the mirror, was the dead man's photograph. Poole felt a shudder of repugnance pass through him—what sort of mentality must the man have to plant in his own bedroom the likeness of the brother he had killed!

However, psychology was no business of his—except as an aid to deduction. Making a note of the photographer's name and address, and leaving the print where he had found it, Poole left the house, after sternly cautioning Mrs Gubb to say nothing of his visit to anyone—not even to her employer. The photographer was soon found, the negative produced, and within a few hours copies issued to the divisions.

For three more days Poole waited, with growing impatience. By the evening of Saturday, March 2nd, the last report was in—a complete blank. The search had failed.

On Monday morning, Poole had another conference with the superintendent, and it was reluctantly decided that Reginald Gainly must be again interviewed in the hope of getting some admission from him. Poole took a bus to the end of Lewisham High Road, intending to walk till he came to the Gainlys' shop, which he had not yet seen. He had not got far when a man, emerging quickly from the post office, nearly knocked him over. The quick glimpse that the detective had caught of the man's face had suggested something faintly familiar; as he walked along, Poole puzzled his brain to think where he had seen it before. Then it came upon him that the man was Reginald Gainly! But how changed—almost unrecognisable. Poole had seen a stooping, sallow-faced, shifty-eyed creature who seemed—like his chair—afraid to come into the room. This man had burst out of the post office, walked vigorously away with his arms swinging; his back was nearly straight, his eyes were alive, there was colour in his cheeks. He was a different man!

All inside a week! What a deadly influence his younger brother must have had on him, crushing his spirit, almost his body. A week's freedom, independence, better food, perhaps, and he was a changed man—a— Poole stopped dead, a flood of understanding breaking over his face.

'By gad, that's it!' he exclaimed. 'By jove, I'm going to find where that money is!'

Turning out of the stream of foot traffic, Poole planted himself in front of a bookseller's window, apparently studying its contents, but really deep in thought. Why had the police not been able to find the safe deposit used by Herbert Gainly? For he felt sure that that was how the money had been 'banked'—if he were paying no income-tax on it, that was as good as a twenty per cent investment. But why had his colleagues failed to find it? Why the Metropolitan area only? There were safe deposits outside London—in every big town. Why should Herbert Gainly not have used one—and if so, which?

Poole's brain was racing now—his recording thoughts could hardly keep pace with it. If he had gone to some outside town, how would he go? By car? There was no evidence of his having one. By train—much simpler.

Poole went into the shop and bought a map of London, and on the back, 'fifty miles round London.' Where was he? Lewisham. Where was the Gainlys' house? Here somewhere, near Peckham Rye. What would their station be? Honor Oak? That only took one to the Crystal Palace. But Honor Oak Park, that was on the main line, London, Brighton, and South Coast, as the out-of-date map called it. London, Brighton—Brighton! A local train would take him to Croydon, and from there it was but an hour's run to Brighton—an easy afternoon trip, there and back—and miles from the prying eyes of the Metropolitan Inspector of Taxes.

The detective signalled to a passing cab. 'Honor Oak Park Station, quick!' he said.

Ten minutes later, Poole was on a hot trail. Booking-office clerk and porter at Honor Oak Park both knew Herbert Gainly well by sight; he frequently travelled from there to Brighton—about once every three weeks. It was easy to get a connection with an express at Croydon East—the train now signalled would connect with the 12.5 p.m.

Poole needed no further incentive—he had the photograph of Herbert Gainly with him—he would see to it himself this time. He bought a ticket, trundled slowly to Norwood and Croydon, and thence rapidly to Brighton. Calling a taxi, he asked if the man knew a safe deposit—he did—the Brighton Security, Marine Terrace. Within a few minutes, Poole was in the manager's office.

Dimly he felt as if he were fitting in the last few pieces of a jig-saw puzzle—they fell together so quickly, so automatically. The manager recognised the photograph at once; Mr Henry Godfrey, of East Grinstead, had had a safe in the company's depository—two safes, in fact—for three years— came about once a month, perhaps more often. When had he been last? Would inquire.

The manager rang a bell—a clerk appeared. When had Mr Henry Godfrey last been to his safe? He was there now; had come in two minutes ago, and asked for the check key—without which no safe could be opened.

There now! Poole's heart leaped.

'Quick!' he exclaimed. 'Show me the way; come with me, Mr Manager—tell your clerk to have the outer doors shut—we must get this man!'

Giving a sharp order, the manager led the way down a steep staircase, through a steel door at the bottom, opened by a uniformed porter, and along a narrow, electrically-lit passage with steel compartments on each side. Round a corner they came upon a man in the act of closing a steel safe door—a tall man with a black moustache.

'Mr Godfrey,' said the manager. 'This gentleman wants a word with you.'

Poole stepped forward.

'Reginald Gainly,' he said, 'I must ask you to come with me to a police station. I hold no warrant for your arrest, but I must detain you until one is issued. You will be charged with the murder of your brother, Herbert Gainly, on February 26th. I must warn you that anything you say will be taken down and used as evidence.'

As his hand touched Gainly's arm, the man suddenly wrenched himself aside, hurled Poole against the manager, and started down the passage. He did not get two yards; quick as lightning, Poole shot out his foot. Gainly stumbled over it, and before he could recover, Poole was on his back, bringing him crashing to the ground. The manager and porter joined in the scrimmage, and within a few minutes Gainly was secured.

That evening, after Poole had safely seen his prisoner lodged in the Camberwell Police Station, he reported his doing to Superintendent Flackett. The latter listened in silence to the bald narrative which was all that Poole allowed himself. When it was over, the senior officer held out his hand and firmly shook that of his subordinate.

'And now tell me why you departed from your instructions and suddenly went off on this happy thought,' he said.

'Well, sir,' replied Poole, 'it was like this. When Reginald Gainly came out of that post office, I didn't recognise him at first—he was so changed—grown—developed in every way. Even when I realised who he was, I had a feeling that it was someone else he had first called to my mind. Suddenly I realised who it was—Herbert Gainly, the younger brother, though without his moustache. Then it came to me why he had had that photograph of his brother on his mantelpiece—in front of a mirror. He was trying to make himself as like his brother as he could. Why? So that he could present himself at the safe deposit *as* his brother and get the money out. With a false moustache he could now pass any but close scrutiny. That put me on the safe deposit idea again, and somehow it worked out at once—to Brighton. He evidently slipped our 'watcher'; I must look into that.

'Of course, it was sheer chance that Gainly came for the money that day—we must have travelled by the same train and he walked from the station while I drove. They were all Treasury notes, sir; two safes stacked with them. Gainly had a suit-case with him; no doubt he was going to move the stuff gradually—too dangerous to leave it there. In a week or two he'd have got it all away; after that he'd have done a bolt. We only got him just in time, superintendent.'

The Avenging Chance

Anthony Berkeley

*Anthony Berkeley Cox (1893–1971) was one of the most inno-
vative crime authors of the Golden Age, and his ironic view of
justice influenced a host of successors. Writing as Francis Iles, he
published three excellent fictional studies of criminal psychology,
while as Anthony Berkeley, he created the breezy novelist and
amateur detective Roger Sheringham. Sheringham often comes
up with solutions to mysterious crimes which prove, despite their
ingenuity, to be mistaken.*

*'The Avenging Chance' is a deservedly famous whodunit,
and Berkeley liked the plot so much that he expanded it into
a witty and engaging novel,* The Poisoned Chocolates Case.
*A master of the unexpected ending, he came up with no fewer
than six different explanations of the crime in the book-length
version of the murder mystery. The correct answer proves to be
different from the solution in this story.*

When he was able to review it in perspective Roger Sheringham was inclined to think that the Poisoned Chocolate
Case, as the papers called it, was perhaps the most perfectly

planned murder he had ever encountered. Certainly he plumed himself more on its solution than on that of any other. The motive was so obvious, when you knew where to look for it—but you didn't know; the method was so significant, when you had grasped its real essentials—but you didn't grasp them; the traces were so thinly covered, when you had realised what was covering them—but you didn't realise. But for the merest piece of bad luck, which the murderer could not possibly have foreseen, the crime must have been added to the classical list of great mysteries.

This was the story of the case, as Chief Inspector Moresby told it one evening to Roger in the latter's rooms in the Albany a week or so later. Or rather, this is the raw material of Moresby's story as it passed through the crucible of Roger's vivid imagination:

〉〉〉

On Friday morning, the fifteenth of November, at half-past ten in the morning, Graham Beresford walked into his club in Piccadilly, the very exclusive Rainbow Club, and asked for his letters. The porter handed him one and a couple of circulars. Beresford walked over to the fireplace in the big lounge to open them.

While he was doing so, a few minutes later, another member entered the club, a Sir William Anstruther, who lived in rooms just round the corner in Berkeley Street and spent most of his time at the Rainbow. The porter glanced at the clock, as he always did when Sir William entered, and, as always, it was exactly half-past ten to the minute. The time was thus definitely fixed by the porter beyond all doubt. There were three letters for Sir William and a small parcel, and he also strolled over to the fireplace, nodding to Beresford but not speaking to him. The two men only knew each other very slightly, and had probably never exchanged more than a dozen words in all.

Having glanced through his letters Sir William opened the parcel and, after a moment, snorted with disgust. Beresford looked at him, and Sir William thrust out a letter which had been enclosed in the parcel, with an uncomplimentary remark upon modern trade methods. Concealing a smile (Sir William's ways were a matter of some amusement to his fellow members), Beresford read the letter. It was from a big firm of chocolate manufacturers, Mason and Sons, and set forth that they were putting on the market a new brand of liqueur chocolates designed especially to appeal to men; would Sir William do them the honour of accepting the enclosed two-pound box and letting the firm have his candid opinion on them?

'Do they think I'm a blank chorus-girl?' fumed Sir William. 'Write 'em testimonials about their blank chocolates, indeed! Blank 'em! I'll complain to the blank committee. That sort of blank thing can't blank well be allowed here.' Sir William, it will be gathered, was a choleric man.

'Well, it's an ill wind so far as I'm concerned,' Beresford soothed him. 'It's reminded me of something. My wife and I had a box at the Imperial last night and I bet her a box of chocolates to a hundred cigarettes that she wouldn't spot the villain by the end of the second act. She won. I must remember to get them this morning. Have you seen it, by the way—*The Creaking Skull*—? Not a bad show.'

'Not blank likely,' growled Sir William, unsoothed. 'I've got something better to do than sit and watch a lot of blank fools with phosphorescent paint on their faces popping off silly pop-guns at each other. Got to get a box of chocolates, did you say? Well, take this blank one. I don't want it.'

For a moment Beresford demurred politely and then, most unfortunately for himself, accepted. The money so saved meant nothing to him, for he was a wealthy man; but trouble was always worth saving.

By an extraordinarily lucky chance neither the outer wrapper of the box nor its covering letter were thrown into the fire, and this was the more fortunate in that both men had tossed the envelopes of their letters into the flames. Sir William did, indeed, make a bundle of wrapper, letter and string, but he handed it over to Beresford with the box, and the latter simply dropped it inside the fender. This bundle the porter subsequently extracted and, being a man of orderly habits, put it tidily away in the waste-paper basket, whence it was retrieved later by the police. The bundle, it may be said at once, comprised two out of the only three material clues to the murder, the third of course being the chocolates themselves.

Of the three unconscious protagonists in the impending tragedy, Sir William was without doubt the most remarkable. Still a year or two under fifty he looked, with his flaming red face and thick-set figure, a typical country squire of the old school, and both his manners and his language were in accordance with tradition. There were other resemblances too, but always with a difference. The voices of the country squires of the old school were often slightly husky towards late middle-age; but it was not with whiskey. They hunted, and so did Sir William. But the squires only hunted foxes; Sir William was more catholic. Sir William, in short, was no doubt a thoroughly bad baronet. But there was nothing mean about him. His vices, like such virtues as he had, were all on the large scale. And the result, as usual, was that most other men, good or bad, liked him well enough (except a husband here and there, or a father or two) and women openly hung on his husky words.

On comparison with him Beresford was rather an ordinary man, a tall, dark, not unhandsome fellow of two-and-thirty, quiet and reserved; popular in a way but neither inviting nor apparently reciprocating anything beyond a rather grave friendliness. His father had left him a rich man, but idleness did not appeal to him. He had inherited enough of the parental energy and drive not to allow his money to lie softly in gilt-edged securities and had a finger in a good many business pies, out of sheer love of the game.

Money attracts money. Graham Beresford had inherited it, he made it, and, inevitably, he had married it too. The daughter of a late ship-owner in Liverpool, with not far off half a million in her own right. That half-million might have made some poor man incredibly happy for life, but she had chosen to bring it to Beresford, who needed it not at all. But the money was incidental, for he needed her and would have married her just as inevitably (said his friends) if she had not a farthing.

She was so exactly his type. A tall, rather serious-minded, highly cultured girl, not so young that her character had not had time to form (she was twenty-five when Beresford married her, three years ago), she was the ideal wife for him. A bit of a Puritan, perhaps, in some ways, but Beresford, whose wild oats, though duly sown, had been a sparse crop, was ready enough to be a Puritan himself by that time, if she was. To make no bones about it, the Beresfords succeeded in achieving that eighth wonder of the modern world, a happy marriage.

And into the middle of it there dropped, with irretrievable tragedy, the box of chocolates. Beresford gave her the chocolates after the meal as they were sitting over their coffee in the drawing-room, explaining how they had come into his possession. His wife made some laughing comment on his meanness in not having bought a special box to pay his debt, but approved the brand and was interested to try the new variety. Joan Beresford was not so serious-minded as not to have a healthy feminine interest in good chocolates.

She delved with her fingers among the silver-wrapped sweets, each bearing the name of its filling in neat blue lettering, and remarked that the new variety appeared to consist of nothing but Kirsch and Maraschino taken from the firm's ordinary brand of liqueur chocolates. She offered him one, but Beresford, who had no interest in chocolates and did not believe in spoiling good coffee, refused. His wife unwrapped one and put it in her mouth, uttering the next moment a slight exclamation.

'Oh! I was wrong. They are different. They're twenty times as strong. Really, it almost burns. You must try one, Graham. Catch!' She threw one across to him and Beresford, to humour her, consumed it. A burning taste, not intolerable but far too strong to be pleasant, followed the release of the liquid filling.

'By Jove,' he exclaimed, 'I should think they are strong. They must be filled with neat alcohol.'

'Oh, they wouldn't do that, surely,' said his wife, unwrapping another. 'It must be the mixture. I rather like them. But that Kirsch one tasted far too strongly of almonds; this may be better. You try a Maraschino too.' She threw another over to him.

He ate it and disliked it still more. 'Funny,' he remarked, feeling the roof of his mouth with the tip of his tongue. 'My tongue feels quite numb.'

'So did mine at first,' she agreed. 'Now it's tingling rather nicely. But there doesn't seem to be any difference between the Kirsch and the Maraschino. And they do burn! The almond flavouring's much too strong too. I can't make up my mind whether I like them or not.'

'I don't,' Beresford said with decision. 'I shouldn't eat any more of them if I were you. I think there's something wrong with them.'

'Well, they're only an experiment, I suppose,' said his wife.

A few minutes later Beresford went out, to keep a business appointment in the City. He left her still trying to make up her mind whether she liked the new variety or not. Beresford remembered that conversation afterwards very clearly, because it was the last time he saw his wife alive.

That was roughly half-past two. At a quarter to four Beresford arrived at his club from the City in a taxi, in a state of collapse. He was helped into the building by the driver and the porter, and both described him subsequently as pale to the point of ghastliness, with staring eyes and livid lips, and his skin damp and clammy. His mind seemed unaffected, however, and when they had got him up the steps he was able to walk, with the porter's help, into the lounge.

The porter, thoroughly alarmed, wanted to send for a doctor at once, but Beresford, who was the last man in the world to make a fuss, refused to let him, saying that it must be indigestion and he would be all right in a few minutes. To Sir William Anstruther, however, who was in the lounge at the time, he added after the porter had gone: 'Yes, and I believe it was those infernal chocolates you gave me, now I come to think of it. I thought there was something funny about them at the time. I'd better go and find out if my wife's all right.'

Sir William, a kind-hearted man, was much perturbed at the notion that he might be responsible for Beresford's condition and offered to ring up Mrs Beresford himself, as the other was plainly in no fit state to move. Beresford was about to reply when a strange change came over him. His body, which had been leaning back limply in his chair, suddenly heaved rigidly upright; his jaws locked together, the livid lips drawn back in a horrible grin, and his hands clenched on the arms of his chair. At the same time Sir William became aware of an unmistakable smell of bitter almonds.

Believing that the man was dying under his eyes, Sir William raised an alarmed shout for the porter and a doctor. The other occupants of the lounge hurried up, and between them they got the convulsed body of the unconscious man into a more comfortable position. They had no doubt that Beresford had taken poison, and the porter was sent off post-haste to find a doctor. Before the latter could arrive a telephone message was received at the club from an agitated butler asking if Mr Beresford was there, and if so would he come home at once as Mrs Beresford had been taken seriously ill. As a matter of fact she was already dead.

Beresford did not die. He had taken less of the poison than his wife, who after his departure must have eaten at least three more of the chocolates, so that its action in his case was less rapid and the doctor had time to save him. Not that the latter knew then what the poison was. He treated him chiefly for prussic acid poison, on the strength of the smell of bitter almonds, but he wasn't sure and threw in one or two other things as well. Anyhow it turned out in the end that he could not have had a fatal dose, and by about eight o'clock that night he was conscious; the next day he was practically convalescent. As for the unfortunate Mrs Beresford, the doctor arrived too late to save her and she passed away very rapidly in a deep coma.

At first it was thought that the poisoning was due to a terrible accident on the part of the firm of Mason & Sons. The police had taken the matter in hand as soon as Mrs Beresford's death was reported to them and the fact of poison established, and it was only a very short time before things had become narrowed down to the chocolates as the active agent. Sir William was interrogated, the letter and wrapper were recovered from the waste-paper basket, and, even before the sick man was out of danger, a detective inspector was asking for an interview just before closing-time with the managing director of Mason & Sons. Scotland Yard moves quickly.

It was the police theory at this stage, based on what Sir William and two doctors had been able to tell them, that by an act of criminal carelessness on the part of one of Mason's employees, an excessive amount of oil of bitter almonds had been included in the filling mixture of the chocolates, for that was what the doctors had decided must be the poisoning ingredient. Oil of bitter almonds is used a good deal, in the cheaper kinds of confectionery, as a flavouring. However, the managing director quashed this idea at once. Oil of bitter almonds, he asserted, was never used by Mason's. The inspector then produced the covering letter and asked if he could have an interview with the person or persons who had filled the sample chocolates, and with any others through whose hands the box might have passed before it was dispatched.

That brought matters to a head. The managing director read the letter with undisguised astonishment and at once declared that it was a forgery. No such letter, no such samples had been sent out by the firm at all; a new variety of liqueur chocolates had never even been mooted. Shown the fatal chocolates, he identified them without hesitation as their ordinary brand. Unwrapping and examining one more closely, he called the inspector's attention to a mark on the underside, which he suggested was the remains of a small hole drilled in the case through which the liquid could have been extracted and the fatal filling inserted, the hole afterwards being stopped up with softened chocolate, a perfectly simple operation.

The inspector agreed. It was now clear to him that somebody had been trying deliberately to murder Sir William Anstruther.

Scotland Yard doubled its activities. The chocolates were sent for analysis, Sir William was interviewed again, and so was the now conscious Beresford. From the latter the doctor insisted that the news of his wife's death must be kept till the next day, as in his weakened condition the shock might be fatal, so that nothing very helpful was obtained from him.

Nor could Sir William, now thoroughly alarmed, throw any light on the mystery or produce a single person who might have any grounds for trying to kill him. The police were at a dead end.

Oil of bitter almonds had not been a bad guess at the noxious agent in the chocolates. The analysis showed that this was actually nitrobenzene, a kindred substance. Each chocolate in the upper layer contained exactly six minims, the remaining space inside the case being filled with a mixture of Kirsch and Maraschino. The chocolates in the lower layers, containing the other liqueurs to be found in one of Mason's two-pound boxes, were harmless.

❭❭❭

'And now you know as much as we do, Mr Sheringham,' concluded Chief Inspector Moresby; 'and if you can say who sent those chocolates to Sir William, you'll know a good deal more.'

Roger nodded thoughtfully. 'It's a brute of a case. The field of possible suspects is so wide. It might have been anyone in the whole world. I suppose you've looked into all the people who have an interest in Sir William's death?'

'Well, naturally,' said Moresby. 'There aren't many. He and his wife are on notoriously bad terms and have been living apart for the last two years, but she gets a good fat legacy in his will and she's the residuary legatee as well (they've got no children). But her alibi can't be got round. She was at her villa in the South of France when it happened. I've checked that, from the French police.'

'Not another Marie Lafarge case, then,' Roger murmured. 'Though of course there never was any doubt as to Marie Lafarge really being innocent, in any intelligent mind. Well, who else?'

'His estate in Worcestershire's entailed and goes to a

nephew. But there's no possible motive there. Sir William hasn't been near the place for twenty years, and the nephew lives there, with his wife and family, on a long lease at a nominal rent, so long as he looks after the place properly. Sir William couldn't turn him out if he wanted to.'

'Not a male edition of the Mary Ansell case, then,' Roger commented. 'Well, two other possible parallels occur to me. Don't they to you?'

'Well, sir,' Moresby scratched his head. 'There's the Molineux case, of course, in New York, where a poisoned phial of bromo-seltzer was sent to a Mr Cornish at the Knickerbocker Club, with the result that a lady to whom he gave some at his boarding-house for a headache died and Cornish himself, who only sipped it because she complained of it being bitter, was violently ill. That's as close a parallel as I can call to mind.'

'By Jove, yes.' Roger was impressed. 'And it had never occurred to me at all. It's a very close parallel indeed. Have you acted on it at all? Molineux, the man who was put on trial, was a fellow member of the same club, if I remember, and it was said to be a case of jealousy. Have you made enquiries about any possibilities like that among Sir William's fellow members at the Rainbow?'

'I have, sir, you may be sure; but there's nothing in it along those lines. Not a thing,' said Moresby with conviction. 'What were the other two possible parallels you had in mind?'

'Why, the Christina Edmunds case, for one. Feminine jealousy. Sir William's private life doesn't seem to be immaculate. I daresay there's a good deal of off with the old light-o'-love and on with the new. What about investigations round that idea?'

'Why, that's just what I have been doing, Mr Sheringham, sir,' retorted Chief Inspector Moresby reproachfully. 'That was the first thing that came to me. Because if anything does stand out about this business it is that it's a woman's crime. Nobody but a woman would send poisoned chocolates to a man. Another man would never think of it. He'd send a poisoned sample of whiskey, or something like that.'

'That's a very sound point, Moresby,' Roger meditated. 'Very sound indeed. And Sir William couldn't help you?'

'Couldn't,' said Moresby, not without a trace of resentment, 'or wouldn't. I was inclined to believe at first that he might have his suspicions and was shielding some woman. But I don't know. There may be nothing in it.'

'On the other hand, there may be quite a lot. As I feel the case at present, that's where the truth lies.'

Moresby looked as if a little solid evidence would be more to his liking than any amount of feelings about the case. 'And your other parallel, Mr Sheringham?' he asked, rather dispiritedly.

'Why, Sir William Horwood. You remember that some lunatic sent poisoned chocolates not so long ago to the Commissioner of Police himself. A good crime always gets imitated. One could bear in mind the possibility that this is a copy of the Horwood case.'

Moresby brightened. 'It's funny you should say that, Mr Sheringham, sir, because that's about the conclusion I'm being forced to myself. In fact I've pretty well made up my mind. I've tested every other theory there is, you see. There's not a solitary person with an interest in Sir William's death, so far as I can see, whether it's from motives of gain, revenge, hatred, jealousy or anything else, whom I haven't had to rule out of the question. They've all either got complete alibis or I've satisfied myself in some other way that they're not to blame. If Sir William isn't shielding someone (and I'm pretty sure now that he isn't) there's nothing else for it but some irresponsible lunatic of a woman who's come to the conclusion that this world would be a better place without Sir

William Anstruther in it—some social or religious fanatic, who's probably never even seen Sir William personally. And if that's the case,' sighed Moresby, 'a fat lot of chance we have of laying hands on her.'

Roger reflected for a moment. 'You may be right, Moresby. In fact I shouldn't be at all surprised if you were. But if I were superstitious, which I'm not, do you know what I should believe? That the murderer's aim misfired and Sir William escaped death for an express purpose of providence: so that he, the destined victim, should be the ironical instrument of bringing his own intended murderer to justice.'

'Well, Mr Sheringham, would you really?' said the sarcastic chief inspector, who was not superstitious either.

Roger seemed rather taken with the idea. '*Chance, the Avenger*. Make a good film title, wouldn't it? But there's a terrible lot of truth in it. How often don't you people at the Yard stumble on some vital piece of evidence out of pure chance? How often isn't it that you are led to the right solution by what seems a series of sheer coincidences? I'm not belittling your detective work; but just think how often a piece of brilliant detective work which has led you most of the way but not the last vital few inches, meets with some remarkable stroke of sheer luck (thoroughly well-deserved luck, no doubt, but *luck*), which just makes the case complete for you. I can think of scores of instances. The Milsom and Fowler murder, for example. Don't you see what I mean? Is it chance every time, or is it Providence avenging the victim?'

'Well, Mr Sheringham,' said Chief Inspector Moresby, 'to tell you the truth, I don't mind what it is, so long as it lets me put my hands on the right man.'

'Moresby,' laughed Roger, 'you're hopeless. I thought I was raising such a fruitful topic. Very well, we'll change the subject. Tell me why in the name of goodness the murderess (assuming that you're right every time) used nitrobenzene, of all surprising things?'

'There, Mr Sheringham,' Moresby admitted, 'you've got me. I never even knew it was so poisonous. It's used a good deal in various manufactures, I'm told, confectionery for instance, and as a solvent; and its chief use is in making aniline dyes. But it's never reckoned among the ordinary poisons. I suppose she used it because it's so easy to get hold of.'

'Isn't there a line of attack there?' Roger suggested. 'The inference is that the criminal is a woman who is employed in some factory or business, the odds favouring an aniline dye establishment, and who knew of the poisonous properties of nitrobenzene because the employees have been warned about it. Couldn't you use that as a point of departure?'

'To interrogate every employee of every establishment in this country that uses nitrobenzene in any of its processes, Mr Sheringham? Come, sir. Even if you're right the chances are we should all be dead before we reached the guilty person.'

'I suppose we should,' regretted Roger, who had thought he was being rather clever.

They discussed the case for some time longer, but nothing further of importance emerged. Naturally it had not been possible to trace the machine on which the forged letter had been typed, nor to ascertain how the piece of Mason's notepaper had come into the criminal's possession. With regard to this last point, Roger suggested, as an outside possibility, that it might not have been Mason's notepaper at all but a piece with a heading especially printed for the occasion, which might give a pointer towards a printer as being concerned in the crime. He was chagrined to learn that this brilliant idea had occurred to Moresby as a mere matter of routine, and the notepaper had been definitely identified by Merton's, the printers concerned, as their own work. He produced the piece of paper for Roger's inspection, and the latter commented on the fact that the edges were distinctly yellowed, which seemed to suggest that the sheet was an old one.

Another idea occurred to Roger. 'I shouldn't be surprised, Moresby,' he said, with a certain impressiveness, 'if the murderer never *tried* to get hold of this sheet at all. In other words, it was the chance possession of it which suggested the whole method of the crime.'

It appeared that this notion had also occurred to Moresby. If it were true, it only helped to make the crime more insoluble than before. From the wrapper, a piece of ordinary brown paper with Sir William's name and address hand-printed on it in large capitals, there was nothing at all to be learnt beyond the fact that the parcel had been posted at the office in Southampton Street, Strand, between the hours of eight-thirty and nine-thirty p.m. Except for the chocolates themselves, which seemed to offer no further help, there was nothing else whatsoever in the way of material clues. Whoever coveted Sir William's life had certainly no intention of purchasing it with his or her own.

If Moresby had paid his visit to Roger Sheringham with any hope of tapping that gentleman's brains, he went away disappointed. Rack them as he might, Roger had been unable to throw any effective light on the affair.

To tell the truth Roger was inclined to agree with the chief inspector's conclusion, that the attempted murder of Sir William Anstruther and the actual death of the unfortunate Mrs Beresford must be laid to the account of some irresponsible criminal lunatic, actuated by a religious or social fanaticism. For this reason, although he thought about it a good deal during the next few days, he made no attempt to take the case in hand. It was the sort of affair, necessitating endless enquiries, that a private person would have neither the time nor the authority to carry out, which can only be handled by the official police. Roger's interest in it was purely academic.

It was hazard, two chance encounters, which translated this interest from the academic to the personal.

The first was at the Rainbow Club itself. Roger was lunching there with a member, and inevitably the conversation turned on the recent tragedy. Roger's host was inclined to plume himself on the fact that he had been at school with Beresford and so had a more intimate connection with the affair than his fellow members. One gathered, indeed, that the connection was a trifle closer even than Sir William's. Roger's host was that kind of man.

'And just as it happened I saw the Beresfords in their box at the Imperial that night. Noticed them before the curtain went up for the first act. I had a stall. I may even have seen them making that fatal bet.' Roger's host took on an even more portentous aspect. One gathered that it was by no means improbably due to his presence in the stalls that the disastrous bet was made at all.

As they were talking a man entered the dining room and walked past their table. Roger's host became abruptly silent. The newcomer threw him a slight nod and passed on. The other leant forward across the table.

'Talk of the devil! That was Beresford himself. First time I've seen him in here since it happened. Poor devil! It knocked him all to pieces, you know. I've never seen a man so devoted to his wife. Did you notice how ghastly he looked?' All this in a hushed, tactful whisper, that would have been far more obvious to the subject of it, had he happened to have been looking their way, than the loudest shouts.

Roger nodded shortly. He had caught a glimpse of Beresford's face and been shocked by it even before he learned his identity. It was haggard and pale and seamed with lines of bitterness, prematurely old. 'Hang it all,' he now thought, much moved, 'Moresby really must make an effort. If the murderer isn't found soon it'll kill that chap too.'

He said aloud, somewhat at random and certainly without tact: 'He didn't exactly fall on your neck. I thought you two were such bosom friends?'

His host looked uncomfortable. 'Oh, well, you must make allowances, just at present,' he hedged. 'Besides, we weren't *bosom* friends exactly. As a matter of fact he was a year or two senior to me. Or it might have been three. We were in different houses, too. And he was on the modern side of course, while I was a classical bird.'

'I see,' said Roger, quite gravely, realising that his host's actual contact with Beresford at school had been limited, at the very most, to that of the latter's toe with the former's hinder parts.

He left it at that.

The next encounter took place the following morning. Roger was in Bond Street, about to go through the distressing ordeal of buying a new hat. Along the pavement he suddenly saw bearing down on him Mrs Verreker-le-Flemming. Mrs Verreker-le-Flemming was small, exquisite, rich and a widow, and she sat at Roger's feet whenever he gave her the opportunity. But she talked. She talked, in fact, and talked, and talked. And Roger, who rather liked talking himself, could not bear it. He tried to dart across the road, but there was no opening stream. He was cornered.

Mrs Verreker-le-Flemming fastened on him gladly. 'Oh, Mr Sheringham! *Just* the person I wanted to see. Mr Sheringham, *do* tell me. In confidence. *Are* you taking up this dreadful business of *poor* Joan Beresford's death? Oh, don't—*don't* tell me you're not!' Roger was trying to do so, but she gave him no chance. 'It's too dreadful. You must—you simply *must* find out who sent those chocolates to that dreadful Sir William Anstruther. You *are* going to, aren't you?'

Roger, the frozen and imbecile grin of civilised intercourse on his face, again tried to get a word in; without result.

'I was horrified when I heard of it—simply horrified. You see, Joan and I were such *very* close friends. Quite intimate. We were at school together—Did you say anything, Mr Sheringham?'

Roger, who had allowed a faint groan to escape him, hastily shook his head.

'And the awful thing, the truly *terrible* thing is that Joan brought the whole business on herself. Isn't that *appalling*?'

Roger no longer wanted to escape. 'What did you say?' he managed to insert, incredulously.

'I suppose it's what they call tragic irony. Certainly it was tragic enough, and I've never heard anything so terribly ironical. You know about that bet she made with her husband of course, so that he had to get her a box of chocolates, and if he hadn't Sir William would never have given him the poisoned ones and he'd have eaten them and died himself and good riddance? Well, Mr Sheringham—' Mrs Verreker-le-Flemming lowered her voice to a conspirator's whisper and glanced about her in the approved manner. 'I've never told anybody else this, but I'm telling you because I know you'll appreciate it. You're interested in irony, aren't you?'

'I adore it,' Roger said mechanically. 'Yes?'

'Well—*Joan wasn't playing fair!*'

'How do you mean?' Roger asked, bewildered.

Mrs Verreker-le-Flemming was artlessly pleased with her sensation. 'Why, she ought not to have made that bet at all. It was a judgment on her. A terrible judgment, of course, but the appalling thing is that she did bring it on herself, in a way. She'd seen the play before. We went together, the very first week it was on. She *knew* who the villain was all the time.'

'By Jove!' Roger was as impressed as Mrs Verreker-le-Flemming could have wished. 'Chance the Avenger, with a vengeance. We're none of us immune from it.'

'Poetic justice, you mean?' twittered Mrs Verreker-le-Flemming, to whom these remarks had been somewhat obscure. 'Yes, it was, wasn't it? Though really, the punishment was out of all proportion to the crime. Good gracious, if every woman who cheats over a bet is to be killed for it, where would any of us be?' demanded Mrs Verreker-le-Flemming with unconscious frankness.

'Umph!' said Roger, tactfully.

'But Joan Beresford! That's the extraordinary thing. I should never have thought Joan *would* do a thing like that. She was such a *nice* girl. A little close with money, of course, considering how well off they were, but that isn't anything. Of course it was only fun, and pulling her husband's leg, but I always used to think Joan was such a *serious* girl, Mr Sheringham. I mean, ordinary people don't talk about honour, and truth, and playing the game. Well, she paid herself for not playing the game, poor girl, didn't she? Still, it all goes to show the truth of the old saying, doesn't it?'

'What old saying?' said Roger, hypnotised by this flow.

'Why, that still waters run deep. Joan must have been deep, I'm afraid.' Mrs Verreker-le-Flemming sighed. It was evidently a social error to be deep. 'I mean, she certainly took me in. She can't have been quite so honourable and truthful as she was always pretending, can she? And I can't help wondering whether a girl who'd deceive her husband in a little thing like that might not—oh, well, I don't want to say anything against poor Joan now she's dead, poor darling, but she can't have been quite such a plaster saint after all, can she? I mean,' said Mrs Verreker-le-Flemming, in hasty extenuation of these suggestions, 'I do think psychology is so *very* interesting, don't you, Mr Sheringham?'

'Sometimes, very,' Roger agreed gravely. 'But you mentioned Sir William Anstruther just now. Do you know him, too?'

'I used to,' Mrs Verreker-le-Flemming replied, with an expression of positive vindictiveness. 'Horrible man! Always running after some woman or other. And when he's tired of her, just drops her—biff!—like that. At least,' added Mrs Verreker-le-Flemming hastily, 'so I've heard.'

'And what happens if she refuses to be dropped?'

'Oh, dear, I'm sure I don't know. I suppose you've heard the latest?' Mrs Verreker-le-Flemming hurried on, perhaps a trifle more pink than the delicate aids to nature on her cheeks would have warranted. 'He's taken up with that Bryce woman now. You know, the wife of the oil man, or petrol, or whatever he made his money in. It began about three weeks ago. You'd have thought that dreadful business of being responsible, in a way, for poor Joan Beresford's death would have sobered him up a little, wouldn't you? But not a bit of it; he—'

'I suppose Sir William knew Mrs Beresford pretty well?' Roger remarked casually.

Mrs Verreker-le-Flemming stared at him. 'Sir William? No, he didn't know Joan at all. I'm sure he didn't. I've never heard her mention him.'

Roger shot off on another tack. 'What a pity you weren't at the Imperial with the Beresfords that evening. She'd never have made that bet if you had been.' Roger looked extremely innocent. 'You weren't, I suppose?'

'I?' queried Mrs Verreker-le-Flemming in surprise. 'Good gracious, no. I was at the new revue at the Pavilion. Lady Gavelstoke had a box and asked me to join her party.'

'Oh, yes. Good show, isn't it? I thought that sketch *The Sempiternal Triangle* very clever. Didn't you?'

'*The Sempiternal Triangle?*' wavered Mrs Verreker-le-Flemming.

'Yes, in the first half.'

'Oh! Then I didn't see it. I got there disgracefully late, I'm afraid. But then,' said Mrs Verreker-le-Flemming with pathos, 'I always do seem to be late for simply everything.'

Once more Roger changed the subject. 'By the way, I wonder if you've got a photograph of Mrs Beresford?' he asked carelessly.

'Of Joan? Yes, I have. Why, Mr Sheringham?'

'You haven't got one of Sir William too, by any chance?' asked Roger, still more carelessly.

The pink on Mrs Verreker-le-Flemming's cheeks deepened half a shade. 'I—I think I have. Yes, I'm almost sure I have. But—'

'Would you lend them to me some time?' Roger asked, with a mysterious air, and looked around him with a frown in the approved manner.

'Oh, Mr Sheringham! Yes, of course I will. You mean—you mean you *are* going to find out who sent those chocolates to Sir William?'

Roger nodded, and put his finger to his lips. 'Yes. You've guessed it. But not a word, Mrs Verreker-le-Flemming. Oh, excuse me, there's a man on that bus who wants to speak to me. *Scotland Yard,*' he hissed in an impressive whisper. 'Good-bye.' He dived for a passing bus and clung on with difficulty. With awful stealth he climbed up the steps and took his seat, after an exaggerated scrutiny of the other passengers, beside a perfectly inoffensive man in a bowler hat. The man in the bowler hat, who happened to be a clerk in the employment of a builder's merchant, looked at him resentfully: there were plenty of quite empty seats all round them.

Roger bought no new hat that morning.

For probably the first time in her life Mrs Verreker-le-Flemming had given somebody a constructive idea.

Roger made good his opportunity. Getting off the bus at the corner of Bond Street and Oxford Street, he hailed a taxi, and gave Mrs Verreker-le-Flemming's address. He thought it better to take advantage of her permission at a time when he would not have to pay for it a second time over.

The parlour-maid seemed to think there was nothing odd in his mission, and took him up to the drawing room at once. A corner of the room was devoted to the silver-framed photographs of Mrs Verreker-le-Flemming's friends, and there were many of them. Roger, who had never seen Sir William in the flesh, had to seek the parlour-maid's help. The girl, like her mistress, was inclined to be loquacious, and to prevent either of them getting ideas into their heads which might be better not there, he removed from their frames not one photograph but five, those of Sir William, Mrs Beresford, Beresford himself, and two strange males who appeared to belong to the Sir William period of Mrs Verreker-le-Flemming's collection. Finally he obtained, by means of a small bribe, a likeness of Mrs Verreker-le-Flemming herself and added that to his collection.

For the rest of the day he was very busy.

His activities would have seemed, no doubt, to Mrs Verreker-le-Flemming not merely baffling but pointless. He paid a visit to a public library, for instance, and consulted a work of reference, after which he took a taxi and drove to the offices of the Anglo-Eastern Perfumery Company, where he enquired for a certain Mr Joseph Lea Hardwick and seemed much put out on hearing that no such gentleman was known to the firm and was certainly not employed in any of their numerous branches. Many questions had to be put about the firm and its branches before he consented to abandon the quest. After that he drove to Messrs. Weall and

Wilson, the well-known institution which protects the trade interests of individuals and advises its subscribers regarding investments. Here he entered his name as a subscriber, and explaining that he had a large sum of money to invest, filled in one of the special enquiry forms which are headed Strictly Confidential.

Then he went to the Rainbow Club, in Piccadilly.

Introducing himself to the porter without a blush as connected with Scotland Yard, he asked the man a number of questions, more or less trivial, concerning the tragedy. 'Sir William, I understand,' he said finally, as if by the way, 'did not dine here the evening before?'

There it appeared that Roger was wrong. Sir William had dined in the club, as he did about three times a week.

'But I quite understood he wasn't here that evening?' Roger said plaintively.

The porter was emphatic. He remembered quite well. So did a waiter, whom the porter summoned to corroborate him. Sir William had dined rather late, and had not left the dining-room till about nine o'clock. He spent the evening there too, the waiter knew, or at least some of it, for he himself had taken him a whiskey-and-soda in the lounge not less than half an hour later.

Roger retired.

He retired to Merton's, in a taxi.

It seemed that he wanted some new notepaper printed, of a very special kind, and to the young woman behind the counter he specified at great length and in wearisome detail exactly what he did want. The young woman handed him the book of specimen pieces and asked him to see if there was any style there which would suit him. Roger glanced through it, remarking garrulously to the young woman that he had been recommended to Merton's by a very dear friend, whose photograph he happened to have on him at that moment. Wasn't that a curious coincidence? The young woman agreed that it was.

'About a fortnight ago, I think my friend was in here last,' said Roger, producing the photograph. 'Recognise this?'

The young woman took the photograph, without apparent interest. 'Oh, yes. I remember. About some notepaper too, wasn't it? So that's your friend. Well, it's a small world. Now this is a line we're selling a good deal of just now.'

Roger went back to his rooms to dine. Afterwards, feeling restless, he wandered out of the Albany and turned down Piccadilly. He wandered round the Circus, thinking hard, and paused for a moment out of habit to inspect the photographs of the new revue hung outside the Pavilion. The next thing he realised was that he had got as far as Jermyn Street and was standing outside the Imperial Theatre. The advertisements of *The Creaking Skull* informed him that it began at half-past eight. Glancing at his watch he saw that the time was twenty-nine minutes past that hour. He had an evening to get through somehow. He went inside.

The next morning, very early for Roger, he called Moresby at Scotland Yard.

'Moresby,' he said without preamble, 'I want you to do something for me. Can you find me a taximan who took a fare from Piccadilly Circus or its neighbourhood at about ten past nine on the evening before the Beresford crime, to the Strand somewhere near the bottom of Southampton Street, and another who took a fare back between those points. I'm not sure about the first. Or one taxi might have been used for the double journey, but I doubt that. Anyhow, try to find out for me, will you?'

'What are you up to now, Mr Sheringham?' Moresby asked suspiciously.

'Breaking down an interesting alibi,' replied Roger serenely. 'By the way, I know who sent those chocolates to

Sir William. I'm just building up a nice structure of evidence for you. Ring up my rooms when you've got those taximen.'

He strolled out, leaving Moresby positively gaping after him. Roger had his annoying moments.

The rest of the day he spent apparently trying to buy a secondhand typewriter. He was very particular that it should be a Hamilton No. 4. When the shop people tried to induce him to consider other makes he refused to look at them, saying that he had had the Hamilton No. 4 so strongly recommended to him by a friend, who had bought one about three weeks ago. Perhaps it was at this very shop? No? They hadn't sold a Hamilton No. 4 for the last three months? How odd.

But at one shop they had sold a Hamilton No. 4 within the last month, and that was odder still.

At half-past four Roger got back to his rooms to await the telephone message from Moresby. At half-past five it came.

'There are fourteen taxi drivers here, littering up my office,' said Moresby offensively. 'They all took fares from the Strand to Piccadilly Circus at your time. What do you want me to do with 'em, Mr Sheringham?'

'Keep them till I come, Chief Inspector,' returned Roger with dignity. He had not expected more than three at the most, but he was not going to let Moresby know that. He grabbed his hat.

The interview with the fourteen was brief enough, however. To each grinning man (Roger deduced a little heavy humour on the part of Moresby before his arrival) he showed in turn a photograph, holding it so that Moresby could not see it, and asked if he could recognise his fare. The ninth man did so, without hesitation. At a nod from Roger Moresby dismissed the others.

'How dressed?' Roger asked the man laconically, tucking the photograph away in his pocket.

'Evening togs,' replied the other, equally laconic.

Roger took a note of his name and address and sent him away with a ten shilling tip. 'The case,' he said to Moresby, 'is at an end.'

Moresby sat at his table and tried to look official. 'And now, Mr Sheringham, sir, perhaps you'll tell me what you've been doing.'

'Certainly,' Roger said blandly, seating himself on the table and swinging his legs. As he did so, a photograph fell unnoticed out of his pocket and fluttered, face downwards, under the table. Moresby eyed it but did not pick it up. 'Certainly, Moresby,' said Roger. 'Your work for you. It was a simple case,' he added languidly, 'once one had grasped the essential factor. Once, that is to say, one had cleared one's eyes of the soap that the murderer had stuffed into them.'

'Is that so, Mr Sheringham?' said Moresby politely. And yawned.

Roger laughed. 'All right, Moresby. We'll get down to it. I really have solved the thing, you know. Here's the evidence for you.' He took from his note-case an old letter and handed it to the chief inspector. 'Look at the slightly crooked s's and the chipped capital H. Was that typed on the same machine as the forged letter from Mason's, or was it not?'

Moresby studied it for a moment, then drew the forged letter from a drawer of his table and compared the two minutely. When he looked up there was no lurking amusement in his eyes. 'You've got it in one, Mr Sheringham,' he said soberly. 'Where did you get hold of this?'

'In a secondhand typewriter shop in St. Martin's Lane. The machine was sold to an unknown customer about a month ago. They identified the customer from that photograph. By a lucky chance this machine had been used in the office after it had been repaired, to see that it was OK, and I easily got hold of that specimen of its work. I'd deduced, of course, from the precautions taken all through this crime, that the typewriter would be bought for that one special purpose and then destroyed, and so far as the murderer could see there was no need to waste valuable money on a new one.'

'And where is the machine now?'

'Oh, at the bottom of the Thames, I expect,' Roger smiled. 'I tell you, this criminal takes no unnecessary chances. But that doesn't matter. There's your evidence.'

'Humph! It's all right so far as it goes,' conceded Moresby. 'But what about Mason's paper?'

'That,' said Roger calmly, 'was extracted from Merton's book of sample notepapers, as I'd guessed from the very yellowed edges might be the case. I can prove contact of the criminal with the book, and there is a gap which will certainly turn out to have been filled by the piece of paper.'

'That's fine,' Moresby said more heartily.

'As for that taximan, the criminal had an alibi. You've heard it broken down. Between ten past nine and twenty-five past, in fact during the time when the parcel must have been posted, the murderer took a hurried journey to that neighbourhood, going probably by bus or underground, but returning, as I expected, by taxi, because time would be getting short.'

'And the murderer, Mr Sheringham?'

'The person whose photograph is in my pocket,' Roger said unkindly. 'By the way, do you remember what I was saying the other day about Chance the Avenger, my excellent film-title? Well, it's worked again. By a chance meeting in Bond Street with a silly woman I was put, by the merest accident, in possession of a piece of information which showed me then and there who had sent those chocolates addressed to Sir William. There were other possibilities of course, and I tested them, but then and there on the pavement I saw the whole thing, from first to last. It was the merest accident that this woman should have been a friend of mine, of course, and I don't want to blow my own trumpet,' said Roger modestly, 'but I do think I deserve a little credit for realising the significance of what she told me and recognising the hand of Providence at work.'

'Who was the murderer, then, Mr Sheringham?' repeated Moresby, disregarding for the moment this bashful claim.

'It was so beautifully planned,' Roger went on dreamily. 'We were taken in completely. We never grasped for one moment that we were making the fundamental mistake that the murderer all along intended us to make.'

He paused, and in spite of his impatience Moresby obliged. 'And what was that?'

'Why, that the plan had miscarried. That the wrong person had been killed. That was just the beauty of it. The plan had *not* miscarried. It had been brilliantly successful. The wrong person was *not* killed. Very much the right person was.'

Moresby gaped. 'Why, how on earth do you make that out, sir?'

'Mrs Beresford was the objective all the time. That's why the plot was so ingenious. Everything was anticipated. It was perfectly natural that Sir William would hand the chocolates over to Beresford. It was foreseen that we should look for the criminal among Sir William's associates and not the dead woman's. It was probably even foreseen that the crime would be considered the work of a woman; whereas really, of course, chocolates were employed because it was a woman who was the objective. Brilliant!'

Moresby, unable to wait any longer, snatched up the photograph and gazed at it incredulously. He whistled. 'Good heavens! But Mr Sheringham, you don't mean to tell me that—Sir William himself!'

'He wanted to get rid of Mrs Beresford,' Roger continued, gazing dreamily at his swinging feet. 'He had liked her well enough at the beginning, no doubt, though it was her money he was after all the time. But she must have bored him dreadfully very soon. And I really do think there is some excuse for him there. Any woman, however charming otherwise, would bore a normal man if she does nothing but prate about honour and playing the game. She'd never have overlooked the slightest peccadillo. Every tiny lapse would be thrown up at him for years.

'But the real trouble was that she was too close with her money. She sentenced herself to death there. He wanted it, or some of it, pretty badly; and she wouldn't part. There's no doubt about the motive. I made a list of the firms he's interested in and got a report on them. They're all rocky, every one of them. They all need money to save them. He'd got through all he had of his own, and he had to get more. Nobody seems to have gathered it, but he's a rotten business man. And half a million—Well!

'As for the nitrobenzene, that was simple enough. I looked it up and found that beside the uses you told me, it's used largely in perfumery. And he's got a perfumery business. The Anglo-Eastern Perfumery Company. That's how he'd know about it being poisonous of course. But I shouldn't think he got his supply from there. He'd be cleverer than that. He probably made the stuff himself. I discovered, quite by chance, that he has at any rate an elementary knowledge of chemistry (at least, he was on the modern side at Selchester) and it's the simplest operation. Any schoolboy knows how to treat benzol with nitric acid to get nitrobenzene.'

'But,' stammered Moresby, 'but Sir William—He was at Eton.'

'Sir William?' said Roger sharply. 'Who's talking about Sir William? I told you the photograph of the murderer was in my pocket.' He whipped out the photograph in question and confronted the astounded chief inspector with it.

'Beresford, man! Beresford's the murderer, of his own wife.' Roger studied the other's dumbfounded face and smiled secretly. He felt avenged now for the humour that had been taking place with the taximen.

'Beresford, who still had hankerings after a gay life,' he went on more mildly, 'didn't want his wife but did want her money. He contrived this plot, providing, as he thought, against every contingency that could possibly arise. He established a mild alibi, if suspicion ever should arise, by taking his wife to the Imperial, and slipped out of the theatre at the first interval (I sat through the first act of the dreadful thing myself last night to see when the interval came). Then he hurried down to the Strand, posted his parcel, and took a taxi back. He had ten minutes, but nobody was going to remark if he got back to the box a minute or two late; you may be able to find that he did.

'And the rest simply followed. He knew Sir William came to the Club every morning at ten thirty, as regularly as clockwork; he knew that for a psychological certainty he could get the chocolates handed over to him if he hinted for them; he knew that the police would go chasing after all sorts of false trails starting from Sir William. That's one reason why he chose him. He could have shadowed anyone else to the Club if necessary. And as for the wrapper and the forged letter, he carefully didn't destroy them because they were calculated not only to divert suspicion but actually to point away from him to some anonymous lunatic. Which is exactly what they did.'

'Well, it's very smart of you, Mr Sheringham,' Moresby said, with a little sigh but quite ungrudgingly. 'Very smart indeed. By the way, what was it the lady told you that showed you the whole thing in a flash?'

'Why, it wasn't so much what she actually told me as what I heard between her words, so to speak. What she told me was that Mrs Beresford knew the answer to that bet; what I deduced was that, being the sort of person she sounded to be, it was almost incredible that Mrs Beresford should have made a bet to which she knew the answer. Unless she had been the most dreadful little hypocrite (which I did not for a moment believe), it would have been a psychological impossibility for her. *Ergo*, she didn't. *Ergo*, there never was such a bet. *Ergo*, Beresford was lying. *Ergo*, Beresford wanted to get hold of those chocolates for some reason other than he stated. And, as events turned out, there was only one other reason. That was all.

'After all, we only had Beresford's word for the bet, didn't we? And only his word for the conversation in the drawing room—though most of that undoubtedly happened. Beresford must be far too good a liar not to make all possible use of the truth. But of course he wouldn't have left her till he'd seen her take, or somehow made her take, at least six of the chocolates, more than a lethal dose. That's why the stuff was in those meticulous six minim doses. And so that he could take a couple himself, of course. A clever stroke, that. Took us all in again. Though of course he exaggerated his symptoms considerably.'

Moresby rose to his feet. 'Well, Mr Sheringham, I'm much obliged to you, sir. I shall make a report of course to the assistant commissioner of what you've done, and he'll thank you officially on behalf of the department. And now I shall have to get busy, because naturally I shall have to check your evidence myself, if only as a matter of form, before I apply for a warrant against Beresford.' He scratched his head. 'Chance, the Avenger, eh? Yes, it's an interesting notion. But I can tell you one pretty big thing Beresford left to Chance, the Avenger, Mr Sheringham. Suppose Sir William hadn't handed over the chocolates after all? Supposing he'd kept them, to give to one of his own ladies? That was a nasty risk to take.'

Roger positively snorted. He felt a personal pride in Beresford by this time, and it distressed him to hear a great man so maligned.

'Really, Moresby! It wouldn't have had any serious results if Sir William had. Do give my man credit for being what he is. You don't imagine he sent the poisoned ones to Sir William, do you? Of course not! He'd send harmless ones, and exchange them for the others on his way home. Dash it all, he wouldn't go right out of his way to present opportunities to Chance.

'If,' added Roger, 'Chance really is the right word.'

They Don't Wear Labels

E. M. Delafield

E. M. Delafield was the pseudonym of Edmee Elizabeth Monica de la Pasture (later Dashwood) (1890–1943), who achieved a degree of literary immortality as the author of the witty and entertaining Diary of a Provincial Lady *(1930). This semi-autobiographical journal of an upper-class woman, living in a Devon village but sometimes venturing further afield, was followed by three more books recording the Provincial Lady's exploits.*

Although known as a humorous writer, Delafield had a deep and abiding interest in criminology, and she was the author of Messalina of the Suburbs, *a study of the Thompson-Bywaters case. She was close to Anthony Berkeley Cox, who shared her fascination with true crime. There are faint echoes in this story of one aspect of the Thompson-Bywaters case, and also of a novel written by Berkeley's alter ego, Francis Iles,* Before the Fact, *which was filmed by Alfred Hitchcock as* Suspicion.

›››

Everybody in the house, almost, liked him—and didn't care very much about her. That was the truth of the matter. Naturally, I didn't offer any opinion myself. A woman who takes in paying-guests has to keep most of her opinions to herself—particularly those that relate to her guests.

There was no denying that *he* was very easy to get on with, very pleasant and friendly, and on the whole quite good about settling up their account promptly.

Mrs Peverelli was ready enough to be friendly, in a manner of speaking, but her idea of being friendly was to talk about her miseries, and her poor health, and after a time people got tired of it, although one couldn't help feeling sorry for her—she looked so white and frightened, with her great dark eyes, and rabbit mouth, and narrow, hunched shoulders.

When they first took the front first-floor room, Mr Peverelli had explained that his wife wasn't strong and would often want her meals upstairs, and he was quite ready to pay a little extra for the trouble.

I agreed to that, of course, and asked if she was an invalid, or likely to get stronger.

He looked at me with those very brown eyes—regular Italian eyes they were, though I believe only one of his parents had come from Italy, and he'd never set foot there himself—and gave me that pleasant, taking smile he had, showing splendid white teeth.

'Between ourselves, Mrs Fuller, there is nothing organically wrong with my wife at all. She's seen one doctor after another, and they've all told me the same thing. It's her nerves. Mind you, I don't mean that she's putting it on. Far from it. She really does feel all the miseries she complains of, and of course the more she diets, and lies awake, and worries about herself, the worse she feels. It's a vicious circle.'

'Surely,' I said, 'something could be done to help her.'

'I've tried everything,' he answered sadly. 'She doesn't feel up to housekeeping, so we haven't got a home, and I've tried various places—we're always moving about. She seemed to like the country at first, but she's got tired of every place in turn. And, of course, it was lonely for her while I was away.'

He was a commercial traveller.

'It's lucky your job is what it is, though,' I couldn't help pointing out. 'It isn't everybody who can manage a change of locality.'

'I know that, Mrs Fuller, and even in my case we have to keep within a certain radius of town. But now she's got an idea that she wants to be in London, and to mix with people more. I hope she'll make some friends here.'

I hoped so too. I had one or two very nice permanents in the house— a widowed Mrs Gordon with her little girl, Joan, and two ladies who worked every day at the Lister Institute, and a couple of single gentlemen, both middle-aged. They all got on very well together and often had a game of cards in the evenings or made up a party to go to the pictures.

Mrs Peverelli seemed ready enough to join in with them at first, although she wasn't much of a Bridge player.

Mr Peverelli played a very good game and at the week-ends, when he was at home, he was always ready to make a fourth. He and his wife would be partners, and one thing we all of us liked about him was the way in which he put up with her bad play, never getting cross about it, and only pointing out, in a chaffing kind of way, some of her worst mistakes.

Many a husband, I used to think, wouldn't have hesitated to haul her over the coals after she'd thrown away one good game after another.

But Mr Peverelli never did that.

He'd wait on her, too, coming down himself to the kitchen sometimes to say she fancied a cup of something or other, and offering to get it ready and take it up himself to save trouble.

I let him do it. He was quick and quiet, and I knew the girls had plenty to do without additional running up and down stairs.

Then one night, when he was away, something happened.

Mrs Gordon's little girl, Joan, who'd been in bed three hours at least and ought to have been asleep, came running down into my kitchen in her pyjamas and dressing-gown, and said that Mrs Peverelli had sent her to ask for a cup of hot cocoa, because she couldn't sleep.

'Sent *you*!' I exclaimed. 'Why couldn't she have rung her bell, I should like to know? Did she call out to you, or what?'

Joan slept in a small room on the landing, next door to the Peverellis.

'I heard her,' said Joan. 'She was crying.'

'Crying!'

'Yes, really she was. I've often heard her before, but sometimes I go to sleep. But to-night it sounded so sad, that I—I got up. I thought I'd fetch mummie.'

'Mummie's out,' I told her—for Mrs Gordon had gone to spend the evening with some friends.

'I know, but I forgot. And when I opened the door it creaked, you know how it does, and she called me and so I went in.'

'Well, you hop straight back to bed. You'll catch your death of cold, a night like this!'

'Can't I wait and take her the cocoa?'

'I'll see to the cocoa,' I said—shortly enough, for I was vexed. The idea of sending a little thing of seven years old running errands about the house at ten o'clock on a December night!

I made some cocoa and poured it into a covered jug and then I went upstairs with it. I didn't grudge the trouble, or the time, but I thought Mrs Peverelli was a selfish woman and that it wouldn't do her any harm to be told so.

She looked wretched enough, poor soul. Her face was glazed with crying, and she was one of those women who scatter powder all over everything in a bedroom, and leave soiled handkerchiefs lying about.

The room was a nice room, but she'd somehow made it look sordid and forlorn.

'I've brought you the cocoa, Mrs Peverelli, but I've sent Joan off to her bed. It's too late, and too cold, for a delicate child like that to be running up and down stairs. I'm afraid you're not feeling well.'

'No,' she said—and I thought what a hunted look her eyes had—'No, I don't feel particularly well. And I can't sleep.'

I suggested aspirin.

'Nothing does me any good,' she said. 'It's my mind, more than my body.'

And she began to cry again.

I begged her to try and brace herself. I told her that she'd a good deal to be thankful for, with her husband in a good job, and always ready to do what would please her, and no anxieties like poor Mrs Gordon, a widow obliged to work for herself and a child who wasn't any too strong.

'And,' I couldn't help adding, 'your own health, if I may say so, would surely improve if you didn't fret yourself so much over nothing.'

Rather to my surprise, she didn't resent that.

'It isn't nothing,' she said, in a kind of whisper. 'You don't know. I'm so frightened.'

'What is it that frightens you?' I asked, feeling as though I were trying to reason with a rather tiresome child.

She shivered, and cried a little more, and looked all round her with her poor, swollen eyes before her answer came. When it did, I don't mind admitting that I was a bit startled.

'I'm not safe,' she whispered. 'My life isn't safe. There—there are people who want me out of the way.'

Well, as I've said, I was startled because, neurotic though I knew her to be, I hadn't thought she was as near the border-line as all that.

'You've been reading detective stories,' I said. 'You know very well you're talking nonsense. Who should want you out of the way?'

Of course, she couldn't answer that. So she poured out a whole flood of nonsense, about her being of no use to anybody, and having no friends, and people hating her because she was difficult, and nervous, and 'they' said she was always making scenes.

'"They,"' I repeated. 'I don't want to force your confidence, Mrs Peverelli, but you started this of your own accord. Who are 'they?' You don't mean your husband, surely?'

She gave a sort of smothered shriek. It sounded to me very forced and unreal, like somebody play-acting.

'You think he's a good, kind husband to me, don't you, Mrs Fuller? Everyone does.'

'It's not my business to offer any opinion on such a question, and I'm astonished you should ask it,' I retorted. 'But since you *have* asked it, I think you're very lucky. Mr Peverelli is good-tempered, and patient—which is more than every man would be, in all the circumstances—and though I dare say he has his ways, like most gentlemen, I don't think you'd find many would say you had much to complain of.'

'You wouldn't believe me, would you, if I told you that he's tried, over and over again, to poison me?'

'I wouldn't believe you, Mrs Peverelli, and I should think you were either a very wicked, or a very silly, woman—or both—for letting yourself imagine such things, let alone saying them.'

She burst out crying again and threw herself back on the pillow.

'Sometimes I know it isn't true. I know I'm just what he says—morbid, and letting my imagination run wild. Oh, I think I shall go mad!'

She was twisting about, working herself into a state—but I was thinking of what her words implied.

'You don't mean to tell me, Mrs Peverelli, that you've accused your husband of trying to poison you? My, I wonder he hasn't had you certified!'

'He wouldn't do that,' she said wildly. 'He wouldn't do that. Locked away I shouldn't be worth anything to him. But if I die first, he gets the money, and he's free—free to marry somebody young, and pretty, and amusing.'

I was beginning to see daylight.

'You're one of these jealous wives, is that it? It's a terrible thing, jealousy—that I do know—and doesn't let you see anything straight or in its true proportions. But what you've just been saying is nonsense, and you know it.'

'Then why was I ill, before we left Essex? Why are we always moving from one place to another so that I never have time to get to know anybody? Why is he always making me try new patent foods, and drinks to make me sleep?'

'And why,' I asked in my turn, 'if you really believe the rubbish you've been talking, do you drink them?'

'He stands over me. He makes me. But after I'd been so ill, before we left Essex, I wouldn't touch anything he brought me. He knew why, though we never spoke of it.'

'All this talk out of books isn't getting us anywhere,' I said. 'You're making up a kind of drama, Mrs Peverelli, with yourself at the centre of it, and it doesn't take one of these psycho-analyst doctors to tell you that if you do that kind of thing long enough, you end by believing in your own imaginings. And where *that* leads to, I leave you to guess. Now honestly, don't you *know* that this nonsense about being poisoned is none of it true? Such things just don't happen.'

'I keep on telling myself that,' she answered, in a weak, exhausted kind of whisper. 'Sometimes I look at him and I tell myself it isn't any of it true. It just can't be true.'

'Of course it can't,' I told her. 'Use your common sense. If you *really* believed it, why—you'd have left him. It's surely the very first thing you'd have done.'

'No,' she said, rolling her eyes at me like someone on the stage. 'You don't understand. I love him.'

I had her then, I thought.

'If you loved him, you wouldn't believe things like that about him. And if you really believed them, you couldn't still love him,' I said, feeling I'd scored rather neatly. I was sorry for her, in a way, but her wild way of talking, like a schoolgirl trying to make herself sound like someone in a story, was irritating. It was against common sense, too.

'Try and be rational,' I advised her. 'Poison isn't at all easy to come by, in this country, and I can assure you that nobody tampers with the food in this house.'

She stared at me without saying a word, and I suddenly remembered how Mr Peverelli had sometimes come down and mixed her a hot drink himself.

As the thought crossed my mind I felt indignant—as though she'd infected me with her own silliness.

'I've just made the cocoa for you with my own hands,' I said hastily. 'Drink it up, before it's cold.'

I poured it out for her and she drank it, and thanked me.

Poor, silly, neurotic thing, I thought—and I felt sorry for her. But thinking it over afterwards, as I was bound to do, I felt much sorrier for *him*. Well I knew that if she'd work herself up like that with me, a comparative stranger, she'd make scenes—much worse and more often—with her own husband.

Two days later he was back, for the week-end.

I must say it gave me a queer feeling to think of seeing them together, after what she'd said. But it was just as usual.

Mrs Peverelli looked ill and nervous, as she always did, and Mr Peverelli was cheerful and ragged her a little—but not too much.

He was in very good form at tea on Sunday afternoon, and told some funny stories that amused everyone very much. Only his wife didn't laugh with the others, but just sat back in an armchair, with her eyes half-closed.

Mrs Gordon said to me afterwards:

'She's a kill-joy all right, isn't she?' and I had to agree that she was.

'But,' I said, 'I don't think she's wholly responsible for her moods. Neurotic, that's what she is, and full of fancies. She invents dramatic situations, if you know what I mean, and goes on brooding over them till she begins to believe they're really true.'

'What sort of situations?' Mrs Gordon asked.

When I told her she was shocked.

'And he's *so* nice and patient with her!' she said. 'What a horrible woman.'

I told her she mustn't let it go any further, and she promised she wouldn't.

Only her manner towards Mrs Peverelli was rather cold afterwards, and she was more friendly towards him. Partly, I suppose, because she felt very sorry for him, and partly because he was kind to little Joan, making a fuss of her and sometimes bringing back a toy or a few sweets for her.

Just before Christmas something happened.

Mr Peverelli came down to the kitchen, as he'd sometimes done before, and he'd got a cardboard container in his hand with one of his favourite patent foods.

'I believe it'll help my wife to sleep, and she's in a very nervous, highly strung mood to-night,' he said, his usually cheerful face wearing a worried look.

I held out my hand for the packet.

'If I may have the jug, and a spoon, and take some water from the kettle—' he began.

'I'll do it, Mr Peverelli.'

'But you're busy,' he said.

'No,' I said, 'I can do it.' And I did.

He just thanked me and took it upstairs.

The next morning was Christmas Eve.

Joan was to have a little Christmas Tree, and her mother and I dressed it in the evening after she'd gone to bed. Mr Peverelli came into the sitting-room and he'd brought some of those coloured glass balls and little ornaments for the tree, and a lot of crackers.

'He *is* a kind man!' said Mrs Gordon, after he'd gone. 'Joan'll be delighted, and don't they make a difference to the look of the tree!'

We'd only had cotton-wool and coloured paper and a couple of gilt stars, to decorate it, besides candles.

'They're pretty,' I agreed. 'Look at that red globe—and the string of green balls. I've always liked this kind of thing, though I know it's trumpery.'

We were a small party, because everyone except the Peverellis and Joan and her mother went away to spend Christmas.

It was on Boxing Day that Mr Peverelli told me he was very much afraid they'd have to move again. His wife's nerves were getting worse, and that always meant she wanted to try a change.

'I'm very sorry, Mrs Fuller,' he said wistfully. 'You've made us very comfortable here. But haven't you noticed that she's been less well lately? More—how shall I put it—more inclined to get worked up over nothing?'

He looked at me quite pleadingly.

'I think she lets herself go, Mr Peverelli, if I may say so without unkindness. Lets herself—fancy things.'

He nodded his head.

'I thought so,' he said.

The very next day they suddenly went—Mr Peverelli paying me the extra week in lieu of proper notice, and saying how sorry he was.

I was helping Joan to put away the things from her tree at the time, and I didn't want to go into any of it before the child. Besides, if they'd decided to go, there really was nothing I could say.

And I was sorry for him—he seemed so distressed and helped us roll the things up in tissue paper, very kindly, before going off to his packing.

He came down later to get her a hot drink before the journey, and I told him I was sorry they were going.

'So am I,' he said. 'So am I, Mrs Fuller.'

Mrs Peverelli, when they went off, looked worse than ever—sallower and more frightened.

She hardly said a word to anybody.

Just as the taxi moved off I remembered that he'd left no address, in case any letters came—but it was too late then.

However, he'd promised to let me hear from them.

Not that I set much store by that.

I went up to the first-floor front room, and couldn't help remembering the night I'd gone up to Mrs Peverelli and she'd poured out all that hysterical rubbish.

I looked round the room, and it seemed as if they'd taken everything.

Something caught my eye, gleaming in a corner, and I stooped down. It was a tiny fragment of—what was it? For a minute I couldn't think of what the brilliant colour reminded me.

Then I remembered Joan's tree, and the glass balls.

It seemed as though one of them had got smashed up in the Peverellis' room, and I looked round for the other pieces to have them swept up, knowing what fine powdered glass can do.

But I never found them.

The Unseen Door

Margery Allingham

Margery Allingham (1904–1966) was born in Ealing to writer parents; her father, Herbert, was editor of The New London Journal. *She published her first novel,* Blackerchief Dick, *whilst still in her teens, and introduced the enigmatic Albert Campion in* The Crime at Black Dudley *(1929). Originally a minor character, he became Allingham's series detective and was played by Peter Davison in a television series that first aired in 1989. Allingham is often ranked alongside Agatha Christie, Dorothy L. Sayers, and Ngaio Marsh as one of the 'Crime Queens' of the Golden Age of detective fiction.*

Allingham lived in both London and East Anglia, and her best work is set against one or other of those backgrounds. The Tiger in the Smoke, *featuring both Campion and the criminal Jake Havoc, is particularly atmospheric. The Margery Allingham Society remains highly active, and celebrated the author's centenary in 2004 with the unveiling by American crime writer Sara Paretsky of a plaque at the home of the Allinghams from 1916 to 1925, 1 Westbourne Terrace, Little Venice.*

⟨⟩⟨⟩⟨⟩

It was London, it was hot and it was Sunday afternoon. The billiard room in Prinny's Club, Pall Mall, which has often been likened to a mausoleum, had unexpectedly become one.

Superintendent Stanislaus Oates glanced down at the body again and swore softly to Mr Albert Campion who had just been admitted.

'I hate miracles!' he said.

Campion drew the sheet gently back from the terrible face.

'Our friend here could hardly have been taken by this one,' he murmured, his pale eyes growing grim behind his horn rimmed spectacles. 'Strangled? Oh yes, I see—from behind. Powerful fingers. Horrid. Who done it?'

'I know who ought to have done it.' Oates was savage. 'I know who's been threatening to do it for months and yet he wasn't here. That's why I sent for you. You like this four-dimensional stuff. I don't. See anyone in the hall as you came up?'

'About forty police experts and two very shaken old gentlemen, both on the fragile side. Who are they? Witnesses?'

The Superintendent sighed. 'Listen,' he commanded. 'This club is partly closed for cleaning. The only two rooms unlocked are the vestibule downstairs and this billiard room up here. The only two people in the place are Bowser, the doorkeeper, and Chetty, the little lame billiard marker.'

'The two I mentioned?'

'Yes. Bowser has been in the vestibule all the time. He's a great character in clubland. Knows everybody and has a reputation for infallibility. You couldn't break him down in the witness box.'

'I've heard of him. He gave me a particularly baleful stare as I came in.'

'That's his way. Does it to everybody. He's become a bit affected as these old figureheads do in time. He's been a power here for forty years, remember. Surly old chap, but he never forgets a face.'

'Beastly for him. And who's this?' Campion indicated the white mound at their feet. 'Just a poor wretched member?'

'That,' Oates spoke dryly, 'is Robert Fenderson, the man who exposed William Merton.'

Campion was silent. The story of the Merton crash, which had entailed the arrest of the flamboyant financier after a thousand small speculators had faced ruin, was still fresh in everyone's mind. Merton had been taken to the cells shouting threats at Judge, jury and witnesses alike, and photographs of his heavy jaw and sultry eyes had appeared in every newspaper.

'Merton broke jail last night.'

'Did he, by Jove!' Campion's brows rose. 'Was he a member here once?'

'Until his arrest. Knows the place like his own house. More than that, someone sent Fenderson a phony message this morning telling him to meet the club secretary here this afternoon at three. The secretary is away this weekend and knows nothing about it. I tell you Campion, it's an open and shut case—only Merton hasn't been here unless he flew in by the windows.'

Campion glanced at the casements bolted against the heat.

'He hardly flew out again.'

'Exactly, and there's nowhere for him to be hidden. Bowser swears that he went all over the club after lunch and found it deserted. Since then he's been on the door all the time. During the afternoon only one member came in, and that was Fenderson. The only other living soul to cross the threshold was Chetty, who is far too frail to have strangled a cat, let alone a man with a neck like Fenderson's. Bowser has a perfect view from his box of the street door, the staircase and this door. He insists he has neither slept nor left his seat. He's unshakeable.'

'Has the unyielding Bowser a soft spot for Merton?'

Oates was nettled. 'I thought of that at once, naturally,' he said acidly, 'but the evidence is all the other way. One could even suspect Bowser of having a grudge against the chap. Merton made a complaint about him just before the crash. It was a stupid, petty quarrel—something about who should say 'Good morning' first, member or club servant? Merton is like that, very self important and a born bully. Bowser is a graceless, taciturn old chap, but I swear he's speaking the truth. He hasn't seen Merton this afternoon.'

Mr Campion glanced round the spacious room, its walls lined with cue-racks and an occasional bookcase.

'All of which leaves us with the lame marker, I take it,' he ventured.

'The perishing little fool!' The Superintendent exploded. 'He isn't helping. He's gone to pieces and is trying to say he hasn't been here this afternoon. He lives in the mews at the back of the building, and he's trying to say he played hooky after lunch today—says he thought no one would be in to play. Actually anyone can see what did happen. He dropped in, found Fenderson didn't want a game, and went out again very sensibly. Now he doesn't want to appear as the last man to see the poor chap alive. I've told him he's doing himself no good by lying. Hang it all. Bowser *saw* him.'

'And so…?'

'And so there must be another way into this room, but I'm damned if I see it.' The Superintendent stalked over to the windows again and Campion stood watching him.

'I'd like a word with Bowser,' he murmured at last.

'Have it. Have it by all means.' Oates was exasperated. 'I've put him through it very thoroughly. You'll never shake him.'

Campion said nothing, but waited until the doorkeeper came in a few minutes later, stalking gravely behind the sergeant who had been sent to fetch him. Bowser was a typical man of trust, a little shaky now and in his seventies, but still an imposing figure with a wooden expression on a proud old face, chiefly remarkable for its firm mouth and bristling white eyebrows. He glowered at Campion and did not speak, but at the first question a faint smile softened his lips.

'How many times have I seen Chetty come into the club in my life, sir? Why, I shouldn't like to say—several thousand, must be.'

'Has he always been lame?'

'Why yes, sir. It's a deformity of the hip he's had all his life. He couldn't have done this, sir, any more than I could—neither of us has the strength.'

'I see.' Mr Campion went over to a bookcase at the far end of the long room and came back presently with something in his hand.

'Mr Bowser,' he said slowly, 'look at this. I suggest to you that it is a photograph of the man you really saw come in and go out of the club this afternoon when Mr Fenderson was already here.'

The old man's hand shook so violently that he could scarcely take the sheet, but he seized it at last and with an effort held it steady. He stared at it for a long time before returning it.

'No sir,' he said firmly, 'that face is unknown to me. Chetty came in and went out. No one else, and that's the truth, sir.'

'I believe you think it is, Bowser.' Mr Campion spoke gently and his lean face wore a curious expression in which pity predominated. 'Here's your unseen door, Superintendent,' he spoke softly. Oates snatched the paper and turned it over.

'Good God! What's this?' he demanded. 'It's a blank brown page—from the back of a book, isn't it?'

Mr Campion met his eyes.

'Bowser has just told us it's a face he doesn't know,' he murmured. 'You see, Oates, Bowser doesn't recognise faces, he recognises voices. That's why he glares until people speak. Bowser didn't *see* Chetty this afternoon, he heard his very distinctive step—a step which Merton could imitate very easily. I fancy you'll find that when there was that little unpleasantness earlier in the year, Merton guessed something which no one else in the club has known. When did it come on, Bowser?'

The old man stood trembling before them.

'I—I didn't want to have to retire from the club, sir,' he blurted out pathetically. 'I knew everyone's voice. I could still do my work. It's only got really bad in the last six months— my daughter comes and fetches me home at night. It *was* Chetty's step, sir, and I knew he could never have done it.'

'Blind!' The word escaped the Superintendent huskily. 'Good Lord! Campion, how did you know?'

It was some time before Mr Campion could be prevailed upon to tell him, and when he did he was slightly diffident.

'When I first passed through the hall,' he said, 'Bowser glared at me as I told you, but as I came upstairs I heard him say to a constable: 'Another detective, I suppose?'.'

He paused, and his smile was engaging as he flicked an imaginary speck from an immaculate sleeve.

'I wondered then if there was something queer about his eyesight—no offence, of course, no offence in the world.'

Cheese

Ethel Lina White

*Ethel Lina White (1876–1944) was born in Abergavenny,
and worked in the Ministry of Pensions before deciding to
concentrate on writing fiction. She died in Chiswick just six
years after her novel* The Wheel Spins *was transformed into*
The Lady Vanishes, *a light-hearted thriller which became one
of Alfred Hitchcock's most popular films. Two years after her
death, her book* Some Must Watch *became another highly
successful movie,* The Spiral Staircase, *this time directed by
Robert Siodmak.*

*White's speciality was 'woman in jeopardy' suspense fiction,
and her ability to evoke a mood of mounting fear has seldom
been matched. Her short stories are little known and mostly hard
to find, but 'Cheese' demonstrates her knack of involving the
reader in the terror experienced by a woman who faces a cruel
adversary, but proves strong and courageous enough to fight back.*

This story begins with a murder. It ends with a mouse-trap.

The murder can be disposed of in a paragraph. An attractive girl, carefully reared and educated for a future which

held only a twisted throat. At the end of seven months, an unsolved mystery and a reward of £500.

It is a long way from a murder to a mouse-trap—and one with no finger-posts; but the police knew every inch of the way. In spite of a prestige punctured by the press and public, they had solved the identity of the killer. There remained the problem of tracking this wary and treacherous rodent from his unknown sewer in the underworld into their trap.

They failed repeatedly for lack of the right bait.

And unexpectedly, one spring evening, the bait turned up in the person of a young girl.

Cheese.

〉〉〉

Inspector Angus Duncan was alone in his office when her message was brought up. He was a red-haired Scot, handsome in a dour fashion, with the chin of a prize-fighter and keen blue eyes.

He nodded.

'I'll see her.'

It was between the lights. River, government offices and factories were all deeply dyed with the blue stain of dusk. Even in the city, the lilac bushes showed green tips and an occasional crocus cropped through the grass of the public-gardens, like strewn orange-peel. The evening star was a jewel in the pale green sky.

Duncan was impervious to the romance of the hour. He knew that twilight was but the prelude to night and that darkness was a shield for crime.

He looked up sharply when his visitor was admitted. She was young and flower-faced—her faint freckles already fading away into pallor. Her black suit was shabby, but her hat was garnished for the spring with a cheap cowslip wreath.

As she raised her blue eyes, he saw that they still carried the memory of country sweets…Thereupon he looked at her more sharply for he knew that of all poses, innocence is easiest to counterfeit.

'You say Roper sent you?' he enquired.

'Yes, Maggie Roper.'

He nodded. Maggie Roper—Sergeant Roper's niece—was already shaping as a promising young Stores' detective.

'Where did you meet her?'

'At the Girls' Hostel where I'm staying.'

'Your name?'

'Jenny Morgan.'

'From the country?'

'Yes. But I'm up now for good.'

For good?…He wondered.

'Alone?'

'Yes.'

'How's that?' He looked at her mourning. 'People all dead?'

She nodded. From the lightning sweep of her lashes, he knew that she had put in some rough work with a tear. It prejudiced him in her favour. His voice grew more genial as his lips relaxed.

'Well, what's it all about?'

She drew a letter from her bag.

'I'm looking for work and I advertised in the paper. I got this answer. I'm to be companion-secretary to a lady, to travel with her and be treated as her daughter—if she likes me. I sent my photograph and my references and she's fixed an appointment.'

'When and where?'

'The day after tomorrow, in the First Room in the National Gallery. But as she's elderly, she is sending her nephew to drive me to her house.'

'Where's that?'

She looked troubled.

'That's what Maggie Roper is making the fuss about. First, she said I must see if Mrs Harper—that's the lady's name—had taken up my references. And then she insisted on ringing up the Ritz where the letter was written from. The address was *printed*, so it was bound to be genuine, wasn't it?'

'Was it? What happened then?'

'They said no Mrs Harper had stayed there. But I'm sure it must be a mistake.' Her voice trembled. 'One must risk something to get such a good job.'

His face darkened. He was beginning to accept Jenny as the genuine article.

'Tell me,' he asked, 'have you had any experience of life?'

'Well, I've always lived in the country with Auntie. But I've read all sorts of novels and the newspapers.'

'Murders?'

'Oh, I love those.'

He could tell by the note in her childish voice that she ate up the newspaper accounts merely as exciting fiction, without the slightest realisation that the printed page was grim fact. He could see the picture: a sheltered childhood passed amid green spongy meadows. She could hardly cull sophistication from clover and cows.

'Did you read about the Bell murder?' he asked abruptly.

'Auntie wouldn't let me.' She added in the same breath, 'Every word.'

'Why did your aunt forbid you?'

'She said it must be a specially bad one, because they'd left all the bad parts out of the paper.'

'Well, didn't you notice the fact that that poor girl—Emmeline Bell—a well-bred girl of about your own age, was lured to her death through answering a newspaper advertisement?'

'I—I suppose so. But those things don't happen to oneself.'

'Why? What's there to prevent your falling into a similar trap?'

'I can't explain. But if there was something wrong, I should know it.'

'How? D'you expect a bell to ring or a red light to flash 'Danger'?'

'Of course not. But if you believe in right and wrong, surely there must be some warning.'

He looked sceptical. That innocence bore a lily in its hand, was to him a beautiful phrase and nothing more. His own position in the sorry scheme of affairs was, to him, proof positive of the official failure of guardian angels.

'Let me see that letter, please,' he said.

She studied his face anxiously as he read, but his expression remained inscrutable. Twisting her fingers in her suspense, she glanced around the room, noting vaguely the three telephones on the desk and the stacked files in the pigeon-holes. A Great Dane snored before the red-caked fire. She wanted to cross the room and pat him, but lacked the courage to stir from her place.

The room was warm, for the windows were opened only a couple of inches at the top. In view of Duncan's weather-tanned colour, the fact struck her as odd.

Mercifully, the future is veiled. She had no inkling of the fateful part that Great Dane was to play in her own drama, nor was there anything to tell her that a closed window would have been a barrier between her and the yawning mouth of hell.

She started as Duncan spoke.

'I want to hold this letter for a bit. Will you call about this time tomorrow? Meantime, I must impress upon you the need of utmost caution. Don't take one step on your own. Should anything fresh crop up, 'phone me immediately. Here's my number.'

When she had gone, Duncan walked to the window. The blue dusk had deepened into a darkness pricked with lights. Across the river, advertisement-signs wrote themselves intermittently in coloured beads.

He still glowed with the thrill of the hunter on the first spoor of the quarry. Although he had to await the report of the expert test, he was confident that the letter which he held had been penned by the murderer of poor ill-starred Emmeline Bell.

Then his elation vanished at a recollection of Jenny's wistful face. In this city were scores of other girls, frail as windflowers too—blossom-sweet and country-raw—forced through economic pressure into positions fraught with deadly peril.

The darkness drew down overhead like a dark shadow pregnant with crime. And out from their holes and sewers stole the rats…

〉〉〉

At last Duncan had the trap baited for his rat.

A young and pretty girl—ignorant and unprotected. Cheese.

When Jenny, punctual to the minute, entered his office, the following evening, he instantly appraised her as his pro-spective decoy. His first feeling was one of disappointment. Either she had shrunk in the night or her eyes had grown bigger. She looked such a frail scrap as she stared at him, her lips bitten to a thin line, that it seemed hopeless to credit her with the necessary nerve for his project.

'Oh, please tell me it's all perfectly right about that letter.'

'Anything but right.'

For a moment, he thought she was about to faint. He wondered uneasily whether she had eaten that day. It was obvious from the keenness of her disappointment that she was at the end of her resources.

'Are you sure?' she insisted. 'It's—very important to me. Perhaps I'd better keep the appointment. If I didn't like the look of things, I needn't go on with it.'

'I tell you, it's not a genuine job,' he repeated. 'But I've something to put to you that is the goods. Would you like to have a shot at £500?'

Her flushed face, her eager eyes, her trembling lips, all answered him.

'Yes, please,' was all she said.

He searched for reassuring terms.

'It's like this. We've tested your letter and know it is written, from a bad motive, by an undesirable character.'

'You mean a criminal?' she asked quickly.

'Um. His record is not good. We want to get hold of him.'

'Then why don't you?'

He suppressed a smile.

'Because he doesn't confide in us. But if you have the courage to keep your appointment tomorrow and let his messenger take you to the house of the suppositious Mrs Harper, I'll guarantee it's the hiding-place of the man we want. We get him—you get the reward. Question is—have you the nerve?'

She was silent. Presently she spoke in a small voice.

'Will I be in great danger?'

'None. I wouldn't risk your safety for any consideration. From first to last, you'll be under the protection of the Force.'

'You mean I'll be watched over by detectives in disguise?'

'From the moment you enter the National Gallery, you'll be covered doubly and trebly. You'll be followed every step of the way and directly we've located the house, the place will be raided by the police.'

'All the same, for a minute or so, just before you can get into the house, I'll be alone with—*him*?'

'The briefest interval. You'll be safe at first. He'll begin with overtures. Stall him off with questions. Don't let him see you suspect—or show you're frightened.'

Duncan frowned as he spoke. It was his duty to society to rid it of a dangerous pest and in order to do so, Jenny's co-operation was vital. Yet, to his own surprise, he disliked the necessity in the case of this especial girl.

'Remember we'll be at hand,' he said. 'But if your nerve goes, just whistle and we'll break cover immediately.'

'Will *you* be there?' she asked suddenly.

'Not exactly in the foreground. But I'll be there.'

'Then I'll do it.' She smiled for the first time. 'You laughed at me when I said there was something inside me which told me—things. But I just know I can trust *you*.'

'Good.' His voice was rough. 'Wait a bit. You've been put to expense coming over here. This will cover your fares and so on.'

He thrust a note into her hand and hustled her out, protesting. It was a satisfaction to feel that she would eat that night. As he seated himself at his desk, preparatory to work, his frozen face was no index of the emotions raised by Jenny's parting words.

Hitherto, he had thought of women merely as 'skirts'. He had regarded a saucepan with an angry woman at the business end of it, merely as a weapon. For the first time he had a domestic vision of a country girl—creamy and fragrant as meadowsweet—in a nice womanly setting of saucepans.

〉〉〉

Jenny experienced a thrill which was almost akin to exhilaration when she entered Victoria station, the following day. At the last moment, the place for meeting had been altered in a telegram from 'Mrs Harper'.

Immediately she had received the message, Jenny had gone to the telephone-box in the hostel and duly reported the change of plan, with a request that her message should be repeated to her, to obviate any risk of mistake.

And now—the incredible adventure was actually begun.

The station seemed filled with hurrying crowds as she walked slowly towards the clock. Her feet rather lagged on the way. She wondered if the sinister messenger had already marked the yellow wreath in her hat which she had named as her mark of identification.

Then she remembered her guards. At this moment they were here, unknown, watching over her slightest movement. It was a curious sensation to feel that she was spied upon by unseen eyes. Yet it helped to brace the muscles of her knees when she took up her station under the clock with the sensation of having exposed herself as a target for gun-fire.

Nothing happened. No one spoke to her. She was encouraged to gaze around her...

A few yards away, a pleasant-faced smartly dressed young man was covertly regarding her. He carried a yellowish sample-bag which proclaimed him a drummer.

Suddenly Jenny felt positive that this was one of her guards. There was a quality about his keen clean-shaven face—a hint of the eagle in his eye—which reminded her of Duncan. She gave him the beginnings of a smile and was thrilled when, almost imperceptibly, he fluttered one eyelid. She read it as a signal for caution. Alarmed by her indiscretion, she looked fixedly in another direction.

Still—it helped her to know that even if she could not see him, he was there.

The minutes dragged slowly by. She began to grow anxious as to whether the affair were not some hoax. It would be not only a tame ending to the adventure but a positive disappointment. She would miss the chance of a sum which—to her—was a little fortune. Her need was so vital that she would have undertaken the venture for five pounds. Morever, after her years of green country solitude, she felt a thrill at the mere thought of her temporary link with the underworld. This was life in the raw; while screening her as she aided him, she worked with Angus Duncan.

She smiled—then started as though stung.

Someone had touched her on the arm.

◇◇◇

'Have I the honour, happiness and felicity of addressing Miss Jenny Morgan? Yellow wreath in the lady's hat. Red Flower in the gent's buttonhole, as per arrangement.'

The man who addressed her was young and bull-necked, with florid colouring which ran into blotches. He wore a red carnation in the buttonhole of his check overcoat.

'Yes, I'm Jenny Morgan.'

As she spoke, she looked into his eyes. She felt a sharp revulsion—an instinctive recoil of her whole being.

'Are you Mrs Harper's nephew?' she faltered.

'That's right. Excuse a gent keeping a lady waiting, but I just slipped into the bar for a glass of milk. I've a taxi waiting if you'll just hop outside.'

Jenny's mind worked rapidly as she followed him. She was forewarned and protected. But—were it not for Maggie Roper's intervention—she would have kept this appointment in very different circumstances. She wondered whether she would have heeded that instinctive warning and refused to follow the stranger.

She shook her head. Her need was so urgent that, in her wish to believe the best, she knew that she would have summoned up her courage and flouted her fears as nerves. She would have done exactly what she was doing—accompanying an unknown man to an unknown destination.

She shivered at the realisation. It might have been herself. Poor defenceless Jenny—going to her doom.

At that moment she encountered the grave scrutiny of a stout clergyman who was standing by the book-stall. He was ruddy, wore horn-rimmed spectacles and carried the *Church Times*.

His look of understanding was almost as eloquent as a vocal message. It filled her with gratitude. Again she was certain that this was a second guard. Turning to see if the young commercial traveller were following her, she was thrilled to discover that he had preceded her into the station yard. He got into a taxi at the exact moment that her companion flung open the door of a cab which was waiting. It was only this knowledge that Duncan was thus making good his promise which induced her to enter the vehicle. Once again her nerves rebelled and she was rent with sick forebodings.

As they moved off, she had an overpowering impulse to scream aloud for help to the porters—just because all this might have happened to some poor girl who had not her own good fortune.

Her companion nudged her.

'Bit of all right, joy-riding, eh?'

She stiffened, but managed to force a smile.

'Is it a long ride?'

'Ah, now you're asking.'

'Where does Mrs Harper live?'

'Ah, that's telling.'

She shrank away, seized with disgust of his blotched face so near her own.

'Please give me more room. It's stifling here.'

'Now, don't you go taking no liberties with me. A married man I am, with four wives all on the dole.' All the same, to her relief, he moved further away. 'From the country, aren't you? Nice place. Lots of milk. Suit me a treat. Any objection to a gent smoking?'

'I wish you would. The cab reeks of whisky.'

They were passing St Paul's which was the last landmark in her limited knowledge of London. Girls from offices passed on the pavement, laughing and chatting together, or hurrying by intent on business. A group was scattering crumbs to the pigeons which fluttered on the steps of the cathedral.

She watched them with a stab of envy. Safe happy girls.

Then she remembered that somewhere, in the press of traffic, a taxi was shadowing her own. She took fresh courage.

The drive passed like an interminable nightmare in which she was always on guard to stem the advances of her disagreeable companion. Something seemed always on the point of happening—something unpleasant, just out of sight and round the corner—and then, somehow she staved it off.

The taxi bore her through a congested maze of streets. Shops and offices were succeeded by regions of warehouses and factories, which in turn gave way to areas of dun squalor where gas-works rubbed shoulders with grimed laundries which bore such alluring signs as dewdrop or white rose.

From the shrilling of sirens, Jenny judged that they were in the neighbourhood of the river, when they turned into a quiet square. The tall lean houses wore an air of drab respectability. Lace curtains hung at every window. Plaster pineapples crowned the pillared porches.

'Here's our 'destitution''.'

As her guide inserted his key in the door of No. 17, Jenny glanced eagerly down the street, in time to see a taxi turn the corner.

'Hop in, dearie.'

On the threshold Jenny shrank back.

〉〉〉

Evil.

Never before had she felt its presence. But she knew. Like the fumes creeping upwards from the grating of a sewer, it poisoned the air.

Had she embarked on this enterprise in her former ignorance, she was certain that at this point, her instinct would have triumphed.

'I would never have passed through this door.'

She was wrong. Volition was swept off the board. Her arm was gripped and before she could struggle, she was pulled inside.

She heard the slam of the door.

'Never loiter on the doorstep, dearie. Gives the house a bad name. This way. Up the stairs. All the nearer to heaven.'

Her heart heavy with dread, Jenny followed him. She had entered on the crux of her adventure—the dangerous few minutes when she would be quite alone.

The place was horrible—with no visible reason for horror. It was no filthy East-end rookery, but a technically clean apartment-house. The stairs were covered with brown linoleum. The mottled yellow wallpaper was intact. Each landing had its marble-topped table, adorned with a forlorn aspidistra—its moulting rug at every door. The air was dead and smelt chiefly of dust.

They climbed four flights of stairs without meeting anyone. Only faint rustlings and whispers within the rooms told of other tenants. Then the blotched-faced man threw open a door.

'Young lady come to see Mrs Harper about the sitooation. Too-teloo, dearie. Hope you strike lucky.'

He pushed her inside and she heard his step upon the stairs.

In that moment, Jenny longed for anyone—even her late companion.

She was vaguely aware of the figure of a man seated in a chair. Too terrified to look at him, her eyes flickered around the room.

Like the rest of the house, it struck the note of parodied respectability. Yellowish lace curtains hung at the windows which were blocked by pots of leggy geraniums. A walnut-wood suite was upholstered in faded bottle-green rep with burst padding. A gilt-framed mirror surmounted a stained marble mantelpiece which was decorated with a clock—permanently stopped under its glass case—and a bottle of whisky. On a small table by the door rested a filthy cage, containing a grey parrot, its eyes mere slits of wicked eld between wrinkled lids.

It had to come. With an effort, she looked at the man.

He was tall and slender and wrapped in a once-gorgeous dressing-gown of frayed crimson quilted silk. At first sight, his features were not only handsome but bore some air of breeding. But the whole face was blurred—as though it were a waxen mask half-melted by the sun and over-which the Fiend—in passing—had lightly drawn a hand. His eyes drew her own. Large and brilliant, they were of so light a blue as to appear almost white. The lashes were unusually long and matted into spikes.

The blood froze at Jenny's heart. The girl was no fool. Despite Duncan's cautious statements, she had drawn her own deduction which linked an unsolved murder mystery and a reward of £500.

She knew that she was alone with a homicidal maniac—the murderer of ill-starred Emmeline Bell.

In that moment, she realised the full horror of a crime which, a few months ago, had been nothing but an exciting newspaper-story. It sickened her to reflect that a girl—much like herself—whose pretty face smiled fearlessly upon the world from the printed page, had walked into this same trap, in all the blindness of her youthful confidence. No one to hear her cries. No one to guess the agony of those last terrible moments.

Jenny at least understood that first rending shock of realisation. She fought for self-control. At sight of that smiling marred face, she wanted to do what she knew instinctively that other girl had done—precipitating her doom. With a desperate effort she suppressed the impulse to rush madly round the room like a snared creature, beating her hands against the locked door and crying for help. Help which would never come.

Luckily, common sense triumphed. In a few minutes' time, she would not be alone. Even then a taxi was speeding on its mission; wires were humming; behind her was the protection of the Force.

She remembered Duncan's advice to temporise. It was true that she was not dealing with a beast of the jungle which sprang on its prey at sight.

'Oh, please.' She hardly recognised the tiny pipe. 'I've come to see Mrs Harper about her situation.'

'Yes.' The man did not remove his eyes from her face. 'So you are Jenny?'

'Yes, Jenny Morgan. Is—is Mrs Harper in?'

'She'll be in presently. Sit down. Make yourself at home. What are you scared for?'

'I'm not scared.'

Her words were true. Her strained ears had detected faintest sounds outside—dulled footsteps, the cautious fastening of a door.

The man, for his part, also noticed the stir. For a few seconds he listened intently. Then to her relief, he relaxed his attention.

She snatched again at the fiction of her future employer. 'I hope Mrs Harper will soon come in.'

'What's your hurry? Come closer. I can't see you properly.'

They were face to face. It reminded her of the old nursery story of 'Little Red Riding Hood'.

'What big eyes you've got, Grandmother.'

The words swam into her brain.

Terrible eyes. Like white glass cracked in distorting facets. She was looking into the depths of a blasted soul. Down, down…That poor girl. But she must not think of *her*. She must be brave—give him back look for look.

Her lids fell…She could bear it no longer.

She gave an involuntary start at the sight of his hands. They were beyond the usual size—unhuman—with long knotted fingers.

'What big hands you've got.'

Before she could control her tongue, the words slipped out.

The man stopped smiling.

But Jenny was not frightened now. Her guards were near. She thought of the detective who carried the bag of samples. She thought of the stout clergyman. She thought of Duncan.

At that moment, the commercial traveller was in an upper room of a wholesale drapery house in the city, holding the fashionable blonde lady buyer with his magnetic blue eye, while he displayed his stock of crêpe-de-Chine underwear.

At that moment, the clergyman was seated in a third-class railway carriage, watching the hollows of the Downs fill with heliotrope shadows. He was not quite at ease. His thoughts persisted on dwelling on the frightened face of a little country girl as she drifted by in the wake of a human vulture.

'I did wrong. I should have risked speaking to her.'

But—at that moment—Duncan was thinking of her.

〉〉〉

Jenny's message had been received over the telephone wire, repeated and duly written down by Mr Herbert Yates, shorthand-typist—who, during the absence of Duncan's own secretary, was filling the gap for one morning. At the sound of his chief's step in the corridor outside, he rammed on his hat, for he was already overdue for a lunch appointment with one of the numerous 'only girls in the world'.

At the door he met Duncan.

'May I go to lunch now, sir?'

Duncan nodded assent. He stopped for a minute in the passage while he gave Yates his instructions for the afternoon.

'Any message?' he enquired.

'One come this instant, sir. It's under the weight.'

Duncan entered the office. But in that brief interval, the disaster had occurred.

Yates could not be held to blame for what happened. It was true that he had taken advantage of Duncan's absence to open a window wide, but he was ignorant of any breach of rules. In his hurry he had also written down Jenny's message on the nearest loose-leaf to hand, but he had taken the precaution to place it under a heavy paperweight.

It was Duncan's Great Dane which worked the mischief. He was accustomed at this hour to be regaled with a biscuit by Duncan's secretary who was an abject dog-lover. As his dole had not been forthcoming he went in search of it. His great paws on the table, he rooted among the papers, making nothing of a trifle of a letter-weight. Over it went. Out of the window—at the next gust—went Jenny's message. Back to his rug went the dog.

The instant Duncan was aware of what had happened, a frantic search was made for Yates. But that wily and athletic youth, wise to the whims of his official superiors, had disappeared. They raked every place of refreshment within a wide radius. It was not until Duncan's men rang up to report that they had drawn a blank at the National Gallery, that Yates was discovered in an underground dive, drinking coffee and smoking cigarettes with his charmer.

Duncan arrived at Victoria forty minutes after the appointed time.

It was the bitterest hour of his life. He was haunted by the sight of Jenny's flower-face upturned to his. She had *trusted* him. And in his ambition to track the man he had taken advantage of her necessity to use her as a pawn in his game.

He had played her—and lost her.

The thought drove him to madness. Steeled though he was to face reality, he dared not to let himself think of the end. Jenny—country-raw and blossom-sweet—even then struggling in the grip of murderous fingers.

Even then.

Jenny panted as she fought, her brain on fire. The thing had rushed upon her so swiftly that her chief feeling was of sheer incredulity. What had gone before was already burning itself up in a red mist. She had no clear memory afterwards of those tense minutes of fencing. There was only an interlude filled with a dimly comprehended menace—and then this.

And still Duncan had not intervened.

Her strength was failing. Hell cracked, revealing glimpses of unguessed horror.

With a supreme effort she wrenched herself free. It was but a momentary respite, but it sufficed for her signal—a broken tremulous whistle.

The response was immediate. Somewhere outside the door a gruff voice was heard in warning.

'Perlice.'

The killer stiffened, his ears pricked, every nerve astrain. His eyes flickered to the ceiling which was broken by the outline of a trapdoor.

Then his glance fell upon the parrot.

His fingers on Jenny's throat, he paused. The bird rocked on its perch, its eyes slits of malicious eld.

Time stood still. The killer stared at the parrot. Which of the gang had given the warning? Whose voice? Not Glass-eye. Not Mexican Joe. The sound had seemed to be within the room.

That parrot.

He laughed. His fingers tightened. Tightened to relax.

For a day and a half he had been in Mother Bargery's room. During that time the bird had been dumb. Did it talk?

The warning echoed in his brain. Every moment of delay was fraught with peril. At that moment his enemies were here, stealing upwards to catch him in their trap. The instinct of the human rodent, enemy of mankind—eternally hunted and harried—prevailed. With an oath, he flung Jenny aside and jumping on the table, wormed through the trap of the door.

Jenny was alone. She was too stunned to think. There was still a roaring in her ears, shooting lights before her eyes. In a vague way, she knew that some hitch had occurred in the plan. The police were here—yet they had let their prey escape.

She put on her hat, straightened her hair. Very slowly she walked down the stairs. There was no sign of Duncan or of his men.

As she reached the hall, a door opened and a white puffed face looked at her. Had she quickened her pace or shown the least sign of fear she would never have left that place alive. Her very nonchalance proved her salvation as she unbarred the door with the deliberation bred of custom.

The street was deserted, save for an empty taxi which she hailed.

'Where to, miss?' asked the driver.

Involuntarily she glanced back at the drab house, squeezed into its strait-waistcoat of grimed bricks. She had a momentary vision of a white blurred face flattened against the glass. At the sight, realisation swept over her in wave upon wave of sick terror.

There had been no guards. She had taken every step of that perilous journey—alone.

Her very terror sharpened her wits to action. If her eyesight had not deceived her, the killer had already discovered that the alarm was false. It was obvious that he would not run the risk of remaining in his present quarters. But it was possible that he might not anticipate a lightning swoop; there was nothing to connect a raw country girl with a preconcerted alliance with a Force.

'The nearest telephone-office,' she panted. 'Quick.'

A few minutes later, Duncan was electrified by Jenny's voice gasping down the wire.

'He's at 17 Jamaica Square, SE. No time to lose. He'll go out through the roof…Quick, quick.'

'Right. Jenny, where'll you be?'

'At your house. I mean, Scot—Quick.'

As the taxi bore Jenny swiftly away from the dun outskirts, a shrivelled hag pattered into the upper room of that drab house. Taking no notice of its raging occupant, she approached the parrot's cage.

'Talk for mother, dearie.'

She held out a bit of dirty sugar. As she whistled, the parrot opened its eyes.

'Perlice.'

〉〉〉

It was more than two hours later when Duncan entered his private room at Scotland Yard.

His eyes sought Jenny.

A little wan, but otherwise none the worse for her adventure, she presided over a teapot which had been provided by the resourceful Yates. The Great Dane—unmindful of a little incident of a letter-weight—accepted her biscuits and caresses with deep sighs of protest.

Yates sprang up eagerly.

'Did the cop come off, chief?'

Duncan nodded twice—the second time towards the door, in dismissal.

Jenny looked at him in some alarm when they were alone together. There was little trace left of the machine-made martinet of the Yard. The lines in his face appeared freshly re-tooled and there were dark pouches under his eyes.

'Jenny,' he said slowly, 'I've—sweated—blood.'

'Oh, was he so very difficult to capture? Did he fight?'

'Who? That rat? He ran into our net just as he was about to bolt. He'll lose his footing all right. No.'

'Then why are you—'

'*You.*'

Jenny threw him a swift glance. She had just been half-murdered after a short course of semi-starvation, but she commanded the situation like a lion tamer.

'Sit down,' she said, 'and don't say one word until you've drunk this.'

He started to gulp obediently and then knocked over his cup.

'Jenny, you don't know the hell I've been through. You don't understand what you ran into. That man—'

'He was a murderer, of course. I knew that all along.'

'But you were in deadliest peril—'

'I wasn't frightened, so it didn't matter. I knew I could trust you.'

'Don't Jenny. Don't turn the knife. I failed you. There was a ghastly blunder.'

'But it *was* all right, for it ended beautifully. You see, something told me to trust you. I always know.'

During his career, Duncan had known cases of love at first sight. So, although he could not rule them out, he always argued along Jenny's lines.

Those things did not happen to him.

He realised now that it had happened to him—cautious Scot though he was.

'Jenny,' he said, 'it strikes me that I want someone to watch *me*.'

'I'm quite sure you do. Have I won the reward?'

His rapture was dashed.

'Yes.'

'I'm so glad. I'm rich.' She smiled happily. 'So this can't be pity for me.'

'Pity? Oh, Jenny—'

Click. The mouse-trap was set for the confirmed bachelor with the right bait.

A young and friendless girl—homely and blossom-sweet.

Cheese.

You Can't Hang Twice

Anthony Gilbert

*Anthony Gilbert was, like Anne Meredith and J. Kilmeny Keith,
a pen name used by Lucy Beatrice Malleson (1899–1973). She
was a Londoner by birth, and when her family ran into financial
difficulties, she became a shorthand typist to earn money while
she struggled to establish herself as an author. Success did not
come quickly or easily, but her career blossomed in the 1930s,
when she was elected to the prestigious Detection Club, and
created the solicitor and amateur detective Arthur Crook, who
subsequently appeared in most of her books.*

    *Gilbert's friend and fellow Detection Club member, the
solicitor Michael Gilbert, wrote in her obituary for* The Times
*that Crook 'behaved in a way which befitted his name and
would not have been approved by the Law Society', whilst noting
that his relations with the police were excellent. Crook's blend of
roguishness and remorselessness is to the fore in this atmospheric
story, which was a prize winner in a contest organised by* Ellery
Queen's Mystery Magazine.

> > >

The mist that had been creeping up from the river during the early afternoon had thickened into a grey blanket of fog by twilight, and by the time Big Ben was striking nine and people all over England were turning on their radio sets for the news, it was so dense that Arthur Crook, opening the window of his office at 123 Bloomsbury Street and peering out, felt that he was poised over chaos. Not a light, not an outline, was visible; below him, the darkness was like a pit. Only his sharp ears caught, faint and far away, the uncertain footfall of a benighted pedestrian and the muffled hooting of a motorist ill-advised enough to be caught abroad by the weather.

'An ugly night,' reflected Arthur Crook, staring out over the invisible city. 'As bad a night as I remember.' He shut the window down. 'Still,' he added, turning back to the desk where he had been working for the past twelve hours, 'it all makes for employment. Fogs mean work for the doctor, for the ambulance driver, for the police and the mortician, for the daring thief and the born wrong 'un.'

Yes, and work, too, for men like Arthur Crook, who catered specially for the lawless and the reckless and who was known in two continents as the Criminals' Hope and the Judges' Despair.

And even as these thoughts passed through his mind, the driver was waiting, unaware of what the night was to hold, the victim crept out under cover of darkness from the rabbit-hutch-cum-bath that he called his flat, and his enemy watched unseen but close at hand.

In his office, Mr Crook's telephone began to ring.

The voice at the other end of the line seemed a long way off, as though that also were muffled by the fog, but Crook, whose knowledge of men was wide and who knew them in all moods, realized that the fellow was ridden by fear.

'Honest, he shuddered so he nearly shook me off the line,' he told Bill Parsons next day. 'It's a wonder a chap like that hasn't died of swallowing his own teeth.'

'Mr Crook,' whispered the voice and he heard the pennies fall as the speaker pressed Button A. 'I was afraid it would be too late to find you…'

'When I join the forty-hour-a-week campaign I'll let the world know,' said Crook affably. 'I'm one of those chaps you read about. Time doesn't mean a thing to me. And in a fog like this it might just as well be nine o'clock in the morning as nine o'clock at night.'

'It's the fog that makes it possible for me to call you at all,' said the voice mysteriously. 'You see, in the dark, one hopes he isn't watching.'

Hell, thought Crook disappointedly. Just another case of persecution mania, but he said patiently enough, 'What is it? Someone on your tail?'

His correspondent seemed sensitive to his change of mood. 'You think I'm imagining it? I wish to Heaven I were. But it's not just that I'm convinced I'm being followed. Already he's warned me three times. The last time was to-night.'

'How does he warn you?'

'He rings up my flat and each time he says the same thing. 'Is that you, Smyth? Remember—silence is golden'; and then he rings off again.'

'On my Sam,' exclaimed Crook, 'I've heard of better gags at a kids' party. Who is your joking friend?'

'I don't know his name,' said the voice, and now it sounded further away than ever, 'but—he's the man who strangled Isobel Baldry.'

Everyone knows about quick-change artists, how they come on to the stage in a cutaway coat and polished boots, bow, go off and before you can draw your breath they're back in tinsel tights and tinfoil halo. You can't think how it can be done in the time, but no quick-change artist was quicker than Mr Crook when he heard that. He became a totally different person in the space of a second.

'Well, now we are going places,' he said, and his voice was as warm as a fire that's just been switched on. 'What did you say your name was?'

'Smyth.'

'If that's the way you want it…'

'I don't. I'd have liked a more distinguished name. I did the best I could spelling it with a Y, but it hasn't helped much. I was one of the guests at the party that night. You don't remember, of course. I'm not the sort of man people do remember. She didn't. When I came to her house that night she thought I'd come to check the meter or something. She'd never expected me to turn up. She'd just said, 'You must come in one evening. I'm always at home on Fridays,' and I thought she just meant two or three people at most.…'

'*Tête-à-tête* with a tigress,' said Crook. 'What are you, anyhow? A lion-tamer?'

'I work for a legal firm called Wilson, Wilson and Wilson. I don't know if it was always like that on Fridays, but the house seemed full of people when I arrived and—they were all the wrong people, wrong for me, I mean. They were quite young and most of them were either just demobilized or were waiting to come out. Even the doctor had been in the Air Force. They all stared at me as if I had got out of a cage. I heard one say, 'He looks as if he had been born in a bowler hat and striped p-pants.' They just thought I was a joke.'

And not much of one at that, thought Mr Crook unsympathetically.

'But as it happens, the joke's on them,' continued the voice, rising suddenly. 'Because I'm the only one who knows that Tom Merlin isn't guilty.'

'Well, *I* know,' Mr Crook offered mildly, 'because I'm defendin' him, and I only work for the innocent. And the young lady knows or she wouldn't have hauled me into this—the young lady he's going to marry, I mean. And, of course, the real murderer knows. So that makes four of us. Quite a team, in fact. Suppose you tell us how you know?'

'Because I was behind the curtain when *he* came out of the Turret Room. He passed me so close I could have touched him, though, of course, I couldn't see him because the whole house was dark, because of this game they were playing, the one called Murder. I didn't know then that a crime had been committed, but when the truth came out I realized he must have come out of the room where she was, because there was no other place he could have come from.'

'Look,' said Mr Crook. 'Just suppose I've never heard this story before.' And probably he hadn't heard this one, he reflected. 'Start from page one and just go through to the end. For one thing, why were you behind the curtain?'

'I was hiding—not because of the game, but because I—oh, I was so miserable. I ought never to have gone. It wasn't my kind of party. No one paid any attention to me except to laugh when I did anything wrong. If it hadn't been for Mr Merlin, I wouldn't even have had a drink. And he was just sorry for me. I heard him say to the doctor, 'Isobel ought to remember everyone's human,' and the doctor—Dr Dunn—said, 'It's a bit late in the day to expect that.''

'Sounds a dandy party,' said Crook.

'It was—terrible. I couldn't understand why all the men seemed to be in love with her. But they were. She wasn't specially good-looking, but they behaved as though there was something about her that made everyone else unimportant.'

Crook nodded over the head of the telephone. That was the dead woman's reputation. A courtesan *manquée*—that's how the Press had described her. Born in the right period, she'd have been a riot. At it was, she didn't do so badly, even in 1945.

'It had been bad enough before,' the voice went on. 'We'd had charades, and of course I'm no good at that sort of thing. The others were splendid. One or two of them were real actors on the stage, and even the others seemed to have done amateur theatricals half their lives. And how they laughed at me—till they got bored because I was so stupid. They stopped after a time, though I offered to drop out and just be audience; and then I wanted to go back, but Miss Baldry said how could I when she was three miles from a station and no one else was going yet? I could get a lift later. Murder was just as bad as the rest, worse in a way, because it was dark, and you never knew who you might bump into. I bumped right into her and Tom Merlin once. He was telling her she better be careful, one of these days she'd get her neck broken, and she laughed and said, 'Would you like to do it, Tom?' And then she laughed still more and asked him if he was still thinking of that dreary little number—that's what she called her—he'd once thought he might marry. And asked him why he didn't go back, if he wanted to? It was most uncomfortable. I got away and found a window on to the flat roof, what they call the leads. I thought I'd stay there till the game was over. But I couldn't rest even there, because after a minute Mr Merlin came out in a terrible state, and I was afraid of being seen, so I crept round in the shadows and came into the house through another window. And that's how I found myself in the Turret Room.'

'Quite the little Lord Fauntleroy touch,' observed Crook admiringly. 'Well?'

'Though, of course, all the lights were out, the moon was quite bright and I could see the blue screen and I heard a sound and I guessed Miss Baldry was hidden there. For a minute I thought I'd go across and find her and win the game, but another second and I realized that she wasn't alone, there was someone—a man—with her.'

'But you don't know who?'

'No.'

'Tough,' said Crook. 'Having a good time, were they?'

'I don't know about a good time. I think the fact is everyone had been drinking rather freely, and they were getting excited, and I never liked scenes—I haven't a very strong stomach, I'm afraid—so I thought I'd get out. They were so much engrossed in one another—'You have it coming to you, Isobel'—I heard him say. I got out without them hearing me—I did fire-watching, you know, and one learns to move quietly.'

'Quite right,' assented Crook. 'No sense startling a bomb. Well?'

'I went down a little flight of stairs and on to a landing, and I thought I heard feet coming up, so I got behind the curtain. I was terrified someone would discover me, but the feet went down again and I could hear whispers and laughter—everything you'd expect at a party. They were all enjoying themselves except me.'

'And Isobel, of course,' suggested Crook.

'She had been—till then. Well, I hadn't been behind the curtain for very long when the door of the Turret Room shut very gently, and someone came creeping down. He stopped quite close to me as if he were leaning over the staircase making sure no one would see him come down. I scarcely dared breathe—though, of course, I didn't know then there had been a murder—and after a minute I heard him go down. The next thing I heard was someone coming up, quickly, and going up the stairs and into the Turret Room. I was just getting ready to come out when I heard a man calling, 'Norman! Norman! For Pete's sake…' and Dr Dunn—he was the R.A.F. doctor, but of course, you know that—called out, 'I'm coming. Where are you?' And the first man—it was Andrew Tatham, the actor, who came out of the Army after Dunkirk—said, 'Keep the women out. An appalling thing's happened.'"

'And, of course, the women came surgin' up like the sea washin' round Canute's feet?'

'A lot of people came up, and I came out from my hiding-place and joined them, but the door of the Turret Room was shut, and after a minute Mr Tatham came out and said, 'We'd better all go down. There's been an accident.' And Dr Dunn joined him and said, 'What's the use of telling them that? They'll have to know the truth. Isobel's been murdered, and we're all in a spot.'"

'And when did it strike you that you had something to tell the police?' inquired Crook drily.

'Not straight away. I—I was very shocked myself. Everyone began to try and remember where they'd been, but, of course, in the dark, no one could really prove anything. I said I was behind that curtain. I wasn't really playing, but no one listened. I might have been the invisible man. And then one of the girls said, 'Where's Tom?' and Mr Tatham said, 'That's queer. Hope to Heaven he hasn't been murdered, too.' But he hadn't, of course. He joined us after a minute and said, 'A good time being had by all?' and one of the girls, the one they call Phœbe, went into hysterics. Then Mr Tatham said, 'Where on earth have you been?' and he said he was on the leads. He wasn't playing either. They all looked either surprised or—a bit disbelieving, and Dr Dunn said, 'But if you were on the leads you must have heard something,' and he said, 'Only the usual row. Why? Have we had a murder?' And Mr Tatham said, 'Stop it, you fool.' And then he began to stare at all of us, and said, 'Tell me, what is it? Why are you looking like that?' So then they told him. Some of them seemed to think he must have heard noises, but Dr Dunn said that if whoever was responsible knew his onions there needn't be enough noise to attract a man at the farther end of the flat roof, particularly as he'd expect to hear a good deal of movement and muttering and so on.'

'And when the police came—did you remember to tell them about the chap who'd come out of the Turret Room; or did you have some special reason for keeping it dark?'

'I—I'm afraid I rather lost my head. You see, I was planning exactly what I'd say when it occurred to me that nobody else had admitted going into that room at all, and I hadn't an atom of proof that my story was true, and—it isn't as if I knew who the man was…'

'You know,' said Crook, 'it looks like I'll be holding your baby when I'm through with Tom Merlin's.'

'I didn't see I could do any good,' protested Mr Smyth. 'And then they arrested Mr Merlin and I couldn't keep silent any longer. Because it seemed to me that though I couldn't tell them the name of the murderer or even prove that Mr Merlin was innocent, a jury wouldn't like to bring in a verdict of guilty when they heard what I had to say.'

'Get this into your head,' said Crook, sternly. 'They won't bring in a verdict of guilty in any circumstances. I'm lookin' after Tom Merlin, so he won't be for the high jump this time. But all the same, you and me have got to get together. Just where do you say you are?'

'On the Embankment—in a call box.'

'Well, what's wrong with you coming along right now?'

'In this fog?'

'I thought you said the fog made it safer.'

'Safer to telephone, because the box is quite near my flat.' He broke suddenly into a queer convulsive giggle. 'Though as a matter of fact I began to think the stars in their courses were against me, when I found I only had one penny.

Luckily, there was one in my pocket—I keep one there for an evening paper...'

'Keep that bit for your memoirs,' Crook begged him. 'Now all you've got to do is proceed along the Embankment....'

'The trams have stopped.'

'Don't blame 'em,' said Crook.

'And I don't know about the trains, but I wouldn't dare travel by Underground in this weather, and though I think there was one taxi a little while ago...'

'Listen!' said Crook. 'You walk like I told you till you come to Charing Cross. You can't fall off the Embankment and if there's no traffic nothing can run you down. The tubes are all right, and from Charing Cross to Russell Square is no way at all. Change at Leicester Square. Got that? You can be in my office within twenty-five minutes. I'm only three doors from the station, and anyone will tell you my address. I'm better known after dark than any house in London, bar none.'

'Wouldn't to-morrow...?' began Smyth, but Crook said, 'Not it. You might have had another warning by to-morrow and this time it might be a bit more lethal than an anonymous telephone message. Now, don't lose heart. It's like going to the dentist. Once it's done, it's over for six months. So long as X. thinks you're huggin' your guilty secret to your own buzoom you're a danger to him. Once you've spilt the beans you're safe.'

'It's a long way to Charing Cross,' quavered the poor little rabbit.

'No way at all,' Crook assured him. 'And never mind about the trams and the taxicabs. You might be safer on your own feet at that.'

Thus is many a true word spoken in jest.

'And now,' ruminated Mr Crook, laying the telephone aside and looking at the great potbellied watch he drew from his pocket, 'First, how much of that story is true? And second, how much are the police going to believe? If he was a pal of Tom Merlin's, that's just the sort of story he would tell, and if it's all my eye and Betty Martin, he couldn't have thought of a better. It don't prove Tom's innocent, but as he says, it's enough to shake the jury. Pity is, he didn't tell it a bit sooner.'

It was also, of course, the sort of story a criminal might tell, but in that case he'd have told it at once. Besides, even the optimistic Mr Crook couldn't suspect Mr Smyth of the murder. He wasn't the stuff of which murderers are made.

'No personality,' decided Crook. 'Black tie, wing collar, umbrella and brief case, the 8.10 every weekday—Yes, Mr Brown. Certainly, Mr Jones. I will attend to that, Mr Robinson. Back on the 6.12 regular as clockwork, a newsreel or pottering with the window boxes on Saturday afternoons, long lie-in on Sunday"—that was his programme until the time came for his longest lie-in of all.

And at that moment neither Mr Smyth nor Arthur Crook had any notion how near that was.

Crook looked at his watch. 'Five minutes before the balloon goes up,' he observed. It went up like an actor taking his cue. At the end of five minutes the telephone rang again.

〉〉〉

As he made his snail's pace of a way towards Charing Cross Mr Smyth was rehearsing feverishly the precise phrases he would use to Mr Crook. He was so terrified of the coming interview that only a still greater terror could have urged him forward. For there was nothing of the hero about him. The Services had declined to make use of him during the war, and it had never occurred to him to leave his safe employment and volunteer for anything in the nature of war work. Fire-watching was compulsory.

'The fact is, I wasn't born for greatness,' he used to assure himself. 'The daily round, the common task...I never wanted the limelight.' But it looked as though that was precisely what he was going to get. For the hundredth time he found himself wishing he had never met Isobel Baldry, or, having met her, had never obeyed the mad impulse which made him look up the number she had given him and virtually invite himself to her party. The moment he arrived he knew she had never meant him to accept that invitation.

'And oh, if I hadn't, if I hadn't,' he moaned to himself.

The darkness seemed full of eyes and ears. He stopped suddenly to see whether he could surprise stealthy footsteps coming after him, but he heard only the endless lapping of black water against the Embankment, the faint noise of the police launch going downstream, and above both these sounds, the frenzied beating of his own heart. He went on a little way, then found to his horror that he could not move. In front of him the darkness seemed impenetrable; behind him the atmosphere seemed to close up like a wall, barring his retreat. He was like someone coming down the side of a sheer cliff who suddenly finds himself paralysed, unable to move a step in either direction. He didn't know what would have happened, but at that moment a car came through the fog travelling at what seemed to him dangerous speed. It was full of young men, the prototype of those he had met at Isobel Baldry's ill-starred party. They were singing as they went. That gave him a fresh idea, and without moving he began to call 'Taxi! Taxi!' Someone in the car heard him and leaned out to shout, 'No soap, old boy,' but now panic had him in its grip. And it seemed as if then his luck changed. Another vehicle came more slowly through the darkness.

'Taxi!' he called, and to his relief he heard the car stop.

Relief panted in his voice. 'I want to go to Bloomsbury Street. No. 123. Do you know it?'

'Another client for Mr Cautious Crook.' The driver gave a huge chuckle. 'Well, well.'

'You—you mean you know him?'

'All the men on the night shift know about Mr Crook. Must work on a night shift 'imself, the hours 'e keeps.'

'You mean—his clients prefer to see him at night?' He was startled.

'Yerss. Not so likely to be reckernized by a rozzer, see? Oh, 'e gets a queer lot. Though this is the first time I've bin asked to go there in a fog like this.' His voice sounded dubious. 'Don't see 'ow it can be done, guvnor.'

'But you must. It's most important. I mean, he's expecting me.'

'Sure? On a night like this? You should worry.'

'But—I've only just telephoned him.' Now it seemed of paramount importance that he should get there by hook or crook.

'Just like that. Lumme, you must be in a 'urry.'

'I am. I—I don't mind making it worth your while…' It occurred to him that to the driver this sort of conversation might be quite an ordinary occurrence. He hadn't realized before the existence of a secret life dependent on the darkness.

'Cost yer a quid,' the driver said promptly.

'A pound?' He was shocked.

'Mr Crook wouldn't be flattered to think you didn't think 'im worth a quid,' observed the driver.

Mr Smyth made up his mind. 'All right.'

'Sure you've got it on you?'

'Yes. Oh, I see.' He saw that the man intended to have the pound before he started on the journey, and he fumbled for his shabby shiny notecase and pulled out the only pound it held and offered it to the driver. Even in the fog the driver didn't miss it. He snapped on the light inside the car for an instant to allow Mr Smyth to get in, then put it off again, and his fare sank sprawling on the cushions, breathing as hard as a spent racer. The driver's voice came to him faintly as he started up the engine.

'After all, guvnor, a quid's not much to save yer neck.'

He started. His neck? His neck wasn't in danger. No one thought he'd murdered Isobel Baldry. But the protest died even in his heart within a second. Not his neck but his life— that was what he was paying a pound to save. Now that the car was on its way he knew a pang of security. He was always nervous about journeys, thought he might miss the train, get into the wrong one, find there wasn't a seat. Once the journey started he could relax. He thought about the coming interview; he was pinning all his faith on Arthur Crook. He wouldn't be scared; the situation didn't exist that could scare such a man. And perhaps, he reflected, lulling himself into a false security, Mr Crook would laugh at his visitor's fears. That's just what I wanted, he'd say. You've solved the whole case for me, provided the missing link. Justice should be grateful to you, Mr Smyth....He lost himself in a maze of prefabricated dreams.

Suddenly he realized that the cab, which had been crawling for some time, had now drawn to a complete standstill. The driver got down and opened the door.

'Sorry, sir, this perishin' fog. Can't make it, after all.'

'You mean, you can't get there?' He sounded incredulous.

'It's my neck as well as yours,' the driver reminded him.

'But—I must—I mean are you sure it's impossible? If we go very slowl...'

'If we go much slower we'll be proceedin' backwards. Sorry, guvnor, but there's only one place we'll make to-night if we go any farther and that's Kensal Green. Even Mr Crook can't 'elp you once you're there.'

'Then—where are we now?'

'We ain't a 'undred miles from Charing Cross,' returned the driver cautiously. 'More than that I wouldn't like to say. But I'm not taking the cab no farther in this. If any mug likes to try pinchin' it 'e's welcome. Most likely wrap 'imself round a lamppost if he does!'

Reluctantly, Mr Smyth crawled out into the bleak street; it was bitterly cold and he shivered.

'I'll 'ave to give you that quid back,' said the driver, wistfully.

'Well, you didn't get me to Bloomsbury Street, did you?' He supposed he'd have to give the fellow something for his trouble. He put out one hand to take the note and shoved the other into the pocket where he kept his change. Then it happened, with the same shocking suddenness as Isobel Baldry's death. His fingers had just closed on the note when something struck him with appalling brutality. Automatically he grabbed harder, but it wasn't any use; he couldn't hold it. Besides, other blows followed the first. A very hail of blows in fact, accompanied by shock and sickening pain and a sense of the world ebbing away. He didn't really appreciate what had happened; there was too little time. Only as he staggered and his feet slipped on the wet leaves of the gutter, so that he went down for good, he thought, the darkness closing on his mind forever, 'I thought it was damned comfortable for a taxi.'

⟩⟩⟩

It was shortly after this that Arthur Crook's telephone rang for the second time, and a nervous voice said, 'This is Mr Smyth speaking. Mr Crook, I'm sorry I can't make it. I—this fog's too thick. I'll get lost. I'm going right back.'

'That's all right,' said Crook heartily. 'Don't mind me. Don't mind Tom Merlin. We don't matter.'

'If I get knocked down in the fog and killed it won't help either of you,' protested the voice.

'Come to that, I dare say I won't be any worse off if you are.'

'But—you can't do anything to-night.'

'If I'm goin' to wait for you I shan't do anything till Kingdom Come.'

'I—I'll come to-morrow. It won't make any difference really.'

'We've had all this out before,' said Crook. 'I was brought up strict. Never put off till to-morrow what you can do to-day.'

'But I can't—that's what I'm telling you. I'll come—I'll come at nine o'clock to-morrow.'

'If he lets you,' said Crook darkly.

'He?'

'He might be waiting for you on the doorstep. You never know. Where are you, by the way?'

'In a call box.'

'I know that. I heard the pennies drop. But where?'

'On the Embankment.'

'What's the number?'

'It's a call box, I tell you.'

'Even call boxes have numbers.'

'I don't see…'

'Not trying to hide anything from me, Smyth, are you?'

'Of course not. It's Fragonard 1511.'

'That's the new Temple exchange. You must have overshot your mark.'

'Oh? Yes. I mean, have I?'

'You were coming from Charing Cross. You've walked a station too far.'

'It's this fog. I thought—I thought it was Charing Cross just over the road.'

'No bump of locality,' suggested Crook kindly.

'I can't lose my way if I stick to the Embankment. I'm going straight back to Westminster and let myself into my flat, and I'll be with you without fail at nine sharp to-morrow.'

'Maybe,' said Crook pleasantly. 'Happy dreams.' He rang off. 'Picture of a gentleman chatting to a murderer,' he announced. 'Must be a dog's life, a murderer's. So damned lonely. And dangerous. You can't trust anyone, can't confide in anyone, can't even be sure of yourself. One slip and you're finished. One admission of something only the murderer can know and it's the little covered shed for you one of these cold mornings. Besides, you can't guard from all directions at once, and how was the chap who's just rung me to know that Smyth only had two coppers on him when he left his flat to-night, and so he couldn't have put through a second call?'

The inference was obvious. Someone wanted Mr Crook to believe that Smyth had gone yellow and that was why he hadn't kept his date. Otherwise—who knew?—if the mouse wouldn't come to Mahomet, Mahomet might go looking for the mouse. And later, when the fog had dispersed, some early workman or street cleaner, perhaps even a bobby, would stumble over a body on the Embankment, and he—Crook—would come forward with his story and it would be presumed that the chap had been bowled over in the dark—or even manhandled for the sake of any valuables he might carry. Crook remembered his earlier thought—work for the doctor, for the ambulance driver, for the mortician—and for Arthur Crook. Somewhere at this instant Smyth lay, deprived forever of the power of passing on information, rescuing an innocent man, helping to bring a guilty one to justice, somewhere between Temple Station and Westminster Bridge.

'And my bet 'ud be Temple Station,' Crook told himself.

It was a fantastic situation. He considered for a moment ringing the police and telling them the story, but the police are only interested in crimes after they've been committed, and a murder without a corpse just doesn't make sense to them at all. So, decided Mr Crook, he'd do all their spade-work for them, find the body and then sit back and see how they reacted to that. He locked his office, switched off the lights and came tumbling down the stairs like a sack of coals. It was his boast that he was like a cat and could see in the dark, but even he took his time getting to Temple Station. Purely as a precaution, he pulled open the door of the telephone booth nearby and checked the number. As he had supposed, it was Fragonard 1511.

There was a chance, of course, that X. had heaved the body over the Embankment, but Crook was inclined to think not. To begin with, you couldn't go dropping bodies into the Thames without making a splash of some sort, and you could never be sure that the Thames police wouldn't be passing just then. Besides, even small bodies are heavy, and there might be blood. Better on all counts to give the impression of a street accident. Crook had known of cases where men had deliberately knocked out their victims and then ridden over them in cars. Taking his little sure-fire pencil torch from his pocket, Crook began his search. His main fear wasn't that he wouldn't find the body, but that some interfering constable would find him before that happened. And though he had stood up to bullets and blunt instruments in his time, he knew that no career can stand against ridicule. He was work-ing slowly along the Embankment, wondering if the fog would ever lift, when the beam of his torch fell on something white a short distance above the ground. This proved to be a handkerchief tied to the arm of one of the Embankment benches. It was tied hard in a double knot, with the ends spread out, as though whoever put it there wanted to be sure of finding it again. He looked at it for a minute before its obvious significance occurred to him. Why did you tie a white cloth to something in the dark? Obviously to mark a place. If you didn't, on such a night, you'd never find your way back. What he still didn't know was why whoever had put out Smyth's light should want to come back to the scene of the crime. For it was Smyth's handkerchief. He realized that as soon as he had untied it and seen the sprawling letters 'Smyth' in one corner. There was something peculiarly grim about a murderer taking his victim's handkerchief to mark the spot of the crime. After that it didn't take him long to find the body. It lay in the gutter, the blood on the crushed forehead black in the bright torchlight, the face dreadful in its disfigurement and dread. Those who talked of the peace of death ought to see a face like that; it might quiet them a bit, thought Mr Crook grimly. He'd seen death so often you'd not have expected him to be squeamish, but he could wish that someone else had found Mr Smyth.

Squatting beside the body like a busy little brown elephant, he went through the pockets. He'd got to find out what the murderer had taken that he had to return. Of course, someone else might have found the body and left the handkerchief, but an innocent man, argued Crook, would have left his own. You'd have to be callous to take things off the body of a corpse. There wasn't much in the dead man's pockets, a notecase with some ten-shilling notes in it, a season ticket, some loose cash, an old-fashioned turnip watch—that was all. No matches, no cigarettes, of course, no handkerchief.

'What's missing?' wondered Mr Crook, delving his hands into his own pockets and finding there watch, coin, purse notecase, identity card, tobacco pouch, latchkey....'That's it,' said Mr Crook. 'He hasn't got a key. But he talked of going back and letting himself in, so he had a key....' There was the chance that it might have fallen out of his pocket, but though Crook sifted through the damp sooty leaves he found nothing; he hadn't expected to, anyhow. There were only two reasons why X. should have wanted to get into the flat. One was that he believed Smyth had some evidence against him and he meant to lay hands on it; the other was to fix an alibi showing that the dead man was alive at, say, 10.30, at which hour, decided Mr Crook, the murderer would have fixed an alibi for himself. He instantly cheered up. The cleverest criminal couldn't invent an alibi that an even cleverer man couldn't disprove.

He straightened himself, as he did so he realized that the corpse had one of its hands folded into a fist; it was a job to open the fingers, but when he had done so he found a morsel of tough white paper with a greenish blur on the torn edge. He recognized that all right, and in defiance of anything the police might say he put the paper into his pocketbook. The whole world by this time seemed absolutely deserted; every now and again a long melancholy hoot came up from the river from some benighted tug or the sirens at the mouth of the estuary echoed faintly through the murk; but these were other-worldly sounds that increased rather than dispelled the deathlike atmosphere. As to cause of death, his guess would be a spanner. A spanner is a nice anonymous weapon, not too difficult to procure, extraordinarily difficult to identify. Only fools went in for fancy weapons like swordsticks and Italian knives and loaded riding crops, all of which could be traced pretty easily to the owners. In a critical matter like murder it's safer to leave these to the back-room boys and stick to something as common as dirt. Crook was pretty common himself, and, like dirt, he stuck.

'The police are going to have a treat to-night,' he told himself, making a beeline for the telephone. His first call was to the dead man's flat, and at first he thought his luck was out. But just when he was giving up hope he could hear the receiver being snatched off and a breathless voice said, 'Yes?'

'Mr Smyth? Arthur Crook here. Just wanted to be sure you got back safely.'

'Yes. Yes. But only just. I decided to walk after all.'

'Attaboy!' said Mr Crook. 'Don't forget about our date to-morrow.'

'Nine o'clock,' said the voice. 'I will be there.'

Mr Crook hung up the receiver. What a liar you are, he said, and then at long last he dialled 999.

The murderer had resolved to leave nothing to chance. After his call to Mr Crook's office he came back to the waiting car and drove as fast as he dared back to the block of flats where he lived. At this hour the man in charge of the car park would have gone off duty, and on such a night there was little likelihood of his encountering anyone else. Carefully he ran the car into an empty space and went over it carefully with a torch. He hunted inside in case there should be any trace there of the dead man, but there was none. He had been careful to do all the opening and closing of doors, so there was no fear of fingerprints, but when he went over the outside of the car his heart jumped into his mouth when he discovered blood-marks on the right-hand passenger door. He found an old rag and carefully polished them off, depositing the rag in a corner at the further end of the car park. This unfortunately showed up the stains of mud and rain on the rest of the body, but he hadn't time to clean all the paintwork; there was still a lot to be done and, as he knew, there is a limit to what a man's nervous system can endure. Locking the car, he made his way round to the entrance of the flats. The porter was just going off; there wasn't a night porter, labour was still scarce, and after 10.30 the tenants looked after themselves.

'Hell of a night, Meadows,' he observed, drawing a long breath. 'I was beginning to wonder if I'd be brought in feet first.'

The porter, a lugubrious creature, nodded with a sort of morbid zest.

'There'll be a lot of men meeting the Recording Angel in the morning that never thought of such a thing when they went out to-night,' he said.

His companion preserved a poker face. 'I suppose a fog always means deaths. Still, one man's meat. It means work for doctors and undertakers and ambulance-men....' He didn't say anything about Arthur Crook. He wasn't thinking of Arthur Crook. Still under the man's eye he went upstairs, unlocked the door of his flat, slammed it and, having heard the man depart, came stealing down again, still meeting no one, and gained the street. So far everything had gone according to plan.

It took longer to get to Westminster than he had anticipated, because in the fog he lost his way once, and began to panic, which wasted still more time. His idea was to establish Smyth alive and talking on his own telephone at, say, 10.30 p.m. Then, if questions should be asked, Meadows could testify to his own return at 10.30. On his way back, he would return the key to the dead man's pocket, replace the handkerchief, slip home under cover of darkness....He had it worked out like a B.B.C. exercise.

Luck seemed to be with him. As he entered the flats the hall was in comparative darkness. It was one of those houses where you pushed a button as you came in and the light lasted long enough for you to get up two floors; then you pushed another button and that took you up to the top. There wasn't any lift. As he unlocked the door of the flat the telephone was ringing and when he unshipped the receiver there was Arthur Crook, of all the men on earth, calling up the dead man. He shivered to think how nearly he'd missed that call. He didn't stay very long; there was still plenty to do and the sooner he got back to his own flat the more comfortable he'd feel. And how was he to guess that he would never walk inside that flat again?

He congratulated himself on his foresight in tying the handkerchief to the arm of the bench; in this weather he might have gone blundering about for an hour before he found the spot where Smyth lay in the gutter, his feet scuffing up the drenched fallen leaves. As it was he saw his landmark, by torchlight, without any trouble. It was then that things started to go wrong. He was level with the seat when he heard the voice of an invisible man exclaim, 'Hey there!' and he jumped back, automatically switching off his torch, and muttering, 'Who the devil are you?'

'Sorry if I startled you,' said the same voice, 'but there's a chap here seems to have come to grief. I wish you'd take a look at him.'

This was the one contingency for which he had not prepared himself, but he knew he dared not refuse. He couldn't afford at this stage to arouse suspicion. Besides, he could offer to call the police, make for the call box and just melt into the fog. Come what might, he had to return the dead man's key. He approached the kerb and dropped down beside the body. Crook watched him like a lynx. This was the trickiest time of all; if they weren't careful he might give them the slip yet.

'Have you called the police?' inquired the newcomer, getting to his feet. 'If not, I…' But at that moment both men heard the familiar sound of a door slamming and an inspector with two men hovering in the background came forward saying, 'Now then, what's going on here.'

'Chap's got himself killed,' said Crook.

X. thought like lightning. He made a slight staggering movement, and as Crook put out his hand to hold him he said, 'Silly—slipped on something—don't know what it was.' He snapped on his torch again, and stooping, picked up a key. 'Must have dropped out of his pocket,' he suggested. 'Unless,' he turned politely to Crook, 'unless it's yours.'

Crook shook his head.

'Which of you was it called us up?' the Inspector went on.

'I did,' said Crook. 'And then this gentleman came along and…' He paused deliberately and looked at the newcomer. It was a bizarre scene, the men looking like silhouettes against the grey blanket of fog with no light but the torches of the civilians and the bull's-eyes of the force. 'Seeing this gentleman's a doctor…' As he had anticipated there was an interruption.

'What's that you said?'

'Penalty of fame,' said Crook. 'Saw your picture in the papers at the time of the Baldry case. Dr Norman Dunn, isn't it? And perhaps I should introduce myself. I'm Arthur Crook, one of the three men living who *know* Tom Merlin didn't kill Miss Baldry, the others bein' Tom himself and, of course, the murderer.'

'Isn't that a coincidence?' said Dr Dunn.

'There's a bigger one coming,' Crook warned him. 'While I was waitin' I had a looksee at that little chap's identity card, and who do you think he is? Mr Alfred Smyth, also interested in the Baldry case.'

The doctor swung down his torch. 'So that's where I'd seen him before? I had a feeling the face was familiar in a way, only…'

'He is a bit knocked about, isn't he?' said Crook. 'What should you say did that?'

'I shouldn't care to hazard a guess without a closer examination. At first I took it for granted he'd been bowled over by a car....'

'In that case we ought to be able to trace the car. He can't have gotten all that damage and not left any of his blood on the hood.'

There was more noise and a police ambulance drove up and spewed men all over the road. Crook lifted his head and felt a breath of wind on his face. That meant the fog would soon start to lift. Long before morning it would have gone. The inspector turned to the two men.

'I'll want you to come with me,' he said. 'There's a few things I want to know.'

'I can't help you,' said Dunn sharply, but the inspector told him, 'We'll need someone to identify the body.'

'Mr Crook can do that. He knows him.'

'Always glad to learn,' said Crook.

'But you...' He stopped.

'You don't know the police the way I do,' Crook assured him. 'Just because a chap carries an identity card marked Alfred Smyth—that ain't proof. I never set eyes on him before.'

'Mr Crook's right,' said the inspector. 'We want someone who saw him when he was alive.'

They all piled into the car, Crook and Dunn jammed together, and no one talked. Dunn was thinking hard. Sold for a sucker, he thought. If I hadn't tried so hard for an alibi—perhaps, though, they won't touch Meadows. Meadows will remember, all the same. He'll think it's fishy. And the car. Of course there was blood on the car. If they examine it they'll notice it's washed clean in one place. They'll want to know why. No sense saying I was coming back from the pictures. Meadows can wreck that. Besides, Baron, the man who looks after the cars, may remember mine hadn't come in when he went off duty. Round and round like a squirrel in its cage went his tormented mind. There must be some way out, he was thinking, as thousands have thought before him. They've no proof, no actual proof at all. Outwardly he was calm enough, maintaining the attitude that he couldn't imagine why they wanted him. But inside he was panicking. He didn't like the station surroundings, he didn't like the look on the inspector's face, most of all he feared Crook. The police had to keep the rules; Crook had never heard of Queensbury. To him a fair fight was gouging, shoving, and kicking in the pit of the stomach. A terrible man. But he stuck to it, they hadn't got anything on him that added up to murder. He'd had the forethought to get rid of the spanner, dropped it in one of those disused pig buckets that still disfigured London streets; but he'd had to use the one near his own flats, because in the dark he couldn't find any others. He thought now the river might have been safer.

He tried to seem perfectly at ease, pulled off his burberry and threw it over the back of a chair, produced his cigarette case.

'Of course, our own doctor will go over the man,' the inspector said, 'but how long should you say he'd been dead, Dr Dunn?'

He hesitated. 'Not so easy. He was a little chap and it's a bitter cold night. But not long.'

'But more than twenty minutes?' the inspector suggested.

'Yes, more than that, of course.'

'That's screwy,' said the inspector. 'I mean, Mr Crook was talking to him on the telephone in his flat twenty minutes before you happened along.'

He couldn't think how he'd forgotten that telephone conversation. That, intended for his prime alibi, was going to ball up everything.

'I don't see how he could,' he protested. 'Not unless the chap's got someone doubling for him.'

'You know all the answers,' agreed Crook. 'Matter of fact, the same chap seems to be making quite a habit of it. He rang me a bit earlier from Fragonard 1511 to tell me Smyth couldn't keep an appointment to-night. Well, nobody knew about that but Smyth and me, so how did X. know he wasn't coming, if he hadn't made sure of it himself?'

'Don't ask me,' said Dunn.

'We are asking you,' said the inspector deliberately.

The doctor stared. 'Look here, you're on the wrong tack if you think I know anything. It was just chance. Why don't you send a man round to Smyth's flat and see who's there?'

'We did think of that,' the inspector told him. 'But there wasn't anyone...'

'Then—perhaps this is Mr Crook's idea of a joke.'

'Oh no,' said Crook looking shocked. 'I never think murder's a joke. A living perhaps, but not a joke.'

Dunn made a movement as though to rise. 'I'm sorry I can't help you...'

'I wouldn't be too sure about that,' drawled Crook.

'What does that mean?'

'There's just one point the inspector hasn't mentioned. When I found that poor little devil to-night he'd got a bit of paper in his hand. All right, inspector. I'll explain in a minute. Just now, let it ride.' He turned back to Dr Norman Dunn. 'It was a bit of a Treasury note, and it seemed to me that if we could find the rest of that note, why then we might be able to lay hands on the murderer.'

'You might. And you think you know where the note is?'

'I could make a guess.'

'If you think I've got it...' Dunn pulled out his wallet and threw it contemptuously on the table. 'You can look for yourself.'

'Oh, I don't expect it would be there,' replied Crook, paying no attention to the wallet. 'But—every murderer makes one mistake, Dunn. If he didn't, God help the police. And help innocent men, too. And a man with murder on his hands is like a chap trying to look four ways at once. Now that note suggested something to me. You don't go round carrying notes in a fog, as if they were torches. You'd only get a note out if you were going to pay somebody, and who's the only person you're likely to want to pay in such circumstances? I'm talking like a damned politician,' he added disgustedly. 'But you do see what I'm drivin' at?'

'I'm only a doctor,' said Dunn. 'Not a professional thought-reader.'

'You'd pay a man who drove you to your destination—or tried to. There was some reason why Smyth had a note in his hand, and my guess is he was tryin' to pay some chap off. That would explain his bein' at Temple Station. On his own feet he wouldn't have passed Charing Cross, not a chap as frightened of the dark as he was. While he was offerin' the note, X. knocked him out, and realizin' that funny questions might be asked if the note was found with him, he'd remove it. You agree so far?'

'I don't know as much about murder as you do, Mr Crook,' said Dunn.

'That's your trouble,' Mr Crook agreed. 'That's always the trouble of amateurs setting up against pros. They're bound to lose. Let's go on. X. removes the note. So far, so good. But he's got a lot to remember and not much time. He can't be blamed if he don't remember it's trifles that hang a man. If I was asked, I'd say X. shoved that note into his pocket, meanin' to get rid of it later, and I'd say it was there still.'

'You're welcome to search my pockets,' Dunn assured him. 'But I warn you, Crook, you're making a big mistake.

Your reputation's not going to be worth even the bit of a note you found in Smyth's hand when this story breaks.'

'I'll chance it,' said Crook.

At a nod from the inspector, the police took up Dunn's burberry and began to go through the pockets. During the next thirty seconds you could have heard a pin drop. Then the man brought out a fist like a ham, and in it was a crumpled ten-shilling note with one corner missing!

'Anything to say to that?' inquired Crook, who didn't apparently mind hitting a man when he was down.

Dunn put back his head and let out a roar of laughter. 'You think you're smart, don't you? You planted that on me, I suppose, when we were coming here. But, as it happens, Smyth's note was for a pound, not ten shillings. You didn't know that, did you?'

'Oh, yes,' said Crook, 'I did—because I have the odd bit of the note in my wallet. One of the old green ones it was. What I'm wondering is—*how did you?*'

◇◇◇

'That was highly irregular, Mr Crook,' observed the inspector, drawing down the corners of his mouth, after the doctor had been taken away.

'It beats me how the police even catch as many criminals as they do,' returned Crook frankly. 'Stands to reason if you're after a weasel you got to play like a weasel. And a gentleman—and all the police force are gentlemen—don't know a thing about weasels.'

'Funny the little things that catch 'em,' suggested the inspector, wisely letting that ride.

'I reckoned that if he saw the wrong note suddenly shoved under his nose he wouldn't be able to stop himself. It's what I've always said. Murderers get caught because they're yellow. If they just did their job and left it at that, they might die in their beds at ninety-nine. But the minute they've socked their man they start feverishly buildin' a little tent to hide in, and presently some chap comes along, who might never have noticed them, but gets curious about the little tent. When you start checking up his story I bet you'll find he's been buildin' alibis like a beaver buildin' a dam. And it's his alibis are goin' to hang him in the end.'

His last word in this case was to Tom Merlin and the girl Tom was still going to marry.

'Justice is the screwiest thing there is,' he told them. 'You're not out of chokey because Norman Dunn killed the Baldry dame, though he's admitted that, too. Well, why not? We know he got Smyth, and you can't hang twice. But it was his killing Smyth that put you back on your feet. If he hadn't done that, we might have had quite a job straightenin' things out. Y'know the wisest fellow ever lived? And don't tell me Solomon.'

'Who, Mr Crook?' asked Tom Merlin's girl, hanging on Tom's arm.

'Brer Rabbit. And why? Becos he lay low and said nuffin.' And then they tell you animals are a lower order of creation!"

CPSIA information can be obtained at www.ICGtesting.com
Printed in the USA
BVOW02s1426110916

461799BV00005B/134/P